BORDER WAR

BORDER
WAR

LOU DOBBS

JAMES O. BORN

A TOM DOHERTY ASSOCIATES BOOK

NEW YORK

This is a work of fiction. All of the characters, organizations, and events portrayed in this novel are either products of the authors' imaginations or are used fictitiously.

BORDER WAR

Designed by Mary A. Wirth

A Forge Book
Published by Tom Doherty Associates, LLC
175 Fifth Avenue
New York, NY 10010

www.tor-forge.com

Forge® is a registered trademark of Tom Doherty Associates, LLC.

Library of Congress Cataloging-in-Publication Data

Dobbs, Lou.
Border war / Lou Dobbs and James O. Born. — First Edition.
    p. cm.
  "A Tom Doherty Associates Book."
  ISBN 978-0-7653-2771-0 (hardcover)
  ISBN 978-1-4299-8669-4 (e-book)
  1. Government investigators—Fiction.   2. Murder—Investigation—Fiction.
3. Suspense fiction.   I. Born, James O.   II. Title.
  PS3604.O2264B67 2014
  813'.6—dc23
                                                    2013029608

Forge books may be purchased for educational, business, or promotional use.
For information on bulk purchases, please contact Macmillan Corporate
and Premium Sales Department at 1-800-221-7945, extension 5442,
or write specialmarkets@macmillan.com.

First Edition: May 2014

Printed in the United States of America

0 9 8 7 6 5 4 3 2 1

For my grandchildren, Malaya, Devon, Miliana, Austin, and Sarah

ACKNOWLEDGMENTS

I am grateful to Tor Books's brilliant executive editor Bob Gleason for coming up with the idea of doing this book. Bob's intellect and energy make the editorial process always helpful and fun. Thanks to Tom Doherty, president and publisher of Tom Doherty Associates, which publishes Tor Books. Tom's passion and vision make all of us who work with him fortunate indeed for the experience. And a special thanks to my collaborator and coauthor, Jim Born, who is impressive whether at work as a Florida state law enforcement officer, or in the creation and writing of imaginative, thrilling fiction. I appreciate Jim's willingness to patiently teach and make it all a hoot. I'm proud to call Bob, Tom, and Jim good friends all.

And thanks to my representative, Wayne Kabak, for his counsel, and my wife, Debi, for keeping her sense of humor, and me, after all these many years.

BORDER WAR

"It would do my stress level some good to punch an asshole smuggler really hard. Hearing you bitch about how this surveillance sucks doesn't help."

FBI Special Agent Tom Eriksen withheld a smile from his older partner and instead said, "I didn't say it sucks, I said it *stinks.* This place physically stinks. Just a comment, not a complaint." Behind him was one of the safest cities in America, and in front of him the little highway that ran southeast of El Paso next to the Rio Grande River. He had no idea what caused the odor he was currently battling, but it did seem to be traveling on the light southern wind just to slap him in the face. It smelled like a mix of industrial chemicals and poor waste disposal.

His partner, John Houghton, a veteran agent of Homeland Security, said, "Sure it stinks. That over there is Juárez—just as deadly as El Paso is safe. Figured you'd be used to the stench of corruption after spending three years in D.C." John's dark face was barely visible in the ambient light.

The terrain was nothing like the grassy hills near Baltimore where he had grown up. This hard, rock-covered ground looked like it couldn't support weeds, let alone the giant cacti and bushes that sprang up everywhere. The uneven ground provided cover while they looked down on the low valley where they expected trouble.

Eriksen was happy to smell something other than the alcohol on John's breath as he looked over the scrub brush and scanned the road and trails in this isolated industrial area. Technically it wasn't part of El Paso, but there was nothing else around to call it. He couldn't even see the reflected light from the city. Another half mile east were the well-guarded grounds of TARC, the Technology and Research Center; a few miles to the west, residential areas started to spring up. This was a favorite spot for Mexican coyotes to smuggle undocumented people across the border. Plenty of access points and room to flee if needed.

John Houghton sighed loudly.

Eriksen said, "C'mon, John, where would you be if not out here on this?"

"At home watching Bill O'Reilly."

"That's what a hotshot federal agent does with his free time?"

Houghton smiled. "The smart ones do." He checked the ridge they were watching one more time. "Besides, he's a Harvard man like you. I'd think you'd like him."

"I do, but scheduling is a problem." Now he checked the ridge and stared in wonder at the Texas landscape he still wasn't used to.

Tom Eriksen didn't care how dusty it got here, how much it stank, or how many nights he had to work, he'd still take it over Washington, D.C., anytime. At least under the circumstances he'd faced before his transfer.

John said, "Why you bitchin', anyway? I thought you were a real cop, not the typical FBI college boy. You can do more than read spreadsheets, can't you?"

"College boy? You went to college, too."

"Yeah, if you can call ASU a college. Not a super-special Ivy League school like you went to. Besides, I'm a black man working for the Immigration and Customs Enforcement. That gives me the right to bitch. Not enough brothers to have any power and too many to claim discrimination. No one pays any attention to me. That's why I drink so much."

"You do okay. Last I checked you were at the top of the pay grade. GS-13, topped out, you gotta be pulling in about a hundred and thirty grand. Somehow I think you'll survive."

"You'll get there. The feds rely on longevity to make money. Just takes time. Besides, having a degree from Harvard makes people take notice."

"Not too much notice. I'm still sitting here on the border with you."

His partner smiled, filling out the laugh lines on his fifty-three-year-old face. "Look at me. I was a Customs agent for fifteen years till that day they merged us into the goddamn Homeland Security and I became an Immigration and Customs Enforcement agent. Now I'm technically an agent for Homeland Security Investigations and looking for illegals on a stupid task force, in a shitty town, with a whining partner." He held up his hand and said, "I know, I know, the term 'illegal' is no longer politically correct, but that's what we've used for years, and it'll take an old-timer like me some time to correct it. That doesn't change the fact that my talents have been wasted."

Eriksen had to laugh out loud at that one.

John continued, "It's a crime. A damn bureaucratic crime. Someone should go to jail for wasting our talent out here like this."

Tom Eriksen just nodded at his partner on this border task force he'd been exiled to. But John was right. It wasn't the stress of violence that ruined most cops, it was the bureaucracy. He felt like the FBI had been trying to kill him for the past two years. It was a long way from what he dreamed of doing.

Eriksen stretched his arms and looked over to the three Border Patrol agents sitting with them. They were all about his age, in their late twenties and close to his six feet. One was pudgy, one looked like he spent too much time in the gym and liked to show off his biceps in a tailored shirt, and the last one had a lean runner's look like Eriksen. The radio crackled, and then Eriksen heard one of the Border Patrol agents in the other group, a few hundred yards south of them, say, "We got movement."

Tom Eriksen liked the Border Patrol guys. They were tough and smart and worked hard at a job seemingly no one wanted them to succeed at. He'd heard more than a few senior ICE or HSI guys say all federal agents should have to start their career in the Border

Patrol. Be assigned an impossible job, informed they wouldn't be allowed to actually secure the border, and told not to apprehend too many undocumented people or risk their careers if they tried. Their bosses took care of the real bullshit: keeping a straight face while the politicians told the public what they wanted to hear, that the border was finally secure. The Border Patrol bureaucracy tended to weed out the weak. At least they learned to speak Spanish, and the ones who survived and then moved on to another federal job appreciated what they had. He knew most of the FBI agents and even some of the HSI guys thought they were too good for this kind of duty. Not his partner, John Houghton. He just wanted to work. He would prefer to work something more substantial, at least in his mind, like narcotics or money laundering, but if they assigned him to a task force to cut off the flow of people entering the country improperly, he threw himself into it as best he could.

Eriksen admired that. His father had instilled the need to work hard in all of his children. Eriksen's sister was at the Johns Hopkins University School of Medicine. His older brother was a federal prosecutor in Baltimore, and his younger brother was finishing up his business degree at Columbia. They all worked hard and they all felt sorry for Tom. He would've preferred to be working hard by fighting terrorists, but now he was just glad to have a job. Punching a supervisor usually turned out worse. Thank God for the FBI's desire to maintain its public image.

Now, looking through binoculars, he saw some movement by the supposedly secure culvert that ran under the highway. Smugglers had dug hundreds of tunnels along the border, and many connected directly to storm sewers. Here the Rio Grande kept that from happening, but they had still found a way over. His heart beat a little faster even though he dreaded the idea of chasing fleeing women with little children in their arms or old men just looking for a job in the land of opportunity.

Maybe this time it would be different.

———

Joe Azeri's neck cartilage clicked as he scanned the ridge from inside the smelly drainage pipe. For a career criminal from New Jersey, he felt like he had hit the Lotto with this gig. The corporation didn't ask that much of him, so he let late nights like this slide by without complaint.

He'd been told there would be immigration officers on the ridge tonight but to go ahead with the plans anyway. It was a complicated way to handle things. If he were in charge, operations would be much more direct and to the point. But this is how they wanted it done, using a porous spot along the border near El Paso, with ways to come through wide open desert, across the highway, or through one of a dozen gullies. Every time the Border Patrol figured out one route, the ingenious smugglers came up with something new. Tunnels were all the rage for a while, but they took time and money to build. They didn't want to waste it on illegals. The tunnels were mainly used to smuggle dope across to the U.S. and sometimes to bring money back to Mexico. Lots of money. It was the poor freelancers that got caught at the border crossings. The cartels all had ways around the checkpoints.

Even close to the city of El Paso, this was wild country as far as he was concerned. There were coyotes (the real canine ones, not the human smugglers like him), snakes, and even a pack of wild dogs that made the news occasionally. The rolling hills had a sharp edge to them, and the ground had just enough loose rocks and gravel to make any upward trek a scary proposition.

Joe Azeri had used this same culvert to help get deeper into the U.S. before emerging with illegals. It was part of a drainage system that started right on the Rio Grande. The high culvert stank, and he imagined armies of roaches crawling up the walls and along the top of the pipe. In fact, he had only seen a few insects and three rats. It was the green mold that worried him now. What would shit like that do to his lungs?

He felt a soft tap on the shoulder and turned to see the youngest of his assistants, a twenty-year-old from Chihuahua who spoke much more English than he ever let on. No matter how many times he had told the young man to dress in simple, dark clothes, the boy had to express himself with neon-bright Nike running shoes and always wore an orange Texas A&M baseball cap.

The young man said, "*Estamos listos*, Cash."

Everyone called Joe "Cash."

He just nodded. Then, when he turned back to look out the culvert grille, a smile crept across his face. He liked his nickname. He didn't make friends with the men he worked with, at least not the Mexicans, and he never gave them his name. At first they just called him *jefe*, Spanish for "boss," Then not quite a year ago, on one of his first runs, he didn't have time to change and wore a black dress shirt when they brought across thirteen Mexicans. He liked it that the shirt was so hard to see at night and started wearing only black clothing. After that they started calling him Cash because they were all fans of the American country star Johnny Cash, who always wore black. He still heard "Ring of Fire" and "I Walk the Line" playing in Mexican bars.

His Spanish was outstanding, but he kept his commands short and to the point. As a result, his Mexican assistants somehow formed the opinion that he was originally from Colombia and not Passaic, New Jersey. His dark hair and eyes—a gift from his Italian father—made him look Hispanic. He liked the idea that if one of them ever got caught, all they could say was they worked for a Colombian named Cash. It could not have worked out better if he'd planned it.

At the moment, Cash was just happy they had a culvert big enough to walk in. He couldn't stand all the way up; his five-foot-eleven frame wouldn't allow it. But on the other hand, his thirty-eight-year-old body didn't complain too much about walking hunched over compared to crawling through a damn tunnel. This wasn't a bad job tonight.

Tonight he had eleven widgets, which was how he liked to think of the people he brought across the border. If this was a business, they were his product. He didn't want to talk to them, get to know them, or have any of them be able to identify him other than a vague description. Three of the widgets had extra value to the company: the older couple and the tall, lanky guy, who wasn't even Mexican but slipped back and forth across the border on a regular basis. Cash knew a little bit about the guy named Eric, but kept it to himself.

Cash also had three of his assistants with him. Only one of them had anything on the ball, and he was going to be the scout for the group tonight.

He moved forward and peered through the steel grating that covered the culvert. They were passing one of the tunnels that cartel members had cut into the drainage system of El Paso in a dozen places. None of them had ever been found by the Border Patrol. Just the outline was visible as they walked past. A crude gray paste was spread across the edges of the board concealing the tunnel entrance.

He had been told what to expect, but one thing he'd learned on this job was never listen to anyone who told you exactly how things were going to work out.

Cash looked behind him and called one of his helpers to the front. He motioned for the others to move the group back a dozen feet. He leaned in close to his comrade and said in a low voice, speaking English, "All right, Vinnie. You and Juan are going to scout ahead of us and call for us when it's time. We're not taking any chances, so keep your pistols out and be ready to lay down fire if we have to run."

Vinnie ran a hand across his long face and said with his thick Brooklyn accent, "I don't want to be running wetbacks for the rest of my life. This ain't what I signed up for."

"So you've been saying to anyone who'll listen. I don't care what plans you have in the future, but tonight you gotta get your head out of your ass and do what I say. This is not the time to be discussing your career path." Cash looked down the line to make sure everyone was ready to move. He pulled out the key that unlocked the giant padlock holding the grid in place.

Vinnie said, "How'd you get the key?"

Cash smiled. "Easy. A week ago I used bolt cutters to take off the real lock and changed it with one that looked like it. The Border Patrol doesn't check each lock every day. It's the flood control and water utility people who insist on the culverts and maintain them." He left the lock open as the door swung out. He gave Vinnie a shove to let him know what he thought of him being overqualified for the job at hand. It was this kind of bullshit that made management a pain.

———————

John Houghton made a few comments about the odors and the bugs so his partner knew he was alert. The catclaw acacia bush he was crouching behind with Tom Eriksen and the Border Patrol agent smelled like a skunk and had thorns that pricked his cheek. He made sure to joke about it. Houghton liked to give off the vibe that he was disgruntled, but in fact he was as happy as a Baptist during Prohibition when he could do real police work like this. He didn't care that much about the undocumented people from across the border; it was the coyotes he was after, the smugglers, who would rob and kill the refugees as often as they would deliver them safely. He understood what it was to be out of place. As a black man raised in the southwestern United States, he never felt completely comfortable. But he also listened to his mother's stories about growing up in South Carolina, and with each generation before her, the stories became more horrific. Now John had a job where he could, at least occasionally, protect the helpless. He had a hard time not thinking about his own son or daughter when he looked at the young Mexicans crossing with their parents.

Sitting here under the star-splashed night sky in close quarters behind the ridge with a cool breeze blowing in from the north made him appreciate all he had in his life, even if it wasn't perfect. He liked it.

He also liked this sharp FBI agent. Tom Eriksen was a hard worker and didn't complain. It was something they needed to teach more thoroughly at the FBI Academy in Quantico. There seemed to be an institutional arrogance that filtered through many of the agents, but this kid from Baltimore was smart and, more importantly, tough. He also had a light sense of humor that would serve him well in the harsh world of law enforcement. John wondered why the FBI dickhead who supervised the agents on task forces treated him so badly. The supervisor wasn't so much stupid as dismissive and insisted on knowing everything the young FBI agent was doing. The tubby FBI supervisor, whose name was Mike Zara, claimed that he treated all the agents under him the same and it was important for him to know what each task force was doing. John thought it was more of a babysitting job.

Tom Eriksen would be a good boss one day. He was interested in catching criminals, not bullying people to prove he was in charge. He was twenty-nine but looked younger, with light hair and blue eyes. If the kid wasn't so serious about his job he'd have women lined up to date. But he worked eighty hours a week and had to work out another ten. Throw in time to sleep and eat and that didn't leave much time to chase women.

John focused his attention down the hill toward the culvert and scanned the area with his powerful Browning binoculars. It took him a moment to notice that the grate on the culvert was wide open. Before he could see the smugglers, one of the Border Patrol agents called over the radio, "We've got two males creeping toward you guys from the culvert."

John Houghton scanned directly in front of him until he saw the two men, one of them with something in his hand, scurrying along the edge of the brush, scouting the area.

Tom Eriksen whispered in his ear, "We could grab those two before they knew we were here."

John shook his head. "Those are just scouts. God knows how many are stuck down the culvert. Let's give 'em a chance to all come out and see what we're dealing with."

John pulled his SIG Sauer .40 caliber from a tactical holster. He liked the feel of the heavy metal pistol in his right hand. He'd kept the gun from when he was still part of the U.S. Customs Service. Unlike most of the other federal agencies, which dictated a narrow selection of handguns, the Customs Service always allowed its agents to show their creativity in arming themselves. Tonight the pistol was going to be more for show, because these guys didn't want to tangle with law enforcement agents who were lying in wait.

No one ever did.

TWO

Tom Eriksen surveyed the valley where he thought the smugglers would emerge. He could imagine a pitched battle between cavalry and Comanche a hundred and thirty years ago, with the horses stumbling over the loose rocks and the nearest decent medical treatment still a hundred years in the future. It was dark, even with unobstructed stars and a slight glow from the lights of El Paso. Ciudad Juárez, which was about the same distance away and eight times as big, was dimmer. It was more of a sprawling barrio with few commercial lights.

Now, as he and Houghton crouched behind a patch of brush, with time to consider where they were and what was about to happen, his heart rate picked up. Eriksen didn't have much experience on the border, or working operations like this, but he could tell the young border patrolman was itching to move. He had crept over from their right and wanted to see some action. He was no different than any other young cop. The money was okay in most law enforcement jobs, but that's not why people joined a police agency. They wanted to do things most of the public only saw on TV. They wanted to shoot guns, drive fast, and chase people.

Eriksen felt the excitement grow inside him, but he still realized the inherent danger of interrupting a crime in the middle of the night. The coyotes would have guns. One of the illegals could be armed and panic, or it could be a drug-smuggling group who would protect their load at all costs.

Now he could see the whole line of people. These weren't drug runners. It was a mix of people, male and female, with the first few appearing more upright and walking normally as opposed to the shuffling, slouched people in the rear of the line. The coyotes were spaced a few yards apart to the side. There were at least three, but Eriksen realized there could be more waiting in the culvert.

John Houghton looked over to the young, dark-haired border patrolman and said, "Hang on there, partner. Let's give them a chance to move up the hill. Between your guys and us, we'll corral everyone easy enough."

Eriksen liked the way John could impart his experience without sounding like he was talking down to anyone. He had used the same tone to explain to Eriksen why this duty wasn't as futile as Eriksen thought it was. The older HSI agent had explained that the porous nature of the U.S.–Mexican border made it a perfect place for a terrorist to enter the country, cause all kinds of havoc, and then scoot back across. Given that it was two thousand miles long, policing it was a mighty task. The fact that the Border Patrol stopped and returned 350,000 undocumented border crossers each year was an indication of how many got across safely.

It may not have been directly investigating terrorists, but working the border for undocumented crossers had a certain value if viewed with the right attitude. Eriksen did what he could to look at his assignment in the best possible light.

Eriksen noticed the young border patrolman pull his issued Heckler & Koch P2000 from his heavy-duty belt and ease forward. Before either he or John could tell him to wait, the radio came to life as someone in the other group of law enforcement officers said, "Let's move."

One of the Border Patrol guys jumped up from cover across the sloping ravine. Before he even took a step, gunfire erupted from the bottom of the ravine and was immediately answered by the border officers on that side.

John sprang forward and motioned his two companions to follow him while the smugglers were focusing their attention on the other group. They raced down the slope silently, covered by shadows.

Now it was clear who the smugglers were and who the poor un-documented people were. The smugglers all stood tall and fired a variety of small arms, from handguns to a semiautomatic that looked like a Ruger Mini-14. The firing eased dramatically as this man with the Mini-14 ducked back into the culvert. It was suicide to chase him, but the two who had initially fired on the Border Patrol agent were stuck in the gully. A border patrolman was down. For a moment it was all Eriksen could focus on. He changed direction to go to the man's aid. One of the people being smuggled across the border fell to his knees next to the wounded agent. Eriksen picked up his pace and shouted at him. He couldn't tell if the man was hurting the agent or trying to help. He raised his gun as he contin-ued to sprint toward the fallen man.

Cash stood just outside the five-foot-tall cement pipe they had just traversed. The shadows along the walls of the canyon could hide an army. His feet were unsteady on the uneven ground after walking on the stable culvert floor. Then he heard the shots he had expected and ducked back into the culvert. A few of the wetbacks pushed past him to race back to Mexico at the other end. He paid no atten-tion. This wasn't his normal job anyway. He didn't like doing things in such a convoluted manner, but circumstances dictated that one of his assistants, Vinnie, be left out there on his own. The backup plan required Cash to slide to the culvert and move southeast about four hundred yards in case he had underestimated the Border Patrol agents' ability to shoot. Management had decreed that Vinnie would not come back tonight, and it was necessary to make it look like the cops killed him. Cash would do his best.

He had thought the three "special widgets" he was required to bring over would run back into the culvert, but so far he had only seen one of them, the tall guy named Eric. It was chaos. More than he imagined when he presented his plan to his employers. He'd been in a number of shootouts with everyone from the New Jersey State Police to Nicaraguan border agents. It took a few times for him to realize the cops always had rules and guidelines they had to follow, but he could just fire away and not worry about who he was going to hit. He wasn't going to get in any more trouble after shooting at the police. In the States, he'd probably get twenty years in prison if he didn't kill anyone, and south of the border, very few cops would take him prisoner after he popped off a couple of rounds. The rest of the world mocked the good old U.S. of A. about its prison population, but he could tell you from a different perspective it had the most professional cops he'd ever dealt with. One of his buddies in New York shot and killed a New York City patrolman, and he was taken into custody two days later without injury. Cash knew for a fact that kind of shit wouldn't happen anywhere south of Texas. And sometimes not even in Texas.

Vinnie had specific orders and was too stupid not to follow them. That was what made him such a valuable asset most of the time. He did exactly what people told him and rarely thought for himself. That's why it had come as a surprise that the knucklehead would cause enough trouble at the office for Cash to be told to deal with him.

A bullet pinged off the metal grate of the culvert, and Cash knew it was time to fall back to the rally point on the other side of the border.

———————

Vinnie DiMetti didn't like the way Cash had set this whole thing up. Right now he was stranded about thirty yards from the culvert and separated from the rest of the group except one of the Mexican assistants. He had never gotten used to open spaces and the lack of pavement. This was definitely not Long Island. He knew this kind of shit could happen on the border, he just hoped it wasn't going to happen to him. He had fired a gun at another human three times in his life, and two of those times that human was tied up, on his knees, and facing away from Vinnie. The third time he had thrown a few rounds toward a Boston cop and taken a few rounds in return, but no one was hurt.

This was different. The way the bullets were flying, he might as well be in combat. The cops or Border Patrol agents or whoever the hell they were didn't seem panicked by a few shots fired their way. He knew there was no way he was going to die for a few illegals. All he wanted to do was shoot and scoot. He moved toward the gully Cash had told him to run to. It was an old wash that rolled directly into the Rio Grande, where he could swim across into the safety of Mexico. He popped off a couple of rounds at a guy in the green uniform but didn't know if it was a sheriff's deputy or a Border Patrol agent. He didn't wait to see if he hit the man.

Then he looked around at the scrambling people and decided this was nothing but bullshit. He'd done two years in a community college on Long Island. He should have a cushy office job. He had paid his dues and didn't understand why he was still stuck doing menial tasks like this. That's why he had barked like an agitated dog at his bosses. Now they had to listen.

He screamed to his Mexican assistant, "Forget the people, let's go."

Eriksen was about to knock the middle-aged man away from the wounded Border Patrol agent, but he paused for a moment because it looked like the man knew what he was doing. Then he sank to his knees to see if he could do anything, but the man snapped in English, "I'm a doctor. Let me help this man." There was something about his bearing and manner that instantly convinced Eriksen to let him do his job.

Another Border Patrol agent raced up, taking a moment to assess the situation and deferring to the man who was carefully searching for the source of blood under the Border Patrol agent's shirt. It looked like a bullet had slipped under his arm and above his ballistic vest.

John Houghton rolled past and called for Eriksen to follow him. For an older guy, he could move pretty fast. Eriksen left the doctor helping the Border Patrol agent and tried to keep up with his partner. He had played lacrosse at Harvard, and it helped him immensely at the FBI Academy in Quantico with the daily physical training and the rigorous fitness tests, but it had been tough to keep that level of fitness in the real world.

John ignored the terrified people crossing the border and dashed toward two fleeing bandits running southeast into an old river wash. The little valley cut under an old highway and ran directly into the Rio Grande, or as it looked here, the Rio Mierda.

A round kicked up dirt directly in front of them, and both federal agents dropped to a prone position and returned fire. A lot of fire. Eriksen recalled his FBI firearms instructor screaming at them on the range, "The only reason to stop shooting at sixteen rounds is if you don't have seventeen." His finger squeezed the trigger and the pistol bucked in his hand over and over as his partner did the same to his left. There were muzzle flashes from the front as the bandits returned fire.

An empty bullet casing from John's pistol bounced off Eriksen's face, making him jump when he thought he'd been hit. He took a moment to glance to his right and realized his casings had popped onto the ground next to him as well. Then the breech of his pistol locked back, and Eriksen rolled to his side to grab his spare magazine with his left hand as he ejected the empty magazine with his right. In a matter of seconds he was ready to roll back into position and continue firing. He purposely took a deep breath to stay calm, and he realized the shooting had stopped. His ears rang as if he were in the tower of Notre Dame, but there was no sign of firing coming from in front of him and no movement to either side.

He took a moment to scan the area with his pistol up, then turned to John Houghton and said, "Did we scare them off or hit them?"

There was no answer from his partner.

Eriksen turned to his left and saw John lying perfectly still in the dirt.

THREE

Cash looked around the luxurious office of his boss and felt a pang of jealousy. This was what he wanted. Big oak desk, shelves filled with management books, framed photos of a cute family. The wide office had two layers of executive assistants in front of it, making contact with a regular employee unlikely. His boss's view of the open prairie that led to the border and the open spaces of Mexico provided an image like one from the pages of *National Geographic*. From inside the climate-controlled office, set at precisely seventy degrees, the bright sunlight outside looked beautiful. He knew if he was out there in the sun, he'd be sweating like an Englishman at the dentist, but from in here it was spectacular. Cash felt anxious in front of his boss, even though the guy in the three-thousand-dollar Valentino suit sitting behind the ornate desk wasn't the type who would seek physical retribution. He was a businessman, and a damn good one. But if there was dirty work to be done, he relied on Cash to do it.

His boss, Rich Haben, pulled his glasses off and set them on the desk. He took a moment to massage his temples with the heels of his palms, then sighed and looked up at Cash. "So it didn't go as we planned. Is that a fair assessment?"

"Yes, sir, Mr. Haben, that's a fair assessment."

Another silence made Cash tense. In North Jersey a few years ago, if his boss had been silent this many times during a conversation, he wouldn't expect to be walking down the street afterward, at least not without a limp.

Haben said, "Did you get the three people we needed across?"

Cash shook his head.

"We need to get our hands on the tall computer geek, Eric Sidle."

"Yes, sir. I know how important it is. I'll jump on it right away." He hadn't been told about the computer guy. It was a mistake not to emphasize his importance. Luckily, his boss realized it had been a communication error.

Now the stern middle-aged man said, "Did Mr. DiMetti make it back?"

"No, sir."

"Well, that's something at least." Then there was more silence as another idea popped into the executive's head. He looked at Cash and said, "You didn't manage to shoot any cops, did you?"

Cash hesitated, then said, "Vinnie fired. Remember, he was told to."

"We should've thought this through a little bit more. I don't need the attention a dead cop would bring. At least an American cop. Mexico loses dozens every week, but if one cop in the U.S. gets shot, it's national news and those media assholes like Dempsey jump all over it. You'd think Dempsey of all of them would quit harping about a border war that he knows America lost years ago."

Cash knew his boss hated the popular TV host. Hated him for bringing the border and drugs and immigration to the forefront of the national debate. Ted Dempsey had taken on all the issues that seemed to drive both political parties nuts: trade deficits and debt, outsourcing of middle-class jobs, education, the wars in Iraq and Afghanistan, illegal immigration. And man, did the independent, conservative commentator piss off presidents, both Republican and Democrat. Left- and right-wingers both tried to shut him up on illegal immigration, trying to paint Dempsey as an economic isolationist, a protectionist, a racist, and none of it had stuck, because Americans weren't quite as dumb as Washington liked to believe. Cash was sure his boss had helped finance some of those efforts to shut down the media on the border, and to shut down the politicians as well.

The big money thought the recent election would end the discussion, that business would return to normal on the border, but, incredibly, Texas voters elected a new senator who was already causing trouble in Washington. Senator Elizabeth Ramos had fallen in love with the sound of her own voice, and her voice was loudest on two subjects: terrorism and immigration. To make her more controversial, she was educated and knew the subjects from all angles. Being the granddaughter of Mexican immigrants inoculated her against some of the harsh rhetoric from critics over her tough stance on illegal immigration. Plus, she was attractive.

It didn't matter how hot she was, though, her message was getting tiresome. And he knew the company didn't need the heat from stepped-up border security. Finally, Cash said, "We should probably lay low for a little while."

Haben looked at him with cold brown eyes and said, "Laying low eats into profits. But you may be right in this situation." The executive looked out his front window onto the wide expanse of the open Texas prairie and Mexico not far beyond. "Now that you handled DiMetti so well, we should be able to convince his wife he was killed by the police. That should keep her quiet. Then, at least, his threat will be neutralized." He looked back at Cash and said, "I need you to take care of any loose ends on this deal. Is that understood?"

"Clearly understood, sir." Cash didn't like his boss's tone or what he might have to do, but this was the job he had signed on for.

———————————

The room was plain, bright, and typical of a government office. Piles of old magazines were stacked in one corner, and shelves full of out-of-date statute books crowded the far wall. A single wobbly table with four chairs filled the center of the room.

The overhead fluorescent lights of the Border Patrol office hurt Tom Eriksen's eyes as he sat there hoping to appear calm. In fact, he had shit calm out two hours ago in the men's room. Now he was close to complete confusion. He'd never been in a firefight before. Most cops never have to fire their guns during their entire careers, and even fewer FBI agents get into shootouts. He'd been in fights and didn't back down from trouble, but the aftermath was a bitch.

It'd been a night of shocks. Seeing his partner so still on the ground next to him had shocked him almost as much as when he popped up a few seconds later to assess the situation. As a veteran of four shootings, John knew to lie flat when he had expended all of his ammunition.

Right now the administrators had him and John in separate rooms like criminals they were trying to break so they could compare their stories. No one had been rude to him, though. In fact, the Border Patrol agents had appreciated his efforts at stopping the man who killed one of their comrades—the doctor hadn't been able to save him. Eriksen had already heard that the young agent was married and left behind two children. The reporters always seemed to skip over such facts and to focus instead on whether the agents involved had justification in shooting.

Eriksen's immediate supervisor, Mike Zara, waddled into the room, his face a deeper red than normal and his pinched face showing his irritation. The senior FBI man said, "I just love being called out in the middle of the night for foolishness like this."

"I don't think I'd call a dead Border Patrol agent foolish."

Zara didn't say anything. Instead he looked at his BlackBerry, then changed his focus back to Eriksen and asked, "Do you have anything to say for yourself?"

"You make it sound like I'm under arrest."

"If I had my way, you might be."

Now Eriksen took a moment to assess his supervisor. The word around the Bureau in West Texas was that Zara couldn't be trusted with an operational squad so he'd been put over a dozen agents who were all out on task forces. He wasn't known for backing up his agents.

Eriksen said, "Why would you want me to be arrested?"

"We found the two coyotes you shot."

"So? They fired first."

"We'll never know."

"Why not?"

"Because their bodies are on the Mexican side of the border where they died."

FOUR

Surveillance from inside a car had to be the worst. Even a classy car like this. Fortunately, the cool night air had taken the edge off the unpleasant task. El Paso's climate was mild three months a year. Tonight it was an even seventy as the heat of the day dissipated.

It was just after nine at night when Cash realized he was dead tired. He wasn't sure if it was his years or the way he had lived them that had turned him into an old man. He tried to stay at his fighting weight of 185 and told people he was six feet tall, even though he was only five eleven, but the late nights and hard partying had taken their toll. Maybe his boss saw it, too, and that was why he had assigned a stooge named Ari to help him out on his project. Maybe not so much a stooge as a thug. He'd been contracted and didn't have an official position with the corporation. Ari was an Israeli with just a slight accent and claimed to have been a member of the Mossad. Every Israeli Cash had ever met claimed to be a former Mossad agent. But that didn't mean Ari wasn't tough. Mr. Haben said Ari usually didn't do the dirty work, but Cash had the sense that he enjoyed it.

He looked through the windshield of his Cadillac CTS at the cute young woman from Chicago who was now the widow of Vinnie DiMetti. Her bleached blond hair dripped into her face as she tossed a bag into the garbage can in front of the pleasant-looking three-bedroom, two-bath house in the suburban El Paso community known as Canutillo.

Ari said, "She's got some nice curves, doesn't she?"

Cash chose not to answer.

"Ari thinks he would have fun with someone like her."

He hated the way this guy always spoke in the third person. Cash said, "This is business. If she doesn't cause any more trouble, we've got nothing more to do with her."

A sly smile swept across Ari's face and he raised his eyebrows. "Ari hopes she causes some more trouble."

The stocky little guy gave Cash the creeps. But he had heard Ari could handle himself in a tight situation, so he wouldn't come down too hard on the jerk right now. With any luck they'd never have to talk to Carol DiMetti about work again. He'd listened carefully to any hint of anger or threat when he told her about Vinnie catching a bullet from one of the Border Patrol agents. Just like he had planned, she had seen it on the news as well. He did notice that she didn't seem all that broken up about her dimwitted husband ending up dead. The news had no details about the dead coyotes since they had wound up in Mexico, but he had explained the whole situation to her. He knew not to push too hard just yet. He'd come by and casually speak to her again in the next few days, once he got rid of Ari.

The fact that Vinnie was a moron made it all the more surprising that he had caused a load more trouble than he should have been capable of. Apparently, he had seen one too many mob movies and thought he was living one himself.

As Cash watched Carol walk away from the garbage can, she lifted her cell phone to her ear. She didn't seem too distraught. He just hoped she could keep her mouth shut. For her sake.

———

It had been eight days since the shooting, and Tom Eriksen was still sulking at his apartment on Sun Trail Drive. The three-room detached building, behind an older house, was cheap as well as private. It had plenty of windows, although at the moment the vast amount of sunshine flooding in did nothing for his mood. All it did was illuminate the fact that he had very little in the way of furnishings not scrounged from his landlord, and his eleven-novel book collection looked feeble. He still basically lived like a college student.

The family that lived in the house in front of him loved the idea of an FBI agent renting their little apartment. They were part of a three-generation pool-building family that still had Sunday night dinner all together. The oldest son, Marty, had taken Eriksen out for beers a couple of times to show him the town. The twenty-five-year-old laughed at the idea of a family employing twenty members building pools in a place like El Paso. Despite the slowdown in the economy they had made it work with determination and effort. Eriksen respected that.

The house sat near Sal Berroteran Park, surrounded by bland cookie-cutter houses in developments. Along with a few others, it had been there before developers shoved identical single-family homes into every available space. Eriksen had been lucky to find it.

He thought about going home to see his folks, but didn't want to give the impression he was running away or worried that he'd done something wrong. That was the reason he hadn't hired an attorney, against the advice of virtually everyone he knew in law enforcement. Even John Houghton had consulted an attorney. He said it was the sensible thing to do.

It wasn't like Eriksen had wasted his time off. He had caught up on his back issues of financial magazines and a journal of accounting he had subscribed to since his early days in the business school at Harvard. He occasionally caught a whiff of regret from his parents that he had not become an accountant at one of the Big Four firms in either New York or Baltimore. But his dad had also been in public service, even with his engineering degree from MIT. It was as if the whole side of the family were trying to make amends for the actions of one distant relative a hundred and fifty years ago.

Eriksen had also used his time off to help the elderly couple that lived in the little house next door. The husband had emphysema and had difficulty getting around, so Eriksen gladly drove their ancient Lincoln Town Car to a Firestone store close to downtown. He got a great deal on a decent set of Michelins, and the sweet old woman had made him a different dessert every night. She had even been watching a news story about the shooting when he returned the car, but she made no connection between him and the incident being analyzed on TV.

Eriksen had been allowed to speak to the man who had helped the fallen Border Patrol agent. Luis Martinez had been a doctor in Mexico when he went to work for a drug cartel, tending to the wounded employees and treating the occasional case of common diarrhea or flu. He said it was a pleasant job with phenomenal pay until he was not able to save the kingpin's oldest son when he had overdosed on their own product. The drug kingpin, known as the Dark Lord of the Desert, had placed a price on the doctor's head and forced him to flee.

Dr. Martinez had been told by someone in the computer manufacturing business that he could work in the U.S. for a company with lots of undocumented employees. He didn't know the name of the company and had few details, but had jumped at the chance to live.

The Immigration Service had appreciated his efforts to save their wounded man so much they had put up Dr. Martinez and his wife, Concepción, in an apartment near downtown El Paso with a temporary visa and the promise of a more permanent status if he provided the government with all the information he could remember about the drug cartel.

Eriksen was happy the doctor and his pretty wife had a chance to straighten out their life.

Now Eriksen stood from his recliner and tossed his final financial magazine onto the lone table in his living room. The TV caught his attention when the news anchor started talking about the increased danger for federal agents working on the border. The network's most popular commentator, Ted Dempsey, appeared on the screen talking in his usual calm, direct manner about the need to support Border Patrol agents and other law enforcement personnel risking their lives for the security of the entire nation. The footage running behind Dempsey was of the aftermath of Eriksen's shooting.

Dempsey, arguing with a heavyset man with stringy hair, said forcefully, "I don't care which side of the border the smugglers ended up on, they were on U.S. soil when they shot and killed a young Border Patrol agent with a wife and kids."

Eriksen couldn't keep the smile from forming on his face after hearing the words of support. But just as quickly the smile faded when he saw the footage of protests in Ciudad Juárez over the killing of two Mexican nationals, by U.S. authorities, on what the protesters thought was Mexican soil.

Juárez and El Paso were the sister cities on the border in this part of the country. Unlike most U.S. and Mexican sister cities, El Paso was much smaller than the sprawling and densely populated Ciudad Juárez.

Then the news story switched to some do-nothing comedian from Los Angeles who was advocating the extradition of Houghton and Eriksen to Mexico to face charges of murder.

Before he could curse out loud, a knock at his front door grabbed Eriksen's attention.

———

Ramón Herrera rarely used his full name, Ramon Jesús Herrera Zapata. It had become too complicated when dealing with *norteamericanos* who didn't understand the Hispanic system of paternal and maternal surnames. He liked the sound of the honorific "Don Herrera" when people addressed him. Although he considered himself an industrialist and businessman, much of his income came from the narcotics trade, kidnappings, and siphoning off oil from Pemex, the Mexican government-run oil company.

Now, wrapped in a silk dressing robe, he slouched further into the leather lounger in his personal office while he sipped from a glass of Maestro Dobel Extra-Añejo tequila, aged and distilled from ten-year-old blue agaves, each bottle numbered and labeled with the name of the ranch where the agave was harvested. The Jalisco, Mexico, bottling plant provided him with whatever he needed as a courtesy to one of the country's most powerful men.

As he let the warmth of the tequila seep through his body, a beautiful young girl massaged his feet to ease the stress of the day. Her straight black hair hung to one side, brushing her ample breasts as she stroked his feet as if it were an act of love.

This hacienda was one of the few places he felt absolutely secure. It was his favorite retreat. Nestled in the mountains near Creel, Chihuahua, the twenty-six-room, multilevel hacienda was almost identical to one he owned outside Loreto, on Mexico's Baja Peninsula. Both were designed by the famed architect Alberto Kalach.

The views from each hacienda were entirely different. This one looked out over the beautiful mountains and valleys. The hacienda near Loreto had a vista of the Gulf of California and its calm waters.

The forty-three-year-old Herrera worked diligently to stay in shape, and the tequila was one of only two vices that affected his health. The other was cigars made for him personally by a master craftsman outside Havana. But he only smoked out on the balcony overlooking the foothills of the mountains.

The reason he could relax here was the outstanding security. Some said it was even more effective than the security surrounding the president of the United States. Why not? He wielded nearly as much power, and people were much more obvious about wanting to kill him.

Until the day when the killing finally stopped, he had the narrow mountain road leading to his house protected by fifty Mexican Army combat troops, and the entrance to his hacienda and the surrounding grounds patrolled by thirty private security officers who were loyal only to him, plus a detail of twelve men who would lay down their lives for him at any time. He was never in a room where one of those twelve men was not within shouting distance. Right now one stood just outside the door to his office while he enjoyed this exquisite foot rub by the eighteen-year-old actress he had brought from Mexico City.

The twelve men each commanded four others, and that sixty-man group made up his personal security force that handled not only his safety but most of the dirty work he needed done. They were, in effect, his Praetorian Guard. They would do anything he asked, kill anyone he wanted, die on his simple command. But he still kept some secrets from these men. Occasionally it was good to have contract help. Sort of a checks-and-balances system.

His vast wealth was one source of influence, but these dedicated, ruthless men were his real power, and the people who needed to be afraid of them were. Only he knew the exact size of his "security team," as he liked to call them. They were more like his personal Delta Force. He made sure he chose men who were already connected by bonds like family and former military service, and tied tighter with good pay and benefits most Mexican citizens couldn't fathom.

Even though he thought it might be overkill, there was an Oerlikon 35 mm twin cannon antiaircraft artillery site set up on either side of the hacienda that included surface-to-air missiles and radar, covering every direction for two hundred miles. The German manufacturer of the cannons held him hostage on a price until Herrera was able to have one of the executive's sons "detained" while on vacation in Acapulco. The price became much more reasonable after that.

His private airfield accommodated anything up to a 727, but he preferred to travel in his personal Learjet. He liked the ability to be anywhere within Mexico in less than three hours.

His personal cell phone rang, and he sighed as he saw who was calling. The early proto version of the next generation of iPhones had been a gift from his partner in an American computer company. How he got it was a mystery, but the phone was like something from the future. It always had decent service, and the video and voice were crystal clear. Still, he hated to let the world seep into this quiet time. He let the phone ring three times before he decided to answer, then let it ring twice more to show the caller how insignificant he was.

Herrera said, "Yes, Pablo."

From what sounded like a jungle in Africa with little reception, Herrera heard his man Pablo Piña calling from Ciudad Juárez.

"*Hola,* Don Herrera."

He hated it when a cheap cell phone degraded communication with his iPhone. "What is it you need, Pablo?" He had started to get frustrated with the man who supposedly ran Juárez, who seemed to have more and more excuses on all aspects of their business. Piña was not part of the enforcement arm of his security force, but Herrera still depended on men like him to do their jobs and expend their own resources to handle different areas of the country. As long as these lieutenants knew their place and did as they were told, Herrera rarely interfered with their day-to-day operations. That gave them a sense of power and responsibility.

"I just wanted to tell you before you heard it from someone else that there was a shooting on the border last night between El Paso and Juárez. We think our American partners were bringing over some workers."

"Did you know about it?"

"No, sir."

"Why not?" Herrera smiled at the silence the question caused. People never expected that question when they had nothing to do with the screw-up. In this case, Pablo should know everything that went on in his sphere of influence.

"This man, Haben, is not as open with me as he is with you. He never gave me a fancy phone like you got."

"Why do you think that is the case?"

"He probably views me as a drug thug and you as a business-man."

"Very good, Pablo. At least you are thinking. Now you can proceed with more knowledge. I want the business with this American company to continue. This is not a business deal I should have to babysit. Understand?"

"Yes, Don Herrera."

Herrera smiled as he hung up. He was gratified that Pablo knew his role in life.

Herrera was called an industrialist by the media, but his various positions were much more complicated than that. He sat on the board of Pemex, the state-owned petroleum company, which had more than $400 billion in assets. In fact, Herrera was involved in a number of businesses, including a role in both the Gulf and Juárez cartels. Although on the face of it they appeared to be competing entities, he had found there was room to control people in both organizations. He and others were working tirelessly to establish a détente between all the cartels and control the violence that was spreading in Mexico. For now each cartel viewed the frightening murder rate as a sort of cleansing and believed that Mexico would be more competitive once the process was completed.

His liaison with the cartels was as important as his liaison with the government. Especially since, at present, the Mexican government was merely an impotent referee in any squabbles between the powerful cartels.

Herrera's net worth was roughly the same as the Mexican government's liquid assets. He just didn't flaunt it. Much. Places like this were a retreat. He lived much of his life in regular mansions near the big cities, with the only obvious sign of his wealth being the extraordinary security measures at each location.

He looked forward to staying at his various mansions because he had a literal harem spread across seven different properties. Herrera paid one German woman nearly $300,000 a year. She then managed to negotiate one week a month off and all of December as vacation. She also got free air travel in a private jet each week. She even had a 401(k). No one complained about wages and benefits like that.

He looked down at the pretty face of the young girl massaging his bare feet and said, "That's enough for now, my dear." He couldn't help but watch her walk out of the room, her spectacular body swaying like a ship on rough seas.

Herrera stood up and stretched, enjoying the tingling in his feet as he stepped toward his balcony and took in the aroma of the thousand heirloom tulips that had been planted for him in special climate-controlled boxes beneath his private quarters because he liked the way they smelled.

He took one more breath of fresh mountain air, then turned back to his office. He tried to keep up with the more important American news shows and recorded them on his DVR. It was just another aspect of his job, and even though he would prefer to retire with one of the girls from the hacienda, now he had to catch up on what his least favorite of American commentators was saying that might slow his business and make life complicated.

The American commentator, Ted Dempsey, seemed to have sources in every field and was not shy about expressing his opinion on any subject. He criticized his own government constantly, and Herrera agreed with much of what he said. But recently the infuriating man was pointing out the flaws in Mexico and how they could be fixed. Herrera didn't care for that at all.

Ted Dempsey had become far more than a nuisance. Sometimes, it seemed as if Dempsey were describing Herrera on his show, as he talked about escalating border violence, a lost war on drugs, and what now was unchecked illegal immigration. The fool Dempsey actually thought that the U.S. could still secure its borders.

Herrera would've thought that September 11 would have taught the Americans that security was an illusion. And why was the man so concerned about violence in Mexico? It was none of his business.

Tonight's show was twice as bad as usual because Dempsey had on his favorite guest, Senator Elizabeth Ramos, the good-looking Latina. She'd been born in Texas, but with her dark hair and high cheekbones she was clearly of Mexican descent. But Herrera had to hand it her, she knew her material: illegal immigration, terrorism, drugs, and strengthening the U.S. military. Just about every subject Herrera wanted her to ignore.

The dapper, professional Dempsey said, "The drug cartels are responsible for the deaths of about seventy thousand Mexican citizens since 2006. The Mexican people don't know which way to turn—they're caught in a spiral of violence and corruption that most Americans can't even imagine. The Mexicans returned the long-ruling PRI to power. Their new president has offered no new ideas and may bargain a truce with the cartels. Will Mexico remain a democracy? Or will it slide into dictatorship? Or an oligarchy, like

Russia after the fall of Communism? Or outright anarchy? Not pleasant possibilities for either Mexico or America."

The pretty senator said, "At least then we wouldn't have opposition to better border security."

Herrera's fist clenched involuntarily as he listened to the debate start. These people shouldn't worry about Mexico when they had their own problems north of the border. It was maddening to hear this trash. He had to get control of himself.

He wished he could say either one of them was an idiot, but it was clear they were both intelligent and well educated. Usually, he had Pablo Piña handle anything with the Americans. After all, Piña was based next to the border in Juárez. He could do dirty work or send messages, but Herrera hated to waste resources on nothing more than a nuisance. He was a patient man. He never would've reached this position without patience. He would never have the new business ventures in the U.S. without patience and intelligence.

Herrera listened to a few more minutes of the show before he mashed the remote in disgust. There was a gentle knock at his door, and a smile spread across his face when the young blonde dressed in silky, erotic lederhosen lingerie with tall, tight leather boots and almost nothing else smiled then said, "*Guten Abend*, Herr Herrera."

FIVE

Tom Eriksen was surprised when he opened the front door of his little apartment and his former girlfriend Trudy Martin stepped through to give him a big hug and a kiss on the lips. Not that he didn't appreciate her exaggerated feminine form against him, or the intensity of the kiss, it was just that he didn't expect it.

As the kiss ended he took a step away and said, "Trudy, what are you doing here?"

"What a silly question."

"I don't think it's silly."

"Why wouldn't I be here? I'm your girlfriend, aren't I?"

Eriksen took a second to consider that statement and, looking in this girl's beautiful eyes, wondered if he should refute it, but that wasn't part of his personality. "I thought you broke up with me two weeks ago."

"Why would you think that?"

"Because you told me we were through and you were tired of being ignored for police work." He looked up and scratched his chin for dramatic effect. "Oh yeah, you said I was too cheap, and your parting shot involved me being too immature to ever commit to a relationship." He looked her in the eye again and said, "I'm pretty sure I got all that right. Now what's changed?"

"I saw the news and was worried about you, baby."

He eyed his Kardashian-loving, reality-show-junkie ex-girlfriend and suddenly realized why she had appeared. He controlled his temper and said calmly, "I'm not allowed to speak to the media, and the whole thing is just about over."

"Not according to Ted Dempsey. He says you guys are heroes. He's been talking about it on his show for the last few days."

"Talking about what?"

"You and your HSI buddy and the whole border. He says he's gonna come down and do a show in a few weeks right here on the border. You're gonna be famous."

"Trudy, I promise I'm not gonna be famous. I also promise I'm not going to become mature enough to commit to a relationship and I'm not going to start ignoring police work. You walked out on me for all the right reasons. You should keep your dignity and leave right now." He wasn't much for being tough on friends and loved ones, and the puppy-dog look on her face cut into him as bad as anyone had in the past week. He wanted nothing more than the chance to hold a beautiful girl like Trudy, but he wanted to do it for the right reasons. His mother kept telling him the right girl was out there for him, but he was starting to have his doubts.

———————

John Houghton sat at his scarred wooden desk inside the Homeland Security Investigations office near the main port of entry on the border. The office was a typical federal workplace with dull paint, thin carpet, and an air conditioner that smelled like mold. Every desk had a phone, but in today's world no agents answered them. If a call was important, it came to your cell.

He had been reassigned to an ordinary HSI squad, which focused on money laundering. No one in the Department of Homeland Security had questioned his version of the events, and aside from a standard three-day administrative leave to make sure he wasn't traumatized, he'd come right back to the job he bitched about but loved. It also strengthened his faith in the DHS. So far, since the merger, they'd acted like a bunch of dickheads toward the former Customs agents. There was a strong bias toward the immigration side of the agency, which felt its mission far outweighed anything the U.S. Customs Service once claimed as its turf. But for some reason they had backed him up on the shooting. He wished he could say the same thing about his friend Tom Eriksen. The FBI still had him on leave, and his supervisor, Mike Zara, didn't seem interested in letting him come back to work anytime soon. It was a shame to waste such a hard-charging, smart young man. But that's what the FBI was famous for. They could be awfully harsh in their policy judgments.

John had spent his week off either drunk or pestering his wife to move back into the house. The two activities overlapped several times and gave his estranged wife a reason to stop talking to him. Now he was popping Xanax and had used a few Ambien to sleep. It was getting harder to deal with his everyday life.

Using what little pull he had, John had at least gotten Tom Eriksen transferred to a new unit. It wasn't necessarily operational, but that's why the FBI was willing to risk letting Eriksen come back.

He had managed to dodge most of the coverage of the shooting on TV except for the Ted Dempsey show. That son of a gun could get fixated on an issue like a bloodhound on the trail of a wounded deer.

John looked up and noticed the show happened to be on TV now. Senator Elizabeth Ramos was being interviewed again. Immigration was her big cause, and she didn't even acknowledge the shooting except to say the U.S. government shouldn't waste resources investigating something like that.

The senator's other pet peeve was the lack of focus in the war on terror. It didn't seem to matter who the president was, if nothing happened, the whole threat of terror faded from everyone's minds. With the economy in the dumper, all anyone cared about was jobs. But John knew it would only take one truckload of dynamite driven into a government building or a teaspoon of anthrax in the air-conditioning system of a major mall and the whole country would be interested in the topic of terrorism again.

This young, good-looking senator had realized that a politician can never go wrong harping about undocumented aliens and terrorism. Who would ever come out in favor of those issues?

John had to get Eriksen back to work before he started to feel sorry for himself or think he did something wrong. It happened all too often in law enforcement.

———

Pablo Piña liked his role as thug for Don Herrera. He enjoyed the respect he felt from the local residents and even enjoyed occasionally killing a rival or cop who wouldn't do as he was told. But being a father was his favorite job, and he smiled at his six-year-old daughter as she scampered out of the room to play with her cousins in the estate's backyard. He appreciated this office he had set up in his twenty-four-room hacienda because where his desk sat, he had a round panel of windows installed so he could look into the sprawling rear yard and watch his children play. One acre right next to the house had been designated a sanctuary for the children where they were never to see men with guns or hear rough language. It held two giant swing sets, a trampoline, a pool, and a full soccer field. Beyond the kids' area his men patrolled day and night, and there were always two men on the roof with Barrett .50 caliber sniper rifles that could kill a target more than a mile away.

As soon as he looked up at his chief adviser and enforcer, a wiry man with a quiet intelligence, Piña lost all good humor. He snapped, "Manny, I hear this so-called *doctor* is in El Paso."

Manny just nodded.

Piña spoke Spanish with an aristocratic flair even though he had been raised on the streets of Ciudad Juárez. He had lived a life as hard as anyone in Mexico. He'd killed his first man at thirteen, using just a knife strapped to a long pole. He pretended he was striking a lance into a dragon as the knife plunged into the man's chest. Piña drove him back into the wall of a small shop and pinned him there while others watched. It was a warning of what would come from the young man as he forged a name in the ruthless world of crime in Mexico.

Piña had even slipped across the border and killed four people, four different times in four different American cities. But as he got older and mellowed, he learned the value of education, and to set an example for his growing brood, he had continually taken courses and brought in tutors to help him with his language and math skills. He even had a manners coach who taught him how to act in certain situations so he was presentable at any party, even ones thrown by the governor, who called frequently.

Now those courses helped him when he had to deal with Don Herrera, who trusted him to run Juárez and the businesses associated with the area. Although Piña claimed to be afraid of no man, he always excluded Herrera when he said it. He also worked hard to show the powerful man that he was cultured and not just a killer from the barrio. But he held an old-style, hard-core grudge. Once he had it in his mind that someone had crossed him or insulted his family, Piña would never let a slight go. This was the sort of grudge that no amount of education could ease. It was personal. Dr. Luis Martinez had failed in the only job that he ever really needed to accomplish: to save Piña's seventeen-year-old son after he'd overdosed on a combination of prescription pills and cocaine. The doctor had failed, and now Piña's son was in the small family cemetery that held his father, his mother, and his one-year-old daughter who died of leukemia thirteen years ago.

Piña snapped back to reality, looked at Manny, and said, "Can you and a few boys cross the border and deal with this *puto* and his wife?"

"It won't help business at all. We've already ruined his life."

"He ruined mine."

Manny said, "He tried to save Pablito, but the boy was too far gone."

Now Piña dropped his voice, his warning that he was on the edge of saying or doing something less sophisticated than his recent education would predict. "This is not an argument. Do it."

Manny had worked for his boss for sixteen years and knew when to keep his mouth shut. All he said was, "Yes, boss."

"What do you need from me?"

"Just give me a few days to locate him and build the right team." After a short pause he added, "Can I look for Enrique while I'm across the border? Martinez may know where he is."

Piña just nodded. He wasn't worried about U.S. retribution and what the authorities might have on him. Enrique, the computer whiz, might manage to hurt Piña's American partners, but not him. It was one less thing to weigh on his mind. With six daughters and one son, he had plenty to worry about. Plus he had his employees who depended on his business sense and his ruthless reputation for security. Of all the murders in Ciudad Juárez, only one was one of his employees—and twenty-six men died because of it. Two had their heads chopped off and planted on spikes at the edge of the city. It was this kind of attitude that kept his people safe in the long run.

He knew Manny was hesitant because the killing would have to take place in the U.S., and the soft *norteamericanos* frowned on murder. But for something like this he would take the heat.

———

Not long after Eriksen had shown Trudy the door, he was sitting on his porch, trying to gain some perspective and relax as he read the online copy of the *Harvard Crimson* on his iPad. He heard a vehicle screech into the driveway in front of the main house, then a second vehicle roar up as well. After some doors slammed he could hear shouting and obscenities from the front of the house. It was the middle of the day in the middle of the week. The family in the main house worked hard, and no one ever came home before six in the evening.

Wearing shorts, a T-shirt, and tennis shoes, Eriksen wandered down the extended driveway until he saw the family's oldest son, Marty, standing behind his brand-new Camaro as if avoiding someone. As Eriksen came around the corner of the house he saw three burly men dressed in construction clothes standing next to a Ford F-250 diesel pickup truck pulled onto the front yard. One man started to move toward Marty, and Eriksen called out, "Hold on, what's the problem here?" He had no weapon and technically no authority whatsoever while he was on suspension, but since he'd been a little kid there was something about bullies and mismatched fights that kept him from minding his own business.

The man at the front of the truck turned and glared at Eriksen. The sign on the side of the truck said LOPEZ BUILDING SUPPLY. All three men had brown or light hair, and none appeared to be Hispanic. Eriksen couldn't help asking, "Which one of you is Mr. Lopez?"

The man at the front of the truck said, "We all are. We're brothers, you moron." He had the typical Texas drawl Eriksen had become used to.

Eriksen crept closer to Marty, who was clearly shaken by the confrontation. "Okay, Mr. Lopez, what's the problem?"

"Just who in the hell are you?"

"I'm the family adviser. And if you don't dial it back a few notches I'm gonna advise Marty to call 911."

Now the thick, six-foot-two man gave a chuckle and said, "You don't want the police involved."

Marty shook his head frantically and said, "I'm trying to make this right, Curtis."

Now Eriksen had to hold up his hands to calm everyone down and say, "Your name is *Curtis* Lopez? I gotta ask how you came by that moniker."

"Any family that lived on the border a long time has a mix of Mexican and American heritage. Just because my last name's Lopez don't mean my mama didn't want to give me a family name, too. Now I'm telling you to get out of the way and let us teach this little shithead a lesson."

Eriksen lowered his voice and turned to Marty and said, "Jesus, what are you involved with?"

"Nothing illegal, I swear. Just a little side job that's slow in paying, and now I owe Lopez Supply a few grand that I don't have."

All three men moved closer to them, and Curtis said, "A few grand! Try thirteen thousand bucks. And we've let this slide for over nine months. Just like Marty over here, we went through the whole deal without telling our pop what we were doing."

Now Eriksen had a clear picture of what had happened. It was a case of the younger generation of two established businesses trying to strike out on their own. Eriksen doubted Marty had that kind of money. Without consulting Marty he said, "What if you took his new Camaro until he gets the money together?"

"We're not in the car rental business. We want our cash, and the interest is gonna be a few broken bones." Now all three of the men rushed forward.

As Curtis Lopez reached across with both hands to grab Eriksen by the shoulders, the more agile FBI agent used his years of karate and seemingly endless self-defense training from the Bureau to slip to one side, twisting one of Curtis's arms behind his back as he did. Instead of releasing Curtis, he ran the big man forward like a battering ram into the second man, who was advancing on Marty. The two men crashed into each other, sending the second man against the hood of the Camaro. Eriksen pulled Curtis back a few feet and then slammed him into the man again. Then Eriksen released Curtis's arm, stepped back, and kicked him hard on the side of the leg between the knee and the hip, striking a vital nerve and causing the big man to tumble to the ground.

Without waiting for the second man to react, Eriksen threw a left elbow across his jaw, knocking him across the hood of the Camaro and onto the ground near his brother. Now the third man completely ignored Marty and rushed Eriksen, who easily sidestepped him and brought a foot up into his solar plexus. When the man bent over and exhaled violently, Eriksen grabbed him by the shoulders and redirected him between his two brothers already sprawled on the ground.

Eriksen straightened to his full six feet and tried to stay as calm as possible as he said, "Now are you guys ready to listen to reason?"

Each of the men was holding a different part of his body as Curtis looked up and said, "Dang, you didn't have no reason to do that to us. We were just trying to collect what's ours."

"But I can't have you beating up on Marty here. His family's been too good to me."

"What are we gonna tell our pop when he sees the loss of inventory?"

Eriksen slowly helped the men to their feet one at a time, even brushing off dead grass from their clothes. He was still ready to send a more serious message, but at least these guys weren't on alert for another attack. He led them back to the giant pickup and noticed a computer on the front seat.

"You got the store ledgers and inventory on the laptop?"

The men all nodded. The three brothers looked at each other sheepishly. Finally Curtis said, "Yeah. We put a password on the files so Pop didn't get a shock seeing them. We need to look at them for big jobs, so we always have a computer handy. Pop won't worry about it until he wants to look them over. That's gonna happen any day now."

Eriksen said, "Can I take a look? I'm good with finances. Maybe I can help, and we'll get you the money as soon as we can."

It took some more convincing and a lot of conversation between the brothers, but Curtis fired up the machine and opened the files.

Eriksen had spent his years at Harvard learning the ins and outs of finance and accounting. The FBI had shown him what to look for if someone was hiding money. This was simple. He just did what he was trained to do in reverse. The language of finance and numbers had always come easily to him, and compared to some of the records he had seen, these were simple.

Lopez Building Supply was a profitable family business with what must have been a giant warehouse. Eriksen looked down and moved several numbers around until the total inventory and sales balanced. He showed it to Curtis, who stood slack-jawed at the speed and effectiveness of Eriksen's little changes. Curtis said, "Oh snap, bro, where'd you learn to do that?"

"It's a magical place called college."

"Don't be a dick, we all three went to college."

"What school?"

"Texas A&M."

Eriksen managed to withhold any witty comments. Instead he said, "So are we all good?"

Curtis used his size and glare to show his concern. "We still need to get paid."

Eriksen said, "What if I give you my word we'll figure out a way to pay you?"

"And what do we get in return for waiting?"

"Right off the bat, you won't get any more black eyes and I won't toss you around the front yard like old furniture. How's that sound?"

Slowly Curtis nodded. "What are we supposed to do for money till then?"

"You still have your job at Lopez Supply. And if we have to we'll go to Marty's dad to see about getting an advance on his salary."

Tentatively Curtis stuck out his hand, and as Eriksen shook it, the big man said, "We ain't in no position to argue with you right now."

Eriksen stood his ground until all three men had piled back into the big pickup truck, backed carefully out of the yard, and headed down the street. Marty stepped up behind him and said, "I can't thank you enough, Tom."

Eriksen didn't even look back at him as he said, "Shut it. I don't know what kind of scam you were running, but you're sure as shit gonna pay those guys back so we don't have to go through this exercise again. Understood?" He turned to give Marty a hard look.

"Yes, sir."

"I just committed a felony to keep all of you in good with your parents. I gotta get back to work. I'm turning into a day care teacher."

SIX

Tom Eriksen took in his surroundings as he followed his FBI supervisor, Mike Zara, into his new post of duty. For the first time since he had been with the FBI, Eriksen had a chance to use his degree in international finance to assess the situation. He decided the building they were in looked like either a really nice Charles Schwab office or a run-down Merrill Lynch office. Dozens of neatly but casually dressed men and women worked in cubicles, and each window gave a decent view of downtown El Paso. Every government worker's dream is to have a view of El Paso, Texas.

The building itself gave no outward sign that it was related to the federal government. There was nothing on the inside that indicated it was a law enforcement office. In fact, in Eriksen's mind, it wasn't. It was an *intelligence unit*. A unit that looked into rumors and didn't make arrests. They handed off the operational cases to other agencies and moved on to the next assignment to determine the connections between narcotics-trafficking groups and terror groups, or whatever someone dreamed up. The old-timers in the Bureau called it "the rubber gun squad." Great.

Zara could barely contain his glee at Eriksen getting an even shittier assignment than his last. He wasn't that much older than Eriksen, probably his midthirties, but he had the attitude and demeanor of a sixty-year-old, coupled with the pettiness and jealousy of a five-year-old. And he always spoke a little too loudly.

As a supervisor, Zara was probably what federal agencies liked. He tended to be a micromanager and insisted on knowing every detail of Eriksen's day. He was terrified of tactical operations because he didn't have any experience in them. That was probably one of the reasons Zara looked so happy. By definition, an intelligence unit didn't participate in tactical operations and therefore had very little chance of bringing attention to itself with a shooting or something else that Zara would find distasteful.

Most of the personnel in the drab but comfortable commercial building were analysts who could navigate computers and public records to make connections between people and groups. Eriksen recognized their work was vital and difficult; he just didn't want to be part of it. He was surprised at the number of agencies represented in the office. Even the secretive National Security Agency had analysts working at computers in an office in front of a room filled with equipment that monitored a number of communications satellites and radio transmissions. As they walked along what felt like a quarter mile of plush carpet, Eriksen noticed rooms with computers that searched keywords entered into the different search engines in real time. An attractive blond woman looked up and smiled as he lingered at the door, marveling at the computers, which generated so much heat they required extra air-conditioning pumped into the secure room.

He couldn't say he wasn't impressed by the computers, and he'd told himself he would adopt John Houghton's positive attitude about seeing the good side of any assignment. Then the smile on Zara's face turned more menacing as they rounded a corner and he said, "This is where *you'll* be working." He had the sound of a man about to open the door on a surprise party.

Eriksen stepped into the room crammed with desks and felt like he was stepping into the seventies through a time portal with cheap carpet, a popcorn ceiling, and Formica desktops.

Five men and three women turned to see who had entered their lair, but only one showed any interest. A striking young woman with long dark hair stood from the nearest desk and said in a curt tone, "I'm Lila Tellis, DEA. Welcome to the Island of Misfit Cops."

After the harrowing border crossing, Dr. Luis Martinez, sitting in the clean one-bedroom apartment, couldn't believe how comfortable the U.S. authorities had made him and his wife. The building had been built in the sixties, and it had thick walls and a sturdy fire escape that ran up to their fifth-floor apartment. The deep carpet was new, and the bed felt like a cloud. It was the perfect way for the U.S. government to show gratitude for his efforts to save the wounded Border Patrol agent.

The Border Patrol in particular appreciated how hard he'd worked in his futile effort to save the agent shot by the human traffickers. Once they had heard the story of his former employer, Pablo Piña, other agencies were very interested in speaking with him. He was careful not to let out too much information at once, and now that he and his wife were secure in the pleasant apartment near the Federal Building in downtown El Paso, he would use the information to keep this level of comfort.

Of the people that had interviewed him so far, he liked a young female DEA agent who spoke Spanish well but with an odd accent he couldn't place. Her business card indicated that she was in some kind of special intelligence task force, and he could tell by her sharp dark eyes and intensity that the girl was intelligent herself.

Even with the beautiful DEA agent, Dr. Martinez had held back information. The time would come when he would have to remind U.S. authorities how valuable he was. For example, he still had not told them anything about his U.S. employer, and he hoped to keep that secret unless revealing it was absolutely necessary. If he was somehow able to wrangle a long-term visa, he still hoped to work for them.

He had been careful during the debriefing not to mention his friend Enrique, or, as he had confided in the doctor, Eric. Eric already lived in the United States and had to cross the border frequently, but his employer wanted no record of it. Dr. Martinez wondered if his young computer friend was safe. He was going to call the special phone Eric had said only a few people knew about. He didn't want to trade his friend to the government, but he would if he had to. Family meant too much to him.

Luis Martinez had called his daughter to tell her she could cross legally with her husband and their two children. The Border Patrol had worked out all the details. But her husband insisted that his family be allowed to come as well, and that made the crossing more problematic. Soon, with extended family, he wanted to bring more than forty people with him and refused to leave without all of them. Dr. Martinez's daughter didn't feel she could cross without her husband, and so now they were at an impasse.

Dr. Martinez made a few notes and looked down, wondering what information he could trade for visas. He didn't think three or four visas were any issue at all, but once he started multiplying it and including cousins and aunts, he knew he'd have to come up with something good.

In the meantime, he'd settle down on the comfortable couch and watch a few more minutes of ESPN on the big-screen TV. Not only was it relaxing, but he justified it by telling his wife it was helping him with his English.

Driving his Cadillac in downtown El Paso still felt odd to Cash. The Caddy seemed more at home in Boston or even L.A. Here all he saw were sport utilities and Jeeps. The cold General Motors air-conditioning fought to overcome the heat of the day but did nothing against the stench of garlic coming off his new partner, Ari.

Cash had never felt he was anti-Semitic. In Jersey and New York, he had lived and worked with Jewish people his whole life. He also recognized that most people south of Philly couldn't tell the difference between a New York Italian and a New York Jew. But Cash had decided that if he had to spend too much more time with Ari, he might summon some righteous prejudice.

Now Ari was saying, "Ari's hungry." Not *I'm hungry*. He sounded like a conceited NFL wide receiver.

"We ate two hours ago."

"Is there a law we can't eat again? Ari needs protein to fuel these legs." Ari patted his thick thighs. He let his gaze linger on his lap as if he were admiring all the work he did in the gym.

Cash sighed and said, "They want us to tie up loose ends. That means finding the doctor and his wife, as well as the goddamn computer guy named Eric we lost track of."

"And you're sure they didn't go back to Mexico?"

"The computer guy is from Chicago originally, but he spends a lot of time in Juárez."

"Got any other ideas?"

Cash said, "No one has seen them. The boss gets info somehow. He was checking around. But the whole reason the doctor was willing to come across the border was that his life wasn't worth ten cents in good old Mexico. The young computer guy is a different story. Maybe he slipped past the Border Patrol agents and made it to the U.S. I screwed up not keeping better track of him. If he shows up at the main office, there's no problem. That means he's loyal, but if he's trying to leverage information, he'll end up on the shit list on both sides of the border. Seems like a lot of people think they can get over on the company lately."

Ari turned and looked at his partner, who was a good five inches taller, and said, "Ari wants to handle DiMetti's wife personally."

"We don't even know if there's anything to handle yet."

"Why risk it? Are you going soft on us? Ari would kill them all and be done with it."

"But Ari's not in charge."

Cash could hear the young Israeli mutter, "Yet."

———

Tom Eriksen had a twinge of apprehension about Lila Tellis. He suspected a lot of men felt that way based on her looks, but his impression was based on her attitude, which she showed without hesitation. The squad bay they were sitting in didn't ease his anxiety.

The walls were a tad too close and the puke green paint was anything but calming.

When Mike Zara started to sit down at one of the desks, Lila said, "You have to go through a class and sign a confidentiality agreement before you have authorization to stay in this room. This is the most classified of all the offices in the building. That's why the maintenance and cleaning crews can't come in."

Zara said, "But I'm his supervisor."

Lila winced at his loud voice but shot right back, "And he's mine." She jerked her thumb to a giant man sitting at the rear of the room, wearing a short-sleeve shirt with a tie that came about halfway down his chest. The man's massive arms were matted with thick dark hair, making him look like an extra from a *Planet of the Apes* movie.

The man made a sound like thunder rumbling up from the desert. "She's right."

Zara stammered, "But I have a top secret clearance and I'm with the FBI."

"And I'm with Homeland Security, but I still had to take the class and sign the agreement to come into this room." He turned his massive head to look at Eriksen and said, "He can update you on anything you need to know. That's how it's always worked around here, Mr. FBI."

Zara hesitated, the way he often did. Indecision wasn't acute in the porcine FBI supervisor, it was chronic.

The Homeland Security supervisor said, "What's it gonna be? Class or leave?"

Flustered, Zara looked down at his watch, then mumbled, "I gotta go." As soon as he was out of the room, the big DHS supervisor chuckled, "Just like I thought, no class." He looked at Eriksen and said, "My name is Andre."

Immediately, Eriksen had to wonder if it was a nickname after the wrestler Andre the Giant. He was about to laugh when the big man said, "Make any jokes about my name and you'll fail the class and have to follow your supervisor right out of here."

Eriksen nodded, stifling any comment he'd thought he might make. Finally, he said, "How long is the class?"

Andre looked at Lila, who waved her arm across the office and said, "This is where we work. End of class." She slid a sheet of paper onto the desk next to him. "Sign this agreement and you're good to go."

"That's it?"

Lila said, "Yep. You see, Mr. FBI, we're all here for stepping on our dicks, at least figuratively. Our agencies think we're harmless over here. But we wear it like a badge of honor. Usually the Bureau handles its screw-ups by itself. You're my first FBI agent." She cut him a sly sideways glance with those beautiful eyes and added, "In here, at least."

SEVEN

John Houghton was glad to get a chance to have lunch with his former partner. He still thought the normally cheerful Tom Eriksen looked a little down, but it didn't take long for him to decide it was more a result of the typical FBI bungling a personnel matter than it was an emotional reaction to the shooting. John was careful not to sound too happy about his reassignment, and he didn't let on that he had been instrumental in getting Eriksen back to work.

The perky Tex-Mex restaurant, which sat near the trendy Union Depot, played the obligatory cheesy mariachi music over cheap speakers, but the outdoor tables were well spaced and clean. The Hispanic equivalent of Hooters, it served the best burritos in the Southwest. The smell of roasting vegetables and sizzling skirt steak reminded John of the family dinners he had enjoyed here just a few months ago. He had come early to down a few beers without the reproachful stare of his FBI friend. John was certain that if he worked for the FBI he'd drink a lot more than he already did.

After they ordered, he said to Eriksen, "One thing you have to promise me you'll remember and live by."

Eriksen shook his head, obviously anxious for the wisdom his experienced partner was about to dispense.

"Always have meetings or discuss work over a meal. Always. Saves time, and a good cop never gets hungry or gets wet. Remember that."

Eriksen gave him a good smile. That was enough. Although he was trying to cheer up the young FBI agent, it was also sound advice.

John said, "So what are your coworkers like? I know our guy, Andre Sanders, is a hoot. He'd still be running one of our squads if he hadn't tried to cover for one of his agents who had an accidental discharge with his pistol. The dumbass was cleaning it at home and left one in the chamber after ejecting the magazine. One of his neighbors called the cops when he heard the shot, but Andre smoothed the whole thing over. Then someone ratted him out, and he's serving his penance over at the Border Security Task Force. You could do a lot worse for a boss."

"Everyone over there seems okay. The DEA rep is a tough chick named Lila. I can't figure her out."

John nodded. "I heard she's on the secretive side. No one knows much about her, but she's a hard worker."

"At least I'm not sitting at home."

"I'm glad you're happy with the assignment. Now we gotta do something to clear up the perception that we shot two guys in Mexico."

"How are we going to do that?"

"I'm working on it right now. I keep hearing a rumor that one of the shitheads found dead was American, not Mexican. There's also a rumor that the bullet wounds were inflicted from close range. We never got within thirty yards of them."

"Where are you getting these rumors from?"

John smiled. "I can sure tell you haven't worked in the intelligence squad too long. Rumors come from all sorts of places. Down here everyone calls it border talk. Goes back and forth and everyone hears something about every subject. I've worked the damn border here for over twenty years and have contacts on both sides. The second rule most intel squads have is never reveal your specific source of information."

"What good does it do us to prove one of the coyotes was American? Or that someone else shot them? It feels like my bosses have already decided I'm a liability."

"The first thing it might do is get the FBI off your ass. Maybe you could land back onto a squad that makes arrests. The second thing it would do is keep guys like Ted Dempsey from doing their show live on the border. Our jobs are hard enough without distractions like that."

"Dempsey seems to be sincere, and he's definitely backing us up."

"There's no doubt he's on our side, but it would be best to move past this whole incident. It doesn't matter that much to me, but you got your whole career in front of you. You don't want to be known as 'the guy from the border shooting.'"

John could see his young friend apply his considerable intellect to the issue. He still looked tired and a little older than he should. Maybe this was something John should investigate on his own.

———

Tom Eriksen and his new partner, Lila Tellis, walked through the quiet lobby in complete silence. Eriksen finally realized that as much as he'd talked to Lila Tellis in the last two days, she really hadn't told him much about herself. He'd shared about his family and his hope to work something worthwhile like investigate terrorism and she only told him that she was originally from Toledo and had been with the DEA four years. She had a very youthful face and a lean and athletic body but he didn't think she was older than twenty-eight. He discovered she had a serious mistrust of the FBI. His supervisor, Mike Zara, didn't do anything to convince her otherwise.

Now they were on their way to the apartment where Dr. Martinez and his wife were living. Last week Lila had debriefed the doctor about his life in Mexico and the work he did for the cartels. He had told Lila stories of how he patched up gunshot wounds, set bones broken in car accidents on the twisty mountain roads, and even delivered babies with only the minimum amount of modern equipment and one old, surly Argentine nurse.

This was the kind of work she did every day—talking to people crossing the border. She didn't like to call them illegal aliens. They were just people, usually poor people who were looking for a better life. One of her interests was trying to determine how bad Mexican society in general had become as a result of the drug wars. As part of his indoctrination to the unit, the first statistic she mentioned was that in the last few years almost fifteen hundred people had been killed each year in Ciudad Juárez. A few hundred feet across the border in El Paso there were between ten and twenty-five murders. If that wasn't an indicator of the breakdown of a society, Eriksen didn't know what was.

When they got to the building where Dr. and Mrs. Martinez were being kept by the Immigration Service, Eriksen was surprised at how nice it was. He wondered if all the apartments were rented by the agency.

One of the things Eriksen liked about his new partner was the way Lila moved with confidence and was a complete professional unless she met someone who needed to be put in their place. That's what happened when they walked into the lobby of the apartment building and the rent-a-cop tried to keep them from going directly to the Martinezes' front door.

The pudgy guy with the red face and crew cut worked himself off the stool near the elevator, holding up his hand and saying, "Hold on there, little lady. I've got to announce you before you go up."

Lila let the "little lady" comment slide as she smiled and flipped open her credentials that identified her as a special agent with the U.S. Drug Enforcement Administration. All she said was, "Official business."

"It's my official business to know who comes in and goes out of this building." The guy's attitude made Eriksen check his uniform more closely to make sure he wasn't some sort of government service officer or cop. But his patches clearly identified him as a private security officer, and an ancient Smith & Wesson Model 10 revolver indicated he worked for a cheap company.

Lila sighed and just stepped toward the elevator. The man reached out and wrapped beefy fingers around her arm. In a fluid motion, she simply reached across and grasped the man's hand, twisting his thumb one way and his knuckles another. Somehow the fat security officer spun in place and ended up seated on his stool.

Lila said in an even voice, "The next time you touch a federal agent, you get booked into jail with a broken arm. Is that clearly understood?"

The man nodded his head as he looked up at her and said, "What're you, a Terminator?"

All Lila said was, "Worse, I'm on my period." She turned to Eriksen and gave him a quick wink.

Maybe she was human after all.

A few minutes later they were sitting in the pleasant living room of the apartment shared by Dr. Martinez and his pretty wife. Eriksen still felt like a passenger on this train as he sat back and listened to Lila ask the doctor a few more questions.

She leaned forward from her spot on the couch and looked the doctor in the eye. He was sitting in the matching chair across an old coffee table with rings from the fifties stained into it. Eriksen realized she was putting the doctor at ease and doing a good job of it.

Lila said, "I really need to know who you were going to work for here in the U.S."

The doctor shrugged his shoulders and said, "I don't know. I told you this already." He spoke English with just a slight accent, like many educated people speaking a second language. It sounded more elegant than obtrusive.

Lila said, "Really? You risk the dangerous trip over here without knowing what company you're gonna work for? You told me last week that you were coming over to take a job with a decent salary. How could you possibly know the salary and not know who was paying you?"

"I don't understand why you're questioning me like this. Last week you were so pleasant and supportive, and you only wanted to know about my life in Mexico. The Border Patrol and Immigration people have been treating me like a celebrity because of what I did for their wounded man. Why should a DEA agent be so harsh to me?"

"I'm asking these questions because it could be useful for us to know who's bringing a doctor across to treat workers. That sounds like a really big human trafficker."

The doctor hesitated, then looked across the room to his wife, who was pretending not to listen to the conversation. "Well, it could be really useful to me to get an extra thirty visas for my son-in-law's family."

Lila shook her head and said, "That's a big family and a lot to ask."

"An employer like this would be a big feather in some federal agency's cap."

"And what would a trip back to Mexico be like? Do you think that would put a feather in someone's cap? That's a question you might like to ask yourself, Dr. Martinez." She closed her notebook, stood without preamble, and quietly stalked out of the room.

If Eriksen were the good doctor, he would probably have shit his pants right about now. This girl was pure dynamite.

EIGHT

Tom Eriksen had never watched TV while at work before. This office had an entire room dedicated to three big-screen TVs hanging on separate walls, three computers used for undercover and anonymous Web surfing, and a police scanner that picked up Juárez police activity. Spacious, with beige walls and new carpet, it was called the media room and was probably the nicest space in the office. The door closed snugly so the noise of the televisions or scanner didn't bother anyone.

Eriksen was still trying to figure out his exact job description at the Border Intelligence Unit, which was often referred to as the Border Security Task Force. No one seemed to care what it was called. He knew it wasn't oriented toward operations like arrests and surveillance, but he was just starting to realize how much information came into the center every day. Novels and TV shows made it look like intelligence units did nothing but intercept secret messages and spy on other people, but, in fact, information came from a variety of sources. One of the easiest and most successful was TV news coverage. Fox, both its news and business networks, and most of the other cable channels had reporters and producers posted all over the world. There was no way that even the federal government would ignore efficient and cost-effective resources like that.

At least that's how Tom Eriksen rationalized sitting in a task force media room, watching footage of a protest in Mexico about the shooting of Mexican nationals in Mexico by U.S. law enforcement officials. It was an odd experience for Eriksen to watch the show and know that he was the unnamed focus of it.

Then the giant head of Ted Dempsey filled the screen as he gave an intense promo for a show that evening. "Riots in Mexico, soaring murder rates, and two American heroes under the microscope."

From behind Eriksen someone said, "That's about you, isn't it?"

The voice startled him and made him jerk his head. It was the beautiful blonde with the creamy complexion he'd seen earlier, working in one of the communications offices.

She said, "I'm sorry, I didn't mean to startle you." Her soft voice matched her delicate appearance.

The woman said, "I'm Katharine Gleason, but my friends call me Kat."

"I'm Tom." That was all he could manage in the current situation. He'd never thought he was particularly suave with women, but it would be nice to come up with something other than just his first name. Especially with a knockout like this.

Kat gave him a perfect smile and said, "You think this is purgatory, don't you? I've heard the other law enforcement people call the task force the Island of Misfit Cops."

Eriksen said, "I take it you're not sworn?" Being sworn meant that you had attended a police academy and been "sworn in" as a law enforcement officer. It was usually the difference between carrying a gun and making arrests versus working at computers in the office.

She shook her head and said, "I'm an analyst with NSA."

"No kidding. How'd you end up at the National Security Agency?" He didn't know much about the secretive intelligence agency.

"I was recruited out of school."

"Where'd you go?"

Kat smiled again as she eased into the chair at the other end of the table. "Stanford, the Harvard of the West. What about you?"

"I went to Harvard. The Stanford of the east." Eriksen found himself forgetting about his problems for the first time in days.

She asked, "What did you study?"

"International finance."

Kat said, "That's part of my job."

Eriksen said, "What's the rest?"

"Can't talk about it."

"Maybe we'll get a chance to work together."

"I seriously doubt it. My mandate is to pass on specific information to Homeland Security. And right now you're attracting too much attention for the NSA to be associated with you." She held up her hands. "That's not me, that's the agency and policy. In some ways we're worse than the FBI about maintaining our image."

"I doubt that." He smiled, trying to figure out how to spend a few more minutes with this girl.

Manny had been the chief of operations for Pablo Piña for seven years now. Aside from the remarkable financial rewards, he liked the logistical planning and management. But occasionally he was stuck with a task he didn't care for. Like this.

Manny was walking in the busy square in downtown Juárez. Just looking around at the buildings, a visitor wouldn't know this was considered the "murder capital of the world." People weren't running down the street shooting at each other. It might not have the elegance of New York or the glitz of Los Angeles, but the town conveyed a sense of commerce.

The buildings were not newly painted, and the sidewalks were cracked. The few trees in the park had withered due to a lack of care by the municipal workers. Some people said they were afraid to work in the parks due to the violence. Manny thought it was more likely they were just overworked and a little lazy.

Manny considered his position in the organization. He respected his boss, Pablo Piña, but El Jefe's thirst for retribution against Dr. Martinez was foolish and wasteful. Manny appreciated his role as an adviser and knew when to argue with the Dark Lord of the Desert. And when his boss wasted resources like this, he really earned his nickname.

Few Mexicans could conceive of a man more powerful than

Pablo Piña. He ruled the area around Ciudad Juárez with an absolute iron fist. But Manny knew even Piña had someone to answer
to. He had never met him, but through years of careful attention to
details he had concluded that Piña's boss was Ramón Herrera. The
Pemex board member and industrialist appeared to be above the
violence of Mexico and probably thought he was, but the death toll
was always tied to men like that. Herrera had no idea how most
people lived. Manny was sure he didn't care, either. But Pablo Piña
was afraid of him, and that was an impressive feat.

In order to actually accomplish something while dealing with Dr.
Martinez, Manny intended to put more effort into finding Enrique—or Eric, as his American friends called him—than he let on.
The computer geek could affect business whether Piña thought so
or not. Business was all Manny thought about. Grudges were for
teenagers and Italians, not businessmen looking for respect.

They had cocaine and marijuana to run, even the occasional load
of farm workers looking for a better life in the United States. Usually he took them across, because his conscience would not allow
the coyotes to prey on them like bloodsucking parasites. He had no
idea who Martinez had contracted to take him and his wife across
the border, but they had stumbled right into a hornet's nest of border cops. Even if Piña was blind to the realities of business, Ramón
Herrera was not. He would ask questions about why the deal with
the American company soured if the computer engineer was not
found and the information protected.

Manny knew the protests going on here were being staged. The
only odd thing was he didn't know who was staging them. It could
be the government looking for some benefit from the United States
or hoping the different U.S. federal agencies back off the border so
they could start lining their pockets again, but it had the feel of a
more effective guiding hand like one of the other drug lords. It
didn't really affect him, but he found it curious that anyone cared
about a couple of dead coyotes and that the federal agencies in the
United States would take the shooting so seriously. Here in Mexico
cops shot people all the time on purpose and by accident, and rarely

had to do much more than apologize to the family if it was a mistake.

Right now all Manny cared about was getting the product processed and shipped over to their best markets. It took an amazing amount of money to get this accomplished. It was an endless circle. They made money by smuggling drugs. They needed money to buy equipment and men and police (at least in Mexico), and if they had no money the *federales* would descend upon them, and then no one would work. Hundreds of families would go hungry, and no one in Mexico or the United States would care.

Manny had studied economics at the University of Chihuahua and understood the basics of any economic model. Killing a helpless doctor was not part of the basics. It did nothing for their bottom line.

Now, strolling in the busy square in the northeast section of Juárez, Manny knew exactly who he needed to come with him to kill the doctor. If it were here, in Mexico, there were dozens of men he could use, but in El Paso, under the watchful eye of a competent police force, he had to be careful. He knew the doctor was still in El Paso. One of his many sets of eyes had seen him. They'd have an exact location soon.

He plopped down into a comfortable chair at an outdoor café next to a hulking man with short gray hair. The man barely turned his pockmarked face as Manny said, "I could use you, Hector."

"When?"

The man's voice sounded like it was rumbling out of a troll's lair. "In the next few days."

The man just nodded. After a few seconds of silence he said, "My cousin will come, too."

"Can you control him, Hector?"

The big man rumbled, "He needs the work."

Manny just nodded. It was the same story everywhere. Things were getting tight because the government was cracking down. They were bowing to pressure from the United States. He said, "I know. The new senator from Texas is causing us a lot of grief."

Hector said, "The woman? Doesn't she have family in Mexico that can be pressured?"

Manny just shrugged.

"Why would her husband let her do something as degrading as politics? And why does she have to pick on us?"

"The people in the United States are always looking for causes. If terrorism isn't hot, then immigration is. It just happens that this woman is stuck on both, and that attitude is a lethal combination for a country that listens to singers and actors about politics." Manny paused and added, "I wish I was going to use you on something important, because that might be good for business. Instead, the boss has us handling a personal vendetta."

The big man chuckled and said, "As long as I get paid, I don't care what the reasons are."

————

Ramón Herrera felt secure strapped into the Bell JetRanger helicopter he owned through one of his corporations. The comfortable commercial helicopter was unmarked but fitted with a new system to buffer the interior noise of the rotors. There was also a 7.62 mm six-barreled M134 Minigun that could be deployed from a hidden compartment on the side of the helicopter if there was trouble. The weapon, manufactured by General Electric and capable of firing up to four thousand rounds per minute, would solve most problems Herrera might run across while flying.

The pilot, dressed in an off-the-rack JCPenney business suit, was a former U.S. Marine helicopter pilot, and the two well-dressed men in the back were part of Herrera's personal security force. Herrera made the pilot swing over Juárez so he could get a look at the city before landing on the southern edge at the office complex used by Pablo Piña. The sprawling barrios, made up of rickety buildings and shacks pasted together with scrap metal, spilled over the low rolling hills all the way to the Rio Bravo de Norte, which the Americans called the Rio Grande.

Right now he was gazing down at the protests he had arranged.

The crowd of about a thousand gathered near the municipal complex and attracted the attention of local police and army troops as well. It gave the masses something to scream about. If they were focused on the supposed killing of Mexicans by U.S. police, it took their minds off so many other problems. It made Herrera feel like a Roman emperor, giving his subjects entertainment. That idea coincided with him regarding his security force as his Praetorian Guard. But no Roman ever had access to an arsenal like his. Even the helicopter had a .30 caliber machine gun mounted on it.

The protests served a secondary purpose of reminding the American government how careful it had to be when dealing with issues on the border.

He had several reasons for being in Juárez today, but his main purpose was to talk face-to-face with his chief thug in the area. Pablo Piña had a leaky organization, and Herrera wanted to know what he was going to do about the snitch that passed on all kinds of information to someone in the U.S. government. It usually had nothing to do with drugs, and Herrera was very disturbed by the inside knowledge the U.S. could use against his business interests.

Herrera knew he would eventually discover who the snitch was. He had spent too much time and too much money developing sources in the United States. His main target of recruitment was U.S. federal law enforcement officers. He chose them *because* they were hard to break. Unlike their Mexican counterparts, they made excellent salaries and had outstanding training. They also endured extensive background investigations before they were hired, which meant Herrera had to get to them after they were already in their positions. He was methodical and relentless, taking small steps, but never going too far until he had someone firmly in his grasp. It was the same way the Central Intelligence Agency recruited spies from across the globe.

He would start with a simple dinner party or a free meal and slowly escalate to a small gift like a leather wallet or expensive sunglasses. Once he got through those steps, Herrera would move on to something bigger, like a woman for the night. The best and quickest way was to offer a woman for the night who was expendable. All he needed was one drunken, pissed-off, twice-divorced federal agent to kill a prostitute and he owned him. It had happened more than once. Or at least, he had convinced more than one man it had happened. Alcohol and barbiturates with the right dead girl could have a great effect on a man's sense of reality.

If, on the other hand, one of the federal agents rejected a small gift early on in their relationship, he would just write it off as Herrera being a rich, generous Mexican. He had used the phrase "part of our culture" regarding the gifts on a number of occasions.

The days of blackmailing with a photograph of an indiscretion or simple embarrassment were long gone.

It wasn't like Mexico, where they lived by the motto "silver or lead." Every cop knew it. You can either take money and do what you're told, or risk being shot. It was brutal but simple. There were no games, and it didn't waste time.

Herrera preferred not to meet men like Pablo in public or at their offices. He didn't want to be associated with the drug business in any way. If you were labeled a criminal or a "drug lord," it would greatly interfere with your other pursuits. He had too much work to do with the government and legitimate businesses to be a fugitive like the head of the Sinaloa Cartel, Joaquin Guzmán, known to the masses as "El Chapo." Rich and powerful, he was a folk hero to the people of Sinaloa. He was also the most wanted man in Mexico. Of course, that didn't keep him from walking in public occasionally. It was really all public relations how you were labeled. "Businessman" sounded better than "drug lord." To Herrera, "freedom" sounded better than "fugitive."

Pablo Piña rushed out to greet him at the helicopter like an eager child. His ill-fitting suit told Herrera that Pablo didn't usually dress for work but was trying to impress him. The landing pad was between his five-story office building and a slum of second-rate businesses that included mechanics and reupholstering shops.

Herrera kept quiet until they were in the comfort of the air-conditioned lobby of Piña's building. Then he simply said, "How is the business with Mr. Haben?"

Piña's hesitation said it all. Then the ruddy-faced thug said, "Good. It's going good."

Herrera nodded and said, "I wish to expand it." When it was obvious Piña had nothing further to add and seemed at a loss for words, Herrera said, "I want to talk to you about the potential for informers inside your organization. But I have heard you're on a particular crusade with more bodies than usual."

"Who told you that?"

"Don't worry about it. Worry about how to dispose of the bodies."

Now a smile crept over Piña's crooked face. It was unnerving, and Herrera suddenly understood why so many people could be intimidated by him.

Piña said, "If you have a moment, Don Herrera, I would love to show you our ingenious solution to that."

Herrera was intrigued, and in spite of his better judgment, he nodded, then followed Piña out into the parking lot and through a series of short alleys cutting between businesses. His security men trailed him, drawing their weapons to be on the safe side. Herrera liked the fact that they were always on edge.

He was rarely in places like Juárez. He never got to see things up close. Now he smelled the stale odor of urine and noticed the incredible number of bullet holes in virtually every old building. All different calibers and sizes had shredded some buildings and merely maimed others. Some bullet holes made crazy patterns, almost like clouds drifting across the sky.

Finally, behind an auto repair business, the group stopped at a wide, open lot with rusted cars lining the six-foot-high cement wall. It was remote and secure. In the middle of several vehicles was what looked like a small swimming pool filled with a dark, bubbling liquid.

Herrera said, "What's this, Pablo? Your new Jacuzzi?"

They both laughed at his little joke, but Piña was obviously enjoying giving his boss a tour. He said, "This is where the bodies go."

"They're hidden in the pool?"

"It's not a pool. It's twenty-five feet deep and is filled with a mixture of acids, lye, and motor oils. Nothing of any value could ever be recovered from a body dropped in here. And none of the thirty-five bodies we have dumped in it are left intact."

Just the idea of the acid-filled pool made Herrera's skin crawl. "It's a human stew?"

"Brilliant, isn't it?"

Herrera could only nod in agreement. Was this what Mexico had come to?

NINE

Tom Eriksen sat in the Border Security Intelligence Unit's media room and continued to watch TV, but mainly because Kat was sitting with him in the empty room. He knew very little of what the National Security Agency really did. They weren't the CIA and didn't use operatives for the most part, but they were the king of communications. They could listen in to anything from a satellite to a couple of kids using tin cans and string. He'd heard stories since he first started with the FBI about tidbits of information from the NSA that helped prevent calamitous attacks.

All the public focused on was terror attacks that hit the news. They had no idea how many potential attacks were defused well before they came to the attention of the media. The fact was that since September 11, 2001, jihadists and others had continuously attempted to cause havoc with everything from simple plans like driving a tanker loaded with fuel into a crowded building to complex schemes for releasing bioweapons in the subways of New York. In each case, the FBI had uncovered the plot before completion, and certainly some of that heads-up came from the National Security Agency and their ability to listen to conversations halfway around the world.

His interest in the NSA right now concerned the young woman with a soft, pleasant manner that made him think of a character from a Jane Austen novel. But his attention was diverted back to the TV when Ted Dempsey welcomed the relatively new senator from Texas. She was very pretty, with dark features and a professional demeanor, but the first thing Eriksen noticed was that she didn't have a Texas accent.

He said, "Where is she from?"

Kat said, "Third-generation Texan. Her ancestors are from around Mexico City. She's from the Dallas area originally, but she lived back east."

From the TV, the appealing senator looked like a bank teller as she crossed her legs, leaned toward Ted Dempsey, and said in a very calm voice, "We must close the border until our visitors understand they must sign our guest registry on entry. We live in perilous times and have no idea who crosses our borders. Everyone from criminals to terrorists has easy access. The whole idea frightens me." She gave Dempsey a chance to agree, but didn't look like she cared if he did. The senator continued, "As much as fifty billion dollars is laundered across the border. That's billion with a *B*. Over two hundred U.S. cities have Mexican drug cartels and Central American gangs operating in them, which are responsible for hundreds of homicides. The sister city to El Paso, Juárez, Mexico, is the murder capital of Mexico— more than fifteen hundred homicides each year. Now they don't even keep track of them. The U.S. Border Patrol stopped over three hundred and twenty thousand illegal, undocumented border crossers last year. That's a lot of tax dollars spent on policies that encourage people to risk the trip."

Dempsey had to interrupt the monologue. "As to your last point, Senator, don't we want border officers working?"

"Yes, Ted, we do, but the seventeen thousand or so Border Patrol agents can be more effective other ways. If we just close the border, even for a short period, we could use the military and have different rules of engagement. Technically the Posse Comitatus Act, which restricts the use of U.S. armed forces to enforce state laws, only applies to the U.S. Army and Air Force. The National Guard could easily be used for law enforcement duties. But I think this is a national security issue and the army could be used with the right support. It would send a serious message to the Mexican government about how serious the U.S. is about security. As a Mexican American, I respect the border as well as the differences between the countries."

Eriksen looked at Kat and said, "Where the hell did she live back east?"

"Jersey. She went to Princeton."

"Figures," he mumbled.

Then one of the task force members popped his head in the room and said, "There's someone here to see you, Tom."

———————

Manny decided he liked sitting at the café with Hector, the large assassin he'd just hired. He was also surprised the giant man had such an interest in U.S. politics.

Hector said, "This Senator Ramos, she never shuts up. Our politicians are afraid of her. Can you imagine that? I hear from some of our people that some of the radical Islamists we've taken across the border are more concerned about her than anybody else. She's a hard woman."

Manny nodded and said, "It would be nice if someone got her to tone down her rhetoric. She should be talked to."

"She should be slapped down." The tenor of his deep voice showed that it was no idle joke.

Manny shrugged. "Maybe one day soon."

The big man said, "I hear she speaks in El Paso all the time."

"Where did you hear that?"

"It's my business to know what's going on close to the border. Why else would you come to me for a job in El Paso? My English is good, but I'm clearly Mexican. You like the fact that I pay attention."

Manny nodded as he considered the comment. Then he noticed four men at the same time his companion did. They sat across the narrow, crowded street at a restaurant known to serve the police.

The big man growled, "I know that black man. He's an American federal police officer. The other man, the one as big as me, I've never seen before."

Manny studied the fit-looking man who was just over fifty. His name was Houghton, and he was sitting with two of the commanders for the local police.

The big man said, "Why does he sit with the local police if he is a federal agent?"

Manny said, "Relax, he works for the U.S. Customs or whatever they're called now. He's concerned with border issues, so it makes sense for him to talk to these policemen. If he were with the DEA, I might worry, but the U.S. Customs cares only about what comes across the border, not what we do here."

The big man nodded and said, "I once collected a bounty on an informer for the DEA. They never forgot I snatched their eyes and ears in Juárez. They did everything they could to find out who'd taken one of their informers and sold him to the drug lords. The DEA proved to be dangerous and smart, and they had many contacts on this side of the border."

Manny said, "This man Houghton has a reputation for being fair and honest. I wouldn't worry about him. Let us focus on our job in El Paso. I'll find you tomorrow." The big man merely nodded.

———

John Houghton looked at the sheets of paper provided by the two commanders of the Juárez police force. He'd spoken to the men in the Spanish he'd been practicing for more than twenty years on the border.

The two local cops constantly shifted their eyes, checking for threats. Being seen with two Americans could be dangerous because no one would know who John and Andre were and what they wanted. The food at the small cantina was good, but Houghton noticed no one came into the cantina while they were sitting there. The other restaurants filled up, but they remained isolated at the table with a good, open view of the street.

John felt like he was accomplishing something now that he had identified the dead man from fingerprints. His name was Vincent DiMetti, and he was a wannabe gangster from Long Island. Somehow that didn't sound so tough. The Bronx or Brooklyn made tough guys sound scarier, but the phrase "I'm going to get someone from *Long Island* to visit you" didn't sound as terrifying.

Now John had something to go on in his personal investigation into the men who killed the Border Patrol agent and were later found dead across the river. One was, in fact, a Mexican national, but this other fella, DiMetti, had no business being involved in any kind of human trafficking.

Technically, John was still under investigation for the shooting. At least the case had not been officially closed. He also knew that Tom Eriksen was doing okay. His friend on the Border Security Task Force said a pretty, young DEA agent had become Eriksen's unofficial partner. Eriksen hadn't told him about her himself. Maybe he had more on his mind than just police work.

His two police buddies dropped them off near the main crossing point between Juárez and El Paso. It used to be more open, and the entry to Mexico from the U.S. side had been very easy. Juárez depended on tourists, but they didn't flood in like they used to. That was a shame, because Mexico was a lovely place and had a lot to offer. Its people were sincere, and the restaurants and cantinas served incredible food. But it was the damn drug war. Murders had increased to an astronomical rate, but the American media had not helped cities like Juárez by covering the carnage day and night. It was almost as if they took glee in saying how dreadful things had become in Mexico while the U.S. was still safe by comparison. The fact that very few tourists had actually been harmed in any way played no role in any of the stories submitted by the networks.

John separated from Andre when it came time to cross the border. His friend was more by the book and had nothing to hide. He crossed legally, showing his ID. John paused as he looked at the short line of people headed across the border. This was tricky because he didn't want any record of him crossing one way or the other. He decided the best defense was a good offense, so he walked through the main line, where he knew the chief Customs inspector, then waved to the man as if he had just rolled across the border for a moment. The inspector nodded back to him, and just like that he was on U.S. soil.

He realized it should be harder to get back into the country than that. He also needed a drink badly. He popped a little orange pill the doctor had prescribed him for anxiety. That would hold him until he found some tonic to go with the bottle of gin he had at his apartment.

———————

Ramón Herrera sat comfortably in the back of his armored Chevy Suburban as it tooled through the streets of Chihuahua, Mexico. The Chevy was the third car in a row of five vehicles, each with at least three armed men riding in it. The last car in the motorcade was an unmarked military Humvee with the ability to launch rocket-propelled grenades. He spent so much time in Chihuahua that the people were no longer awed by the motorcade. But that only made things go more smoothly. It probably wasn't necessary from a security perspective here in the heart of his own state. The motorcade was like his haciendas; it projected power. He often thought of himself as a Roman ruler, with the haciendas as his fortresses and this motorcade as his horsemen.

He settled back with his secure phone and started to look up the name Pablo Piña. He had concerns about his man in Juárez. He had always been a little odd, acquiring the title Dark Lord of the Desert for killing six police officers and their families. It was a stupid name, but it helped to spread terror and control the populace. If that was all he needed Pablo to do, Herrera wouldn't worry so much about him, but their plans to expand into other businesses, especially into the United States, made him wonder if Pablo could handle it. His pleasure at showing off his acid pool made Herrera wonder about his man's stability.

Herrera put the phone back in the console on the extended rear seat of the Suburban. Maybe Pablo wasn't the right guy to handle something sensitive like this. That was the problem with so many employees. He had plenty of killers; his security force, the Zetas, street thugs, assassins, even the Mexican Army in some situations, but he never liked to get his hands dirty. He had never killed a man himself and didn't intend to start now.

Herrera kept a cadre of men separate from his chain of command. Men no one in his security force realized existed. He never knew when someone within the chain would have to be dealt with severely. None of these men knew each other. Pablo and other middle managers had no idea Herrera could so easily go outside of the organization if he needed dirty work done. It was essential to keep control and stay above the fray. Even with equals who were rivals, like the heads of some of the cartels, relations were cold, but rarely violent. They were basically the heads of state.

He was trying to use his contacts within the Gulf Cartel to clean up its image. They had too many nuts. People who considered themselves witches. That was one of the things that led to the massacre at Matamoros, which got so much play on the U.S. news. It looked bad from a public relations standpoint. Mexico was already floundering in a quagmire of negative media coverage.

Herrera wanted to correct that, and he wanted to keep the United States from interfering in Mexico's business. Once that was accomplished, his investment could shift from cocaine and heroin to oil and other legitimate companies dealing in the high tech industry both in the U.S. and Mexico. This would provide a stable basis for long-term expansion. The drug business was too profitable to ignore, but he needed more capital to move into other industries.

The other big moneymaker that was emerging was "protection," or as he called it, "insurance." Once he got everyone paying the proper premiums, kidnappings and extortion would become extinct and the U.S. media would have much less to complain about.

After careful consideration he snatched the phone from the console and called his most reliable independent contractor. After three rings, a male voice answered, and Herrera said, "*Hola*, Hector."

Sitting in the obsessively neat office of his supervisor at the FBI, Tom Eriksen fidgeted in his hard chair. He had spent surprisingly little time in the FBI office since moving to El Paso. There were only three main squads and the task-force squad supervised by

Mike Zara. All the agents on that squad were scattered across the various task forces every city had. The areas for investigation were broad: fraud, Internet crimes against children, and terrorism—the domain of the Joint Terrorism Task Force, or JTTF.

Eriksen looked around at the plaques and photos that covered the walls. He noticed the plaques were all for time spent on different units, not for exemplary work. Sort of like a participation medal in sports.

Eriksen noticed the wide grin on his supervisor's face as the Department of Justice inspector general, head of a watchdog agency that could cripple an agent's career faster than a DUI, said, "You're going to have to stay on this Border Security Task Force for the foreseeable future." The pudgy IG was all business and seemed to have put some thought into everything he said.

Eriksen didn't want to sound like a whiny kid, but he had to say, "Why? If you're closing the case and I'm not being charged, why do I have to stay on the rubber gun squad?"

The inspector general was a trim, neat man of about forty-five, who looked like he had been born wearing his Brooks Brothers suit. "The reason there are no criminal charges is that Mexico has not been very cooperative and we haven't even seen the bodies of the dead coyotes. And although you may not care about a couple of dead Mexican traffickers, others do. Your assignment to the intelligence task force keeps you low-profile and mitigates some of the hostility being expressed on the Mexican side of the border."

"So I can't conduct any enforcement activities?"

Now his supervisor stepped in and said, "None whatsoever. No surveillances and no crossing the border into Mexico."

The IG added, "And it goes without saying you will make no public comment. We understand several commentators have been following this case closely and might come to El Paso. You will not appear with any of them on TV. Is that clearly understood?"

Eriksen just nodded.

The IG said, "Do you have anything you wish to say?" No matter how he phrased it or what tone he took, it still made Eriksen sound like a defendant.

Eriksen said, "I've heard a few rumors about the coyotes that killed the Border Patrol agent."

Now his supervisor jumped up and said, "What rumors? Where did you hear them?"

Eriksen said, "My old partner, John Houghton, heard it from his informants in Mexico. The wounds don't match ammo we used, and one of the dead men may not even have been Mexican."

The IG took furious notes, but Zara said, "Since when does the FBI listen to anyone at Homeland Security? You worry about the job you've been assigned to at the Border Security Task Force and take my advice: Stay away from John Houghton and any of those morons at HSI. You're in enough trouble already."

Carol DiMetti shuffled around her cute little house doing all the chores that had piled up since she'd learned her husband, Vinnie, had been killed at the border. The three-bedroom home was in a purely residential neighborhood with a shaded backyard and a front porch like the one she played on at her grandmother's, growing up in Chicago.

She always kept the place tidy and the kitchen well stocked. At the moment, she was packing up a box of her dead husband's clothes. She intended to donate them all to the Salvation Army. There was no way she wanted to schlep them back to Chicago with her. There was also no way she was headed back to Long Island, where Vinnie was from. She felt guilty more than she did sad. In fact, she felt guilty because she wasn't sad in the least that Vinnie was dead. It wasn't really his fault. He was a putz, but he could be sweet. He believed he was some kind of Hollywood Mafia thug instead of a nice Italian boy from upper Long Island. His father was a dentist, for Christ's sake. He had no reason to act the way he did and drag her all the way out here to El Paso to work for that stupid company.

El Paso had been too much for her marriage. She'd been planning to leave long before Vinnie had gotten shot, just waiting for something to open up back home in Aurora or Chicago. Now she needed a job and didn't want to move back in with her parents. She had to find some ready cash so she could head back to the civilized world.

She heard the doorbell and took a second to peek through the curtain the way Vinnie had showed her. She was relieved to see it was Vinnie's old boss, dressed, as usual, all in black. He had a nickname, but she couldn't remember it. As Carol opened the door she said, "Hey, Joe. Come on in." She appreciated his long face and quiet demeanor and how carefully he asked how she was doing and gave her a hug even after she said she was doing okay. He was obviously uncomfortable, but she didn't know if it was just around her or around all women. Every time they had ever met he'd been cautious. Vinnie had said Joe was queer, but she didn't think so.

Finally, after she'd gotten him a cup of coffee and they sat in the living room on the decorative couch Vinnie had picked up the first day they were here, Joe said, "What are your plans?"

She shrugged her shoulders, aware that his eyes kept drifting to her cleavage. "I guess I'll move eventually. But I need money to move."

"You need money from the company?"

She shrugged. "That would be nice." She didn't want to push it yet. Now he looked downright anxious.

Carol decided to risk making him a little more uneasy. She said, "Why does the news keep saying the two men shot by the cops were Mexican nationals? My Vinnie was a New Yorker through and through."

Joe shrugged his shoulders and said, "They don't know what they're talking about."

Carol said, "Vinnie was a shitty husband, but a good provider. He usually thought things through. You know what I mean?"

Joe just nodded like a nervous kid on his first date.

Carol hoped he might be motivated enough to go to his bosses and negotiate a severance package.

TEN

Tom Eriksen wondered if his friend John Houghton was playing a joke on him. Although John clearly had a drinking problem, which was not always under control, he had never asked Eriksen to meet him at a bar before. But when he had called and told Eriksen he needed to talk to him and suggested this place called the Border Crossing, it sounded too important to ignore.

The sprawling club was set up like an old-style disco right down to the glittering ball hanging above the giant dance floor. KC and the Sunshine Band blared over the phenomenal sound system as every possible faction of people crowded onto the dance floor. There was the obligatory bachelorette party with a dozen pretty young women swilling tequila shots and dancing as a group. The largest section of dancers appeared to be younger gay men, and a much smaller segment of the population was couples, with the male partner invariably looking somewhat uncomfortable.

Eriksen sat in the rear corner by himself, sipping a Coors and enjoying the various styles of dancing as well as the solid beat of the music. John had said he *needed* to talk, not that he *wanted* to. There was no question that his partner was onto something. Eriksen heard his supervisor's voice in his head saying, "Stay away from John Houghton," but it made no difference to him.

He had just looked down at his watch and noted that John was more than thirty minutes late when a tall woman in a long, shiny dress, plopped down on the couch next to him. She wore heavy eyeliner, and it took a moment for Eriksen to notice her pronounced Adam's apple.

She scooted a little closer, turned her head, and said in a husky voice, "Hello, gorgeous."

Eriksen couldn't help but smile as he said, "Hi."

"Good-looking and not too talkative. You're my kinda guy. Do you come here often?"

Eriksen appreciated the attention, no matter who it was from, and thought she had a pretty face, but he had to ask, "You're a dude, aren't you?"

"Yes." He looked dejected.

Eriksen just nodded, not wanting to insult the tall man.

The man said, "Would it help if I told you my penis doesn't work anymore?"

Eriksen shook his head and said, "Not really."

The man shrugged and said, "To each his own," as he stood quickly and zeroed in on a young man sitting at the edge of the bar.

Eriksen gave him a wave and said, "Good luck," as the man walked away. Then he noticed John walking toward him.

John said, "Making new friends?"

"Not very well. I was dumped for the guy at the bar." He could smell the alcohol on John's breath as he took a seat on the couch where the transvestite had been sitting moments before. After almost a minute of silence, Eriksen leaned in and said, "Why are we here, John?"

"None of your stuffy, stuck-up fellow FBI agents would be caught dead in a place like this. And the music is loud enough that I know we would never be recorded. This is one of the safest places in town to meet."

"I mean what's so important?"

"One of the coyotes was a small-time thug from New York. I want to do some more checking before I say anything else."

"What's a New Yorker doing in Texas running undocumented people across the border?"

"That's the big question. I learned through my associates in

Juárez that he sometimes worked with another guy known only as Cash. He might be Colombian and always wears black. I think your friend Dr. Martinez might know more about what's going on."

Eriksen didn't like the idea of a doctor who tried to do what was right when the Border Patrol agent was shot not being a completely stand-up guy. "What's our next move?"

John hesitated and said, "I'm not sure you should be involved in our next move. I heard you were told to stay away from me, and for the sake of your career you should probably listen. I just didn't want you feeling guilty about a shootout with a wannabe mobster who was probably killed by someone on the other side of the border. You just sit tight and this'll all work out."

"But I want to help."

"Then keep your ears open and let me know if you hear anything important. I'm gonna poke around a little bit more, and I guarantee we'll straighten the shit out." He reached over and drained Eriksen's beer. As he slapped the empty bottle back down on the table, John smiled and said, "Then maybe we can go on Ted Dempsey's show and make a big splash."

Cash didn't like being around Ari, especially at dinnertime. So he didn't mind waiting in his two-year-old Cadillac CTS outside a little fast-food joint called Chicago Street Food. Why on earth some redneck from El Paso thought it would be a good idea to start a restaurant based on Chicago cuisine was beyond him, but Ari loved the place. Cash figured it was probably good, but to spite Ari, he refused to eat there.

The traffic was light, but the restaurant was slammed. It might as well have been the only place to eat in the whole city. He hated crowded restaurants, but he liked this new assignment even less. What the hell was this job coming to? There used to be a certain dignity and honor to his chosen profession. At least that's what the general public thought thanks to writers like Mario Puzo and TV shows like *The Sopranos*. He knew it wasn't that way in real life, but he'd always tried to maintain certain boundaries. He didn't go after a man's family unless they were part of the problem, he didn't deal with addicts, and he didn't kill dogs to slip into people's houses. Surprisingly, out of those three rules, it was the dog one that had screwed him up the most. He'd had to pass on two different hits because of family dogs that made too much noise, but he couldn't justify shooting an innocent hound who was just doing his job.

He had other rules, lots of them, and now the company was asking him to cross one of his self-imposed boundaries. And he didn't like it one bit. He'd quit this job if he thought he'd survive more than a week. But the one way out, the one chance he had to maintain his dignity and still fulfill his obligations, was a muscle-bound little Israeli who got on his nerves more than anyone else he had ever met.

His employers had said to use Ari any way he saw fit. And this was one way he could keep the little jerk-off busy and accomplish a task he'd rather not do himself. It made him wonder how an American company like his employer came across an Israeli with homicidal tendencies like Ari. Cash supposed it wasn't much different than him being hired, except he knew he'd been vetted through a number of sources and he was reliable, trustworthy, and professional. As far as he knew, Ari possessed none of those attributes.

Ari used his stout, short legs to hustle out of the restaurant with a sack full of dinner and a gigantic Coke with a straw pointing straight up. He slid into the front seat and popped out a sausage-and-peppers sub without even asking permission. He jammed the leaky Coke between his legs and wolfed down a tremendous bite of the messy sandwich, dripping some kind of orange sauce onto the front of his T-shirt.

Cash had to swallow hard to control his temper and finally had to ask, "How do you eat so much?"

Ari said, "Is there a law about eating regularly?"

Cash looked aside and said, "There is if we're busy. We got a new job."

Ari turned to him with a leering smile. "Is it the woman, DiMetti? Ari would do her for free. And all night long." His grin, with the sauce from the sandwich, made him look like a creepy clown.

"Give it a rest, Ari. This one is no cakewalk."

"Who is it?"

Cash hesitated, turning it over in his head. Would it be better to hand the job off, or should he break one of his stupid rules and do it himself? It was probably important or his employers wouldn't have sent it to him. He didn't know how much he wanted to tell the little Israeli. He turned to Ari and said, "We have to make this one look like an accident."

Ari shrugged. "So it just takes a little more thought. Who is it?" There was an edge to his voice that gave away his impatience. "Ari never heard of a job he couldn't do."

All Cash could do was shake his head. "I'm gonna let you run with it. This will be *your* special assignment."

———

Manny made it through the short line at the checkpoint going from Juarez to El Paso. He had learned that at this time of the evening, when workers were coming back and forth across the border and the inspectors hadn't gone to dinner yet, there were enough lanes open that there wasn't much delay. He had a good ID and wasn't on any watch lists. Not under the name he was using. He didn't mind coming through the official port of entry because all he intended to do was a quick surveillance to confirm Dr. Martinez's location. He had an address and knew the area pretty well. When it was time to act, tomorrow or the next day, he'd bring Hector and his crazy cousin to do the dirty work.

He still wasn't happy about the assignment, but he had to get it done. All to quiet down a pissed-off Latin father. It was a good thing he respected Pablo Piña overall or this would be a reason for him to walk away. He had enough money in mutual funds and overseas investments that he and his wife could live comfortably for the rest of their lives. He'd already set up his children in their own houses and was ready to pay for private school when they provided him with grandchildren.

He drove a truck that belonged to a landscape company in El Paso and looked perfectly legitimate crossing the border. He knew the arrogant inspectors looked at him like some sort of indentured servant, and that was why he had worn an old T-shirt and slipped on a University of Texas at El Paso baseball cap. Driving down the main street he realized how much he liked El Paso. It reminded him of a smaller Juárez with a vibrant Latin community and a growing reputation as a business center in the Southwest. There were a few too many law enforcement agencies for his taste, though. HSI and DEA maintained large offices to keep an eye on the activity across the border.

No one would look at the downtown and consider it a big city, with the tallest building being the Wells Fargo Business Center, which was a mere twenty-two stories. Manny felt embarrassed that he was going to shatter the quiet calm of the little city with a calcu- lated murder. He wondered if others in his business hesitated with certain jobs.

After several turns he found himself on Arizona Avenue looking for the apartment building near Brown Street. His main objective was to see the apartment complex and the surrounding areas to know what he could use as an escape route if necessary, but as he drove past the three-story building he was shocked to see Luis Mar- tinez step out onto the street and slip into a small red Toyota.

Manny wished he could just pull alongside him and take a quick shot now, but he had not risked bringing any weapons across the border. Somewhere in the back of the truck, along with the rakes and shovels, had to be a machete or something he could use to eliminate the little doctor quickly. He even considered a simple hit- and-run, but then decided to stick to his plan. Piña had been very specific that he wanted to send a message, and that's why Manny had contracted out the hit.

He followed the Toyota for several blocks, feeling almost invisible in the lawn maintenance truck, until Dr. Martinez stopped at a popular market area with a number of cafés and bars. Manny parked across the street and watched, wondering if it was worthwhile to call Hector and see if he would come across the border on such short notice.

Then he felt a hitch in his breathing as he realized who the doctor was meeting. It took a moment for him to recognize the tall man, who had cut his hair very close and wore sunglasses and a baseball cap. The gringo computer guy who had wired the hacienda. The one who had stolen business secrets that could prove vital in the future. The one called Enrique, but he had heard Martinez call him Eric. The computer technician spoke Spanish with no accent, which was a mark of a smart man. But he'd gotten too smart for his own good and thought he found a way to make money on the side.

If Manny had not come across the border at the checkpoint—if there hadn't been video of him in the truck—he would act now and find a way to run down both men at once. Instead, he decided that when he finally did talk to the good doctor he would get some questions answered about Enrique.

Something told him this did relate to business.

Tom Eriksen felt nervous. Not the kind of nerves he'd experienced in the last two weeks with his supervisor and the inspector general breathing down his neck as if he were a suspect, but a few butterflies. He sat in a simple restaurant called the Central Café that had gotten outstanding reviews in the *El Paso Times* and other local newspapers.

Unlike the Border Crossing disco, this place was quiet and, by comparison, boring, but he thought it was appropriate. There were no transvestites asking him onto the dance floor, which he had to admit was at least flattering.

Thinking about the disco made him think about John Houghton. He was worried about his former partner, who'd been acting oddly and drinking way too much. He suspected John was crossing the border against regulations for his own little investigation, but he wasn't sure how to approach his friend, who had more experience and was very bright; he didn't want to come off as an arrogant FBI douche, telling others what to do. John was separated from his wife, but Eriksen didn't know her well enough to ask her for help.

There was no one at the Border Intelligence Unit to give him any guidance because he didn't know anyone well enough to trust yet. He couldn't get a fix on his assigned partner, Lila Tellis. She wasn't rude, but she wasn't friendly. He noticed she preferred to conduct a number of activities on her own, and he didn't know whether he should take it personally or not.

Lila was convinced Dr. Martinez was hoarding information in an effort to trade for visas and other favors from the U.S. government. But Eriksen couldn't figure out who he would lie about to protect. Why keep quiet?

All of these thoughts whirled through his head but faded as soon as he saw his companion for the night enter the restaurant and look right at him. Kat Gleason paused at the front door, looking like an actress on the red carpet with her flowing blond hair and beautiful smile.

Eriksen suddenly felt like things were looking up.

ELEVEN

Sitting alone in his Cadillac, Cash could hardly believe the feeling of relief that Ari wasn't at his heels, either eating or bitching about how soft Americans were. Cash had sent Ari off on his "special assignment," and he didn't want to think about the muscle-bound Israeli, or what he was doing.

Cash was amazed how easy it was to find where the Immigration Service had stashed Dr. Martinez and his wife. He still wasn't crazy about having to deal with Dr. Martinez by himself, but at least this way Mrs. Martinez would escape unharmed. Cash would even try to get her back to Mexico. Ari would've argued she was a witness and had to be dealt with. He wouldn't necessarily be wrong, but it hardly justified killing an innocent woman.

This was the kind of job he had to suck up and complete because it made perfect sense that the company couldn't risk Martinez blabbing about who he was working for. And from what Cash had heard, Martinez would do anything he had to not to return to Mexico and face that crazy-assed drug lord. Pablo Piña's reputation was well-known in the El Paso area, and no one in their right mind thought a simple international border would slow the sociopath down.

Cash had the address on Arizona Avenue and waited a block down in his comfortable Cadillac to see who came and went from the building. It gave him time to wonder what Carol DiMetti was doing now. He knew she was too decent to be involved in any of her dead husband's stupid plans. He couldn't understand how she got mixed up with a moron like Vinnie in the first place.

The front door to Martinez's building opened and knocked Cash out of his philosophical ruminations. For a guy who was concerned for his safety, the doctor didn't seem to pay much attention to anything around him. He slipped into a red Toyota parked directly in front of the building and pulled away from the curb on Arizona Avenue. Cash gave him a few blocks and pulled out to follow him. It only took a minute to realize a beat-up white pickup truck was following the doctor as well.

The short ride took them through some of the side streets in downtown El Paso until Cash caught a glimpse of the Toyota pulling up to a popular and trendy market area. Just as he suspected, the pickup truck parked a block behind, forcing Cash to park even farther down the street. For the moment he was more interested in who was driving the pickup truck.

It took Cash a few minutes to realize he was conducting an honest-to-God surveillance. He wondered if this was how the cops did it. Maybe the guy in the truck was a cop. If he was, that was the greatest undercover vehicle Cash had ever imagined. He lost sight of Dr. Martinez as he walked into the market. It looked like he might've talked to someone at the front door, but Cash couldn't be sure.

Dammit, he wanted to drive by and get a look at the driver of the pickup truck, but he also wanted to scoot into the market. Son of a bitch, it really would be easier with Ari here. Then they could just grab both of them.

There was nothing on earth that would make Cash say out loud that he wanted Ari with him.

———

Luis Martinez liked the touristy marketplace with dozens of booths selling trendy clothing and homemade jewelry. The open-air plaza was a popular spot among the young people of El Paso. No one worried about being gunned down here.

He had made the conscious decision that he was safe over here on the northern side of the border. He didn't want to live his life scurrying around like a cockroach afraid of the light. He knew

Pablo Piña was powerful, but he felt secure under the protection of the United States Immigration Service. He couldn't believe how accommodating they had been, even providing him with a small rental car. But that didn't change the fact that he had business to tend to and needed to know what his future held.

He had one phone number that might reach his friend Enrique. It had taken several days, but finally he spoke to the young computer whiz and convinced him to meet at the market. It was public, but busy, and would make it difficult for anyone to see them meeting.

The first thing out of Enrique's mouth after they had embraced was, "Why did you want to meet?"

Martinez ignored the question and said, "Why are you staying in El Paso?"

"I have family living here locally. No one would think to look for me here."

"Are you going through with your plan? I think that it is suicide."

"Those are the issues I'm trying to figure out now. I think the company would pay a lot of money to have the thumb drive, and I don't think your old boss would care. I can't believe a U.S. corporation with that high of a profile would actually pay to have me killed."

"One thing I've learned is that money makes people and companies do horrible things. It even makes doctors do stupid things."

They eased into one of the picnic-table-like booths and ordered two Coronas. On principle, Martinez usually ordered Corona beer because of the ugly rumors spread by U.S. brewers that Mexicans urinated in the beer during brewing. It fit into a racist stereotype, and too many rednecks along the border bought into it. Martinez now addressed his friend by his given name. "Eric, this is not a game. Are you sure the information is safe?"

The lanky young man said, "It's all on one thumb drive, and I guarantee you it's safe."

"But are we?"

"Have you told anyone who hired us?"

Martinez shook his head.

Enrique said, "Anyone ask about me?"

Again the doctor shook his head.

Enrique said, "You'd never give me up, would you?"

Martinez put on his most solemn expression, raised his right hand, and said, "May I invite the wrath of God if I do."

Enrique just nodded and said, "We probably shouldn't meet like this again."

Martinez knew he needed to be able to get hold of Enrique if things went really bad with the DEA agent and his request for visas. He said, "Keep the phone with you, no?"

The younger man nodded. "For now."

Martinez threw down the rest of his beer and said, "Be safe, my brother."

It seemed natural for both of them to stand and embrace.

––––––––

Eriksen enjoyed the leisurely dinner. He was careful not to drink too much, limiting himself to two beers while Kat sipped red wine. There was something about her manner, even the way she ate, that was graceful and calming. Now they were on the outdoor patio of the trendy sports bar down the street from the Central Café. It cooled off outside as a September breeze blew from the west. It was almost the first night since he'd been in El Paso that he thought the weather and the company were nice. He had dated on and off, with Trudy being his most serious girlfriend, but even she only lasted two months. She might have been pretty, but she had no substance. Sitting here with this bright young woman emphasized that shortcoming even more.

The TV was on a pedestal above their heads, and he glanced up briefly.

Kat said, "I watch so many broadcasts on duty that I don't even own a TV. I couldn't care less if I never saw another news story or political speech. If I need a laugh I watch MSNBC for a few minutes."

"You never feel like watching a movie just to relax?"

She shook her head. "I'm a big reader."

"What sort of stuff do you like to read?"

She almost looked embarrassed as she shrugged and said, "Novels. Especially novels about police work. I don't care what agency or what the crime is, I love police novels. If I wanna read about the LAPD I pick up a Michael Connelly novel. Anything Thomas Harris writes about Hannibal Lecter and the FBI is gold as far as I'm concerned, and I love the novels of W. E. B. Griffin and William Butterworth IV about the Philadelphia Police Department. It's almost like I read about the life I expected to have when I took this job."

Eriksen had to let out a snort of laughter. "I know exactly how you feel. When I graduated the FBI Academy at Quantico I thought I was gonna run out and change the world and see action every day. Now you and I have essentially the same job."

"I wouldn't say that. You're not nearly qualified to have my job." She gave him a sly smile, and they both started to laugh.

"How'd you get into an agency like NSA, anyway?"

"I was interested in communications and technology in college and was considering the navy when I met a lieutenant commander who also worked for the NSA. He's the one who started me looking into it. They liked my degree from Stanford and my engineering background, and next thing I know I'm hooked."

"But how do you feel about El Paso?"

"It's a big change from where I grew up in Pittsburgh and nothing like the crazy atmosphere in the Bay Area, but it does have its own charm."

"It sounds like you're saying except for the weather, violence, and economy, Detroit is not a bad place to live."

"I like El Paso; I just thought it would be bigger. I also would like the task force more if the law enforcement group wasn't completely separated from the intelligence people. I know we're all supposed to be doing the same job, but the sworn people have a certain attitude toward us."

"They haven't exactly warmed up to me either."

"You're working with Lila Tellis, aren't you?"

He nodded his head.

"The rumor is that she's a lesbian, but I think it's ridiculous. She's just all business, and I admire that."

"I'm a little scared of her."

"We all are."

He laughed as he nodded again, appreciating the easy conversation. They had a lot in common, and he felt like he could confide in her. He was hoping he'd develop that feeling toward everyone on the task force.

He glanced up at the news and then asked Kat, "You guys following any interesting trends?"

"It's a lot like following someone on Twitter. The more interest in a subject, the more it attracts our interest in that subject."

"And the big subject now?"

"Immigration."

John Houghton sat uncomfortably on a hard wooden stool at the bar of his favorite watering hole. The one-story cinder-block structure simply had a green neon sign that said PUB. The inside was no fancier, with two TVs over the bar and ten tables, of which rarely more than two were occupied at any time. He was enough of a regular that the bartender knew his first name but not what he did for a living. Anything to do with law enforcement along the border was better kept to one's self.

He casually watched highlights of Major League Baseball on ESPN. The other TV had ESPN2 with the World Series of Poker. John had always been more interested in real athletics than in cards, billiards, or bowling. Pretty much any sport that smoking didn't affect your ability to win was not something he'd watch.

He still didn't pay much attention to baseball except for the Arizona Diamondbacks, which represented the entire Southwest as far as he was concerned, although the Texans loved their Rangers. He sipped on his fourth gin and tonic as he brooded about what he could say or do to convince his wife to allow him back into the house. Ironically, he recognized that cutting down on his drinking might be one of the keys to accomplishing his goal. He argued that the kids needed him around even if they didn't show it. Teenagers never did. He thought he might be getting through to her, but she had been strangely silent on the subject the last few days.

His head was already spinning slightly as a result of the gin. John made the decision to leave his car in the parking lot behind the pub. He could make it the five blocks to his house without being stopped. God knew he'd done it enough times before. That was the main reason he liked this place. Shitty food, fair service, one short ride home. HSI put up with drinking, but a DUI would not only hurt his employment, it would seal the deal with his wife.

The muscular guy sitting next to him raised a glass to the high-light clip of a homer by the Diamondbacks first baseman. He had the look of a military man.

John said, "You've got to be from around here if you're a fan of the Diamondbacks."

The man shook his head and said, "I lived here a while back, but I'm just visiting now."

"What brings you back?"

"Just a little reunion at Fort Bliss."

John nodded, pleased with his ability to evaluate someone accurately. He stuck out his hand and said, "Hi, I'm John."

The man shook his hand with a firm grip and said, "My name is Ari."

TWELVE

Tom Eriksen sat at his desk, reading reports related to Dr. Martinez and other people with recent information on the growing unrest in Mexico. The squad bay held all ten desks of the various law enforcement agents on the task force. Five were HSI agents; that was why the unit had an HSI supervisor. The desks were separated by cheap cubicle dividers that did nothing for the sound that carried across the bay. Generally there were only a few agents in the office at any one time.

Lila had already been at her desk when he arrived at eight, and she grunted her usual greeting, her dark eyes barely flicking up to assess him. She had the ability to focus on a task unlike anyone else he'd ever met.

He leaned back in his rolling chair with a funky wheel, stretched his back, and said, "It seems like no matter how many reports I read, there's always a stack to catch up on."

Lila looked up and said, "Maybe if you spent a little more time reading and less time flirting with the NSA chick in the TV room, you'd be all caught up and we could go out and interview more people instead of waiting for you to get up to speed."

Eriksen stared at her for a moment, wondering if she was pulling his leg like cops tended to do. When he saw she was serious he said, "I didn't realize you were my supervisor and I had to check in with you."

"It doesn't matter if I'm your supervisor or not, I'm your assigned partner. I have a certain pace I want to keep, and having a typical entitled FBI agent in tow slows me down."

"There's more to life than this bullshit."

"Is that right?"

Eriksen just nodded.

"Then why don't you tell me what you do with your free time? Because my guess is you sit at home and sulk about being shipped over here to the Island of Misfit Cops and you talk with your old partner about how you're being shafted by your respective agencies."

Eriksen stared at her, wondering how she knew so much about him. "I manage to do a few other things, too."

"Like sniff around Katharine Gleason?"

"That's none of your business."

"Anything that affects the operations here is my business. Whether you know it or not, this is a vital job, and one day you might come to appreciate it. You need to focus on something real, like information Luis Martinez is providing us. He wouldn't be bargaining unless he had something good. Everything else around here is a smoke screen. Whether it's that crazy Senator Ramos or chatter about a nebulous terrorist threat, it isn't as real as whatever Martinez could give us."

Eriksen had the sense that she wasn't angry as much as anxious for him to figure out the benefits of the assignment.

———

Cash concentrated on driving even though he felt a headache coming on as Ari repeated the story of his "special assignment" and how he engineered his brilliant encounter with the HSI agent they had been told to deal with. The fact that he'd been jabbering away since midmorning had made this one of the most unpleasant workdays Cash had ever experienced.

The little Israeli said, "Ari really researched this one. Ari looked for his weaknesses and saw that he was a drinker, so Ari followed him to a bar where he drank. Just played to his weakness. Nothing unusual or flashy, that's the key to this kind of work."

Cash couldn't help but roll his eyes.

Ari continued. "Told him Ari was a vet here for a reunion at Fort

Bliss and just kept letting him throw back the gin and tonics. He offered Ari a ride, and when we got outside, Ari told him he was too drunk to drive and he bought it. Let me drive you home, Ari said, and I'll call a cab from there. By the time we got to his place he was stumbling drunk. He invited Ari inside to wait, and we had another drink. Then Ari came up with the most brilliant part of the plan."

Cash mumbled, "I can't wait."

"Ari told him he needed an Alka-Seltzer to avoid a hangover. Ari fixed him one, then mashed up a couple of prescriptions that were lying around, Xanax and Ambien and some pink pills. Then Ari made him drink down the whole mixture as quick as he could. He dribbled down his chin and shirt but finished every last drop. By the time Ari left he was barely breathing. Just laid out on his couch. I put the TV on ESPN and crossed his legs. There is not one piece of evidence linking Ari to him. Not that anyone will ever suspect anything. Maybe if the drugs weren't prescribed to him or if he had a reputation as a nondrinker, but Ari did good this time."

"Except he was still alive when you left."

"Don't sweat it, Cash, he's stone cold right this second."

As much as Cash hated to admit it, his little partner had done a good job, and best of all it kept Cash out of the dirty business he wanted no part of. Cops were just doing their job and shouldn't have to face stuff like this.

Now Cash and Ari were looking up at the apartment building where Martinez lived. Cash mumbled, "I don't see the Toyota. And I know there's a security guard inside. Maybe we should wait until we see him walk in the building."

Ari immediately said, "There's a fire escape on the back of the building. We could surprise him and be waiting in the apartment."

Cash looked down at the sheet of paper he had been given with the diagram of the third floor and location of the apartment. He'd seen the fire escape, too. It was at the end of the hallway. There were also smaller escape ladders on each bedroom window. Someone had been afraid of fire. This was a plan that could work, but there was no way he would ever admit it to Ari.

———

Tom Eriksen had spent a troubled morning at his desk after Lila knocked him back to the reality of his job. She wasn't wrong, and he couldn't even say she was nasty about it. But it made him wonder about her background. He'd called a couple of friends with the DEA to see if any of them knew her. He waited while they looked her up on their computers, but no one had had any personal encounters with the beautiful agent. It was odd, because the agency was small enough that they should at least know someone who knew her.

He let it slide and called John Houghton, but got his voicemail. He'd left a message earlier, then again just after lunch, and at two in the afternoon he left another one. It wasn't like his partner to ignore him. Sometimes, in the morning, he was slow to respond if he was sleeping off a night of drinking. Eriksen wondered if he wasn't in some kind of disciplinary meeting or getting dressed down for something he had done.

As he thought about it, John was the only person in the Southwest that Eriksen worried about personally. When he was back home he worried about his parents and his brother and sister, but out here there was only one person for him to look after.

At least for now.

———

Cash was surprised how easy it was to boost Ari up with his hands to grab the lower bar of the fire escape and climb to the third floor and slip in the unlocked window at the end of the long corridor. At the door to apartment H, Cash hesitated. Ari stepped to the other side of the door and reached under his shirt, where Cash knew he had a small semiautomatic handgun. He had seen the Beretta Model 85 and wondered if it was a firearm the Israeli Army used. He liked Berettas himself but carried an older, powerful Colt .45.

Ari was clearly impatient and wanted to kick in the door like a SWAT team, but Cash had a better idea and tapped on the door lightly. They waited for a full thirty seconds before Cash wondered if he would have to force the door open. Just as he reached for the knob, it turned and the door opened a crack. A small woman with dark hair peered out past the chain. He vaguely recognized her from the short trip across the border.

Cash gave her a warm smile. He knew she couldn't see Ari from where she was standing. Mrs. Martinez had never seen Cash clearly in the light, so he doubted she could recognize him, and she was unlikely to expect the man who smuggled her across the border to show up at her comfortable apartment supplied by the Immigration Service.

Cash said, "Mrs. Martinez?"

The pleasant-looking woman nodded and smiled.

"I'm here to check the smoke detector."

Mrs. Martinez hesitated, then shook her head and mumbled, "No English, I sorry." Before Cash could take another tack, Ari came from his side and threw his shoulder into the door, knocking Mrs. Martinez to the floor. Ari pulled his pistol and rushed into the apartment as Cash leaned down to help the woman to her feet.

A few seconds later, Ari stepped back into the living room and said, "He's not here."

Cash frowned, but he knew it was time to sit and wait.

———

Ramón Herrera didn't mind sharing a few personal minutes with the five most influential bankers in all of Mexico. He was not a particular fan of Mexico City, with its sprawling barrios and smoggy air, but the top floor of the Scotia Bank building was not unpleasant. There were other Mexican bank buildings, but the rotating basis of this meeting left Scotia on the schedule.

The palatial conference room, with a sweeping vista of the city, a wet bar, two big-screen TVs playing international news, and a table full of fresh seafood and fruit made the meeting tolerable.

The discussions today had been about the financing of infrastructure across the country. The oldest banker present, Vincent Diaz, was a proponent of spending to create jobs that weren't connected to the drug trade. Herrera thought such notions admirably quaint.

Diaz was sixty years old and had the complexion of a man who had not spent any time outdoors, so he had none of the leatherlike appearance of his contemporaries. His Brooks Brothers suit also indicated his status as a simple banker, not a ruler of the country like Herrera.

The senior financial man had already expressed his concerns about the high casualty rate in the country, noting that in the last four years more than thirty thousand people had been killed. That topped the casualty rate in several of the countries currently engaged in war. It was more than the total fatalities suffered by the Americans and their allies in both Iraq and Afghanistan combined. Herrera dismissed the concerns of Diaz as a sign of weakness.

Herrera said, "I am making efforts to stem the violence in the very near future. There are many factors to consider and many armed men to placate. I have plans for all of this to eventually straighten out."

Everyone at the table knew when Herrera closed a subject for further debate. They moved on quickly.

Diaz hit on his other favorite issue. "Don Herrera, you're on the board of Pemex."

"I am. What's the problem?"

"All of our banks hold stock in the company. We're concerned about the amount of oil that is missing. We know a certain amount will disappear as part of doing business, but this threatens to bankrupt the company."

Another banker, Raul Matos, the only man under forty, with the wide, full build of a man who rarely missed a fine meal, said, "We could all be in the poorhouse."

"That would seem more urgent if you weren't wearing a Brioni suit that costs more than most Mexicans make in two years."

The younger man looked stung by the comment and stepped back, plopping his girth into a wide leather chair.

After an awkward silence, the group moved on to the next topic, the U.S. media coverage of Mexico. To emphasize the point, Matos played a clip from the Ted Dempsey show featuring the Texas senator Elizabeth Ramos. All the men in the room spoke

English virtually without an accent and understood the proceedings on the show, which was apparently taped outdoors in Dallas.

The segment of the show focused on Dempsey, who told all of his panelists, "Forget about immigration. Let's talk about how the average Mexican citizen is forced to live. Ten thousand drug-related murders a year in Mexico, and their government seems powerless or unwilling to stop the cartels. Do we need to assist the Mexican government far more than the past two administrations have? I've even heard contingencies to use U.S. troops if necessary. Would U.S. military intervention really be wise?"

As usual, the first to speak up was the senator from Texas. "No one wants us to get involved in another country's problems, but we've used troops in the past on a limited scale. It worked in Bosnia, and our efforts in the Middle East have contained that powder keg. I would hope things don't get so bad in Mexico that we are forced to take action, but we can never take an option like that off the table."

Herrera found himself fuming at what the senator said, as the men around the table murmured in disbelief.

Diaz said, "They discuss us like we are children."

Herrera said, "Then we must make them see us as equals."

Manny had crossed the border into the United States with impunity over the last twenty years. One thing he'd learned was a simple lesson, to hide in plain sight. He used a trail west of El Paso and called a spotter on the other side on a no-frills cell phone to ensure no one was around when he, the giant assassin, Hector, and his crazy cousin entered the United States. Manny never bothered to remember Hector's cousin's name because he wasn't someone Manny wanted to be associated with. He doubted the guy would be much use today or in the near future.

Hector's cousin, who was only about thirty-five and a good three inches shorter than Manny's five feet ten inches, was known to use only knives and was silent as a snake. That was generally a plus in this kind of work, but in the United States, where forensics was a true science, the use of the same weapon over and over might lead to identification, or at least the linking of killings. Manny would see what use this man could be soon enough. His only complaint so far was that the car he'd been given to drive in the United States was a two-door Chevy and it was difficult for three grown men to slip in and out of it. Other than that, things had gone smoothly until they drove past the apartment complex where Luis Martinez was being housed with his wife. The red Toyota he had seen the doctor drive was nowhere in sight. It would've been prudent to place surveillance on the apartment complex, but Manny hated to waste resources on a personal vendetta that didn't help business in any way.

Manny eased the car into a spot down the block in the shade of a building. He said, "We'll wait a while and see if he drives up."

Hector said, "And if he doesn't?"

"We'll make a decision then."

Hector said, "I've been in El Paso a couple of times in the past few days. If I'd known this was the area he lived in I could've checked up on our target."

"Why were you in El Paso?"

The big man cut his eyes toward Manny, then said, "You're not the only one I work for, my friend. Some people have a real problem with big mouths in the United States. I scored a big job to shut one of those mouths up."

Manny knew he didn't want to ask any questions. Once they were done here today he could leave his friend to do whatever he wanted.

The afternoon zipped by. Every vehicle attracted his attention, and he appreciated being away from the constant nagging phone calls he got from distributors and suppliers, as well as pilots and everyone else in the organization run by Pablo Piña. The only problem was that Piña didn't run it anymore; he had given all the responsibility to Manny. Just as he felt his stomach rumble with hunger for the first time, and he was about to suggest they eat and come back, the red Toyota pulled past them and parked on the same side of the street, a mere fifty feet away.

THIRTEEN

Tom Eriksen needed to get out of the office for a few minutes. One of the main reasons was the fact that John Houghton had yet to answer his phone and no one at his office had seen him. Eriksen didn't want to set off alarms unnecessarily, and he didn't want to get John in trouble by calling attention to the fact that he had not come to work. The hardest part about leaving the office was turning down an invitation from Kat Gleason to share an afternoon cup of coffee. But he couldn't focus on anything now except his former partner.

When he was done, he and Lila were going over to Dr. Martinez's apartment to have another chat. He decided he didn't want to be stuck at the apartment without his own vehicle in case the interview went late. Lila didn't seem upset that she wouldn't get to ride with him out to the apartment.

Eriksen had only been to John's apartment one time, but he knew it well. There was a joke among the federal agencies that the complex housed all the agents going through divorces, which meant that it housed all the federal agents in El Paso. Known for heavy drinking and the occasional wild party, the complex was notorious among the separated spouses, who in many cases had traveled halfway around the country to get stuck in a "shitty little border town." At least that's how the spouses viewed it.

A careful drive through the parking lot, which showed more than a dozen obvious federal law enforcement vehicles, showed him John's car parked at an odd angle and in a spot not assigned to his apartment.

As Eriksen was about to climb the outdoor stairwell to John's apartment, his phone rang, and he hesitated when he saw it was Mike Zara. He was already in enough trouble to know he couldn't ignore a call from this moron.

He popped the phone open and said, "Tom Eriksen."

His supervisor's loud, unmistakable voice said, "I just called the Border Security Task Force office and they said you were out."

"Hey, Mike, I, um, am on my way to an interview." He didn't want to mention that the target of the interview had been on the disastrous crossing when the shooting had occurred.

"What time will you be done?"

Now Eriksen knew how to answer. If he came up with a time later than five o'clock, it was likely his supervisor wouldn't want to speak to him until tomorrow. "It could be a long one and go as late as seven o'clock. Why? Do you need me to meet you?" That was a nice touch.

There was a long pause over the phone. Then his supervisor said, "No, as long as you're doing what you're supposed to do over on the task force and not getting mixed up in any of your ex-partner's crazy ideas, I'm okay."

After another thirty seconds of small talk, Eriksen was able to get off the phone and knock on John's door. He waited, but there was no answer. He stepped over to the kitchen window and knocked on that, hoping the different sound might attract John's attention. Now he was starting to get concerned and moved back to the door, pounding with the palm of his hand.

When he got no response after almost a minute, Eriksen tried the handle and was surprised to find the door unlocked. He opened it slowly and called out immediately, "John, it's Tom. Are you in there?" He stepped into the dark apartment, comforted by the gun on his hip because something didn't seem right. He called out again, "John." He didn't want to startle an armed, hungover federal agent either.

He stepped all the way into the apartment. It was stuffy, but there was no overwhelming odor. The living room was empty, and the TV was playing ESPN. He eased into the hallway, still calling out to his friend. The bedroom was empty as well.

The door to the bathroom was shut, and it gave Eriksen a chill. He knocked on the door but got no response and immediately turned the handle and pushed the door open. The small bathroom was empty. The whole apartment was empty. He called John's cell phone one more time and could hear it ring in the kitchen. He walked in and picked up the small Verizon phone from the counter.

This wasn't like John Houghton at all.

Eriksen wanted to investigate further, maybe call John's wife and a few friends, but it was getting late and Lila expected him over at the Martinez apartment right now. He glanced at his Timex Ironman watch again and reluctantly shut the door to John's apartment, considering who he should call first to check on his friend.

––––––––––

Luis Martinez pulled into the parking spot that always seemed to be open directly in front of his apartment building. He liked parking the leased Toyota Tercel where the guard in the lobby could see it. Not that he thought one of the heavyset, minimum-wage security officers would actually stand up from the stool by the elevator if someone attempted to steal the car, but he felt better parking in that spot. The sun was just at the top of the low ridge of mountains to the west, and the temperature had dropped out of the low nineties for the first time since midmorning.

He still had a hard time comprehending that the Immigration Service trusted him enough to let him travel anywhere in El Paso freely. The caseworker assigned to him and his wife was a very pleasant young woman whose grandparents had come over from Mexico to work the fields in the fifties. He didn't know if she understood their plight or if she made everyone feel so comfortable. Dr. Martinez realized the sentiment in the United States was turning against immigration, and he could understand it in some circumstances, but the Mexican people had traditionally been a good source of honest labor. He had a hard time understanding why anyone wanted to keep out Mexicans. To work on his English, he had watched a great deal of TV on the small set in their apartment. One commentator, Ted Dempsey, was able to make his points clearly and rationally, unlike many of the partisan pundits who spewed their party's talking points and little else while appearing on TV. Dempsey's view, as usual, was straightforward: create a rational, effective, and humane solution for undocumented people already in the country, and end illegal immigration once and for all. Dempsey said the only way the government could reform immigration was to truly secure and control the border, and then and only then would it be possible to reform U.S. immigration laws and rules. Essentially, he wanted business and the federal government to follow the rules and do it in a common-sense way. And for their refusal to follow the law, Dempsey blamed employers of undocumented immigrants, not the people who understandably were fleeing poverty and violence in their own country. Martinez noticed Dempsey also tended to get a little louder and more demonstrative when he took up the issue of so many American companies outsourcing middle-class American jobs to other countries with cheaper labor costs.

Martinez checked his watch, knowing the lovely DEA woman was supposed to meet with him again this evening. He wondered if she had come up with the visas and hoped he didn't have to give up his friend Enrique. He liked the affable computer engineer but believed the young man should be working for a legitimate computer company, not for the thugs and drug dealers who employed him now. He also wondered if getting locked up wouldn't be a blessing for the reckless young man before he did something that guaranteed he wouldn't see his next birthday.

When Martinez was about halfway between the car and the building's front door, he felt a strong hand around his upper arm. He was startled by the mountain of a man, then recognized Pablo Piña's captain, Manny, standing next to the unknown giant.

Manny simply said, "Come with us."

"Where?"

"Does it matter?"

Martinez felt panic rise in his throat and realized he had to buy time. Maybe the DEA agent could help. Finally he blurted, "I have information to trade." He knew Manny was smart enough to at least consider the statement.

After a moment the older man nodded his head and said, "Like what?"

Martinez tried to think of something of value to these killers from his hometown of Juárez. "I have Enrique's cellular phone number." He could see that caught Manny's attention.

"What is it?"

The direct question threw Martinez for a loop. "I have it up-stairs." As soon as he said it, he realized he'd put his wife in danger as well. But a lot could happen, and they still had to pass the security guard.

Manny considered the offer, looked directly at Martinez, and said, "Get us past the guard or you die in the lobby."

Now Martinez noticed a third man. He was smaller and wiry, with eyes that darted back and forth. A man used to being followed and evading danger. One look in those eyes told Martinez that he was a man used to killing as well.

As Lila Tellis waited on the sidewalk next to her car, down the street from Dr. Martinez's apartment, she grudgingly admitted, at least to herself, that Tom Eriksen didn't act like a typical whiny FBI agent. She had even purposely scheduled this interview late in the afternoon so it would go into the evening. It didn't make him complain. She appreciated that. The FBI had a reputation for rarely working out on the street and for leaving the office at the stroke of five every afternoon. There was even a nickname for FBI administrators on Friday afternoon. They were called HBO. *Home by one.* Lila knew the worst of the stereotypes weren't completely accurate, and some of the jokes made by other agencies were out of spite or jealousy that the FBI got such positive press coverage, but most of the stereotypes had a grain of truth. Tom Eriksen had managed to avoid them all.

This interview with Luis Martinez was important. One of Lila's best sources inside Mexico said Martinez was friendly with a computer genius who had screwed over Pablo Piña. Not a good plan if someone wanted to live very long. Her overriding curiosity focused on what the computer geek had that Pablo Piña wanted. Maybe Martinez could shed some light on it or, if the price was right, lead her to the computer guy. That might be worth a few visas. She had a special interest in Piña. The so-called Dark Lord of the Desert sometimes put her two jobs in direct conflict, so the more she knew about him the better.

Lila looked up at the spreading dusk as Eriksen pulled his Ford Taurus up behind her Chevy Impala, about a block from the building where Martinez lived. She knew they looked like a couple of cops, but they weren't trying to hide it.

As Eriksen approached, she said, "Ready to crack the big one?" Lila even threw him a smile just to cheer him up. For some reason he looked like he could use it.

———

Manny was patient. He needed answers and was prepared to wait to get them. The doctor had lived up to his part of the bargain so far, getting them all past the uninterested security guard downstairs. The presence of the armed guard made him wonder who exactly was housed in the apartment complex.

Now that Manny realized he might get some usable information, he felt better about this assignment. Enrique had stolen information, and no one knew the extent of what was compromised. Piña showed little interest in it, saying it was more a matter for their American partners, but Manny knew it was a potential disaster. He'd lean on Mrs. Martinez to loosen the doctor's tongue. More accurately, he would let Hector's cousin do it. The little creep seemed to enjoy that sort of thing.

He let the doctor unlock the door, the key shaking in his hand. Manny was confident the doctor didn't have the sense to have a gun hidden or have his wife prepared for an armed assault. What he didn't expect was someone else in the apartment besides Mrs. Martinez.

Especially someone with a gun.

———————

Cash controlled his anxiety as he sat on the sofa, which felt like it was out of the 1960s, in the little apartment shared by Dr. Martinez and his wife. He didn't want to hurt Mrs. Martinez, but he was ready to kill Ari. The little Israeli had found a hundred ways to annoy him during the afternoon, and currently he kept twirling his little .380 like a Wild West gunfighter.

Cash didn't want to scare Mrs. Martinez. He didn't like it when women were frightened, and that made him think of Carol DiMetti. She was so sweet and pretty; he didn't want to think what his employer would do to her if he thought she was going to continue with her husband's stupid plan. He just hoped he didn't end up sitting in her house with Ari one afternoon.

He had let Mrs. Martinez dictate what was on the TV, and thought she might watch Spanish-language programming, but she showed no interest as she prayed silently to herself, watching Ari from the corner of her eye.

Cash switched between the various news channels and decided Texas stations only covered three topics: immigration, UT football, and politics. Ever since LBJ, Texans had loved politics, and the newest star on their wide horizon was Elizabeth Ramos. Apparently the crazy bitch was speaking in El Paso soon about the growing threat of terrorism and its ties to immigration.

He was surprised when the door handle turned. Usually he was more alert and would've heard someone walking down the hallway. It took Ari a second to catch on and stand back in the room with his gun in his right hand. As the door opened Cash thought he heard someone speak, and suddenly he realized there were other people with Martinez. He reached for the .45 under his shirt, but it was too late. A giant man stepped in next to Martinez, holding his own pistol, which had an abnormally long barrel. As Cash heard the first, sputtering sound, he realized it was a silencer.

Ari started squeezing off unaimed rounds from the other end of the room, and Mrs. Martinez let out a shriek that seemed to be an excuse to let chaos erupt.

———————

Tom Eriksen met his partner on the street near the Martinez apartment and sensed a slight change in Lila's demeanor from this morning. He wondered if she just relaxed more as the day went by.

Lila said, "We're not leaving Martinez without some answers tonight."

Eriksen nodded, but he was thinking that if she weren't so beautiful, she'd sound a little like Joe Friday.

Lila paused on the sidewalk, touched his arm, and said, "What's wrong? You look worried."

Eriksen hesitated, then decided to tell her the truth. "I can't reach my old partner, and it's not like him. I checked his apartment, but he wasn't there, and he left his cell phone on the kitchen counter. I'm going to start calling around after our interview."

She nodded. "You're a loyal guy."

"John inspires loyalty." She smiled, and it changed her whole persona. Eriksen was amazed.

Lila said, "You ready for a boring interview? It's not a car chase or whatever you FBI guys usually do every day, but I promise you'll see how important a job like this is."

"I believe you." He paused as he heard something in the distance.

"What is it?"

Eriksen said, "Listen." He could hear faint pops. "What is it?"

"Gunfire."

FOURTEEN

Cash reacted instantly as the door opened to the apartment, reaching for the Colt model 1911 he'd carried for the past ten years. He'd taken it from a Dominican guy who'd been sent to kill him in Jersey. That was back before he realized it was better to hire guys to deal with drug mules than do it yourself. The heavy black pistol slipped from his leather inside-the-pants holster and came up toward the front door as he realized there were three men with Dr. Martinez. The only one he could focus on was the big guy with a silenced pistol who was already popping off rounds.

Cash fired as he fell away into the short hallway that led to the bedroom. Out of the corner of his eye he saw Ari, just as startled as he was, bring his little .380 into play. It sounded like a cap gun and barely caught the attention of the men who were in the room now.

The smallest of the three men moved with blazing speed. He was so quick, Cash didn't realize he had a knife in his hand as he lunged at Ari, who had moved and tried to fire again but had taken a tremendous gash in his right arm. Blood began to pour from his upper bicep.

The little knife-wielding man seemed to dance and move without hesitation as his arm popped out again and Mrs. Martinez made a little gasp. As Cash moved back to cover at the end of the hallway he saw her hands reach for her throat and realized the man had just slashed her deeply across the windpipe, just below her chin. She toppled backward, bouncing off the couch and flopping onto the ground.

Cash raised the Colt again and fired three more rounds, this time hitting the oldest of the men. He couldn't see where Ari had fled. The whole scene was terrifying and complete chaos. He experienced classic tunnel vision, able to focus only on the man with a silenced pistol who continued to fire at other people in the room, although he was aware that everyone was moving, and now Ari was screaming and firing wildly, also hitting the older man, who now seemed familiar to Cash.

Dr. Martinez went down, but Cash had no idea who'd shot him.

The lead man was now bleeding from his side and hip and stumbled toward the door shouting orders as Ari ran back toward Cash.

The little Israeli screamed out, "What now?" As if he had to be heard above the gunfire, which was no longer a factor.

"Martinez?"

"Both dead."

Now Cash realized how much blood Ari was losing from the gaping wound in his arm. He looked over his shoulder, then dashed to the window and realized there was a simple escape ladder to the first floor. It wouldn't be as easy as the fire escape but was a chance to get away. He turned to Ari and said, "We gotta get out of here."

The elevator walls seemed to close in on Manny as he took a breath to clear his head. It only made the pain in his side more acute. He'd taken two bullets very close together, and his big concern was whether a bullet had damaged his hip bone. Although it hurt to move, his left leg didn't feel like it had suffered catastrophic damage. He stemmed the blood flow himself as Hector calmly reloaded his pistol and his cousin moved erratically as if trying to burn off energy. Somehow the elevator felt smaller on the ride down even though they no longer had Dr. Martinez with them.

Manny said, "Was I the only one struck by a bullet?"

Hector mumbled, "I'm fine."

His cousin held up his loose shirt to show a bullet hole in the fabric, but he was otherwise unharmed. The round had passed to the side off his bony chest and torn through the billowing shirt.

Manny was impressed with how calm Hector was and realized this was his normal profession, whereas it was more of a sideline for Manny. He was a manager, not an assassin.

The bell sounded and the door to the elevator doors slid apart. The guard was standing next to the door and said, "What the hell is going . . ." He couldn't finish his sentence because Hector's cousin jabbed his knife sideways into the man's throat. The guard made a gurgling sound as he tumbled to the ground clutching at the wound.

Before they had taken three steps toward the front door, a man and a woman darted inside the lobby, holding pistols in their hands. Manny heard the man shout, "Police, don't move."

Then it was chaos again.

––––––––––––––

Tom Eriksen kept his cool, breathing before he stepped through the door of the apartment building into the small lobby. This was where the gunfire had come from, and now he could see three men by the elevator. The government had spent a small fortune training him to be comfortable with a pistol in his hand, but it was the shooting at the border that had transformed him and made him function so well today. There was no substitute for experience.

As Eriksen looked across the simple lobby, he assessed the three targets by the elevators. One was a big man with a silenced pistol. The man saw Eriksen and Lila rush in the door and raised the pistol. Eriksen dove to one side as three quick, buffered shots struck the wall. The sound was still obviously a gunshot, but it didn't have the deafening effect of a gun being fired inside a normal-sized room.

Eriksen returned fire as Lila opened up from the other side of the lobby. They had good positions and were not in the crossfire as they drove the man away from the elevator and down a hallway.

Eriksen figured there was an exterior door at the end of the hallway and rushed to the edge of the lobby where he would have another chance to fire. Eriksen had had enough of people shooting at him and all the associated bullshit. He was pissed.

He charged forward, firing, with Lila falling in behind him. When he reached the corner of the lobby he ducked low and peeked around with his pistol up to see the men just bumping out the side door. He threw a few more rounds their way until the slide locked back on his Glock. He ducked back behind cover and called out, "Mag," as a way to let Lila know that he was going to reload. Just as most cops had been trained, she kept her pistol up to cover the area while her partner slid in a new magazine and released the slide to slam it forward.

As Eriksen was about to stand up and charge the doors, Lila paused at the counter next to the elevators. All she said was, "Man down."

Eriksen stepped to the counter, still pointing his pistol toward the door at the end of the hallway, looked over the edge, and saw the security guard on the ground gurgling as he worked to place his hands over a hole in his throat and blood poured out on the ground. Without thinking, Eriksen holstered his weapon, slipped around the counter, and applied direct pressure as Lila grabbed the desk phone and called for help.

Eriksen murmured to the man, "Just calm down and breathe, I've got you."

The knife, or whatever had caused the injury, had struck at an angle and slipped into the side of the man's throat. Shock was already setting in. Eriksen tried desperately to get the flat of his palm over the open wound and press without cutting out the man's air supply.

Now Lila stepped away from the phone and said, "I've got to go up and check on Martinez."

Eriksen doubted the gunmen would be coming back, and his guess was there were people up in the apartment that needed help, too.

Outside the apartment building, Hector grunted as he carried his limp cousin across his shoulder like a sack of flour and held up Manny, dragging them along at a surprisingly fast pace. Manny knew the cousin was likely dead, having taken at least two rounds from the police near the elevator. He had no idea how serious his own injuries were except that they hurt like he couldn't believe.

Hector cut through the rear parking lot, then through an alley to the next street, where he walked directly to a pickup truck as if it had been parked there for him. There was someone in the cab, and the engine was running. Hector flopped his cousin into the bed of the truck, then turned to Manny and said, "I will not have him left on this side of the border."

Before Manny could answer, a middle-aged, heavyset man popped out of the driver's door and yelled, "What the hell you doing?" in the Texas twang that made English a little more difficult for Manny to understand.

Hector didn't hesitate to use a silenced pistol to shoot the man twice in the chest. Then he looked back at Manny to casually say, "Get in."

When Manny opened the passenger door he saw a girl, no more than twenty years old, staring at the fallen man in shock. Manny hesitated, but Hector leaned in and shot her in the head, then dragged her across the seat and dumped her on top of the dead man on the street.

This time he screamed for Manny to get in the truck.

Manny was horrified, gawking at the dead woman, her lifeless eyes staring at him like an accusation.

Hector seemed not to notice as he turned his head and said, "Get someone to meet us at the trail. The police might try to block the port of entry. Tell them we'll be there in ten minutes."

Manny just stared out the window as the truck sped away from the killing grounds.

Inside the small apartment, Luis Martinez gave his wife one last hug even though she would never feel it or know the sorrow he was experiencing right now. He let out a sigh and quickly moved to stem the blood flowing from his upper chest. He had a single bullet wound on his upper chest, away from any vital organs. He couldn't believe things had turned so badly so quickly as he took another look down at his dead wife.

The apartment looked like it had been the site of combat. Furniture was overturned; blood was splashed across the carpet; the TV set crackled on the floor.

His wound appeared to have been made by a small-caliber pistol, but he still needed medical attention, and he didn't know who was coming back, the coyote named Cash or Piña's enforcer, Manny. Either way he would be dead. He didn't know how long it would be before anyone arrived if he called for help. Now survival was the only thing on his mind. He pushed to his feet and forced himself to look at his wife's open throat, knowing the inspiration it would give him. Now he would tell everything. Not just for visas, but for justice. People on both sides of the border would regret doing something like this.

He rushed out the door of his apartment and hesitated at the elevator, wondering who might be waiting for him at the bottom. He turned down the corridor to the big fire escape at the end of the hallway.

He had to find a way to the hospital.

FIFTEEN

Tom Eriksen sat on an old couch that had been reupholstered in thick vinyl and watched everyone pass by in the lobby, although he had already been up to the apartment and seen the body of Mrs. Martinez. The El Paso cops had this crime scene. It was a clear homicide, and despite the fact that the Martinezes were under the Immigration Service's protection, murder was still a state crime, not a federal crime.

One of the paramedics told Eriksen that his efforts with the security guard saved the man's life, although he had lost a lot of blood. There were blood spatters at the end of the hallway that indicated either Lila or Eriksen had hit the fleeing killers, but they had both decided not to take credit because they didn't want a lengthy suspension while the incident was investigated.

He had already heard about a father and daughter who'd been murdered on the next street, and the assumption was that it was the killers fleeing from this building. That was the kind of shit that made Eriksen's blood boil. Someone was going to pay for this.

In all the confusion, they hadn't noticed Dr. Martinez's red Toyota pull away from the curb. It'd been parked there when they entered the lobby, but after all the commotion and by the time Lila had found Mrs. Martinez, the car was no longer there.

Now Eriksen looked up and was not encouraged to see his supervisor, Mike Zara, obviously exasperated, pushing through the doors to the lobby, badging a uniformed officer and bullying his way onto the scene.

He plopped down in the chair next to the couch where Eriksen was sitting and said, "What the hell did you do now?"

Eriksen gave him a good hard look and said, "My duty."

"Your duty was to work on the Border Security Task Force, not to shoot it out with drug runners in downtown El Paso."

Eriksen didn't bother telling him the circumstances of what had just happened. It would all come out soon enough in an official report. All he could think about now was how he and Lila were going to sort this mess out.

———

Dr. Luis Martinez pulled into an open spot next to the emergency room entrance at the Providence Memorial Hospital in El Paso. It seemed like a palace compared to the grubby clinics he had worked in over the years in Mexico. He knew the attending physician would call the police as soon as the doctor realized it was a bullet wound. That didn't matter, because he wanted to talk to the feds now that he was away from the scene. He wasn't going to lie just because he needed medical attention.

He had not come to grips yet with his wife's death, but his thoughts drifted to his children, and he wondered how safe they were. It was an insidious type of panic that flooded through him. Different from the panic he felt when the guns were fired in his own cozy apartment. He had heard gunfire and seen bodies before, but never anyone close to him, and he had never suffered an injury like this.

At the apartment he had wondered how they had found him. Was this place just like Mexico, where you couldn't trust the police? Then he took a breath to calm himself and knew he could trust the DEA agent. That's who he needed to talk to now. That's who would be able to protect him.

He'd hobbled a few steps from his car when he heard someone say, "I can't believe it. Look who came to visit us at the hospital."

Dr. Martinez jerked his head up and was stunned by who he saw.

———

Lila Tellis had purposely hovered near the entrance to the apartment building, nodding hello to the different cops she knew. The lobby was buzzing with activity. Tom Eriksen looked tired, sitting on a gaudy couch alone. She had made her report to Andre, the supervisor of the Border Security Task Force, and he seemed content to let the El Paso police conduct the investigation into what now looked like a triple homicide. Lila knew the same men had killed the driver of a pickup truck and his nineteen-year-old daughter on the next block. This was exactly the kind of stuff she had been trying to stop.

She saw the portly inspector general from the Department of Justice hustling toward the door. Technically, he had jurisdiction over both the DEA and FBI. But he was one of the few people who understood Lila's unique position, and she knew he'd listen as soon as he pushed through the door.

The short, heavyset man shot her a nervous glance as she reached to take his arm, leading him to the corner of the lobby. All she said was, "We need to stay in play for whatever is going on. No leave while under investigation. Got it?"

The man just nodded his head.

Lila walked behind him and tried to look concerned as he headed toward the FBI supervisor talking to Eriksen. The dickhead supervisor stood up as if the president had just walked into the room.

The first thing the IG said was to Tom Eriksen. "Are you all right, Special Agent Eriksen?"

Eriksen just nodded. Lila liked how he kept his calm and didn't run off at the mouth. She'd decided he'd proven himself all he needed to and could be very useful in the future.

The IG looked from Eriksen to the supervisor and then to Lila and said, "I've talked to my boss and the FBI SAC, as well as the El Paso police detective in charge of the investigation. You're free to leave anytime you want. Do you need any time off to recover?"

Eriksen seemed to brighten at the statement, and he shook his head. Lila hesitated to make it look more realistic before she said, "No." Eriksen's supervisor looked stunned by the statement.

The IG said, "Good, I'll call you if we need anything else. It looks like the local cops have it covered."

Eriksen's supervisor sprang to his feet and said, "Wait a minute. You can't ignore this." He was so excited he sprayed a little spit across them.

The IG gave him a long, cool stare and said, "I'm not."

"I mean, this is a shooting. The second one Eriksen has been involved in during the last month."

The IG looked at Eriksen, then finally said, "It's a good thing he's handy with a pistol. I'll make sure to include it in my report." Then he turned and glared directly at Zara, saying, "I will call you directly if I need anything. Until then you're only in the way on this crime scene."

———————

Cash pressed the accelerator slowly, easing down the road so as not to draw any attention. He couldn't believe their luck in getting away from the scene without being identified. He hesitated to put Ari into his Cadillac because he didn't want blood all over the leather. Instead, he took a workout towel from his trunk and managed to wrap it tightly around the long, straight gash across Ari's bicep. He used a shoelace to tie the bandage in place and a second towel to soak up any blood that was on his arm and shirt.

Ari looked pale and nervous by the time Cash finally agreed to drive away. There was no doubt he needed stitches, but Cash wanted to come up with the right story first. Ari kept his yap shut and started to pant like a dog. Cash wondered if he could do this to his little coworker every day, because he was tolerable in this condition.

They passed by an urgent walk-in clinic because Ari thought he might need more attention than they could provide. Instead, they drove a little farther to the main hospital, counting on the emergency room being quiet on a weeknight.

He parked the car in the lot across from the emergency room, then had to rush to catch up to Ari, who had sprinted out of the car.

He was about to remind the little Israeli not to run off at the mouth when they got inside, but he noticed someone coming from the other side of the entrance. They both froze when they realized it was Luis Martinez, making his own efforts to stem the blood from an upper chest wound.

Martinez stopped, looked up at them, and froze as Ari said, "I can't believe it. Look who came to visit us at the hospital."

He didn't want to make his partner wait for medical attention, but this was too good an opportunity. He stared down the doctor and lifted his shirt to show the handle of his Colt .45. "You can come with us and hope for the best or I'm going to kill you right where you stand."

The doctor shuffled their way. Ari let out a quick groan when he realized what was happening.

SIXTEEN

Ramón Herrera sat at his oversized teak desk in the private office of his hacienda in Creel. He wore a Jay Kos English woolen business suit even though he would not be seeing any business associates today. It just put him in the mind-frame of handling business instead of lounging around the house. The view from the office was spectacular, with the gently sloping mountains reaching ever steeper. The blue Mexican sky melted his stress.

He had spent twenty minutes in his concealed art room in the climate-controlled, perfectly lit art museum built into the side of the mountain with access through the office. He was the only one who ever visited the six Picassos, the two Renoirs, and the da Vinci sketch of a wagon with a sail, seen only by a dozen people in the past 150 years. He wasn't even that much of an art connoisseur; it just made him feel special. He was the only one who would ever see them again. No one else was allowed in the room, and he planned to burn them before he died. Hopefully, when that time came, no one but him would've seen them in fifty years. It made him feel singular. It was such a rush he had plans to have all four versions of *The Scream* by Edvard Munch stolen when the time was right. Three were in museums in Oslo. The only one in private hands was a pastel version sold in May 2012 to Leon Black for almost $120 million. It had been on loan to the Museum of Modern Art in New York, but Herrera had missed his chance to try to grab it there. He was currently forming the greatest ring of thieves in history, purely for the challenge of seeing if he could corral all four paintings. It was more of a hobby than a business undertaking. He had to keep himself busy.

After the downtime in the gallery, Herrera had been looking over figures for his businesses as well as for the government overall. There was an estimate that profits from illegal narcotics smuggling into the United States exceeded $15 billion a year. That made sense because it was the largest consumer of drugs in the world. It was just good fortune that the U.S. sat on a porous border with Mexico.

He had watched several shows on his 60-inch Sony TV that morning about how the president of Mexico had deployed more than eighty thousand troops and federal police to fight the drug lords. The extra troops had made an astounding number of arrests in the past six months. Herrera and others realized that only about 2 percent of those arrested were ever found guilty in Mexican courts. That was disruptive, but not devastating.

The shows' favorite footage always involved narco-police who insisted on wearing ski masks in public while they paraded around with automatic weapons, trying to show everyone how tough they were. If they were so tough, why were there close to fifteen hundred murders in Ciudad Juárez in just one year? El Paso, right across the border, was one of the safer cities in the United States. Aside from rarely authorizing violence across the border unless it was absolutely necessary, Herrera wondered if it had something to do with Texas cities being so well armed. It seemed like every citizen owned a gun. In Juárez, personal firearms were outlawed.

Not that they could do much against the ruthless thugs that invaded houses and had shootouts on the corners, but in El Paso there was no telling what would happen.

Herrera had been worried about the subject since Hector had told him what he and some of Piña's people had to do to escape after trying to execute a former member of Piña's organization.

Now he had Hector, his most effective assassin, on the speaker-phone explaining why there were extra dead bodies in El Paso and the news was talking about a wave of new violence.

When Hector had finished his brief description of the day's

events, Herrera said, "I recognize you hire yourself out to other people. I'm just disappointed Pablo uses you in such minor ways. Avoid him in the future, if possible."

Hector grunted his acknowledgment of the statement. Herrera said, "I understand this is a difficult assignment that I have given you. But I'm telling you, if you complete it the way I want you to, you will be well rewarded." He knew the silence meant that Hector understood him. "I should be able to give you some intelligence about the target. Do you have any problem with the job?"

"No, Don Herrera. I will do what you need." Herrera cut off the phone thinking how easy life would be if everyone just did what he needed.

———

Cash stood in the dark shadow of a secluded gully west of El Paso directly on the border. The fresh air washed away any odor of blood, but not the stain on his conscience. This night wasn't going as planned.

He'd cringed when he pulled off Anapra Road onto a dusty trail. His beloved Cadillac rattled and bumped all the way. Now he worried about the trip back.

There was no effective border fence here. In fact, there was almost nothing except the battered remnants of the fence between the two countries and a dry riverbed that rose to a low hill on the Mexican side. The border from extreme western Texas to almost San Diego had questionable fencing and depended on the open, inhospitable desert to keep people on their respective sides of the border. Cash did worry about the sophisticated electronic surveillance and ground sensors, but he didn't plan to be here long enough to give the Border Patrol a chance to dispatch a car.

The Rio Grande River was curving north this far west and was nowhere in sight. Cash had been careful to position Dr. Martinez so he could see his homeland and realize that if he spilled his guts on every issue Cash asked about there was at least a chance he could go home again.

The whole idea was a better alternative than torture for both the doctor and Cash. The doctor had been most forthcoming so far, and now Cash was down to one vital question. "Do you know where Eric is?"

"Enrique?"

"The computer guy, Eric." Cash worked hard to hide his frustration, mostly as a way to keep Ari quiet. The wounded man had been in favor of shooting Martinez as soon as they saw him, then going in to get treatment for his injured arm. Now, more than an hour later, Ari was approaching desperation for what Cash knew would only be a couple dozen stitches. The towel he had wrapped around the wound was hardly leaking any blood at all now.

Cash repeated the question, "Do you know where Eric is?"

"No." The doctor shook his head and looked at the ground. That was his tell. Until now Martinez had looked Cash in the eye every time he answered a question.

"I don't want to get rough with you, Dr. Martinez, but you could not imagine how important it is right now for you to tell me what you know about Eric. You've already been through enough today. I promise it won't compare to what's about to happen to you if you don't tell me everything you know."

Dr. Martinez looked at him but hesitated.

Now Ari stepped forward, clearly anxious to end this so he could seek medical attention. Cash didn't care if the interrogation went on all night and Ari died of blood loss, but he did need answers, so he let the little Israeli throw the fear of God into Martinez. The rumors had run wild about Eric, the computer guy, and Cash's boss was bat-shit about finding him. He wasn't on any of the books and wasn't listed as an official employee at the company. Cash knew Eric a little bit from all the times he'd crossed into Mexico and back, but they had barely spoken. He was on the last run but had disappeared in the confusion. Cash wished his boss had been honest about Eric's significance, but the company was probably worried about the scam to extort money spreading further. It had already included Vinnie DiMetti and Eric. Cash wondered what the link between the two men was. Vinnie never mentioned that he knew Eric. The computer guy never spoke to Vinnie while crossing the border. What kind of information could he have? Cash wished he was told more about the reasons for his assignments sometimes.

Ari still hung menacingly close to Martinez, but he took no action.

Now Cash put on a big act, saying, "If you don't know where Eric is, then you're not much use to us anymore." He made a show of lifting his shirt and reaching slowly for his Colt. He suppressed a smile as the action took effect on the terrified doctor.

Martinez held his hands up in front of him as if fending off a blow and screamed, "Wait, wait!" He had to take a second to catch his breath. "I have a cell number for him."

Cash nodded to Ari, who dug in his pocket for a little notepad and pencil. They waited as the doctor wrote out the phone number.

Now Ari looked up at Cash and said, "That's it. We don't have any more time to screw with this guy. I need a doctor."

Martinez said, "I *am* a doctor."

"No, I need a nice Jewish doctor."

Cash wanted to laugh at the comment, but he agreed with Ari. It wasn't fair to let this thing drag out. He turned and nodded to Ari, then said to Dr. Martinez, "Cross here and never come back to the U.S." He waited as the doctor took a moment to comprehend what he had just been told. The doctor nodded nervously, turned, and scurried toward the imaginary line between Mexico and the U.S.

In the time it took him to run thirty yards and navigate the dry creek bed, Ari had popped the trunk on the Cadillac CTS, reached in, and retrieved a .308 hunting rifle. The sleek Remington had no scope, but anything less than a hundred yards didn't require one. He leaned on the edge of the heavy car and sighted in on the fleeing doctor. As soon as Martinez had made it to the far side of the dry creek and climbed the first few feet of a small rise, Ari fired one time.

The bullet struck the ground at the apex of the little hill right next to Dr. Martinez, startling him.

Cash mumbled, "Aim lower and to your left." He could see Ari already making the slight adjustment, then squeezing the trigger twice. The heavy rifle bucked in his hands, and the doctor was knocked off his feet and fell out of sight. This was sweet. The body was in Mexico, so there would be little investigation. Things were looking up.

———————

Tom Eriksen was exhausted and needed sleep, but he couldn't relax until he felt better about John Houghton. He decided to cruise past John's apartment complex one more time, and if he wasn't there then he would call John's supervisor and tell him how worried he was. The roads were empty after ten o'clock, and the sound of his pistol seemed to still echo in Eriksen's ears.

He had an odd emotional reaction to the shooting earlier in the evening. He had handled it well, and it made him feel good about himself. He had proven he could stand up to danger and handle the consequences. He was still in shock that the IG had let him off so quickly. He tried not to think what petty retribution his supervisor, Mike Zara, might try to exact over the next week.

The incident also made him realize that somewhere in the back of his mind he had expected to see that kind of action on a regular basis when he joined the FBI. He knew it was the influence of too many TV shows and novels, but it had still caused a great deal of disappointment when he came to grips with what the job really entailed. He'd been mistaken and paying for that mistake ever sense.

He turned the corner to John's apartment building and recognized he was excited to tell his partner what had happened. He appreciated the older veteran's perspective and sought his approval whenever something unusual happened. But as the apartment complex came into view, he saw the emergency vehicles and felt a lump in his stomach.

He parked his car and jogged to the cop standing in the parking lot as two paramedics loaded someone into an ambulance. Eriksen held up his credential case with the badge on the outside and said, "What happened here?"

The cop took a second to make out the FBI badge and said, "Someone found a body in the laundry room. They thought he might still be alive, and we called for fire rescue."

"Do you know the victim's name?"

The cop shook his head. "We haven't identified him yet."

Eriksen nodded, then pushed past the cop and rushed to the paramedic, holding up his badge as he approached. "Do you have any idea what happened?"

The young, lean African American paramedic shook his head and said, "No, sir. He was expired when we got here. We had to move him from the cramped corner of the laundry room to check for vitals and see if there was anything we could do. The cops told us by then we had ruined any potential crime scene and had us load him into the ambulance."

Eriksen said, "I might be able to identify him."

The paramedic didn't hesitate to nod at the ambulance driver over his shoulder and have him wait as he walked to the rear and opened the gate. It only took a second for Eriksen to look inside. He turned to the paramedic and nodded. "His name is John Houghton."

His world was starting to spin.

SEVENTEEN

Tom Eriksen drove around El Paso in a daze before he headed to his apartment in the suburbs. The town had a certain comfortable quality, something that was incredible when considering the violent, sprawling city just across the border. Even most of the streetlights were small and decorative, unlike a lot of the tall, practical cement light poles in many American cities.

He wasn't even sure how long he had driven as all kinds of thoughts raced through his mind, after he'd realized there was nothing else he could do at John's apartment.

He'd spoken briefly to an El Paso police detective who had come to the scene and made a quick assessment based on all the prescriptions and the empty alcohol bottles that John's death was an accident. All homicide detectives wanted to clear cases quickly, and accidents were the fastest way to keep their stats up. Based on John's position in law enforcement, Eriksen had convinced the detective not to jump to any conclusions and at least wait until after the autopsy to make a determination about the cause of death.

The paramedics on the scene had been pretty sharp. When Eriksen had wondered aloud how John's body had ended up in the laundry room, one of the veteran paramedics said, "Drug interactions are a crazy thing. I saw he had a prescription for Ambien. The sleeping pills can do weird shit to people and could explain why your friend's body was found in the laundry room. There is no telling what was going on in his head."

The hardest thing for Eriksen to deal with was the sudden appearance of John's wife and two teenage kids. They had been called to John's apartment by the fire department, but only told there had been an accident. It was the worst kind of bureaucratic foul-up. Eriksen sat and tried to comfort John's wife, although he had only met her once before, and even then briefly. The kids, a young man about sixteen and a girl a few years younger, sat in shock after they discovered the truth. He stayed with them until more relatives came and drove them home.

It was well after midnight when Eriksen pulled into his apartment behind the house in an area locals called Sun Ridge South. Like most of El Paso's neighborhoods, it was flat with some green lawns and a few tall trees. A sedan was parked in his usual spot, causing him to pull his government-issued Taurus to the side of the house. The events of the night and the strange car set off the internal alarm common to everyone in law enforcement. They had all read too many bulletins about home invasions and burglars to dismiss anything out of the ordinary. He stood in the shadow of the bushes and listened for a moment but heard nothing unusual. As Eriksen eased past the car, he moved his right hand, ready to slide the Glock out of the holster on his hip. His left hand brushed the hood of the car and felt just a trace of heat from the engine. The car had been parked for at least an hour.

As he stepped around the corner of the little apartment he saw someone move on his narrow front porch.

———————

Eric Sidle huddled in his cheap, dingy hotel room. The smell of urine in the hallway had almost sent him back to his sister's house, but he didn't want to put her in any danger. He was at least safe here. No one knew he was here, and he didn't have to give his name when he registered and paid cash. The room only contained a double bed, a scratched and scarred dresser with a tube TV on top, and a small table and chair. The bathroom looked like it belonged in a dorm room, with a minuscule stand-up shower, a rust-stained sink, and a toilet tucked between them.

He had seen the news story about the father and daughter gunned down in the middle of El Paso. The kind of stuff just didn't happen here. Juárez, just a few miles south, saw violence like that every day, with more than fifteen hundred murders each year. It was dubbed the most violent city in the world. But El Paso prided itself on its safe reputation and small-town values. Later in the evening, the news stories linked the deaths to another murder close by. The names were not released, but Eric knew his friend Luis Martinez lived in the area, and he'd been unable to reach him at the number the doctor had provided.

The sick feeling in Eric's stomach replaced the thrill he had been experiencing, scheming to play both his employers against each other. It hadn't even been his idea, but now that he was involved, he felt like he owned it. The news of the dead people and a sense of responsibility had thrown a wet blanket on his enthusiasm. He didn't even know why he was doing it for sure. Money was a motivation, but he could make plenty of money at a legitimate computer job. He had gone to Northwestern, for Christ's sake. He might not have been able to enjoy college football but at least he could look down his nose at most other midwestern schools.

The whole thing simply started as a challenge. He loved challenges. Most engineers did. The company he worked for ignored the greater part of his skills, and if he used them to help himself and his family, he didn't see the harm. But now Luis Martinez, if he was one of the dead people, made him see he might be in over his head.

Eric wondered who else could be in danger. His sister knew what was going on because he didn't feel right about living in her house and not being honest with her. Eric also thought that she would be the one in his family who could most use some money. He planned to pay off his parents' house back in Chicago and help his little brother with his expenses at Notre Dame, but his sister was his main concern right now.

He wondered if it was too late to wrap this up quickly with his

U.S. employers and flee before Pablo Piña decided he needed Eric dead as well. He stood up and flipped off the TV on the way to the kitchen to grab a beer and consider his options.

———————

Cash suppressed a smile every time Ari jumped or grimaced while the young doctor stitched up the gash in his arm. The small examination room was neat and clean with a hard wooden chair for a family member to sit on in the corner. He'd finally convinced Ari that they should go to a walk-in clinic where there would be fewer questions about his injury and why it was several hours old. His instinct had been correct when the young Indian doctor had accepted two hundred dollars plus the normal fee to work on the injury and not ask any questions at all.

Cash had considered giving him an extra hundred bucks to not use anesthetic. It would be a good chance to see if Ari was as tough as he claimed to be. But now he realized that if he had to face armed men again, maybe Ari wasn't such a bad guy to have on his side, even though his marksmanship at close quarters hadn't really impressed Cash at all. When it came down to it, Ari could be trusted to act, and he was too stupid to tell the police anything if he was ever caught.

Cash knew he had to have a sit-down with his boss sometime soon. Tomorrow, if possible. He needed to know everyone involved and whether he would have to face any more Mexicans with giant, silenced pistols again.

He wondered if maybe it wasn't time to find a new job.

———————

Tom Eriksen turned and crouched slightly as he peered up onto the porch through the darkness. Before he drew his pistol he saw a sandaled foot kick up near the rocking chair that had been on the porch before he moved in. He stepped around the corner of the building, allowing light from the rear of the main house to illuminate the porch.

Katharine Gleason rocked back and forth easily in the chair, unaware that he was watching.

He cleared his throat as he stepped onto the porch and feigned surprise when she stood from the chair.

Kat said, "I'm so sorry about John. I just came over because I thought you might not want to be alone. I knew if I called, you'd act like any other macho FBI agent and say everything was all right."

Instead of denying the accusation he stepped toward her and took her in his arms. She kissed him and leaned her head against his chest.

She was absolutely right. If she had called he would've told her he needed to be alone, but now that she was here he had never felt more relief in his entire life.

EIGHTEEN

Tom Eriksen was stuck in that pleasant dream world between sleep and wakefulness. The soft couch gave him no interest in starting the day. He felt the warm haze of spending the evening with Katharine Gleason even in this foggy mental land.

She'd listened while Eriksen spouted John's crazy conspiracy theories, but clearly couldn't get on board with Eriksen's idea that he'd been murdered. Kat had a different slant on things and said, "I understand you're upset, and I heard John was a great guy, but he was a serious drinker and he had, like, six prescriptions that didn't mix with alcohol or each other."

Eriksen thought back to what the paramedic had said and realized she made sense as he started to calm down.

He respected her insight. She didn't try to be something she wasn't. She was essentially a very bright engineer working with communications equipment with the National Security Agency. Kat had no experience with the intrigues that could be involved in federal law enforcement and spying agencies. He had heard over the years, before the attacks of 9/11, when the CIA had faced hard times and the Cold War had fizzled into a little-cheered victory for the West, that the new spy agency was the U.S. Drug Enforcement Administration.

At the time, when the drug war was near its height, DEA agents were the ones using high-level informants to infiltrate drug gangs every bit as well funded as countries. They were the new spymasters as they sent armies of paid informers into every country. They also had the muscle, with more than three thousand armed and well-trained agents, to support this shadow army. In contrast, the NSA was more of a collection of very bright geeks than tough field agents who were trained at bases on the East Coast.

They had talked through the night. He told her about growing up in Bowie, Maryland, with his brothers and sister. Saying it out loud made him realize how great his childhood was. His brothers had made him tough, and his sister had taught him patience. It made Eriksen recall something his father had said to him when he turned fourteen.

Eriksen couldn't understand why his sister was crying about a boy who had broken up with her. His father had said that he should always treat women the way he wanted his sister to be treated. The simple statement had taken root in him. It'd hurt him so badly to see his sister cry, even if it was only for one evening and the kid turned out to be a jerk, that he and his brothers tormented the boy for years afterward.

Values were instilled early in life, and they were the foundation of any civilized society. His work at the FBI had shown him that the police can't be everywhere at once and that they see only a fraction of the crime committed in society. It was only people's basic conscience that kept the wheels of life turning without chaos. Like many other agents, he had worked on fraud cases. The fraud douchebags were horrible, preying on the most vulnerable people imaginable. Often their victims were the elderly and lost everything to these ruthless jerks. But most scams were easy to pull off and rarely noticed. Even if a scammer got caught, the courts were hesitant to be harsh on nonviolent offenders.

Eriksen was startled out of his hazy recall of his past as he blinked into the early morning sun streaming through his living room window. He felt stiff and moved his hand and realized he'd fallen asleep sitting up on the couch with Kat nestled under his right arm, her hand draped over his stomach.

She blinked open her pretty eyes and gave him a sweet smile. They were both clothed, and he was happy he hadn't rushed anything, his father's words coming back to him. She pulled herself higher and planted a long kiss on his lips.

Eriksen already felt like he could face the day now. Her one kiss had shown him she was something special. Maybe she was the ingredient that had been missing in his life in El Paso.

Kat stood up and stretched. "I have to go home."

"Why? It's early."

She smiled and said, "I can't go to work in the same clothes. People will get the wrong idea."

"Do you care what people think?"

"I do at work." She looked down at him sitting on the couch and said, "You need to take it easy today."

"We'll see."

"You can't conquer the world in one day."

Eriksen gave her a smile. "I can try."

She smiled back as she picked up her purse. "Don't try too hard," she said, and then she was out the door.

Before Tom Eriksen could get rolling, his cell phone rang and he snatched it off the coffee table, hoping it was Kat Gleason saying she would come back for a while. Instead, it was the supervisor of the Border Security Task Force, Andre. Before the big man even identified himself, Eriksen could tell by the echo of his deep voice and blocked number who it was.

Andre said, "How you doing today, tiger?"

"Just getting ready to come in now."

"That's why I'm calling. I think it's a good idea if you take a couple of days to get your head on straight."

"I'm fine."

"I didn't say you weren't, but you and Lila saw some shit and I don't want you back yet."

"I know you already heard that the FBI cleared me to come back."

"What I heard was the Department of Justice inspector general did some kind of voodoo and didn't force you to take what I always thought was mandatory leave after a shooting."

"Doesn't matter if it's voodoo or sound judgment, I've been cleared to work and that's what I want to do."

"I'm sorry if I gave you the impression it was a suggestion. I'll see how I feel about you coming in tomorrow. But for now you can consider yourself free for the day. Any comments?"

"No, sir." Then he worked up the courage to say, "What about Lila?"

Andre hesitated. "She's different."

"How?"

"I'm afraid of her." There was an awkward pause on the line. Then, in a softer tone, Andre said, "Look, this isn't really about the shooting. It has a lot more to do with John Houghton. I'm taking some time today, too. He was a really good dude."

Eriksen mumbled, "I'll see you in a couple of days."

"Stay in touch. I like to know what each of you guys are up to, and I definitely want to keep track of a guy like you."

"Why's that?"

"I can see trouble coming from way off. Enjoy your personal time." The line went dead.

Instead of looking forward to some free time, Eriksen plopped on his couch, realizing for the first time just how empty his life was.

———————

Cash walked a step behind his employer as they surveyed the production facility just outside El Paso. The building had been constantly expanded over the past two years, and thousands of square feet of production and shipping space were supposed to be online soon.

He appreciated the fact that Mr. Haben wasn't skittish about having a guy like Cash near him in public. He was supposed to be more of a liaison who let employees like Ari do the dirty work, but his job description had evolved, and he couldn't argue with the pay.

This catwalk above the conveyor belts and packing areas was the perfect place to talk because no listening devices could be planted easily and the unending noise from the floor would disrupt any of the new technology used to catch even the most errant sound wave.

Cash looked out over the rows of computers. The parts came

from Taiwan, and they were assembled in Mexico. All the United States was used for was a last check and the boxing of the computers. It took only a fraction of the workers that other computer manufacturers needed to provide the finished product. That's why the corporation's profits had soared even in the face of a near-collapse of the country's economy.

Companies like Intel and Microsoft had to know something was up even though this company was nowhere near their size. Cash wondered if Bill Gates thought about why a company like TARC was so profitable. There were only a few ways to build a computer and the costs were similar. TARC was relatively small, but it was expanding.

Mr. Haben didn't look at him when he said, "I appreciate how you handled the job yesterday."

"I didn't expect the other men."

"That's exactly what I mean. You didn't panic and stayed with it until you accomplished your task. Technically speaking, those other idiots botched it by killing the father and daughter. Anything that attracts negative press can potentially affect profits. Now the problem is if anyone connects our reasons for shutting up Martinez and Piña's reason for silencing the doctor." He turned to face Cash, having to angle his bald head upward to look at the taller man. "And you're certain Martinez is dead."

"As a doornail."

"What about Eric Sidle?"

"We're working on it. I have a cell number for him, and we're seeing what we can find out. I believe he's still in the El Paso area."

Haben shook his head and looked down at the factory floor. "Things were going so smoothly for so long that this is throwing me off my stride. It all seemed to happen at once. And this isn't the only problem. I might need you to do a complicated job. One that could be more public. I can't have people blabbing about immigration right here in our own town without it cutting into our operation."

All Cash said was, "I'll be ready."

"I know you will, Joe." He patted Cash on the shoulder like a father.

This was the first time Cash had ever detected any worry or distress in his employer's voice. It freaked him out a little bit.

———————

Eriksen cleaned up and was considering what to do with his day when he was surprised by a curt knock on his front door. His apartment wasn't so big that he could hide his movements. He was cautious, stopping to pull his Glock from the drawer in the kitchen where he always stored it. The kitchen was in the corner of the living room and in sight of the door. He stayed behind the thick cabinets and called, "Who is it?"

A female voice said, "Eriksen, you decent?"

He recognized Lila Tellis's voice and stepped to the door. When he pulled it open he was surprised to see her smiling and casually dressed in jeans and a simple, loose T-shirt with no makeup. She still looked great with her straight black hair and intense dark eyes. He was confused and hesitated.

Lila dropped her voice low in a mock imitation and said, "You wanna come in, Lila?" In her regular voice she answered herself, "Yes, I do." She stepped inside and assessed him. "How are you doing?"

Eriksen shrugged. "Okay."

"I heard about John Houghton. I'm sorry." Eriksen just nodded.

Lila said, "Are you going to sit here alone and feel sorry for yourself?"

"I didn't have those specific plans."

"Are you as confused as me by what's going on? Your border shooting, the Martinez home invasion, John's rumor about one of the coyotes being a U.S. national."

"Yeah, I am. So what?"

"So do you want to sit here or do you want to do something about it?"

He just stared at the beautiful DEA agent. Somehow he knew she had a plan, and he wanted to be part of it.

NINETEEN

Lila Tellis scanned the half-empty parking lot and felt comfortable no one noticed her or Tom Eriksen. The midmorning sun forced her to slip on her Ray-Bans and shade her eyes with her hand as she swept the area one last time.

She liked how few questions this good-looking FBI agent asked. It'd taken a little time before she was sure he was trustworthy, but now she'd decided to jump into the deep end of the pool.

She'd parked her personal vehicle in a shopping center three blocks from the port of entry between El Paso and Juárez. It had taken her a moment to convince Eriksen to lock his Glock and his badge in her glove compartment. No cop liked the idea of roaming the streets without a firearm handy. Now he followed her dutifully as they walked south toward the main port of entry.

She led him to the far left line for pedestrians and glanced past the first twenty people to make sure it was the correct line. The inspector on the Mexican side of the border looked up and gave her the faintest of nods.

Lila looked at Eriksen and said, "Any questions?" Eriksen just casually shook his head. That made her smile again. She'd found an FBI agent who trusted her enough to lock up his credentials and gun, then walk into Mexico carrying nothing but some cash and his driver's license.

The line moved quickly, especially once the inspector on the Mexican side saw Lila. She already had the four fifty-dollar bills folded in her hand to slip the inspector, who gave Eriksen only a passing glance and waved them both through.

When they were past the port of entry and strolling toward the northern edge of Juárez, an area once teeming with U.S. visitors but now strangely quiet, Lila leaned in close and said, "Hold my hand."

Eriksen turned and stared at her. "What?"

"We're tourists. We are boyfriend and girlfriend or maybe even engaged. Grab ahold of my goddamn hand." She kept a smile on her face while she said it. He had a good grip for holding hands, she realized as they interlocked fingers. Not too strong but not too weak. There was a gentle quality to it that made her imagine him for a moment as her real boyfriend.

Two blocks and twenty Chiclet-selling kids into the Mexican city, she saw the six-year-old Jeep Cherokee right where she expected it. The paint job was beat up, or at least looked like it was. She didn't hesitate to open the rear door and slide all the way across and was happy to see Eriksen was smart enough to slide in with her.

As the car pulled away from the curb, beeping at pedestrians, Eriksen turned to her on the backseat and simply said, "Who are you, Lila?"

Eriksen had learned to keep his mouth shut and eyes open. John Houghton had said that set him apart from other FBI agents. Just the thought of his former partner made him smile. Now he followed Lila through the streets of Ciudad Juárez without comment. She obviously knew who to bribe on the Mexican side of the border, because they hadn't even slowed down at the port of entry. A car was conveniently waiting for them, so she had plenty of contacts.

The DEA was known for international contacts, but this was something else. If Lila had misjudged anything and they were stuck unarmed here in Ciudad Juárez, they'd be in deep shit. But the way she moved and acted told Eriksen he had nothing to worry about.

Juárez was considered the most dangerous city in the world, with murders occurring at all levels of society. The death toll was frightening, even exceeding those in war zones across the globe. Generations of cartel members had been battling for control of northern Mexico and access to the border. The police had failed to stem the violence, and the military was taking a stab at the gargantuan task. By most estimates several of the cartels had more fluid capital than the government, and they certainly didn't have to follow the same rules. Bribes to underpaid officials were difficult to track, and the barrios provided a seemingly unending source of cartel foot soldiers. In 2010, the city administration had tried to fire 25 percent of the police force on suspicion of corruption.

The cartels turned fourteen-year-olds into hit men and drug mules without batting an eye.

Mexico had been ruled by the PRI political party for seventy years before it lost power in the elections of 2000. The PRI had allowed certain cartels to operate as long as violence was kept to a minimum and out of the public eye. Now, with a multiparty ruling system, each party had a tie to a different cartel and violence had burst into the world's view. The hope was to stop it before it became ingrained in society and could never be stopped.

Eriksen had already considered the different explanations he might have to make to his supervisor for why he was on this side of the border. Zara had proven to be by the book and unsympathetic to almost any effort Eriksen took to complete his role as an FBI special agent. At first Eriksen thought he was just testing a new transfer and feeling him out, and he wondered how much of his reputation had preceded him. Now he realized Zara was just lazy and didn't want to be saddled with any extra work. Once again the simplest explanation was the best.

Eriksen took in the views of the city as they drove south, farther and farther from the border. Juárez almost looked like an American town out of the seventies, with lots of low strip malls and off-brand supermarkets, but the stark apartments and shantytowns didn't resemble anything in the U.S. he had ever seen or read about.

Now they turned and stopped at a hotel with a bar on the first floor. They were on the extreme south side of Juárez. This was not a tourist area. A visitor would have to run the gauntlet of the entire city and risk seeing one of the up to five murders that occurred every day. This was a hotel where business was discussed and deals were made.

Eriksen said nothing as Lila reached into the back pocket of the front seat and pulled out an older .45 caliber pistol. It looked like army surplus from the 1960s.

Lila turned, smiled, and winked at him. "Ready to ruffle some feathers?"

"Ready as I'll ever be."

———————

Manny felt a twinge of anxiety when he stepped into the beautiful office where Pablo Piña leaned on the desk, staring out over the fields behind his massive hacienda. He was dead tired, and the pain medicine the company doctor had given him after bandaging his bullet wound had made him even groggier. It was only the sharp stab of agony he felt when he stepped wrong on his right leg that kept him even partially alert.

After what seemed like an eternity, Piña turned and said, "What the hell happened yesterday?"

Manny shrugged, the exhaustion and drugs releasing his inhibitions. "The main thing I remember is being shot while trying to settle a minor personal grudge for my employer." He contained a smile when he saw a twitch in Piña's left eye.

Piña continued, "The only thing that's been on the news in El Paso is the killing of a construction manager and his daughter. They mention another murder a few blocks away, but that's what everyone focuses on. Why did you guys shoot the father and daughter?"

Manny hesitated, not wanting to shift the blame. He was responsible for everything that went on during a job he supervised. Finally he took a breath and said, "I regret it happened, but as I'm sure you know, we ran into other armed men as well as the police. Hector's cousin was killed."

"The crazy one who uses the knives?"

Manny just nodded.

"The thing that bothers me, Manny, is that you didn't come to me and tell me everything that had happened. I had to learn things on my own, and I hate surprises."

"I'm sorry, boss, but I figured once Martinez was dead, you didn't care too much about anything else, and I had to get medical attention."

"So you saw Dr. Martinez dead?"

Manny knew his employer well enough to realize there was some trap in the question. He thought back on the scene and everything that had happened and finally said, "I saw him go down from a bullet to his chest. But truthfully, so much was going on I never got a chance to lean down and take his pulse or make the statement you wanted us to make. I'm sorry, boss."

Piña seemed to consider this response for some time. Finally he said, "I knew you were an honest man, Manny. That's why I accept your version of what happened without question."

Then Manny said, "Why, is someone saying things didn't happen like that?"

Piña leaned down and pressed the intercom button on his phone. "Bring him in." Manny heard the door behind him and turned to see one of Piña's personal security men step into the room, followed by another man who shoved someone from behind. It took a moment for Manny to realize the dusty, dazed man who had been wedged between the security people was Dr. Luis Martinez.

TWENTY

The hotel had a certain cinematic quality, like something out of a Humphrey Bogart film, and Tom Eriksen appreciated the fact that he and Lila now sat in a private room behind the bar, speaking to the second set of men today. The first had clearly been smugglers who told them Pablo Piña had been upset with Luis Martinez, but that it was a personal matter. For some reason the news seemed to bother Lila. She kept trying to break the men's story and make it sound like Piña had been forced to take action.

The two men they were talking to now were off-duty federal police officers. Eriksen didn't know if they realized they were talking to other cops, and he knew it wasn't the time to ask any questions like that. The older of the two men slid a set of photographs across the rough table between them.

He spoke English with an accent, but it was clear to Eriksen. "These are the two men found after the shootout with the border patrol. One man is a local coyote. It looks like he was hit in the chest from a great distance. But this man"—he tapped the second photo—"he had been shot with a .45 caliber from just a few feet away. He had one other bullet hole in his left arm, but he would've survived. They were both left at the scene where they could be found."

Lila checked the photographs and said to the man, "And you have the fingerprints and other information from this coyote killed up close?"

The man nodded but made no other move.

Lila sighed, dug in her pocket, and plopped down a stack of fifty-dollar bills. A smile spread over both men's faces as one slid across an envelope.

The man paused a moment, then said, "You're not the first American *federale* we've given this information to."

Lila just looked at him, waiting for more.

The man said, "One of your Customs agents. A black man, about fifty, named John, asked us the same questions."

Eriksen cut in, showing his first real interest in the conversation. "Do you know his last name?"

The man shook his head. "We try to operate on a first-name basis with everyone. He had another man with him one time we spoke."

Eriksen said, "Who was the other man?"

"I think his name is Andre. Very large, perhaps six and a half feet."

Lila spoke quickly to cut off any more questions from Eriksen. "Anything else I need to know?"

"Yeah, this is not the place to be caught after sundown."

––––––––––

Luis Martinez wondered where in this beautiful hacienda these drab, featureless hallways were. They seemed endless. Unfinished cement with bare lightbulbs every thirty feet. It felt like a dungeon, but that was probably the idea.

He was past the point of fear and almost didn't notice the persistent pain. A bullet had been roughly removed from his upper chest, and a heavier bullet, from the rifle shot when he crossed the border, had passed through his upper shoulder, apparently bounced off his scapula, and left a clean exit wound near his collarbone. Some clumsy male nurse had patched him up and, out of professional courtesy, gave him a decent shot of Demerol, but he recognized the hopelessness of the situation.

Now he walked alongside Manny, the older man showing the same dignity he always did, despite the fact that he had been wounded. There was something about the calm professional that made Martinez believe he had not given the order to have his wife slashed with a knife. But he was still going to pay.

There were no other guards around, yet Martinez knew he had no chance to escape. At least not at this time.

Casually, without even looking at the doctor, Manny said, "What kind of information does Enrique have?"

"I don't know, but he thinks it's valuable. He expects payment for it."

"From us?"

Martinez shook his head. "I think he is looking to embarrass an American company."

Manny stopped and turned toward Martinez. "Piña says we might have a use for you and that I can keep you alive as long as I can explain your value. Please tell me you can help me find Enrique."

"I can try."

Manny just nodded his head.

———

They came back across the border easily. The lines were short, because what sane American would visit the "murder capital of the world"? Just as they got through Customs, Eriksen's cell phone rang, and he answered it. They walked toward a small restaurant district as he talked. Lila eavesdropped enough to know that it was the secretary from the Border Security Task Force and she was asking him where he was.

Eriksen looked up at the sign of the restaurant they were about to enter. He said, "I'm about to walk into a place called the Border Cantina. Why, is something wrong?"

He didn't say anything else, just shut his phone and slipped it back into his pants pocket, so it looked like everything was all right. Lila knew he had a thousand questions, but the first thing she had learned in federal service was that being hungry never helped any situation. It was a slow time of day, after lunch but before dinner, and they took a nice, wide table with a view of the city and Juárez in the distance.

Lila liked this young FBI agent. The guy was smart and funny, with good manners and a dazzling smile. It was too bad she never mixed business with pleasure. She was still in that assessment phase, trying to decide how much she should tell him about anything outside the confines of the task force they were both assigned to. She had already broken a lot of rules by slipping them into Mexico and letting him see two of the best-known informants for the U.S. government. But there were so many things that were none of his business. Lila rarely disclosed more than the DEA line of bullshit she'd learned.

Now, sitting across from him, Lila appreciated someone else who'd gone through the academy at Quantico where both the DEA and FBI trained. And even though he didn't brag about having gone to Harvard, it was obvious Tom Eriksen could be doing anything he wanted, from working at one of the big accounting houses to being a superstar analyst on Wall Street. The fact that he had chosen to be a working agent with the FBI said a lot about him. There seemed to be fewer and fewer people in the U.S. willing to consider the concept of duty and putting the country before themselves. That was why Lila never failed to give up a good seat on an airliner to anyone in the military. They got it. Military personnel understood what made the country and what it would take to keep it safe.

She watched Eriksen shovel some guacamole on a chip as they waited for their fajita platters. "Pretty good Mexican food, isn't it?"

He nodded his approval while he finished his mouthful.

Even having his cheeks filled, he was an extremely handsome man, with a strong jaw and deep-set eyes. It was hard to imagine him ever being lonely. But his laid-back and quiet attitude told her he wasn't on the prowl for women every night. Finally, as he finished swallowing, Eriksen said, "I'm not sure I would trust some of the food we could've gotten in Juárez."

"If you know the right place, you can avoid some of the more serious setbacks, healthwise."

Lila watched him eat. He looked like a damn recruiting poster for the FBI. She could see a Bureau brochure with Eriksen, a black guy, and an Asian woman and some corny slogan like *Today's FBI* or *The FBI cuts across cultures*. Yeah, right, unless you were black in the sixties, Hispanic in the eighties, or Muslim today.

She engaged Eriksen in idle chatter. "Does your supervisor always talk so loud?"

Eriksen nodded and said, "We thought he had a hearing problem and got his hearing tested. Turns out he's just an asshole."

They shared a laugh and then a long, awkward pause. Finally Eriksen said, "You gonna tell me what's going on and how you have connections like that? That wasn't a typical DEA agent interview. And I know you hide a lot of what you're doing from Andre. Don't you trust him?"

Before Lila could answer, she noticed a middle-aged man walking confidently toward them. Wearing a crisp white shirt and dark red tie, he looked like he'd just stepped out of a news studio, and there was something familiar about him. Before it clicked in her head who the man was, he stopped right in front of their table.

Lila wasn't sure she liked this interruption.

TWENTY-ONE

Tom Eriksen was settled at the comfortable booth in the nearly empty restaurant when he noticed Lila look up and realized someone was walking toward them. He let his right hand drift down to the pistol he'd retrieved from Lila's car. It wasn't in his official hip holster but tucked into his waistband in a leather inside-the-pants holster. After everything that had happened in the last month he wasn't about to be surprised. Lila's eyes told the whole story until he saw the man stop in his peripheral vision.

He slid away from the man and turned to his side, but his initial assessment was that there was no threat. The man was in his mid-fifties or a very fit sixty and dressed nicely in a shirt and tie. The man nodded to Lila but turned toward Eriksen and said, "I hope I'm not interrupting."

Eriksen let his eyes coast around the empty restaurant to make sure this guy wasn't here with anyone else. Then, as he focused on the man again, Eriksen realized he looked familiar, and his voice triggered something in Eriksen's subconscious.

Finally Eriksen said, "May I help you, sir?"

The man smiled, then chuckled and said, "I appreciate good manners, especially from a fellow Harvard alum."

"Do I know you, sir?"

Without asking, the man sat down on the bench on Eriksen's side of the table. He reached out his right hand and said, "I'm Ted Dempsey. Nice to meet you."

Kat Gleason sat in her neat cubicle next to the NSA listening post set up inside the Border Security Task Force. It was a plain room that she had tried to brighten with a Stanford pennant, two plants, and photos of her family. No one who didn't work for the NSA was allowed into this part of the office.

She was reviewing transcripts of several intercepts they'd made overnight. She'd been working on a program built on an algorithm that correlated certain phrases over certain forms of communication. Specifically she was tying into cell phone numbers from the northern Sonoran area of Mexico that made calls in two area codes in Texas and Arizona.

These were not wiretaps in the traditional sense. They also had nothing to do with the Patriot Act. None of that really had an impact on her job. The NSA was tasked with monitoring *foreign* communications traffic. Although she had the ability, she had never intercepted a call from within the United States to a destination also within the United States.

Three phone calls made overnight all appeared to be connected. It was far too soon to push the panic button, but the chatter involved hiring someone to come from Mexico into the United States to commit murder. The victim was referred to as a "chatterbox" and a "big mouth." The conversation was entirely in English, and the person on the U.S. side of the call did not have an obvious Texas drawl.

Kat took a break from her work to think about Tom Eriksen. She was a little surprised he had not called during the day. Everyone in the office already knew he'd been told to take a couple of days off because of everything that had happened. She didn't want to be like a schoolgirl and obsess over a guy. But there was definitely something special about Tom Eriksen. He had a certain manner and understated charm that she found intriguing. She could see getting involved with a guy like him.

She'd dated two naval officers since she'd graduated from Stanford. During her brief assignment to the National Security Agency's headquarters at Fort George Meade near Baltimore, she only had contact with navy men for five months. But since she'd moved to El Paso it'd been difficult to meet anyone she found interesting.

Kat sighed and looked back down at the transcripts as she started to compose an intelligence brief to send up the line. At least she had something to focus on and wasn't hoping the phone would ring at any second. Even if that was the truth.

———

Tom Eriksen didn't waste any time before saying, "I'm sorry, Mr. Dempsey, I can't appear on your show." He said it so loudly that a waitress looked up from wrapping silverware on the other side of the restaurant.

"So I understand. But we can still talk, can't we?"

"Off the record?"

"That's how I live the majority of my life, and one of the reasons I've had such a long career is I never break a confidence, minor or large. Sometimes what you don't report is more important than what you do. There's no way I would risk getting a public servant like yourself in trouble by revealing anything that you don't want revealed."

Lila Tellis hadn't been fazed when this bigger-than-life TV commentator sat down so casually and comfortably with them like a regular guy and introduced himself.

Eriksen had asked Dempsey how he knew to come to this restaurant.

Dempsey had given him a warm smile and said, "I have fans everywhere." Eriksen knew this meant that the secretary from the Border Security Task Force, who had called them just before they got to the restaurant, had told Dempsey where he could find the reluctant FBI agent. That was a bit of information Eriksen would file away for future reference.

Eriksen looked at the fit older man and said, "Mr. Dempsey, I appreciate the fact that you stood up for us after the shooting." Before he could continue, Dempsey cut in.

"First, call me Ted. Second, I appreciate what *you* do. I was sorry to hear about your partner's heart attack."

Eriksen didn't say anything. Someone was covering for John and preserving his memory. It was exactly the kind of thing Eriksen would've said if someone asked about John. Let their imaginations come up with the rest. Maybe people would think that the stress of the job was too much for him. That was very possibly the case.

Dempsey continued, "I'm in El Paso for several reasons. It would've been nice to have you on the show, but I completely understand. I was hoping that by showing your side of the story, you could help the general public understand the complex issues of border security enforcement. Maybe it would calm down some of the hotheads on the Mexican side of the border, too."

Now Lila cut in. "I'll ask what some of your other reasons for being here are." Dempsey focused his attention on Lila and flashed her a smile, and Eriksen could see the man forming response, assessing both Lila's likely interest and how much of an answer she would expect. It was comforting for Eriksen to realize this man was also a product of Harvard University. He was no empty suit or talking head. He had substance.

Dempsey said, "There are a few issues I feel are vital to our society. Two of those issues are on perfect display here in El Paso."

"What would those issues be?" Lila looked like she was enjoying this.

"Border security and job outsourcing. Our borders have to be secured, especially our southern border. Not just because undocumented and unsanctioned immigration has a crushing effect on our levels of employment, worker pay, and standard of living, but it's an obvious opportunity for terrorists to enter our country."

Lila gave him a long look. "What crushing effect does undocumented immigration have on prices in our country? Don't the undocumented people help keep prices lower?"

Dempsey smiled at her, pleased by her obvious grasp of the economics, and said, "You're absolutely right about that, but what is the larger result? Illegals take their lower pay, at least the part they can afford, and send it back to their home country, usually Mexico, rather than invest or spend their money here. The businesses that hire the undocumented people pay lower wages, then undercut their competitors. Lower wages sometimes have very high costs to our economy and our legal workers."

She stared at him for a moment before she asked, "If that's so, then why do so many support undocumented immigration?"

Now Dempsey laughed out loud, leaned back in the seat, and raised his hands in surrender, saying, "Your question is spot on. Leaving rationality aside, as so many love to do in America, the outcome of this great debate may be left to those preyed upon by pure propaganda, moved by simple sentiment. The facts be damned and love of country and countrymen forgotten. And we Americans can be a forgetful lot. But the facts are undocumented immigration does drain government resources, disrupts the labor market, and sometimes leads to the creation of new waves of crime."

Lila shot right back, "Are you saying undocumented people are committing more crimes than other people?"

"No, quite the opposite. They become a community of victims who are unable to call the police for help. Those who smuggle them into this country are most often also smuggling drugs, and the Mexican cartels oversee both products, in both markets north and south of the border. Their young women can be forced into prostitution. Whole families often work as indentured servants to pay off the cost of slipping into the United States, and they're an easy source of street robbery victims who can never call for help."

Eriksen could see Lila considering all these points. He cut in by saying, "What about the outsourcing of jobs? Why is El Paso central to that?"

Dempsey gave him a serious look and simply said, "The Technology and Research Center, TARC, is one of the biggest outsourcers in the Southwest. And there are more. Follow any of the four bridges across the river and you'll find the *maquiladoras*, the assembly plants that build wealth for Mexican and American companies, but not our middle class, or for all the folks who want to live the American dream. And most Americans don't know, don't care, and yet wonder why our middle class shrinks, rather than grows. None of it is easy to fix."

Eriksen could see why this guy was so popular.

———————

Cash felt better than he had in days. The couch he sat on didn't hurt his sciatica, and the small house was very inviting. The company wasn't bad either.

He'd given Ari the slip, telling him he was going to question Carol DiMetti alone. Ari had pushed to be included but stopped short of forcing the issue. Cash saw a change in the little Israeli's attitude since the shootout at the Martinez apartment. He seemed a little more open to Cash's ideas and understood that he was the boss.

Instead of grilling Carol about her husband's attempts to blackmail the company and where Vinnie had gotten the information, he savored a home-cooked meal and a bottle of decent Pinot Noir. Now they sat comfortably on the leather couch just enjoying a calm moment.

Carol said, "You're nice to check on me, Joe."

He slipped his left arm around her shoulders. He liked the feel of her smooth skin and smell of her light perfume. He looked down at a photo of Carol and her late husband on the coffee table. "How'd you and Vinnie meet?"

"The usual, I guess. I was a secretary and, well, you know what he did for a living. But my parents were never crazy about him."

"I bet." Cash didn't mean to sound so harsh and was afraid she might react, feeling the need to defend her dead husband. Looking back on it, Cash hadn't felt any remorse when he'd used his .45 to shoot Vinnie as he crawled out of the Rio Grande River and across the nominal border marker Mexico had placed near Juárez. The plan had been for the cops to kill him on the U.S. side of the border. Then Carol wouldn't feel any need to fulfill Vinnie's threat to use the information if someone from the company hurt him. But there was no way Cash could let the loudmouth walk away from the border crossing. His orders were clear, and he had no problem pulling the trigger. Frankly, the chaos and questions the two dead men on the Mexican side of the border had raised had been a blessing in disguise. His sources said cops weren't watching the border as closely and not nearly as many people were trying to cross.

Cash tried to cover his comment by immediately saying, "He never should've brought you in on his plan to blackmail the company."

"Vinnie said to use the computer information if they killed him. I'm still not sure what I intend to do." She scooted away from him on the couch so she could look him in the eye. "Is that why you're here, Joe?"

On impulse he reached across and kissed her on the mouth. He felt her full, moist lips as her tongue probed his. She moved closer, wrapping her arms around his neck.

After a few minutes, Carol broke the embrace and said, "Let's move this to the bedroom."

As she led him down the hallway he looked into the spare bedroom and saw men's clothes tossed on the bed, one sweat shirt with a Northwestern University logo and size twelve tennis shoes on the throw rug. "Whose are those?" he asked without thinking.

Carol gave him a sly smile and said, "Jealous?" Before he could answer she said, "Relax, my brother comes by and stays with me sometimes."

Cash had only one thing on his mind. "But he's not coming by now, is he?"

"No, we're good." She led Cash away from the room into her bedroom, then turned and said to him, "You know, Joe, you're like my knight in shining armor."

Cash embraced her again. He had never been anyone's knight in shining armor before.

TWENTY-TWO

Eriksen enjoyed listening to Ted Dempsey as he explained his philosophy. He could see why the guy was a respected television host and also why he was a lightning rod for those on both the left and the right who would much prefer the American public not bother themselves with the big issues, the big decisions, but simply let the wealthy and powerful, liberal and conservative alike, exercise what they imagine is their right to decide fates and destinies. They had talked for so long the restaurant had started to fill up with the dinner crowd. People occasionally came over to the table for an autograph, and Dempsey was unfailingly polite and pleasant. As he wrote his name on the title page of his latest book for a man who had gone out to his car to retrieve it, Dempsey looked over to Tom and asked, "What about you, Tom? How's a Harvard man end up in the FBI?"

"Thought it was a good use of an economics degree. I wanted to make a difference." He looked down, deciding not to finish his sentence and sound like a whiner. He'd screwed up and gotten transferred. No one to blame but himself.

Dempsey looked at Lila and said, "Harvard College doesn't issue business degrees. We have *economics*."

Lila laughed at his comment and said, "What about you? How did a Harvard guy like *you* get into broadcasting?"

"At first, I have to admit I was drawn to the excitement, to the outright fun of chasing down stories, digging into all that was going on. Then I was fascinated by the interplay between money and power, the politics of it all and the global struggle to assure ideological and economic outcomes. And I get the chance to raise my voice once in a while in favor of a country I love and a people I really like, especially when somebody is screwing with both. Occasionally, I get my butt kicked, but sometimes I win. Being in the arena is a hoot."

Dempsey's comments only made Eriksen think about his transfer from Washington, what he was working for, his desire to work terror cases, and something he didn't say very often, even to himself: his desire to serve his country.

Dempsey said, "Everyone has a job to do, so do it well and wisely." Eriksen watched as the older man gave Lila a knowing wink.

———————

Luis Martinez's hand shook violently as he held the cell phone. Manny had told him that if Enrique didn't answer the phone, Martinez would lose a finger. He had ten chances to reach the computer geek by phone; then his usefulness was over. The little, almost empty room where he sat in a folding metal chair was at the end of the rat maze of hallways. The room was decorated the same way, with one bare bulb and little ventilation. The stench from the hallway had told Martinez that blood had been spilled in this room. Lots of it. The dark stains on the concrete floor weren't from spilled coffee.

When he was a young man, going through medical school and his residency in Mexico City's second-largest hospital, he'd thought the hardest part of his life was already over. Despite everything he'd learned in medical school and saw at the hospital, nothing had prepared him to deal with this sort of pressure. He had a new wave of guilt for all the times he had treated Pablo Piña's torture victims so that they could return to the torture room for another chance to reveal their information. He used to tell himself that no matter what he did, these people would suffer. Now he only hoped God would forgive him.

Luis Martinez didn't like setting up a friend. That was why he had some alternate ideas. All he needed was a few minutes alone with the cell phone. Manny had already ordered Martinez to arrange a meeting with Enrique at the marketplace where they had met before. The trendy tourist attraction had plenty of cafés and stalls where Manny could hide.

His immediate concern, as he heard Enrique's phone ring, was his ability to retain all ten fingers.

Manny looked on placidly. Martinez cringed when Enrique's mail message came on. His heart sank as he left a message hesitantly. "Please call me, Enrique. It's very important." His eyes flicked to Manny, who showed no emotion. At that moment Martinez thought the whole thing might have been a bluff.

Then Manny gave a curt nod to a wiry young man with bad acne. The young man stepped up without hesitation, a folding knife already in his hand. He flicked it open with a quick twist of his wrist, snatched Martinez's left hand, and jerked it up in front of his face.

Martinez felt ill but couldn't keep his eyes off the well-used knife. He cried out, "I can try again. Please don't do this."

From the other side of the small room Manny said, "You can try again in an hour." Martinez felt his entire body sag with relief.

Then Manny said, "You can dial with nine fingers." Martinez tried not to scream. But he failed.

———————

Tom Eriksen sat across from Kat Gleason, holding a turkey-on-whole-wheat sub, in a quiet family-owned sandwich shop a few blocks away from the office. He tried to contain his excitement that she'd accepted his invitation to lunch, hoping to maintain some kind of cool-FBI-agent facade, but just looking across at her beautiful face made him grin like a lawyer suing a tobacco company.

Kat had been telling him about how she had chosen Stanford. Along the way she explained that the tree most people thought was the school's mascot was actually a member of the band. In fact, the school didn't have a mascot. The nickname "the Stanford Cardinal" referred to the color, not the bird. It was a unique lack of tradition that confused pretty much everybody. But then she turned those blue eyes on him and said, "I really don't know much about you. I get the idea you didn't want to come out here from Washington. What made you move?"

He hesitated because he hadn't really talked about it with anyone in El Paso. Finally Eriksen said, "I had a choice to transfer or risk being fired."

She gave him a sly smile and said, "I can't wait to hear this story."

"Not a lot to tell. I had a pretty severe disagreement with the supervisor and may or may not have ended up assaulting him."

She gave him another smile and said, "You're not sure if you assaulted him?"

"For legal reasons, I'm never definitive about that point."

"You definitely have tweaked my curiosity, but I understand if you don't want to tell me the whole story."

He thought about it for a moment, then shrugged and said, "No, I think you might be the first person in El Paso I wanted to tell. Make that the second person. John Houghton knew the story."

She quietly reached across the table and put her soft hand on his.

Eriksen gathered his thoughts and said, "My squad in D.C. thought we were working a kidnapping, but it was, in fact, a human-smuggling case where the family didn't have the money to pay for the teenage girl that had been brought up from the border. Regardless, we had to get the girl, who didn't realize she was in any danger, and in the confusion one of the agents identified the wrong vehicle. My supervisor at the time jumped on the radio and told us to all follow that vehicle even after I came on the radio and said I had seen the girl with two grown men in a blue SUV headed the other direction. He told me to ignore it and fall in with the other surveillance." Eriksen had to stop for a second to contain his anger as he recalled exactly what had happened.

"I didn't respond on the radio, but I ignored his order and followed the vehicle to a shopping center, where I called for help. The supervisor told me I was mistaken and that they were on the correct vehicle. The moron continued to insist I was wrong and broke off the surveillance he was on to come over to scream at me. He absolutely refused to even look for the SUV I had seen in the parking lot. When it started to pull out, my supervisor blocked me from getting back in my car, telling me I was an insubordinate son of a bitch. It was at this point I may or may not have punched him, then shoved him bodily across the hood of his own car so I could follow the blue SUV."

Kat sat still and speechless until she was finally able to say, "What happened to the girl?"

"I was able to get a D.C. cop to help me stop the vehicle, and we rescued the girl. By that time my supervisor had already made a complaint about me, and the Bureau was faced with a dilemma. Do we fire a guy who just rescued a girl being essentially held for ransom, or do we brush it under the rug by transferring him out of the division? Faced with those choices, I decided I would love to see Texas."

Kat gave him a big smile and said, "Sounds like you're a hero. I've often wondered what drives people to go so far above and beyond the call of duty."

"I thought I was just doing my duty, but our family has a chip on their shoulder and always tries to exceed people's expectations."

"Why is that?"

"My father says it goes back to the family's arrival from Norway and the need to prove they could be an asset to their new country. He says it doesn't matter if you're an accountant or a congressman, you always have to do what's right no matter what the consequence. In a way, being transferred out to El Paso is proof to my father that I was willing to live by the motto 'do what's right, not what's easy.'"

"You don't think working in intelligence is the best use of your skills?"

Eriksen shook his head. "I think everyone would be better served by letting me work cases that could affect the security of the country. It's difficult to be free if you're not safe."

———————

Manny stood perfectly straight in front of Pablo Piña, barely able to conceal his scorn. No matter what happened, he intended to end his employment with the so-called Dark Lord of the Desert, and when he crossed back after his assignment, Manny would decide if it was simply a resignation or something more permanent.

Seated behind the enormous oak desk in his study, Piña said, "So Enrique finally answered the phone."

Manny nodded.

"How many men will you take with you across the border?"

"Just one."

"Don't let the doctor leave the market either."

"We might have another problem, *jefe*."

"What's that?"

"A DEA agent was asking questions yesterday at a hotel in Juárez. Some of the *federales* were showing her photographs of the two coyotes killed the night Martinez tried to cross. She might know more about the whole situation."

"It was just an example of our American partners trying to screw us. They wanted both Enrique and Martinez under their control and never told me they were bringing them across. It's ironic that I am now trying to save them any embarrassment by dealing with both these *putos*."

"There are a number of men who would be happy to deal with the DEA agent if she ever thought to come back across the border."

Manny could tell his boss was considering the offer. "Who was this DEA agent?"

"Her first name is Lila, and she is supposed to be quite attractive, maybe thirty years old."

Now Piña perked up, his head snapping so he could look directly at Manny. "Leave her be. Make sure nothing happens to this DEA agent." Then he seemed to take a breath and add, "It would draw too much attention."

Manny nodded and turned toward the door.

Piña said, "Wait. Why don't you take Hector with you. That way I know you have someone reliable to back you up."

"Hector took another job. It sounds like it is something he enjoys doing."

"What job would that giant madman enjoy?"

"I think someone has paid him to assassinate Senator Ramos in Texas."

TWENTY-THREE

Tom Eriksen had never been on the set of a TV news show before, or any kind of show, for that matter. Glass partitions had been put up in the front courtyard of the Bank of America office building to enclose a set built up on a platform facing an audience area with simple wooden benches. More people could crowd in behind the benches if they didn't mind standing. Ted Dempsey had explained that the set was going to be stored in El Paso so he could do a number of shows from the city in the coming months.

A small army of technicians and workers had moved everything into place in just a couple of hours. High-intensity lights flooded the area, and security guards kept people from wandering behind the set, which consisted of two chairs facing each other and a second, smaller space that looked like it was used for news updates.

The excitement of the crowds and the bustling crew as well as memories of his lunch with Kat Gleason had come together to put Eriksen in a good mood.

He had been nervous accepting Ted Dempsey's invitation to visit the set and watch the first live broadcast from El Paso. Mike Zara would have a stroke if he knew Eriksen was anywhere near Ted Dempsey, but Lila had convinced him it would be fun and said she wasn't going to come by herself. In truth, he knew he needed a distraction from dwelling on John Houghton's death. Next week, after the complete autopsy, they were meeting with the El Paso homicide detective, and then he might get some closure. That didn't change the fact that one of the few people he could trust in El Paso was gone.

Lila came up beside him and pointed out how distinct the two different groups of people in front of the set were. They didn't look like protesters, but some carried signs. On one side of the set the signs had slogans like STOP OUTSOURCING or SENSIBLE IMMIGRATION. The other side of the crowd had more of an angry demeanor and signs that said such things as NAZIS WERE ANTI-IMMIGRATION TOO and RAMOS IS A TRAITOR.

Lila said, "This is interesting. I didn't realize his first guest was Elizabeth Ramos."

Eriksen turned from surveying the crowd and said, "The senator?"

"The only senator who's been making headlines for weeks. People either love her or hate her."

Eriksen started surveying the crowd as if he were on a security detail: Every person was a potential assassin and every object a possible weapon. He found himself checking the number of security people and saw that the producers had hired El Paso police officers in addition to the private security force.

Lila's phone spit out the beat she used as one of her ringtones. She looked at the phone, then said to Eriksen, "This is one of my good sources in Mexico. I gotta take this."

Eric Sidle felt a jolt of excitement seeing his friend alive and sitting at one of the picnic benches in the courtyard of the touristy marketplace. He'd been so certain Luis Martinez was dead, seeing him was a little bit of a shock. As he drew closer, Eric realized Martinez looked tired. No, much more than that. He was a shell of the man Eric had seen just over a week before. His left hand was heavily bandaged.

Eric slid onto the bench across from him, and the first thing he said was, "What happened to you?" Then he noticed blood leaking out of the bandage and realized it looked like Martinez was missing his pinky finger.

Martinez shook his head. "You wouldn't believe me if I told you." He looked down and ran his hands across his face. "Concepción is dead."

Eric gave a little nod and said, "She was killed the same day as the father and daughter, wasn't she?"

Martinez just nodded.

"Was it Piña?"

Another nod, and then Martinez looked up at him with red-rimmed eyes. "I'm sorry, my friend."

"For what?" Eric turned his head to see Manny plop down next to him and another man ease onto the bench next to Martinez.

Manny looked at him casually and said, "Hello, Enrique. You have something of ours."

Lila Tellis pulled Tom Eriksen to the rear of the studio set, away from most of the noise, as she tried to explain a more abstract intelligence concept to the very practical, FBI-trained man. She tried to keep exasperation out of her tone, but she'd had this discussion too many times with cops and federal agents who wanted to see everything in black and white. Allegations were either founded or unfounded. People could either be found guilty or not guilty.

Lila sighed, then finally said, "Listen to me, Tom, this is an *unconfirmed* report from a source inside Mexico. It is not necessarily reliable. The source has given me good information in the past, but he has always worked both sides of the street. My usual payment for his information is that I look the other way when he does something illegal for profit."

Eriksen said, "But it sounds specific to me. The threat is that someone is going to kill Senator Ramos. That doesn't sound like speculation."

"It's not the nature of the threat, it's the source who is providing the information. If we act on unconfirmed rumors, soon no one listens to those rumors and intelligence becomes useless border talk. There has to be a happy medium."

Eriksen gave her an odd look. "Wait a minute. How does a DEA agent hear information about an assassination?"

Lila met his stare and said, "Really? That's your concern? If you can't figure it out, you might not be nearly as bright as I thought you were."

Eriksen took a moment as he eased down to sit on a storage crate for a camera. He said, "I had my suspicions."

Lila knelt down so she could be at eye level. "Not one word to anyone."

He didn't waste any time raising his hand and saying, "I swear." Then after a pause he asked, "But why?"

Lila glanced around to make sure they were alone and give herself a moment to commit to telling someone the whole truth. Finally she said, "It's the perfect cover. The CIA is not supposed to operate within the United States. This gives me the opportunity to work on both sides of the border and hear everything. No one interferes, and if I have to make an arrest, I can do it as a DEA agent." She appreciated the expression on Eriksen's face and had to add, "A little more interesting than your FBI job, huh?" She gave him a smile to show him she was okay telling him something like this.

After a few moments he said, "What's our move? Who do we call?"

Lila said, "No one yet."

"What do you mean? If we do nothing, the senator could be killed."

"We've got to check this out ourselves first. I'm not supposed to pass on unconfirmed information unless it's from an extremely reliable source. The one who gave me this would not be considered reliable by anyone."

Eriksen looked troubled by the whole concept of keeping his mouth shut.

Lila had to say, "To be on the safe side, don't tell Andre anything about this."

Eriksen said, "And I can't tell Mike Zara. God knows what he'd do if I did."

Lila said, "Just us for now."

Eriksen looked uneasy but nodded.

That was enough for Lila.

TWENTY-FOUR

Manny appreciated how unusual it was to have a plan like this actually work. He'd been surprised to see Enrique strut right up and sit down across from Dr. Martinez. Manny hadn't trusted the doctor. A man with nothing to lose is a dangerous man. Too bad Piña wouldn't allow Manny to give Martinez some sort of reward. The man had lost his wife, then been shot two times and was missing his left pinky. That was a hell of a punishment.

Manny and his assistant stepped forward and slid onto the bench of the picnic table and drew Enrique's complete attention. Manny was just happy to get the weight off his throbbing right leg. No one in the marketplace noticed the men meeting in the food court's small seating area. It was just turning dark, and the marketplace looked like it was slowing down for the day.

The young man who had come with Manny had shown himself to be ruthless. Even so, Manny would've preferred to have Hector with him. The big assassin made him feel safe. But Hector said he had another assignment tonight, and even though it was somewhere here in El Paso, he couldn't help on this job. Manny hoped to hire Hector again soon.

"Hello, Enrique. You have something of ours." Manny was pleased with his grasp of English with the right inflection of scorn.

Manny waited for Enrique to respond to his greeting. The best the computer engineer could come up with was a stunned stare.

Manny chuckled and said, "Better with computers than people, I see."

Enrique looked from Manny to Martinez to Manny's new assistant. The young man from Chihuahua was not large but had the hard-edged look of a killer. His acne could almost be mistaken for battle scars. The ease with which he had cut off Martinez's pinky told Manny the young man would have no problem pulling the trigger of the pistol he held under the table pointed directly at Enrique.

Manny said, "I'm not sure exactly what you copied off Mr. Piña's computer, but it is not yours, and we need the information to be secure. I don't care if you didn't intend to extort money from us, the information is still stolen." He allowed that to sink into Enrique's brain, then added, "Are you prepared to give us all the information?"

"How do I know you won't kill me once I give you the thumb drive?"

"All I can do is assure you that we *definitely* will kill you if you do not give us the thumb drive."

Enrique's eyes skittered back and forth as he considered his options.

Manny said, "You have to realize there is a pistol pointed at you at this very second. I hope you don't do anything stupid."

Manny felt someone sit down hard next to him on the bench and then felt the pain in his ribs. The new addition to the meeting said, "That's a .45 caliber in your side. I really hope you don't do anything stupid."

Manny turned his head slowly until he could see the face of the man who had just spoken. He swallowed hard before he said, "I know you. Your company has worked with us in the past."

The man said, "My friends call me Cash. And I promise I wouldn't pull something like this unless I had backup. Let's keep calm and resolve this in a businesslike manner."

That sounded exceedingly reasonable to Manny.

Tom Eriksen stood off to the side of the set but couldn't focus on the broadcast of Ted Dempsey's show because he was continually scanning the crowd to see if he could spot anything unusual. Lila had taken up a position on the opposite side of the set and was doing the same thing. He would've felt much more comfortable if they had a dozen more agents out helping them. But some of what Lila had said about information from unreliable sources made sense.

Dempsey had spent the first ten minutes of the show talking about the need for Congress to end government programs that rewarded companies who outsourced jobs to other countries. He used his location in El Paso to single out the computer company known as the Technology and Research Center, or more commonly TARC. The personal computer company did not yet have a heavy market share, but its profits were healthy and attracted investors from across the country. The computers were manufactured in Mexico with only a cursory check and sent on to the packaging plant near El Paso.

Dempsey looked directly into the camera closest to him and said, "Make no mistake, companies like TARC are creating jobs, but not in America, and the offshoring of manufacturing, the outsourcing of jobs, will ultimately devastate our middle class."

That line drew heavy cheers from the live audience. Eriksen thought it made sense, too, especially coming from a guy who had proven to him that he wasn't focusing on these issues for ratings, or ideology. Dempsey believed every word he was saying, and Tom couldn't argue with his conclusions.

Eriksen continued looking through the crowd as Dempsey introduced his guest for the evening. A moment before the introduction was completed, Senator Ramos walked directly past Eriksen as she approached the stage, giving him a nod and a practiced smile. He could see why the young senator would be a political consultant's dream. She was poised, pretty, and obviously very intelligent.

Eriksen listened to the standard early questions but paid much closer attention when Dempsey brought up immigration with the senator.

The senator said, "As the granddaughter of immigrants I think I can speak clearly on this subject. Immigration is one of the severe stressors on our economy right now. With low job-creation levels and high unemployment, we simply can't allow those who would enter our country illegally, no matter how much we sympathize with their economic plight, to take available jobs away from hardworking American citizens. I doubt there's anyone who could disagree with that."

Dempsey gave her a long moment, then said, "I'm afraid I'm going to have to take you up on your challenge. Immigration is not the issue. Immigration has been the lifeblood of this country and shaped not only the national personality, but our values as well. Border security and *illegal* immigration are what concern me, and I believe many more Americans. The idea that anyone can cross either of our major borders without fear of prosecution and with virtually no hope of being detected, frankly, should terrify all Americans."

The senator gave him a forced smile, and much of her Texas accent she had been forcing into her comments seeped out of her voice as she reverted to the debate skills she no doubt learned at Princeton. "You've led me to one of my key issues: terrorism. You're correct that with our open, porous borders there is ample opportunity for terrorists to slip into the country. But I would have to disagree with your assertion that immigration is still as important to an established country like the United States, which now has the world's most advanced knowledge-based economy."

Eriksen couldn't help but look onto the set and away from the crowd as the two educated and opinionated personalities squared off. The senator's deft refusal to directly answer Dempsey's challenge to her restrictionist view of immigration, followed by tying the issue of terrorism to her desire for a closed border, was impressive, and she brought the audience along with her. Terrorism was still one of the few subjects in the country nearly everybody agreed on.

That made Eriksen think the threat against Senator Ramos was probably more reliable than Lila thought.

—————

Hector was sorry to turn down Manny on a job tonight, but he had priorities. The assignment he had been given would help him cover all his debts and prepare for his retirement. He was taking this job seriously and was being incredibly careful. That was the only way to treat a man as powerful as Herrera.

He'd spent most of the afternoon mingling in the crowd before the broadcast of Ted Dempsey's show. Since the set was out in the open, no one had asked to see any identification. His only concern was that since he was more than three inches taller than just about anyone else, if he took any action he could be caught on camera and identified. Hector had been mourning the loss of his cousin and could certainly have used the wild man now. There was nothing he wouldn't have done if Hector had told him it was necessary. The loss had bothered Hector so much that he hadn't even bothered to bring anyone else in on this job. It was too sensitive and secrecy was too important.

He had spent so many years collecting drug debts and sending messages from one drug lord to another that he appreciated the fact that someone wanted him to use his skills for something other than the same old narcotics trade. This was a political issue, and politics was one of his passions. He followed it on both sides of the border. Because of his work with the different drug lords, he realized just how full of shit Mexican politicians were when they said they were going to clean up corruption but accepted campaign contributions from every two-bit smuggler along the border. Hector wondered if the United States was much better. Every day he saw a story about some congressman who got in trouble for chasing women or some other personal lapse in judgment. He didn't see too many stories about outright corruption. That's why this assignment interested him so much. The idea of influencing politics positively thrilled him.

———————

Cash figured a lot of people had gone to the broadcast of the Ted Dempsey show a few blocks down the street at the Bank of America building. The business at the little marketplace went on quietly around them. One couple looked like they were going to buy a taco and sit down at another table, but they moved on.

Cash kept the pistol against Manny's ribs but looked across at

Eric Sidle, the man all of his friends south of the border called Enrique. "We are even more interested in the information you have. And for your sake and my sanity I hope you have it on you."

Eric's hands were shaking uncontrollably on the table as he looked across at the man in front of him.

Manny turned his head slightly and said to Cash, "I'm sorry, I have to ask. How did you find us here at this exact time?"

Cash nodded, considering the question as one professional to another. "You left Dr. Martinez alone with a cell phone. He had my emergency number from when we crossed the border together. Aside from worrying about a trap, I was more than happy to see who showed up." He scanned the market once more to make certain these two were the only muscle on the scene.

Cash had left Ari in reserve and saw him standing at a stall, looking at leather purses directly behind the thin man with a bad complexion. Ari caught Cash's nod and turned, taking two quick steps until he was directly behind the man with acne.

Ari stood directly behind the man, blocking the view of anyone behind him and seeing no one was watching from the front. Without warning he plunged his eight-inch stiletto into the back of the man's neck and up into his head.

Cash was as shocked as the man. He just wanted Ari to be in position to act if anything went bad, not to murder the man silently. It was a slick and professional move, so fast and natural it didn't draw any attention from the few people in the food court. Cash shoved the pistol farther into Manny's ribs to keep him from reacting as the young man went limp right in front of them, and he heard something hit the ground.

He realized the man must've been holding a pistol under the table, and suddenly he wasn't nearly as angry at Ari.

Now the man just looked like another drunk tourist who had passed out. It might have been more common in New Orleans, but it happened everywhere.

Ari gave him a grin and said, "You need Ari to do anyone else at the table?" Cash kept his cool and said, "No, I think you handled it about right. Wait here while we decide who's coming with us." He looked back at Eric and said, "What about it? Do you give up the information and live, or see what it's like to have an eight-inch spike driven into your brain?"

Eric looked sick to his stomach as his eyes took in the scene in front of him. The man with bad skin was facedown on the table as if taking a nap. Ari unfolded the man's collar to cover the single hole in his neck and the dribble of blood.

Eric said, "I can get it easily enough."

"But can you get it in time to save yourself some pain?"

On cue Ari whipped out a switchblade and started cleaning his fingernails. He said, "Ari will get it from him in less than two minutes."

Cash said, "I'm sure you will." He looked at Manny right next to him and dropped his voice. "Now the question is, if we let you go, Manny, can you overlook Ari's enthusiasm? I'm sorry your man is dead. I didn't mean for anyone but Eric to get hurt. You can keep the doctor, and we'll clear up any problems caused by Eric." Manny looked at his dead assistant, then Dr. Martinez, and nodded his head silently.

Cash sat up straight, his hand on his .45 in his windbreaker pocket. "You sit here with your buddy while we take a stroll. I hope we don't have a problem with this later."

All Cash did was glare at Eric and the computer geek started to shake. He slowly reached into his front jeans pocket, making sure Ari didn't overreact to the motion. After a moment of digging, he pulled out a blue thumb drive with the TARC logo. In a small, shaky voice Eric said, "Everything is on this." He slapped it onto the table.

Satisfied, Cash nodded and did a quick survey to see the best way out of the market. He still needed to sweat Eric to see how he got the info in the first place and why he was in league with Vinnie. As Cash was about to stand, he noticed something reflected in the glass around a jewelry stall.

A cop was headed their way.

TWENTY-FIVE

Todd Weicholz had been a patrolman with the El Paso PD for over fifteen months, and he was a little pissed off he'd gotten boxed out of the Ted Dempsey show overtime detail. The administration had kept him with a senior field training officer an extra six months because they said he tended to be "overenthusiastic." He didn't mind the extra few months of supervision under a female officer named Stacy Ibarra. She was understanding and funny, as well as tall and beautiful. Too bad she was dating some goofy construction guy who was into mixed martial arts. But now Weicholz was on his own. Really on his own, as in the only cop assigned to the shitty little touristy market that sold the same crap as the markets in Juárez for about six times the price. The place had added a couple of restaurants and a cutesy café, and now it was the mecca for Southwest arts and crafts.

Weicholz had figured that after his stint in the marines he'd immediately get a slot on the SWAT team and be kicking ass and taking names. Instead, patrolling this little downtown beat, it was more like kissing ass and taking notes. Not the way he thought a police job would be. He wondered if other law enforcement agents felt the same way about their jobs. At five foot eight, Weicholz made up for his lack of height by ensuring his uniform and gun belt were squared away at all times, and he had a half-inch lift in each heel.

As he walked down the main aisle, Weicholz smiled at some of the pretty dress-store employees; he was always on the prowl for a decent phone number. When he stepped into the circular food court, the first thing he noticed was a group of men at one of the six picnic tables. He almost dismissed them as another group of tourists until he noticed one of them passed out on the table. It wasn't much, but it was more exciting than strolling through racks of dresses and flirting with the cute clerks.

None of the men noticed him as he came closer, his right hand slipping to the butt of his Glock on his duty belt in an unconscious show of power. Weicholz knew some of the girls he saw on patrol would be watching from their stalls. He cleared his throat and consciously made sure his voice wasn't squeaky or high-pitched. He called out, "C'mon, fellas, you can't leave him like that." He stepped a little closer. "I'm gonna need some IDs. Right now." He snapped his fingers to emphasize the urgency of his command.

When Cash saw the cop's reflection, he tuned out Eric, the thumb drive, and all other distractions. The cop was a young guy and obviously in good shape. At first, Cash just said a little prayer that maybe he'd walk on past. He noticed Ari tense and mumbled in a low voice, "Be cool, Ari."

Manny, still squeezed up next to him, remained perfectly calm. More than that, he was ice. Cash realized the guy had probably seen more shit than any American thug ever would. His real concern right now was that one of the dumbasses he was threatening, namely Eric or the doctor, would try something stupid. Then he realized the chances of Ari doing something stupid were much greater.

The cop stopped about twenty feet away.

Cash pulled the gun away from Manny's ribs. He would prefer not to shoot a cop, but he wanted to go to jail even less.

The cop yelled out, "C'mon, fellas, you can't leave him passed out like that. I'm gonna need some IDs. Right now." Then he snapped his fingers as if he were talking to an obnoxious waiter. That made Cash tighten his grip on the heavy pistol.

As soon as the show ended, Dempsey stepped off the set and walked directly to Tom Eriksen, who was still standing to the side. He stuck out his hand and seemed genuinely happy to see the FBI agent. Eriksen immediately understood why this guy was so popular. He had the ability to make you feel like the only person in the world at that moment. After they chatted for a minute, Dempsey turned and said, "Let me introduce you to Elizabeth Ramos."

The senator gave Eriksen a dazzling smile. He realized that it was a forced, practiced expression, but she beamed confidence and intelligence, which was probably why she was elected in the first place. Eriksen wasn't sure if that was an act, but since he wasn't registered to vote in Texas, he didn't think it mattered much. Still, it showed him the difference between the two public figures. Dempsey was straight up and sincere, and the senator was pure politician.

She said the obligatory "How nice to speak to the people protecting us."

Eriksen smiled and took her slender hand as Lila approached them from the other side of the set.

The senator said, "One of my main issues is terrorism. It has ruined my family's country of origin. If you can't call what has happened in Mexico terrorism, then what can you call it?" She kept her intense, brown eyes on him. "Do you work any terror cases?"

"Not really." He couldn't help looking down at the ground as he mumbled his response.

The senator said, "Do terror cases interest you?"

"Yes, ma'am." He knew the enthusiasm popped in his voice.

"I have some friends at the FBI. If you're really that interested in working terror-related cases, maybe I can help."

Eriksen's heart skipped a beat. Could this really be his release from purgatory?

As Lila stepped up, she assessed the senator coolly. Dempsey made the introductions, and the senator gave her the same polished greeting.

In the distance, Eriksen heard pops that sounded like gunfire.

TWENTY-SIX

In the market food court, Officer Weicholz stepped up to the picnic table, his eyes on the passed-out man. He couldn't imagine drinking so much in public that he would pass out. It was one of the many things members of the general public did that annoyed him to no end.

He noticed no one at the table was making any effort to find a wallet with some identification. Just as he was about to snap another command, the little stocky guy on the other side of the table reached behind him, as if pulling his wallet.

An instant later, the tall, dark-haired guy at the end of the table turned to face him. There was something about the man's movement that attracted the cop's attention. It took a split second for his brain to register the pistol in the man's hand. Weicholz shouted, "Gun!" He'd been trained to do that anytime he saw a weapon, even if there wasn't anyone else around.

Officer Weicholz stepped to the side as he reached down to draw his issued pistol from the holster, yelling the other phrase that had been drilled into his head in hours and hours of training. As he started to bring his pistol up on target he shouted without thinking, "Drop the gun!" But it was too late. He heard the blast just as his pistol had cleared the holster and started to come on target. Out of reflex, Officer Weicholz squeezed the trigger several times.

He immediately lost the ability to breathe as the first round impacted his torso. He felt himself falling backward and wondered if he could reach the radio mic hooked to his shoulder. He needed help right now.

———————

Cash watched helplessly as Ari reached behind his back. It might look like he was grabbing his wallet, but that was also where he stashed his .380 automatic. So Cash forced himself to calmly turn, trying not to draw the cop's attention. He brought up his heavy pistol and pointed it just as the cop reached for his own weapon.

Time seemed to speed up at that point as the gun bucked in his hands twice. The cop fell backward after popping a few rounds randomly into the air. Ari, seeing the cop dealt with, pointed his small pistol at Dr. Martinez and shouted, "This time you stay dead." He jerked the trigger three times, firing at point-blank range into the doctor's face.

Cash stood up, covering the cop as the other men scattered from the table. He'd heard shouts from all corners of the market. He turned to yell at his partner, but Ari had followed him to the fallen cop. The cop looked like he was still alive, but his pistol was on the ground out of reach.

Ari raised his little gun, aiming at the cop's head as Cash shoved him hard. The one shot Ari fired missed, pinging off the cement sidewalk.

The little Israeli looked at Cash and said, "Why'd you do that?"

"He's no threat. Leave him be. Grab Eric and let's get the hell out of here."

When Cash turned, all he saw was the picnic table with two dead men. There was no one else in sight. They had to get the hell out of there.

———————

Tom Eriksen lingered near Dempsey's set as the crowd dissipated. He was waiting to hear more about a gunfight that had taken place at a market a few blocks away. It had been more than twenty minutes since Eriksen had talked with Senator Ramos and considered her offer to help him get back on terror investigations. Since then most of the cops had gone to the scene of the officer-involved shooting. The cops that were left on the set were on edge and had moved toward the street. One of them held a Remington shotgun.

Lila was chatting with an El Paso PD sergeant she knew. As Eriksen walked up he said, "Any word on what's going on?"

The sergeant said, "One of our cops was shot at the market. There are two dead men at the scene, and at least three other suspects left on foot. We figured out this was the best route to take if you were going to cross back into Mexico quietly."

Eriksen said, "How'd you know the suspects are Mexican?"

The older, heavyset sergeant said, "I don't, but we're stuck here anyway, so why not help out any way we can."

Eriksen liked that kind of attitude. It was cops like this that got things done without making a fuss about it. Eriksen could hear bits and pieces over the radio and was relieved to hear that the cop's ballistic vest had stopped two rounds and he was going to survive. There was a massive search of the downtown under way.

Here on the set, where the crowd spilled out of the courtyard, partially blocking one of the main downtown streets, every pedestrian caught a long look from the cops. A few were asked simple questions like where they had been and what they were doing for the evening. IDs were checked randomly.

Eriksen always heard people complain about the police asking them questions, but they never bothered to look behind the questions and try to understand that cops were just doing their job. Sometimes it was important to gather probable cause for a case or find a fleeing fugitive, and the only way to do that was to ask questions. He could tell by the looks on the faces of some of the pedestrians that they didn't appreciate their interaction with the police, even though the cops were nothing but calm and professional.

Lila nudged Eriksen. He followed her eyes to a lone man walking on the other side of the street. "He look familiar?"

Eriksen studied the man for a moment and nodded his head, saying, "Yeah, he does." He automatically reached back toward his pistol.

It was one of the men from the Martinez apartment shootout.

———————

Eric Sidle panted for air on the empty street a few blocks from downtown El Paso. He had run cross-country in high school. If he still competed, he would've just won the regionals. As soon as he saw Luis Martinez's lifeless, open eyes, and the three bullet holes placed randomly on his face, he knew he had to run farther and faster than he ever had.

When Eric realized what was going to happen to him as soon as Cash and his accomplice finished with the cop, he just started to sprint. His long legs took a moment to fall into rhythm, and he expected a bullet in his back at any moment, but he kept running. He was a little surprised he didn't run out of gas until he was more than ten blocks away from the market and the bloody mess at the food court. Now, as he slowed down, he recognized that he hadn't put any thought into where he was going. He had run north, away from the border, which in this situation was probably the right thing to do. Now that Eric had regained a little composure, he tried to think what he could do to end this whole mess. If he just gave the thumb drive to them, they'd still think he'd copied the information or had seen their secrets. There was no way anyone would let him walk away from a deal like that. He felt another rush of panic and patted his pocket.

He'd left the thumb drive when he fled. It didn't matter, he had a copy, but now they'd know exactly what he had on them, if one of the killers had been able to pick up the drive. He wasn't about to go back to find out.

He couldn't believe he'd been talked into this crazy scheme.

A car racing past made him jump. He looked all around him in a panic and had to lean against the wall to catch his breath.

He couldn't go on like this anymore.

On the street in front of the set Eriksen had the two cops' attention. He pointed at the middle-aged man walking on the opposite sidewalk.

Eriksen said, "That guy. We need to stop him." Eriksen drew his pistol.

The fat sergeant looked at him and said, "Why that guy?"

"He was involved in a shooting the other day, and Lila and I saw him." That was all the cops needed to turn and hustle across the street with Eriksen and Lila next to them.

The big cop with a shotgun yelled, "Hey."

The man now turned to face the cops and obviously knew they had him. He lifted his shirt with his left hand and reached for his waistband with his right.

The cop with the shotgun racked it once, yelling, "Don't!"

But the man kept reaching.

The single shotgun blast stopped him as the pellets from the buckshot ripped through his torso and neck, spinning him until he was a heap on the sidewalk. His pistol dropped a foot from his body.

Eriksen scanned the street for any sign of others. He and Lila had only gotten a good look at this man on the ground. He knew one of the other men from the shootout was big, but he couldn't identify him by his face.

This was all getting very spooky. He wasn't much for conspiracies, but coincidence couldn't explain what had happened over the last few days. Maybe he was involved in some kind of terror case whether he was officially assigned or not.

TWENTY-SEVEN

Tom Eriksen spoke in hushed tones even though it was just him and
Kat Gleason inside his small apartment. Maybe he'd been hanging
out with Lila too much and it was rubbing off on him. She sat next
to him on the long, soft couch that had been there when he moved
in. The light on the small table was bright and made him squint
slightly as he tried to focus on her.

Eriksen said, "I wasn't exactly deceitful, I just didn't tell Andre or
Mike Zara that Lila and I were that involved. The truth is the El
Paso PD did all the work."

Kat cocked her head and gave him one of those looks that usually melted him. "But it was you and Lila who identified the suspect,
wasn't it?" He tried to hide his exasperation. Between the border
shooting and the shootout at the Martinez apartment, Eriksen knew
his FBI supervisor would stop at nothing to have him transferred
again and say it was for Eriksen's own good. The way he and Lila
were telling the story now gave the El Paso PD credit for stopping
one of the men involved in a terrible murder spree.

In the week since a shotgun blast had cut down the fleeing
man tied to the murders, so much had happened that Eriksen was
shocked no one had seen through his and Lila's low-key story. Luckily, the media focus had been on the important parts of the events.
The injured police officer, a feisty little former marine named
Weicholz, identified the suspect shot by the cops. They'd had no
luck with the other suspects. One of the dead men at the crime

scene in the marketplace was Dr. Martinez, but the other man was still unidentified.

The city had calmed down under the impression that the violent gang that had caused so much havoc was now dismantled. The public tended to latch on to any news that reassured them of their safety.

In the week since it had happened, Eriksen and Lila had been busy running down any lead related to the rumor they had heard about Senator Ramos. Lila had managed to get the information to the Texas Department of Public Safety and still remained out of the picture. One unit of the Texas DPS, the famed Texas Rangers, had sent a couple of their people to watch the senator. After a day of close security, Senator Ramos said she would rather risk an assassination attempt than tie up the state's elite police officers. Some saw it as a noble move, but it aroused suspicion in others. There was still nothing to confirm the assassination attempt, but in their efforts to learn more, Lila had subtly taught Eriksen how to stay below the radar and still do his job. No one had noticed them. It was work that meant something and fulfilled Eriksen. He felt he was really going that extra mile.

At the moment he concentrated on Kat sitting across from him at his uneven dining table over an almost homemade meal with two glasses of Pinot Noir.

Kat gave him a warm smile and said, "This fish is great. What's your recipe?"

He could tell from her smile she had caught on to him. He finally said, "You'd have to ask the chef over at the Seafood Hut downtown."

She let out one of the soft laughs he couldn't get enough of, then leaned across the table and planted a long kiss on his lips. They settled back to finish their dinner, and after a few minutes Eriksen finally asked, "Come up with anything interesting at work?"

She gave him her usual answer. "I wish I could talk with you about it."

It felt like Kat enjoyed being able to hold her superior security clearance over his head. It was a small price to pay to spend a few hours with the beautiful girl from Pittsburgh.

Then Kat said the phrase he'd been hoping to hear. "Would you be opposed to the idea of me spending the night with you?"

A broad smile spread across his face as he nodded. For some reason he was wondering what sort of things Kat heard at work that she couldn't talk to him about. He couldn't help being curious.

———

Sitting at a clean table in a little Italian place off Alameda Avenue, Cash found himself in a good mood despite having to watch Ari wolf down his second meatball sub. After the close call in the trendy market he was quite happy to lie low and handle a few minor chores around the office. He had also been relieved the cop he'd shot twice had lived. He couldn't help smiling every time they showed the former marine making a few comments to the media. His heavy ballistic vest had stopped the bullets, but the impact of the heavy .45 caliber rounds had broken two of his ribs.

That hadn't kept Cash's employer from being dismayed. Not that they gave a shit about the life of an El Paso cop; they were worried about the press and pressure something like that would've brought to the area. Cash had managed to make it sound like he had planned on the cops catching Piña's enforcer, Manny, and blaming all the carnage on him. It really couldn't have worked out any better. At least for Cash. Poor Manny. He had no idea it was going to work out so badly for him.

Now he had been directed to find Eric and this stupid thumb drive with the information from Pablo Piña's computer.

None of that seemed to matter to him now. Carol DiMetti had changed his perspective single-handedly. She was a remarkable young woman who had made him reconsider his entire life. Was this really what he wanted to be doing for a living? Hanging out with idiots like Ari? Dodging the cops and hoping his own employers didn't decide to have him eliminated?

His own mom thought he was a stockbroker. He didn't think she even had a clue what he really did for a living. But he had to wonder if it was too late to change.

Ari, with tomato sauce splashed across his round face, said, "When do we start cleaning up the loose ends? Ari would love to do that DiMetti chick."

"Why do you even think she's a problem?"

The short Israeli used a wad of napkins to mop up some of the mess from his face. He shrugged and said, "You may be the corporate guy, but sometimes people feel more comfortable around the contractor. There's no competition. People like to talk to Ari."

"You hear what any of the other loose ends might be?"

"Ari heard they brought in a hitter from Mexico to deal with a problem. We should feel insulted."

Cash barely heard him. He was worrying about the company's plans for Carol DiMetti.

———————

Lila enjoyed the sub at Luther's Sandwiches on North Ochoa Street. It was cool, clean, and close to the office. She'd seen how careful the owner was about freshness and trusted him. That was her biggest issue, trust. She was still getting used to having a partner she could trust and confide in. This was not how she was trained. She tended to work alone and hoard information until she was prepared to use it. She'd seen the results of many of her reports sent back through the channels. Raids on both sides of the border took place, which never would've happened without her information. Although her main duty involved national security, drug activity could be tied to it very easily. She'd even once helped to quietly rescue a young Austrian tourist kidnapped in Mexico, using her contacts to arrange to pay a Mexican police unit to make a lightning strike and kill the kidnappers. The woman was on a plane back to Vienna before there was an official announcement of the rescue. That kind of stuff stayed with Lila.

Now she and Tom Eriksen were conferring over a sandwich.

Increasingly, she felt uncomfortable speaking freely in the Border Security Task Force office. Occasionally they would use the National Security Agency's safe room, but they couldn't do that too many times without attracting attention. Eriksen's girlfriend, Kat Gleason, had proven she could keep her mouth shut, too. Lila liked the pretty analyst with a very high security clearance. But she still hadn't confided her secret profession.

Lila said, "Instead of just avoiding everyone at work, we need to start looking at events and figure out who could have spilled important information. It's no fun to go through life not trusting anyone."

"I thought you guys were trained not to trust anyone."

She looked at Eriksen and grinned. "You've seen too many Jason Bourne movies. One way to look at us is that we're a government agency like anyone else. I've found that my work with the DEA is not too much different than my work with the CIA. It's just the focus of our attention that's different."

Eriksen looked down at a page of notes he'd brought with him, concentrating. Finally he said, "How did anyone know where Dr. and Mrs. Martinez were staying?"

Lila nodded, agreeing with that line of questioning. "They should've been protected and were using an alias. I think they were listed as Mr. and Mrs. Brian Fernandes."

Eriksen said, "Does that mean that someone at Immigration? It seems the simplest explanation."

Lila didn't say it out loud but knew that he was thinking it also provided them with an opportunity to blame someone they didn't know personally. Then she thought of something. "Andre was the one who suggested the apartment. I heard him arranging it the day after the border shooting you were involved in. It was before you even came to our unit."

"That doesn't necessarily mean anything on its own. Wouldn't he be involved in securing someone who is a potential source for you?"

"The apartment was supposed to be secret. And don't forget my source in Juárez who described John Houghton and said that he had a giant man with him."

Now Eriksen said, "But he was John's friend. That's the kind of stuff he would do for another federal agent."

Lila felt herself biting the inside of her lip, a nervous habit she'd had since she was a teenager. Finally she looked at Eriksen and said, "Let's play it safe. We'll keep him at a distance until we can figure everything out."

TWENTY-EIGHT

Tom Eriksen was learning not to be surprised by anything Lila Tellis said or anyone she knew. Of course she had contacts with the El Paso police homicide unit, and now they were in the squad bay of that unit talking to the lead detective who was investigating the deaths at the tourist market the week before. The way the thirty-three-year-old detective looked at Lila, Eriksen had the idea that they were more than just business contacts, but he figured his partner would tell him what she wanted him to know.

The squad bay looked like any working police office: files stacked on top of cabinets, old statute books stuffed under desks, half a dozen detectives working at their desks. There was the constant sound of phones, movement, and chatter. It was great. He had been very impressed with the professionalism of the police department and the pride they took in keeping their streets safe. The town of El Paso was quiet in comparison to the horrible example of the much larger Ciudad Juárez right across the border, and its mounting body count. In fact, the last two weeks had been the bloodiest in the city for the past twenty years. First Mrs. Martinez and the father and daughter a few blocks away, then Dr. Martinez and the unidentified man at the market. The two incidents taken together had set the residents on edge, and this detective was feeling the pressure from above to get some answers. Much like Lila, he appeared ready to step out of bounds of a typical investigation to come up with some answers.

The detective spent most of his time looking at Lila. "We still don't know the identity of the younger guy killed at the market. He'd been stabbed at the base of the head with some kind of ice pick or stiletto. It was a very unusual choice of weapon but apparently didn't draw any attention. The witnesses said all the men just sat talking together at the picnic table. It wasn't until the cop approached that anyone noticed one of the men had his head resting on the table. The guy our cops shot out on the street is a pretty well-known captain for a major drug runner in Mexico named Pablo Piña."

Eriksen noticed Lila react slightly to the name, but she didn't make any notes as she had earlier. "And the other victim at the market was Dr. Martinez. Were you able to find any forensic links between the market and the scene at the Martinez apartment from last week?"

"Ballistics matched on two of the weapons. We dug out some .45 rounds from the wall of the apartment last week. They matched the two slugs that hit our cop. There was also a .380 round that matched. But we have no idea who fired which rounds. There was a fingerprint on the .380 round, but it came up negative in the FBI database."

Lila said, "Is there anything we could do to help you guys?"

Now the detective leaned in closer and said, "We did recover a thumb drive from the scene. It was just sitting on the picnic table. We pulled a single fingerprint off of it, but we haven't been able to match it to anything in the database either."

Eriksen said, "Was there anything on the thumb drive that might point to the identity of the victim or any of the shooters?"

"That's the problem. Our computer guys say there's nothing on it. As a cop, my gut says you don't kill someone over a blank drive."

Eriksen nodded. "You're right."

"Think you might be able to help?"

Eriksen exchanged a silent glance with Lila and hoped she was thinking about Kat Gleason and her agency's ability to look at things like that. He said, "I think we can work something out."

Ted Dempsey hustled through the lobby of the downtown Marriott. He'd moved from the ritzy hotel where he'd originally been staying when he realized the staff was almost all Croatian. That, in itself, wasn't the problem. The problem was that they had been imported as temporary workers for six months at a time, at a much cheaper rate than the hotel would've paid local workers. It was, in effect, outsourcing jobs inside the U.S. His reaction had nothing to do with his public image as a crusader for the middle class and the working man; the practice went against everything he stood for personally. Dempsey now felt very comfortable in the much smaller room at the simple Marriott. He was curious to see how it operated and if the employees liked their jobs.

Dempsey had turned his lifelong natural curiosity into a pretty good living. He had the big house, and expensive vacations when he and his wife wanted. It allowed him to keep his mother in a monstrously expensive assisted-living center in Trenton, New Jersey, and his brother in a house on the coast of Florida, and he paid for college not only for his own four children but for his nieces and nephews as well. Mostly, though, he did his job because he liked it. He enjoyed exposing hypocrites and taking contrarian positions against mainstream ideas. He liked debate. That was one of the things about his time at Harvard he always enjoyed, and there had been plenty to debate in those days.

He sensed a connection with Tom Eriksen and hoped he could help the young FBI agent in some way. Eriksen was quiet and contemplative as opposed to Dempsey's more confrontational style. For that matter, Dempsey would have preferred a country of greater civility, a quieter time. But Washington had set the tone, and the atmospherics weren't going to get any less corrosive soon. Gone were the days in Congress when you could compliment someone on the other side of the aisle or support a bill that didn't originate within your own party. The only time he ever saw a Democrat reference Reagan was to justify a tax increase, and the only time he ever saw a Republican reference Clinton was to justify cutting entitlement programs. The president was in full-time campaign mode now, and the language of politics was increasingly acrid. The president showed no interest in leading all Americans, only in prevailing in the partisan battles that rendered the country ever more polarized. Dempsey knew all this and tried to discuss as much as was sensible on his show.

He had a number of reasons for doing one show every week from El Paso. Initially, it was to help the FBI agent and his friend, who had been accused of murdering a Mexican national on the southern side of the border. Now that that situation didn't seem to be hanging over Tom Eriksen's head, Dempsey liked having a base in the Southwest. Most of the talk shows originated in New York. The danger with that was the overwhelming feeling that living in New York, you were in the center of the country. New York might be a big city, but so was Chicago or Denver or Seattle, and even El Paso. A New Yorker would never agree that any other city, other than perhaps Washington, would be worthy of comparison. By coming to another part of the country, Dempsey left behind his favorite city, but also its sometimes suffocating parochialism. He got to see how other people lived, listen to their ideas and opinions, and show some of it to his audience.

He couldn't believe Elizabeth Ramos had agreed to visit the show each time he broadcast from El Paso. She was a ratings bonanza. Smart, articulate, controversial, and attractive, she was an absolute TV dream and an excellent role model for ambitious young women in every career and walk of life. She also stuck to her convictions. Even if Dempsey didn't agree with everything she said, he could admire her conviction and commitment. She seemed to be doing things for the right reasons. There wasn't much more you could ask of a politician. Agree or disagree, integrity was really all that was important.

The senator's personal story of growing up the daughter of a hardware-store owner who earned an academic scholarship to Princeton was compelling, but her family history of immigration made her difficult to criticize. The senator's critics had been forced to focus on such silly issues as her hairstyle or the sometimes rambunctious behavior of her two teenaged children.

As he headed toward the main door at the front of the lobby, Dempsey heard someone call his name and turned with his ready smile. He paused as he recognized the man in the suit who walked toward him with his hand extended.

The man said, "Rich Haben, with the Technology and Research Center." Dempsey was wary as he grasped the man's hand and gave it a quick shake.

"Nice to meet you, Mr. Haben."

"You probably feel like you already know me since you mention us on your show so frequently."

"Would you like to come on the show and tell your side of the story?"

Haben gave a polished laugh as he patted Dempsey on the shoulder. "There is no 'my side.' I run a business that answers to stockholders. I'm not sure what else you would want me to do."

"Maybe assemble your computers inside the U.S. since this is your primary market for your product."

"Then I'd have to raise the price of each computer considerably and we'd lose what little market share we have."

"Why don't you come on the show and say that?" Dempsey could see all good humor draining from the man's expression.

"You and I both know I can't make a statement like that on television. All I'm asking is that you lay off us for a few months until we get our market share up. If you do that, I'll see what I can do about adding on a few dozen more workers at our factory here in El Paso."

"The way I hear it is that you have more than a hundred undocumented people working for less than minimum wage. If you added on a few jobs, would that mean you're cutting back on your slave labor?"

The man gave him a cold stare and said, "I don't know who's worse, you or Senator Ramos. This is America, Mr. Dempsey. It is based on capitalism. Private industry pushes our massive economy. If you think it should be some other economic model, maybe that's what you should spout on your TV show. Frankly, the rumors and innuendo you spill onto the screen every night do nothing to help people get back to work."

Dempsey held his temper in check. You could insult him, but not his ethics. "Anything I said on the air I can back up. That's why I mention that you employ only one U.S. employee for every nine Mexican employees, yet you sell sixty computers to Americans for every one you sell outside the country. That's a fact I'd like to hear you discuss on air, or prove wrong and we can set the record straight."

Haben gave him a mean stare but didn't say anything.

"I also talk about your corporate statements. You sell computers at a cut rate, yet your profits are healthy. How do you manage such a business miracle?"

"Is any of that helpful to our employees who would lose their jobs if we go belly up?"

Dempsey gave him a TV smile and said, "Maybe not today or tomorrow, but one day, someone speaking up like me will keep guys like you from taking advantage of the workers in both the U.S. and Mexico. I know you say you're just a businessman, that it's all about profits. But you know better, and so do the politicians who look the other way while our trade deficits run up and our trade debt rises. While our middle class loses jobs, and those who want to be in that middle class lose hope. But don't lose sleep, because I blame our elected officials with their bromides and bullshit that our citizens swallow whole. Hell, the truth is you may get away with it all until there's no country for any of us to worry over."

Dempsey could tell by how the man stalked away that he had not made a new friend in industry and commerce. He felt good about that. Hell, you're known as well by your enemies as by your friends. And you have to be particular about both.

TWENTY-NINE

Tom Eriksen took advantage of his visit to the El Paso PD homicide unit to seek out the lead detective handling John Houghton's case. Lila had elected to give him some privacy and chat with the detective handling the market shooting, much to the young detective's delight.

A middle-aged detective with a soft midsection greeted Eriksen at his small office with a smile.

Eriksen said, "How's it going?"

"I'm busier than the lawyer for the University of Florida football team."

"Anything new on John Houghton's death investigation?"

The detective said, "I'm glad you told me to take a closer look at your friend's death. I left it open, and the autopsy results pushed me to go back with a crime scene geek and do a quick check of the apartment."

As Eriksen eased into the chair on the other side of the desk he said, "What'd you find?"

"The autopsy was exactly as we expected, with the cause of death being a mix of prescription drugs and alcohol. All the pills were prescribed directly to the victim, but it was a curious combination. One of the pills in his system was an amphetamine, which was probably what counteracted all of the Ambien and kept him moving. That's how we think he ended up in the laundry room."

Eriksen could hear the man's interest in the case, but he still didn't see the unusual aspect of it.

The detective continued, "Here's the tricky part. The stain on his shirt was water and a mixture of all the drugs, Xanax, Ambien, and the amphetamine. I've spoken to his wife, and there was no indication he was trying to commit suicide."

Now Eriksen said, "No way. He was interested in a big case and talked about it too much to be thinking about ending his own life. He also thought he was going to get back with his wife and kids soon."

"Even if I didn't know that, the biggest factor is that there were no dirty glasses at the apartment. There was one glass, the one I think he drank the water and crushed pills from, that had been hand-washed and was sitting in his sink. Who washes a glass after drinking shit like that?"

Eriksen looked at him and said, "So there had to be a second person at the apartment."

"Exactly."

"Did your crime scene unit pick up any prints or DNA that might identify that person?"

"We're not exactly *CSI: Miami*. We have the victim's exclusionary prints, but we don't have the resources to really check the whole apartment for DNA, and there were no prints on the glass or around the kitchen."

"What if you go back? I know no one else has been in the apartment. His wife can't bring herself to clear out his stuff."

The detective considered the request.

Eriksen pressed him. "I'll go back with you and use my basic fingerprinting skills I learned in the academy. Whatever it takes. There are too many unanswered questions, and as good a homicide guy as you are, I know you can't leave something like this open."

The tubby detective let a smile spread across his face and said, "How can I turn down help from the FBI? It's the first offer we ever had."

Ramón Herrera relaxed in the gigantic Jacuzzi, letting the stress run out of the muscles in his shoulders. The hand-crafted seats in the marble tub held just the right amount of heat. Two naked young women, both of them from Peru, giggled as they exchanged comments on massaging his neck. He had chosen these two girls because of their lack of English skills and his need to conduct business over his utterly untraceable cell phone. He only used the throwaway phone to talk to people over the border. The cheaply made phone had cost about fifty dollars in a department store in El Paso yet defeated the most sophisticated tracking equipment the U.S. government had.

As usual, the phone was answered promptly in two rings. They never used names. Just because the phone couldn't be traced didn't mean it couldn't be listened to. Herrera understood that the process to screen the massive number of calls made over cell phones, even using key phrases and special algorithms, took time. He hoped that most of his immediate concerns could be handled before anyone noticed the conversation.

Herrera was calling the head of the Technology and Research Center, a cautious American named Richard Haben. The man seemed competent enough in the drab business community of computers but never seemed to understand what was involved in other aspects of this complicated world.

His American partner said, "Nice to hear from you."

"Really? It shouldn't be. I only call when there is a problem." He couldn't keep a smile from creeping across his face as he heard the hesitation on the other end of the line and knew the CEO of TARC was scared out of his wits.

"What's the problem?" asked Haben.

Herrera liked how Haben was trying to sound natural and make believe he was calm. Usually his man Pablo Piña would deal with issues like this, but Herrera felt it was important to get more involved in the businesses that had potential to grow. Especially the ones inside the borders of the United States. The partnership they had developed with the Technology and Research Center had many avenues for profit.

He didn't want to waste this opportunity to speak with a wealthy and influential American.

"Your politicians do nothing but criticize us, your citizens shun our tourist attractions, and I can't get your people to pick up even one load of our product for delivery to your factory. Do you have the right man on the job?"

Haben stammered and stuttered, finally saying, "I've been side-tracked by petty criminals who've been trying to blackmail the company."

"Events in real life are usually played out by petty criminals. Men like us work to bend the world to our will only to worry about the minor, ignorant common man who confounds our plans. This is a lesson I learned in my early years and understand all too well now. A random act of violence, a greedy, low-level employee, or an over-zealous police officer can wreck any empire, no matter how big. But you should focus on one thing at a time."

"You're saying I should focus on this one load we have left in Mexico."

"Exactly. Perhaps you need a shakeup in your organization and different people in different management positions. I want your computer company to work and survive. Then our trust in you will show benefits in the long term." Herrera took a moment to let that sink in, then added, "Handle this task better than your attempt to smuggle workers across the border without our knowledge."

Now Haben sounded really flustered. "We did that for other reasons as well. Reasons that helped business. Reasons I didn't think you wanted to be associated with."

"We'll discuss that later. Get this shipment moving now and ensure it is safe or our next conversation will be in person."

Cash found Ari in the little off-site office they sometimes used. It was a convenient place to keep messages and had no connection to the main corporation. The place was only one room with three desks and phones. Cash's desk was always empty because he had nothing to keep there. Ari was sitting at his desk and apparently working on something. It made Cash think of a little kid pretending to have a job.

Cash said, "Let's go out and look for Eric tonight."

Ari kept his head down, focusing on the page he was writing on, saying, "Can't do it tonight. Sorry."

"Why not? You got a date or something?"

"Nope. Ari got another assignment."

"What? What assignment?" He let the frustration stream out in his voice as he stepped next to the desk so Ari had to look up at him. "What the hell are you talking about, you little turd?"

Ari gave him a smug smile as he leaned back in the chair. He knew it would do him no good to stand up because his head would still be four inches lower than Cash's. "I'm supposed to escort a load from the port of entry to the main building tonight at dusk."

"What are you talking about?"

"Does Ari have to explain everything again?"

"He does unless he wants Cash to choke the living shit out of him."

Ari sighed like a teacher trying to get a point across to an adult student. "Mr. Haben told me to wait for the truck to cross through the port of entry, then follow it all the way to the main building and make sure nothing happens to it. I think he's worried about the driver making an unscheduled stop and losing a couple of the packages."

Cash turned to gaze out the window, mainly to hide his astonishment that he had not been told about the assignment. Traditionally this had been his job and his job alone. It was the most secretive of all of the company's activities. It was also one of the most lucrative and ingenious. Semitrailers carrying computers came from Mexico to the factory in El Paso virtually every day. The Customs inspectors became used to the huge trucks and never gave them more than a cursory look. One truck every few weeks carried two thousand computers, and each contained two kilos of cocaine. It was an extra $40 million of untaxed profit that could be increased to every other truck if need be. The biggest risk in any narcotics venture was the distribution, and the company only used two big distributors, which had no links to the company. Those distributors cut the high-grade cocaine into four kilos each, then distributed each kilo individually for an additional giant profit.

The money was one of several revenue streams that kept the company afloat while it tried to expand its market share. It also provided ready cash to keep the lines of communication open with both the Mexican and U.S. authorities.

Now Cash turned back to Ari and summoned the strength to simply say, "Good luck tonight. It would be nice if you let me know about other assignments before they just pop up."

Ari nodded his head and said, "Fair enough. They gave me a heads-up about a couple of loose ends they want me to take care of. I'll let you know if it interferes with anything you and I are doing."

Cash noticed that when Ari wanted to, he could be deadly serious. When he dropped talking in the third person he also sounded much smarter. This could be a problem.

Tom Eriksen couldn't refuse when the detective on John Houghton's case said he had some time and would go by the apartment right then. It would take a few minutes to get some equipment together and recruit a crime scene technician, but Eriksen felt some satisfaction at having John's case looked at a little more closely.

It was obvious the detective had personally selected a crime scene technician he was trying to impress. The plump, pretty, but new technician made the detective look like a puppy dog. Anytime she walked into his line of sight his eyes followed her. She had been all business and very professional, but the detective looked like his heart ached to ask her out. Eriksen hoped he didn't look so obvious around Kat Gleason.

The apartment was no longer marked as a crime scene, but the manager of the building said no one had been inside. There was still time on John's lease, and his wife hadn't felt strong enough to look through his personal effects.

The place was a little stuffy after having been closed up, but with the front door open and the sliding door locked back and sunshine flooding the living room, it didn't seem quite so gloomy. In the big scheme of things the apartment wasn't messy at all. It was a testament to John's Spartan living conditions; he ate most meals out and essentially lived out of a suitcase. It was obvious he never intended this to be a permanent residence and was expecting to get back with his wife soon. One more argument against a possible suicide.

The detective tried to find clever places for the crime scene tech to look for fingerprints. Most of the places the detective found were low to the ground and forced the technician to either bend over or squat low. Eriksen could see the detective had a thing for large, shapely butts. Fingerprints were really their only hope, because unlike how forensics were portrayed on TV, DNA testing was extremely expensive, and on a marginal investigation like this, without any real evidence to point toward the location of the DNA sample, the forensic possibilities were limited.

Eriksen took his own survey of the apartment, slowly walking through the single bedroom, then the hallway, and stopping in the small bathroom with only a toilet, sink, and shower. His eyes settled on the handle to the toilet. He would ask the technician to check it for fingerprints because of an old Burt Reynolds movie he'd seen called *Sharky's Machine*. In the movie, one of the detectives thinks to lift a hit man's fingerprint from the toilet handle because, he says, no one wants to take a leak with rubber gloves on. It was as good advice as any he had heard in the FBI Academy.

As Eriksen moved through the rest of the apartment he found three places he wanted checked for fingerprints: the refrigerator handle, the various prescription bottles sitting on the counter, and the metal on-and-off button on the TV.

Maybe they would get lucky.

Ari stood on the loading dock of a warehouse owned by TARC. The open-air dock allowed up to three semis to back up at one time, but for the moment he had only been trusted with one. The diesel fumes from the big Mack truck were enough to choke him. He hated to think what three would be like. Ari considered himself a valuable employee wherever he worked. His strongest quality was his loyalty. The fact that Mr. Haben had seen fit to put him in charge of bringing this truck from the border to the warehouse made him feel important, and there was no way he would let his boss down.

He'd made sure that one of the older guys loading the truck, who already knew the secrets of the corporation, had heard the story that Ari had been in the Israeli military and was a certified badass. Ari spent a lot of time in the gym to give himself good arms and shoulders to back that story up. He was, in fact, an Israeli citizen, but he had never been in any country's military.

Ari had been smart to stick to the exact same story every time he met someone. He always used the Israeli military instead of the U.S. Marines or Army Rangers. It was much more difficult to check out someone's story from a country halfway around the world that was always hesitant to give out information. The closest he'd come to actual military life was that his family lived near a small base outside Tel Aviv when he was a kid and he was able to pick up a few key terms. Just hanging out with soldiers who called the new recruits *basar tari,* or fresh meat, shaped his view of the Israel Defense Forces. Ari realized that when he dropped the term "IDF" into everyday conversation in the U.S., all he got was pleasant smiles and nods. No one had any idea what sort of questions to ask about his history.

He would throw in comments about Merkava tanks and how a *chopel,* or medic, had stitched up his left shoulder after a mortar fragment had sliced through his uniform. The truth was slightly less heroic. He had fallen off a swing when he was nine and caught his shoulder on its rusty chain. He really did have thirty-one stitches, and they were less than plastic-surgery grade, but the operation was conducted at a civilian clinic in Tel Aviv by a very pleasant Swiss doctor working off some ancestral guilt about the country's lack of interest in the Jews' plight in World War II.

When Ari was twelve, his parents moved to Toronto so his father could work in an electronics shop. Ari spent a very comfortable adolescence in and around a suburb, basking in his local celebrity at a small Jewish school. He was their first and only Israeli student and often used his upbringing in a dangerous and uncertain country as a reason he didn't read on the same grade level as the other kids.

He had gotten into a community college but lost interest when he failed both English and beginning Spanish in the same semester. Starting in and around Toronto he worked in phone-scam boiler rooms, cold-calling people to sell them everything from water-softening devices to penny stocks. He found his lack of conscience a huge bonus in the industry, and his ability to speak with slight accents as the situation dictated made him a top seller.

Just a few hours at the range had taught him enough to feel good with his little .380 caliber pistol. It was easy to slip into the United States from Canada, and he never bothered to officially establish himself. As he slowly moved west, Ari promoted himself as more and more of a tough guy until now he was the veteran IDF soldier.

He liked the persona he'd built. Now, with the experience he'd gotten in a couple of gunfights and having shot someone up close, he was more confident, which translated into his everyday life. That's why the boss had trusted him with this load of computers stuffed with cocaine.

He liked being the enforcer for a company as big as TARC.

THIRTY

Tom Eriksen knocked on the door to Kat Gleason's orderly office and waited for the bolt to slide back and the heavy door to swing open. Like all the other NSA analysts in the building, she worked behind an extra layer of security, in a private office where she could conduct whatever high-level eavesdropping she was supposed to. He hated to admit it, but on some level, not having the clearance to even get a hint about what she was working on bothered Eriksen.

It wasn't like the FBI just hired him off the street. He'd gone through a series of interviews, a polygraph examination, and a battery of psychological and physical tests, and the Bureau had conducted a thorough background investigation, even finding his neighbors from when he was in college. The federal government trusted him with information about Russian spies, but he couldn't know anything about what another federal agency was doing. Sometimes he wondered how the country ran at all.

All that fled from his mind as he saw how Kat's face lit up when she saw him. Her eyes darted from side to side to make certain they were alone as she drew him into the office and gave him a hug and a long, lingering kiss. He felt his own heart rate start to increase as he marveled at the perfection of her smile. It lifted her cheeks slightly, and her teeth were white and straight.

Eriksen said, "What're you doing?"

She groaned in frustration and just tilted her head toward a giant computer screen with a spreadsheet opened. "I can't establish a link between two communication devices we've been monitoring."

He stepped closer, his eyes taking in the spreadsheet. It looked just like a financial ledger, and he interpreted it the way he had been taught. He stepped closer as the spreadsheet became crystal clear.

Kat made a brief attempt to stop him and said, "I'm sorry, I'm not supposed to let anyone see my work product and the material I examine."

He turned away from the screen and gave her a smile as he said, "The second device is communicating with the device in the sixth column."

She moved to the computer and took almost a minute to verify what he was saying, then plopped down into her swivel chair and spun around to look at him. "How on earth did you ever figure that out so fast?"

He shrugged and said, "It's a gift. That looks exactly like a giant bank statement. You just have to look for the common factors." He tried to look humble when he said, "I'm around for any of your harder problems. Don't hesitate to give me a call."

When Kat was through rolling her eyes at this, she said, "Is there a reason you breached security and came into my office?"

"Other than to save you a day of agony looking at a spreadsheet?"

"Yes, other than that."

He dug in his front pocket and pulled out the thumb drive the El Paso homicide detective had given him. "We're not able to figure out the encryption on this thumb drive and look at its contents. Is that something you or one of your coworkers could do?"

She gave him a sly smile. "We might be able to work something out since I have a little free time thanks to you. What case is it?"

He hesitated. He'd never been a good liar. Now Eriksen had to decide if he should invent a story or make Kat decide if she wanted to help on an unsanctioned investigation. After a moment of consideration he knew it had to be her choice.

Eriksen said, "It has to do with the shooting at the market. Since the FBI has no role in it, I was hoping this favor could be done quietly and unofficially. But I'll respect whatever decision you make. I know you guys have incredibly strict guidelines."

She didn't say a word. Instead she reached out and plucked the small thumb drive from his hand and kissed him again.

———————

Cash tooled around the streets of El Paso in his Cadillac listening to some Springsteen on the radio. He had visited three places looking for Eric with no luck but still had a few ideas. The fact that the computer engineer didn't mix with anyone from the corporation made it difficult to come up with the definite location.

It was early evening, and he was getting anxious to see Carol DiMetti. He'd seen the pretty widow virtually every night for the past week. Now she was like a drug to him. He needed to be around her more and more to satisfy his craving. Between that and his annoyance at Ari's assignment to a job that was traditionally his own, he could hardly concentrate on finding Eric.

The third place he stopped was a small Internet café near downtown. Eric had sent some e-mails from its IP address. Cash stepped inside and immediately saw someone slip out of the rear booth and dart through the back door.

Cash hurried through the café and banged out the back door to see an empty alley in both directions. He hadn't gotten a clear look at whoever left and couldn't be sure it was Eric. Besides, the guy could have run in either direction and made one of a dozen turns. There was no point in trying to follow whoever it was. Instead, Cash came back through the same rear door into the now empty café. He gave a hard look at the scrawny kid behind the counter. He was about twenty-three with dozens of piercings and a tattoo running up his neck and onto his face that looked like a crawling vine.

Cash said, "I didn't mean to chase away your customers."

The kid shrugged, saying, "I just work here, I don't own the place. I don't care who comes and goes."

"Good attitude. You'll go far with that." He stood there in silence for a moment, then said, "What about the guy who ran out the back when I came in?"

"What about him?"

"What's his name?"

"Listen, man, I don't talk to cops." The kid looked satisfied with his determination.

"I'm not a cop."

"There's no way you can prove that."

Without any hesitation at all, Cash jerked out his Colt .45 from the holster underneath his loose shirt and whacked the kid right across the face, knocking him onto the floor behind the counter. Cash calmly stepped around the counter to stand over the kid and said, "Would a cop do something like that?"

The kid put his hand to his bloody face. The barrel had caught him on the cheek and the forehead. Blood pooled on his grimy white T-shirt. It took him a full ten seconds to finally say, "What do you want to know, dude?"

"Who ran out the back door when I came in?"

The terrified kid said, "I swear to God I don't know him. He's been in a few times. Usually orders coffee, sometimes a sandwich, and works on his MacBook in the same booth." Tears leaked out of his eyes as they rose to meet Cash's stare.

Cash nodded and said, "Good enough. And if I ever have to come in here again, I hope I don't have to explain I'm not a cop."

The kid shook his head. "I know you're not a cop now."

———————

Tired and annoyed, Cash drove to Carol's house in the quiet suburb of Canutillo without calling. He figured they had to be at that point in their relationship by now. He parked a few houses away on the street, the way he always did, then walked up to her front door. Before he could try the handle she opened the door. Standing there dressed in just a T-shirt and shorts, she looked like a beautiful soccer mom.

The first words out of her mouth were, "Why'd you send Vinnie to scout for you the night he was shot?"

"What?"

"Did you shoot him when he crossed back into Mexico?"

"Where are you getting this?" He could see he wasn't going to get any relaxation tonight. Walking away from her would be like going cold turkey.

———————

Eric was still hiding in the cheap hotel he'd found. This was an area he usually wouldn't frequent. For the time being he had to make an exception. The small room gave off its own set of odors like an old man after Thanksgiving dinner. It was almost like it was alive. Add to that the various creaks and squeaks of other tenants moving and the occasional rodent making itself known, and Eric felt like he was in hell. He was badly in need of sleep, and now on top of that he was panicked. He'd come way too close to running into Cash. He knew a lot about the corporation and knew that Cash's real name was Joe Azeri. Whatever name he went by, the guy was relentless.

Eric knew he had to wrap things up fast. He needed to make his demand to the corporation, collect the money, and hit the road. He didn't care where he went for a few months, just so long it wasn't hot and dry and he didn't hear Spanish. The way his life had been going the last month, just the sound of the language put him on edge.

He couldn't believe how good it felt to sink into the urine-stained mattress in the tiny hotel. His job of convincing the corporation to pay up would be easier if he was in possession of the thumb drive he had lost at the market. At least now he was sure Cash hadn't picked it up. If he had, Eric would've heard about it by now.

THIRTY-ONE

Tom Eriksen looked up from his salad and said, "I can't believe you have time to eat with me before your show." He was sitting with Ted Dempsey near a craft services table behind the set of the TV show in the front courtyard of the Bank of America building.

Dempsey, finishing the last bite of a small turkey sandwich on whole wheat, waved him off and when he finished chewing said, "Are you kidding me? I've got time. Elizabeth Ramos is booked for the show. I'm already prepared for whatever she's gonna say. She only talks about two subjects. But she looks good doing it and is passionate about her beliefs, and that makes for great TV."

"I wish she took the threats to her life a little more seriously."

"I pity the assassin who comes up against her. She'll chew him up and spit him out. But to be on the safe side, the show hired an extra four El Paso police officers for the set tonight. Does that make you feel any better?"

Eriksen nodded but realized he wasn't being entirely truthful. Dempsey said, "Is something bothering you, Tom?"

"I just have a lot of stuff coming across my desk at work. Some of it isn't really official, just a case I'm interested in. I hate misleading anyone, even the supervisor I don't particularly like, so working on the case is causing me a little stress."

"Can an old-timer like me offer you a little advice?"

"Please do."

"Guys like you and I are always going to be under stress because that's the cost of getting things done. When you hear people talk about how relaxed they are all the time, that's because they're not paying attention and don't realize there's a lot of work to do all the time. It's not the whiners and complainers who make this country great, it's the people who shut up and do the hard work."

"No ethical advice to help me ease my conscience about lying?"

"I could give you the standard none-of-us-is-perfect speech, but you and I both know there's a reason you're not telling your supervisor the truth. Sometimes supervisors just don't understand what's important, whether it's in an investigation or on a TV show. You're bright and you know right from wrong. I know you'll make the right decisions when the hard ones come your way."

The words were just what Eriksen needed to hear.

———

Hector took a full twenty minutes assessing Dempsey's set and the security that was in place. Tonight's crowd was similar to the show's audience the last time Hector visited. This time he had brought a well-balanced Browning 9 mm single-action pistol. He'd have several more chances at his target over the next few weeks but had already decided that if there was a chance in a crowd, the easiest course of action would be to take a close up shot, then flee as quickly as possible. He hadn't risked hiring any assistants on this job. It was partially out of pride but also out of his need to keep this quiet.

He had considered using a sniper, but the problem was he didn't know anyone competent enough to make a long shot, and he didn't want to deal with anyone he didn't know well. This was one of the trickiest jobs he had ever accepted in his entire life.

The crowd bumped against him, milling about before the show started. He was comforted by the weight of the pistol under his shirt. His size generally kept him from being shoved too hard, but in this situation it was a hindrance because he would be identified relatively easily. He'd have to stay in Mexico a good long time after this. But the payday was big enough, and he was tired of the work. He could see himself lounging in a cabana somewhere on the West Coast. The lawless Baja area might scare U.S. tourists, but he thought he could carve out a little section for himself. A job like this made him miss his cousin and his friend Manny. He'd trusted the two of them more than just about anyone else in the world.

Some applause and a new light on the set caught his attention. It was still thirty minutes before the show was supposed to begin its live broadcast, but he caught a glimpse of the host and the senator crossing the stage. The young man standing next to them looked familiar. He concentrated on the man's face and finally remembered where he knew him from.

He was one of the cops that shot his cousin dead.

THIRTY-TWO

Tom Eriksen watched the show from the wings, which in this case was between two sets of high-powered lights and a throng of production assistants. He had a nagging anxiety anytime he saw Senator Elizabeth Ramos in public. He'd feel so much more comfortable if she had allowed the Texas Rangers to stay with her as extra security. He wished they could nail down the threat on the senator more clearly, then force the issue with security. But Lila kept insisting her source was unreliable, and as if to reinforce that, she had not been able to reach him on the phone for the past week.

Eriksen was getting used to working with Lila and respected her intelligence and professionalism, but she never divulged anything voluntarily. She had been forced to admit she was a CIA field officer using the cover of a DEA agent. Eriksen realized how subtle and brilliant this cover was. But aside from that, Lila had let him in on very little of her world.

Now he was distracted from the show. He could barely follow the commentary and debate going on as he scanned the crowd for anyone suspicious. The senator, dressed in a sharp, professional skirt suit, sat straight as if she were in an etiquette class at Princeton. She kept her tone even with just a hint of condescension as she debated a weaselly-looking comedian from Los Angeles. Eriksen had a hard time taking the man too seriously because he'd seen the fifty-year-old hitting on two different twenty-year-old production assistants before the show. At five foot five with a long nose and slicked-back, awkwardly long hair, the comedian hardly cut a dashing figure. Nevertheless, Eriksen noticed he lost no determination after being shut down by both the girls.

Eriksen turned his attention to the debate as Dempsey started to hammer home one of his points.

The comedian asked whether we'd need a fence on the northern U.S. border if we found it necessary to build one on the southern border. His smirk after his question made it clear he thought he had just scored a lot of points.

Dempsey looked directly at the comedian and smiled as he said, "You just asked if we needed a fence on the Canadian border. Only if Canadians start flooding over the border into Michigan, Minnesota, or New York. Is it necessary to do everything exactly the same in every circumstance? It's insidious political correctness that is forcing our government to waste billions on expensive and unnecessary measures. U.S. citizens are smart enough to see through smoke screens like that. Having TSA inspectors at the airports searching every third person, just to provide a cover for searching individuals that could be a threat, is a waste of resources."

The comedian cut in and said, "So you're saying we should just search every person of Middle Eastern descent."

The senator let out a slightly exasperated groan and took Dempsey's side. "Ted never once said anything like that. And I know you're trying to confuse the issue and create a sound bite you might use on your show Friday night."

Now the comedian raised his voice. "So you're both suggesting racial profiling."

"No. I'm suggesting common sense." Dempsey even paused to give the comedian a chance to jump in, but he showed restraint and remained silent. "You don't have to search every person of Middle Eastern descent. Just like you don't have to search every third person. By having an experienced police officer at each gate to assess people, to build probable cause, if you will, you can focus resources on those individuals that potentially could cause a threat. Will we miss threats? Absolutely, just like we have in the past. Will it be a better use of our resources? You tell me."

Dempsey glared directly at the comedian, who fumbled with some words before he put together a reply that had nothing to do with the question.

Then the senator responded to Dempsey's question. "We no longer have the resources for window-dressing. We have to take solid, realistic action to prevent terror attacks."

Eriksen must've taken her statement to heart because he immediately focused his attention on the crowd, searching for anyone who could be a potential assassin. After a few minutes of scanning the large crowd of almost five hundred people, his eyes fell on a tall man to the extreme left side of the crowd. He had dark features, and the way his head turned side to side made him seem furtive. That was a favorite word of law enforcement officers trying to build probable cause. A furtive action could be anything and be used to justify any response. Maybe subconsciously he was already trying to explain why he was going to go down into the crowd to talk with the man.

Hector had eased to one side of the crowd, his eyes glued to his target. From where he stood the people on the stage would have to pass within twenty feet of him. There were no cops on this side of the crowd, and he felt his pulse start to increase as he anticipated making his move once the show was completed.

He didn't even pay attention to the debate going back and forth. The *norteamericanos* had no idea how Mexicans felt about their northern neighbor. This jackass comedian had probably not talked to a Chicano on the street in the last fifteen years. The most contact he had with Mexicans was watching them trim his trees and cut his grass. Yet somehow he still felt qualified to spill an opinion on TV.

Hector had little respect for the senator either. What right did a

woman have to try to make policy for a whole country? Even someone like Ramos who had lived in Texas her entire life. The *norteam-*
ericanos were silly and obvious when they elected people like Senator
Ramos. She was pretty with a nice voice, and that was all U.S. citizens seemed to care about.

He had to admit that although Dempsey took many of the same
positions, he at least listened to other points of view. He also responded directly to questions rather than raising new ones or spewing
some prewritten rubbish in order to avoid answering.

Hector turned his head one last time to ensure he could make
the shot, then turn and hustle out of the crowd quickly. This looked
to be a great opportunity.

————————

Eriksen had his hands folded in front of him with his left palm resting on the butt of his pistol. No one would notice he was armed. He
briefly lost sight of the suspicious tall man as he climbed down from
the stage and caught the attention of an El Paso cop to let him slip
past the barricade into the crowd, then spotted him again. He thought
about telling the cop what he was doing, but since it was only a
hunch he didn't want to pull the officer off his post.

Luckily, the suspect he was looking at—and he had to think of
him as a suspect at this point as he built probable cause in his
head—was taller by several inches than many of the people around
him. Everyone was so enthralled in the debate on the stage that
they showed no interest in Eriksen as he mumbled, "Excuse me,"
every few seconds, trying to slip through the crowd as quietly as
possible. He checked his watch and saw that the show had about
three minutes left. He could hear Ted Dempsey wrapping things
up and thanking his guests. But Eriksen kept his attention focused
forward on the suspect, who was now slowly backing up in the
crowd.

Eriksen looked behind the man and tried to figure out where he
was headed and what he was trying to do. The man commanded his
entire attention as Eriksen felt adrenaline surge into his system.

Cash found Ari in their one-room office, playing a game of Angry Birds on one of the two notebook computers permanently sitting on top of one of the ratty wooden desks. The little Israeli didn't even acknowledge Cash coming through the door.

Cash plopped down behind the other desk and finally said, "How did the load go?"

Ari didn't look up from his game. "No problem." After another thirty seconds of silence Ari said, "Did you find Eric?"

"Close."

"You always seem close. No one at the corporation wants to hear 'close.' That's why Ari got the call to handle the load that was bigger than usual. They didn't want it getting close to being unloaded. They needed it all unloaded, and quickly."

Cash shrugged and said as nonchalantly as possible, "Let's see if they use you again."

Now Ari took his eyes off the computer and focused on Cash. "Already got another assignment. They apparently trust Ari enough to do tricky work."

"What's the new assignment?" He tried to sound tired and uninterested, but, in fact, he was concerned about what the assignment could be.

Ari gave him a sly grin and said, "Ari was told not to talk about it with anyone."

Hector focused on the stage as the show ended. Dempsey, the senator, and the comedian all gathered for a few minutes to chat among themselves. Despite the heated debate they seemed to enjoy the informal meeting. Hector couldn't help but let his eyes track down the path he thought they would take. It was almost as if he were willing them to turn to one side and take the clearly marked track between the barricades. Finally, they turned and started walking exactly where he needed them to walk. They turned onto the narrow path leading to him just as he expected, with a tubby, uniformed police sergeant leading the way and a much younger, scrawny officer in the rear. They were single file and slowly headed his direction. Perfect.

Hector used the time to move his hand across his shirt to feel the handle of his Browning. He could picture three quick shots. *Pop, pop, pop.* All into the head of his target. It would be good insurance, and confusing as witnesses might think he was aiming at each of the three celebrities. Then he would turn in the confusion and slip away through the crowd. After that, things would get trickier. The streets were not nearly as crowded as the show area, so he could move faster, but he would also be much easier to see. He had no help or backup here in the United States. His only hope was to make the border and cross. Any way he could.

Now the three talking heads were completely offstage and stopped to greet fans at the barricade. The cops stayed attentive, with their eyes constantly scanning the crowd.

Hector would have to wait his turn.

THIRTY-THREE

After the show ended, Eriksen watched as Dempsey, the senator, and the comedian came down the three steps to the ground level and started to sign autographs for people standing behind the barricade. He wondered if those people had been prescreened, because everyone was well behaved. He could hear a few shouts, but they were mostly coming from people behind those seeking autographs.

The man who had drawn Eriksen's attention had edged closer to the barricade and was still looking in all directions. He had on a loose shirt, but Eriksen couldn't see much detail from this distance. He had to consider how far he could go with no probable cause. He could see himself explaining that any actions he took were based on a hunch. He wondered where he would get transferred from El Paso. As Eriksen pushed through the crowd faster, he realized the man's right hand wasn't visible—it was under his shirt. He started pushing harder as he lowered his shoulder and knocked people out of the way, trying to gain momentum. He would much rather explain bumping into someone and questioning him without probable cause than explain how he allowed a U.S. senator to be assassinated. This was exactly the sort of action his father and grandfather would've preached. Especially in connection with an assassination. It was never clear to him if their relation to the nation's most famous presidential assassin was truly a source of shame or a way to motivate each generation to work as hard as they could. Right now it didn't matter.

He was moving quickly through the crowd, ready to barrel into the much taller man like a pissed-off Ray Lewis, if there was any other kind of Ray Lewis.

———

Hector visualized the action he would take over and over in his mind as his target moved closer and closer, signing fewer autographs along the way. He noticed the differences between the three celebrities. Dempsey had stayed friendly and was still greeting fans. The comedian was doting on pretty girls, his reputation apparently enticing women to offer their breasts for his autograph. The senator was much more detached and had to endure several insulting shouts.

Twenty feet more and he'd have his shot. The insults would turn to screams. The first cop, the one leading the procession, had moved ahead toward a waiting car. The cop in the back was distracted by the women opening their shirts for the comedian's autograph.

This was it.

———

Eriksen was almost to his target. But so were Dempsey and the senator. The comedian was hanging back, talking to someone. Eriksen had tunnel vision, zeroed in on the suspect, who looked up at the last moment.

Eriksen had to decide if he wanted to shout to distract the man or just lower his shoulder and drive into him hard. He decided not to give any warning and got ready for the impact. He turned and started to pick up speed like a bull aiming for a matador.

———

Hector tightened his grip on the handle of the Browning. Now he counted time in heartbeats. Just a few more steps for a clear shot. The only distraction he had was a woman who insisted on leaning into his lower back. He turned around once to give her a dirty look, but it had little effect. The rudeness of these Americans.

Just as he was about to pull his pistol, he saw movement to

his side and realized someone was pushing through the crowd. People moved out of the way as the running man barreled into a tall, awkward-looking *cabrón* a few feet in front of Hector. The action completely broke his concentration and drew the attention of the cops on the other side of the barricade.

It took a moment to realize the man who had just tackled someone was the cop from the Martinez apartment. Hector had to control himself not to pull his pistol and throw a few rounds into him right this second. Despite his feelings, Hector realized this was not the job he was paid for. He could deal with the cop later. The man the cop had tackled was tall and could possibly hurt him, but Hector doubted it.

He turned to assess whether he could still take the shot at his target and live. With the cops rushing toward them and other security personnel shoving his target, he realized he would have to wait for another opportunity.

Even as he pushed through the crowd, Eriksen could see the dark-haired man reaching under his shirt and decided he had to hit him high and solid with a full body block. The man went down hard, and Eriksen landed directly on top of him. He grabbed the man's right wrist. There was something in the man's hand, but it wasn't a gun. Finally, after struggling for a moment, the man grunted and dropped it. Whatever it was shattered on the ground, and Eriksen realized it was a glass jar. Then he smelled the odor. His first thought was that it was some kind of weapon of mass destruction. A cop leaped over the barricade, and Dempsey shouted to him, "He's an FBI agent," in an attempt to keep Eriksen from getting his ass kicked.

Eriksen called out, "I'm on the job." It was an old NYPD expression cops across the country used to informally ID each other. Whether it was Dempsey's warning or Eriksen's comment, the cop understood instantly and helped him subdue the tall man on the ground.

The chubby sergeant looked at Eriksen and said, "What's that smell?"

People shoved away in all directions and fled the area. Rather than start a panic by shouting a warning to the crowd, Eriksen looked at the now-handcuffed man and said, "What was in the jar?"

The man didn't respond.

Now Eriksen shouted it. "What the hell was in the jar?" He wondered if the man spoke English. Was he really a terrorist? Another cop hustled the senator and Dempsey away.

The sergeant called out, "We need a hazmat team. He had a jar of something that spilled on the ground."

Now the man seemed to come to his senses and looked at Eriksen with fear in his eyes. He cried out with no accent, "It's pig poop. It's just pig poop."

Eriksen took a moment to assess the man. "What?"

The man tried to catch his breath as Eriksen pulled him up to a sitting position. "It's not toxic. I was just going to throw pig shit on the senator and shout that it smelled like her views." He swallowed hard as the heavyset sergeant jerked him to his feet. Then the man said, "It was just a way to get on TV. I swear to God, that's all it is."

Eriksen knew immediately the man was telling the truth, but there were certain protocols that went into actions like this. The fire engine pulling up on the street would probably provide some overtime for a few lucky firemen trained in the removal of dangerous material. It didn't matter if it was anthrax or pig excrement, this idiot had just found a way to tie up fire rescue for a few hours.

THIRTY-FOUR

Eriksen maintained his cool as he listened to his supervisor, Mike Zara, become increasingly upset. They were in a conference room at the Border Security Task Force, and he was embarrassed to see people walking past the door and hearing Zara's normally loud voice becoming more agitated and strident. His pudgy face had already turned red, then purple, and now had seemed to lose all color.

Zara said, "What exactly did you not understand about staying away from Ted Dempsey?"

Eriksen tried to counter the frantic tone of his supervisor by speaking in a near-perfect monotone. "With all due respect, I was only told not to *appear* on Mr. Dempsey's show. And from the first time I met him I made it clear that I could never be on air. I don't believe I've done anything unethical."

"Can you explain the man in the county jail with two broken ribs, which he received from you?"

"You mean the man who was about to assault a U.S. senator? A man identified out of the crowd and disarmed without firing my weapon? I can explain anything you'd like about that situation." It almost looked like the last statement might cause Zara to experience an aneurysm. He fumbled with words and appeared to have trouble sucking in enough breath.

Finally Zara lowered his voice and said, "I should've known a guy who would beat up his supervisor in Washington wouldn't listen to his supervisor out here. There are going to be serious repercussions for this action."

Eriksen didn't back down. He looked Zara directly in the eye and said, "It sounds like we should discuss this with the ASAC. I believe I'm in the right here, and I don't know that a rational discussion is possible at this moment."

"Are you calling me irrational?" Zara's voice cracked with the accusation.

"No, sir, but I believe I acted well within my authority."

"Did you make an arrest after you assaulted this man?"

"The El Paso PD made the arrest."

"So you're saying the FBI gets no credit for your *heroic* action."

"I'm saying I was not in a position to transport a prisoner."

"So you were off duty."

Eriksen wondered how many of the subtle traps Zara was going to throw out before he got bored. "No, sir, I am always on duty."

"Then what about your duties here at the Border Security Task Force made you attend the broadcast of the Ted Dempsey show?"

Just then a deep voice from the doorway attracted their attention. "I sent him over there."

Eriksen was amazed at how the massive form of Andre seemed to eclipse all the light in the other room. He stepped into the conference room, then leaned over the table, staring directly at Zara.

Andre said, "Do you have a problem with that, Mr. FBI Supervisory Special Agent?"

Zara tried to hold Andre's stare and said, "Why would you guys care what goes on at Ted Dempsey's show?"

"It sounds like you don't understand anything about intelligence. We gather it everywhere, including wherever there are protests. Dempsey was having Senator Ramos on the show, and she attracts protesters wherever she goes. I sent Tom over to get a feel for the crowd, and now it sounds like it was a lucky thing he was there. In fact, I'm thinking about putting him in for an award."

Eriksen had to conceal a smile when he saw Zara swallow hard like a trainer facing a lion without a whip and chair.

Zara's parting shot was, "I'm going to have to reevaluate Eriksen's purpose over here at the task force. Maybe you guys aren't up to FBI standards in investigations." Eriksen knew that meant he had to start moving faster on the unofficial case he and Lila were working.

———

Herrera stood on a balcony overlooking the mountains in Creel, Chihuahua. It was just getting dark, and the fading sunlight turned the trees a moody green and cast long shadows along the valley floor. The ornate balcony and its decorative railing had been created by Italian artisans Herrera had flown over from Florence several years ago. He appreciated the cool breeze as he spoke on one of his safe phones to Hector, who was obviously stuck in Juárez traffic.

Herrera said, "I see our big mouth is still talking. Another opportunity was missed, no?"

Hector simply said, "I'm sorry, Don Herrera, but the time was not right." Herrera appreciated the professionalism of the hulking assassin and had to respect his assessment of any given situation. But the more he heard his country insulted and the more the Americans were stirred to action, the more determined he became.

"Hector, have I not made the rewards of this assignment clear? You will have money and power beyond your comprehension."

Hector, in his very understated way, said, "I don't want power. I would just like some money. And you would be shocked at what I could comprehend."

"Enough money so you could live comfortably in your villa in La Paz on the Gulf of California?"

Hector hesitated on the phone.

Herrera couldn't contain a little chuckle as he realized the big assassin was trying to figure out how Herrera knew where he owned a villa. In addition, he figured the big assassin was already crossing the location off his list of retirement sites. Nobody wanted others to know where he lived after a career like his.

Finally, Hector said, "I promise I will complete the assignment, Don Herrera."

"This I have no doubt, my friend. That's why I'm paying you so much. But it's all a big circle. I'm paying you that much because you are the only one who can do it."

"Yes, sir."

"And while you're up at the border, I want you to be sure to pass on any information you might come across that relates to Pablo Piña, or Juárez or El Paso."

"Yes, Don Herrera."

Herrera liked his assassin's easy agreement. Information could be more valuable than gold, and sometimes you didn't realize how important it was. All the pieces had to fit together, and he needed to know what others heard and saw. It was the same with any organization.

———

Lila gladly accepted lunch from the handsome homicide detective who'd been working on the market shooting. He took her to an upscale sports bar with fifty TV sets stuck up on the walls and waitresses dressed like cheerleaders.

The detective was from Dallas originally and had stayed here after he flunked out of the University of Texas at El Paso. UTEP seemed to provide a lot of intelligent young people to the area. The detective was two years older than Lila, divorced, and had a four-year-old daughter. That didn't bother her one bit, and she would've gladly accepted his offer of dinner following the lunch except for the fact that he obviously loved himself more than anyone else ever could. That could be a deal breaker.

At one point in her life it would've been an absolute deal breaker. But now, after moving around and having to keep all the secrets of her job, she was starting to feel the effects of loneliness. She went on the occasional date with the local stockbroker or lawyer, but they always proved to be boring or self-centered. There was never anything in between.

She'd heard a number of times that girls always look for men who remind them of their fathers. Maybe that was the problem. Her father had set a very high standard. Although she told people she was an army brat and that's why she had lived in places as far-flung as London, Okinawa, Cairo, and Prague, the truth was that she was a legacy at the CIA. Her father, who was an engineer by trade, used that cover to help build bridges and meet the right people. She didn't learn the truth until after she'd graduated from Virginia Tech. It was quite a realization at the time. She had no interest in any particular subject until she learned exactly what her father had done for a living. Then the CIA seemed like the only thing she was interested in.

She hated to admit it, but her father had streamlined the process for applying. She had a very clean background, and the CIA liked the fact that she spoke several languages, including Spanish. Almost as soon as she was finished training near Langley, Virginia, her immediate supervisor had proposed the idea of using the DEA as a cover. She went directly into the DEA Academy located on the Marine Corps reservation at Quantico, Virginia.

That was where she met a young man who interested her. He was a former marine helicopter pilot and a former San Diego police officer who was also very bright and extremely funny. The confines of the DEA Academy almost forced people into relationships, for better or worse. In this case, Lila thought she had found the perfect guy.

They kept their relationship quiet in the academy. Then he had been sent to the giant Los Angeles field office. For the purposes of her real job, Lila needed to be directly on the border. The long-distance relationship had worked for almost six months; then, for no real reason, it just fizzled out.

Now she was stuck with pale imitations, like this athletic and cute detective. The more time they spent together, the more certain she was that she would not be forming any type of permanent relationship with him. That didn't mean he wouldn't be good for a night or two.

Now Lila looked directly at him and answered his question. "I can't tell you when we'll be done analyzing the thumb drive, but they're working on it."

He gave her a smug smile, and she said, "What's that for?"

"I have some pretty interesting information myself."

"What's that?"

"Your friend the FBI agent went with Chuck and a crime scene tech over to the apartment of the HSI guy who died of a drug overdose."

"John Houghton?"

"Yeah, that's his name. Anyway, your pal insisted they take a print off the TV set on-and-off button."

"And?" Lila hated playing games like this.

"And the thumbprint from the TV matches the thumbprint on the .380 casing found at the market."

The news hit Lila like a slap in the face as she realized this was a conspiracy that was growing every day.

THIRTY-FIVE

Tom Eriksen sat at his desk in the drab Border Security Task Force office thinking about how his meeting with his supervisor had brought him up short. It also made him realize how much he appreciated working on this particular task force and with these particular people. Mike Zara's parting comment about whether the squad's investigative standards were up to the FBI's supposed standards had tweaked something inside him.

Eriksen had always had a plan for his life. As a child, and if he had to admit it, even now, he loved the idea of medieval knights and codes of honor. He had read everything he could ever find about the Knights Templar and the wild injustice committed against them on Friday the thirteenth by the king of France. Whatever their shortcomings or their successes, the original idea of protecting pilgrims on the road to Jerusalem was almost a blueprint for how Eriksen felt about helping people. He wanted to change the world in a positive way and make a difference. And he recognized that many people around him wanted to do the same thing. He had no room for cynicism and the people who looked down at their feet while mumbling about how America's best days were past and there was nothing that could be done to change the future. He just didn't believe that. He didn't believe that America was no longer relevant, and he didn't believe that people wanting to do their best wouldn't help the country. It was largely a perception created by columnists and other people in the media who were nearly as out of touch with the rest of the country as politicians.

He never knew if this feeling of wanting to help people was innate or instilled in him by his father, who took obligations and duties very seriously. Originally, Eriksen thought the military would be an excellent choice, but a scholarship to Harvard was too enticing. It was in his junior year he started considering law enforcement. The FBI had the best news coverage, movie heroes, and TV shows. The Bureau sucked him in and filled his need to contribute. But somehow he didn't feel he was doing enough. Until recently. Now, with the conspiracy swirling around him, he had to see it through. He couldn't give Mike Zara a reason to pull him off the squad.

The FBI wasn't exactly what he thought it would be. But neither was much else in life. The more things he learned, the more things he realized he didn't know. Excellence and achievement seemed to be a component of experience. The perfect example was all the hours he put in on the range with the FBI. He was considered an excellent shot. Two short firefights were able to put all of his training into perspective more than a lifetime of shooting at the range. Now, if he could put the other things he was learning to good use, maybe he could fulfill his lifelong dreams.

Pablo Piña looked out on his estate, watching two of his daughters play on an oversized swing set he had made for them. The slide was so high he had a small elevator built for the kids to use if they got tired of climbing the ladder. Gazing out the huge window was his favorite place to think quietly.

He had never realized how much he had relied on Manny to run his entire operation. He also hadn't expected the older man's death to hit him so hard. Piña's first reaction was to strike back at those who killed him, namely the El Paso Police Department. But he thought about what Manny would have told him to do and realized it was just bad luck that had gotten Manny killed. No one had any idea what had happened in the marketplace. There were other armed men involved, and it appeared that one of them had shot a uniformed patrol officer. That prompted an all-out search, and

Manny got caught in some kind of roadblock near the filming of a TV show.

Piña had already gone to great lengths to make sure Manny's widow was taken care of, but that didn't change the fact that Manny had apparently known all the smuggling schedules off the top of his head, along with contacts and other information Piña had long since given up caring about. He needed another reliable veteran manager. The first person that came to his mind was Manny's friend Hector. The problem was that the giant assassin was difficult to find. It'd been many years since Piña had roamed the streets of Ciudad Juárez on a chore like this. People had been shocked to see the Dark Lord of the Desert appear at different cafés and hotels in his search.

The most he could find out was that Hector had been in the U.S. on some job that required all of his attention.

He'd keep looking. There was no one currently in his organization prepared to step up and run it like Manny, and Piña had already decided Hector was the right man for the job.

His personal cell phone rang, and he checked the number before answering. It was from the United States again, but he didn't feel like talking. He just let it ring.

Katharine Gleason sat in the technical room in the rear of the NSA's suite of offices. The room looked more like an electronics repair shop with half-assembled computers, tools, and gadgets strewn across three workbenches.

The three younger men who worked in here, two graduates of MIT and one from a Russian polytechnic institute, were often referred to as the Three Wise Nerds. The Russian had been a hacker recruited by someone high up in the NSA. The agency had somehow worked out a security clearance to gain access to his remarkable skills at invading computer networks and tracking signals from the other side of the world. The two friends from the Massachusetts Institute of Technology had decided to join NSA together. They both had some kind of electronic engineering degree, but few people understood exactly what that meant. One of the young men, Larry, appeared to be able to diagnose any technical issue and overcome all types of encryption by just looking at a piece of equipment. Of course it wasn't true, but he liked to build up the mythology surrounding his unusual abilities.

Kat had given him the thumb drive from Tom Eriksen and asked if he could pull up the information inside it. As usual, he had taken the drive without looking her in the eyes and mumbled some kind of response. Now, he appeared ready to provide her with the information. It was printed out in a neat thirty-page notebook with an official NSA seal on the front.

Larry said, "Do you have a reference number or case number I can assign to this?"

She hesitated. "No, not really."

"How can you not really have a number for a thumb drive that really does exist?"

"I probably should've thought this through better, but the inquiry was supposed to be low-key and not involve official resources."

Larry made a show of looking around the room crammed with old computers and tools designed to work on the smallest possible devices. "Where did you get the idea that anything inside this room was not an official resource?"

She reached for notebook but Larry pressed his hand down on top of it. He said, "I don't mean to be a dick about this, but they're very sensitive about how we spend our time."

"One of the agencies involved with the Border Security Task Force gave me the thumb drive and just asked to see what was on it. I'm hoping to build a better relationship with other agencies on the task force and not always rub their nose in our higher security clearances. Is there any way, for me, we can just write this off as a favor?" She emphasized the request with a smile and placed her hand on Larry's forearm.

The shy young man, maybe a year or two younger than Kat, swallowed hard and looked around the room again and finally said, "It's nothing but a giant spreadsheet anyway. I don't know if anyone will be able to make heads or tails of it."

Kat smiled and said, "I know someone who will be able to figure it out. He is to spreadsheets what you are to encryption."

"You mean a nerd who hasn't had a date in months?"

"I meant someone who has an unnatural ability in solving specific problems. And don't worry, Larry, there's someone out there just waiting for a guy like you."

Larry looked at her deadpan and said, "It's been my experience through most of my life that the only someone waiting out there for me is a bully. Regardless, you're the prettiest girl to ask me a favor in a long time, and the encryption on this wasn't that crazy, so I'll hide it under another case number. But you have to at least let me show you what I did to get the information."

Kat said, "That's fascinating. I'd love to see what you did." She really did want to pay close attention because she could imagine the look on Tom Eriksen's face when she explained it to him later on.

THIRTY-SIX

Tom Eriksen and Lila were in their favorite fastfood joint, which they called the "cone of silence" because it was safer to talk than any place in their office. None of the health-conscious members of the Border Security Task Force would get caught dead in a place like this because it reeked of fried food and greasy hamburgers. Eriksen doubted he could even get Kat to eat here with him. Plus, it was after lunch, almost three in the afternoon. He knew something was up when Lila suggested the place.

Lila ate with her usual gusto, shoving down a few fries and a bite of burger followed by a gulp of regular Coke. He marveled at her normal appetite and decided that not only was her workout regimen brutal, she had a metabolism faster than a NASCAR champion's Ford. After he had managed to draw her attention from her after-lunch snack for just a moment, Eriksen said, "What was so important we needed to talk in the cone of silence?"

Her eyes darted around the room once before she answered. "You know how I kept telling you to cool it about your conspiracy theories concerning John Houghton."

"Yeah." He continued nodding as he waited for the payoff.

"I heard something very interesting this morning and was told I could pass it on to you."

"What's that?"

"The print you identified on John's TV set is a thumbprint."

"I'm listening."

"It matches a print found on one of the .380 casings from the market shooting."

The news really did stun Eriksen for a moment. "The same .380 casings that were found at the Martinez apartment?"

Lila nodded.

"That means both shootings and John's death are all related."

"And that's how El Paso homicide is approaching the investigation."

"We need to call in the cavalry, too. We can get them all kinds of resources."

"Whoa there, big fella. We still don't know where the leak is coming from in our office. I've already talked to homicide about keeping it in-house. You and I are all the resources they're going to need."

For the first time the idea of an honest-to-God leak in the task force made Eriksen pause and consider the ramifications. The U.S. federal police agencies were remarkably clear of corruption. Only a handful of FBI agents had ever been convicted of corruption, and that included the time before they were at the top end of the public or private wage scale. He didn't think he'd ever been involved in an investigation where he had to hide information from other people on the case. They were sailing in uncharted waters.

Cash was more than a little annoyed that Mr. Haben had included Ari in a tour of the packing facility on the way to the area where he felt comfortable talking. The catwalk looked down on the buzzing facility where workers packaged the laptop and desktop systems largely assembled in Mexico. The air was a little cooler above the fray, but the room was still too warm for a jacket.

The middle-aged CEO looked from Cash to Ari and said, "Boys, we have a lot going on. I'm not trying to insult you, but I'm keeping you out of the loop on purpose. I want you to focus on Eric Sidle."

Cash said, "Is he busy stirring the shit again? I would've thought the incident at the market would scare him into permanent hiding."

"He's proven to be a little tougher than most of the computer engineers I know. Also, one of my Mexican partners wants this handled immediately. I don't want to argue the point."

"We're on it."

"Eric has a partner. I think it's the partner that's pushing him."

"So Vinnie wasn't his only accomplice."

"It appears not." Haben took a moment to look out over the floor where workers scurried around packing computers. The trucks were always unloaded in a different building; only a very select few saw what was coming out of the boxes.

Cash realized that eventually the goal for Mr. Haben was to get the company profitable on computers alone. God knows he was smart enough to work that out. And he had been ruthless enough to get started in a business where the giants regularly squashed the newcomers. The idea to bring in cheap labor and supplement the company's early profits was brilliant.

Cash finally said, "We don't have any idea who his partner is?"

Mr. Haben shook his head and said, "I have no idea. It might be that DiMetti broad. We probably should've done her the same night you shot her husband. But it's too late to worry about now. We need to end this."

Cash had been surprised Ari had been able to stay quiet for so long. The little Israeli wasn't his usual agitated self, walking back and forth, grumbling under his breath. He stood calmly at the railing and looked down onto the floor. Finally he turned and faced their employer and said, "We'll clear all this up for you, Mr. Haben. Don't worry about a thing."

Cash wondered how far Ari was going to take this new role as the responsible contractor.

———

Tom Eriksen was trying to concentrate on the conversation around the table at the Seafood Hut in downtown El Paso. The comfortable restaurant was a little dark and too cold for his taste.

He'd been distracted by the news that John Houghton's death was definitely related to the rash of homicides in El Paso. He had accepted the invitation to dinner with Ted Dempsey earlier in the week, and Lila insisted they continue on with their normal lives so as not to draw any attention. The surprise at dinner was that Senator Elizabeth Ramos had invited herself to come along. She was in town for a meeting with Dempsey, who had mentioned that he was having dinner with the man who kept her from being doused in pig shit.

They were discussing the incident, and Dempsey's view as usual was straightforward. "You can't legislate crazy. No matter what the issue, there is always someone who'll take it too far. When some nut shoots a dozen people, the antigun crowd want to strip every man and woman in the country of their guns, legislate magazine capacity limits, get rid of so-called assault weapons. No one takes into account that the assailant had issues, typically serious mental illness, which motivated the shooting. But the left reflexively exploits the possession of a firearm. Take a look at Chicago—toughest antigun laws in the country and it's the murder capital of America! It's really a simple deal: Outlaw guns and only outlaws will have 'em. And occasionally, there'll be some idiot who brings pig poop to a debate. Crazy, but this time we got lucky."

They all laughed.

The senator placed her delicate hand on Eriksen's forearm and said, "Crazy or not, I'd still be in the shower if he'd been able to complete his task. Thank you so much for your efforts."

"Are you grateful enough to allow the Texas Rangers security detail to start up again?"

"I appreciate your concern. But the fact is most members of the Senate have no security whatsoever. I have several aides who are veterans and can handle themselves. I would rather the Texas Rangers spend their time hunting down fugitives and helping the citizens of Texas." She gave him a smile that looked more genuine than her normal politician's smile as she squeezed his arm.

"I'd like to show my appreciation by helping your career. Have you given any thought to moving to an antiterrorism job?"

Eriksen hesitated, then said, "Of course I've given it thought, but that's all. I'm pretty busy in my current assignment."

"I've been told the Border Security Task Force is a dead end."

"Yeah, some call it the 'rubber gun squad.'"

"The job I'm talking about would mean moving back to Washington, D.C. You still have family back there, right?"

"My parents, sister, and brothers live in Baltimore. It would be nice to be closer." As soon as he said it his mind flashed to the image of Kat Gleason. It was crazy to think their brand-new relationship would enter into a decision to return home and get the job he'd been dreaming about. But it did.

Dempsey picked up that he was uncomfortable and cut into the conversation. "What tipped you off about the guy at the show? How'd you know to rush him like that?"

He didn't want to mention how paranoid he was about a possible assassin in the audience, so he said, "Just a hunch."

Dempsey gave him a big smile. "That's a gift. It's a skill no amount of pay can take into account. Wish we had a thousand like him." He slapped Eriksen on the back and beamed at the senator. Then Dempsey said, "Too bad all your cases aren't as straightforward as this. You guys have to be tricky sometimes."

That made Eriksen think about ways to find the leak in the task force, if there really was one.

Cash knew it was too much to hope that Eric would show up at the same café where he thought he'd seen the computer geek the night before. Staking out the Internet café was more of a way to keep Ari busy. He'd stuck the little Israeli in the alley behind the place, watching the back door. It was petty and useless, but satisfying nonetheless.

The corporate wheels were turning, and he didn't like the direction they were headed. Ari was clearly gaining the respect and attention of his employers. He didn't want to be replaced by the halfwit eating machine. And he really didn't want to have to report to him. The idea of Ari becoming his boss physically turned his stomach.

Cash tried to relax in the front seat of his Cadillac, the Doobie Brothers playing quietly over a soft-rock FM station. He didn't like the fact that he was old enough to appreciate "soft rock" or that people considered the music he liked "oldies." But it was a fact of life that he was getting older, just like it was a fact he'd eventually be replaced. Now he wished he had listened to his mother and stayed in college. He could've ended up going to Rutgers. But that early money, when he was just a kid, was too enticing.

His cell phone rang, and he snatched it up from the console. He answered it the way he always did. "Cash."

Carol DiMetti said, "Joe, is that you?"

His heart immediately started to beat faster when he heard her sweet voice. He wasn't sure how to answer, but he managed to keep cool. "Yeah, it's me, Carol. How are you doing?"

"I'm feeling bad that I freaked out last night. You surprised me, and I've been really stressed out lately. Is there any way you could come over so we could talk?"

He pumped his fist in the car and gave a silent shout of joy. Over the phone he said calmly, "I'm a little tied up right now, but I could be over in the next hour or so. Is that too late?"

"What are you doing?"

"I'm working."

"On what?"

"Just looking for a guy."

"Who?"

He paused for a minute wondering what was with the twenty questions. "Just a guy who's tied up with the corporation. Why do you want to know?"

"Just making conversation. Come by as soon as you can."

After a few more minutes of small talk he closed the phone. Now he couldn't think of anything but Carol. He'd do anything to make her happy. And just being around her made him happy. Maybe it was time to tell her exactly how he felt.

THIRTY-SEVEN

Tom Eriksen plopped onto his couch to relax for a minute before Kat Gleason showed up. She had called him during his dinner with the senator and Dempsey and said she'd meet him about ten at his apartment. It sounded like it had something to do with business, but he could always hope for something more. It really didn't matter. Eriksen just liked being around the beautiful and intelligent NSA analyst.

He heard a soft knock at the front door, then Kat calling out his name as she stepped into his small living room. Somehow he summoned the energy to stand up and greet her halfway across the room with a hug and kiss. She set her bulky purse on the end table and dug out a folder that contained a bound notebook with the NSA logo across the cover.

"What's that?" Eriksen asked, reaching for the notebook.

Kat playfully kept it away from him. "Remember the thumb drive you gave me? This is the data from it."

"There was data on it? I knew it. What was it?"

Her eyes narrowed and she pushed her hair behind one ear. "You could have gotten me in trouble with this. I had to enlist the help of others. Considering what's on here, that doesn't look good."

His anxiety rose to see what three men had died over. He reached for the notebook a second time. Kat pulled it back. "Hold on. I'm serious. You need to hear how well this was encrypted."

"Why does that matter?"

She pulled the file close, holding it tight as if it were filled with money. "Whoever made this formatted it with a Mac. They hid the files in blank sectors on the drive, called file slack, then encrypted it with 256-bit encryption. That's why the PD couldn't see anything."

"What the hell does that mean, Kat? Why should I care about nerd stuff?"

Her eyes narrowed as she pointed a slender finger at him. "Why should you care? Because we had to use some expensive servers to crack it. That raises eyebrows, you know. To make things worse, whoever made this added a script to e-mail themselves when the encryption was broken. Plus, the data on here? The NSA might not like me doing this for you as a favor. A thumb drive trying to e-mail out of the NSA isn't good for my career."

A wave of interest mixed with shock overwhelmed him. All he could think was, *God, I need to get some sleep.* He said, "I didn't think of you getting in trouble, I'm sorry, Kat. Did the e-mail go out?"

She relaxed visibly. "No. We used servers that weren't connected to the outside. Standard protocol. Whoever did this is smart, and from what I can see, they're in over their head."

He held out his hand again to take the file. She paused, then gave it over. He said, "Did you have a look at the e-mail?"

"It's just an anonymous hushmail address. Hushmail is very private, so I can't find anything about it. The information is in this file. I had the tech scrub the servers that decrypted the files. I don't want anyone at the NSA tracking this back to me."

"So you won't get in trouble?"

She shrugged, and he opened the file.

A massive spreadsheet. It was probably the one thing in the world that could distract him from Kat at this moment. He wanted to study it thoroughly but just took a quick look to see that the payments were from one source to hundreds of other bank accounts and businesses. He sat down at the table and started to thumb through it.

Kat said, "You can keep the notebook, but I can't stay very long. I think there is a matter of payment, which involves giving me your full and undivided attention at least for the next hour."

Eriksen had never heard of a better idea.

———

Lila used the secure phone in the back room of the Border Security Task Force office. It was a common room with five secure telephones that could be encrypted to speak to other secure telephones. The room offered no frills; it had plain tan walls and no furniture other than the table with phones and two chairs. The door shut with a secure seal to ensure all calls were completely private in the sound-proof room.

Each line was paid for and operated by a different agency. No one wanted to take responsibility for maintaining a communications link at great expense and then explain why other agencies used it and didn't maintain their own. It didn't look too much different from a normal phone except for a screen showing that the line was encrypted and when it was connected to another encrypted phone.

In this case, the phone was actually operated by the CIA although the placard in front of it claimed the DEA controlled it. In fact, the DEA never got any of the records from this phone. That way no administrator in Washington, D.C., could ask why a drug agent in El Paso made calls to Tel Aviv, Moscow, or Pyongyang, or Toronto, for that matter. Today, Lila was speaking to an analyst back at Langley. This guy was a database specialist who had contacts with everyone from the FBI to the Department of Motor Vehicles in Idaho.

He answered in an unofficial tone. "This is Chuck. My phone has a valid encryption. You may now speak."

"Chuck, it's Lila. How's life back in northern Virginia?"

"I don't mind it, but I would think a Virginia Tech grad like you would miss it very much. Especially if I were thinking about it from the barren wasteland of West Texas."

"Texas has a certain charm about it, and I don't care what anyone says, the people are very nice."

"The people not elected to office. I've been listening to that senator talk nonstop about immigration and terrorism. That woman was not treated kindly by immigrants sometime in her life."

Lila let out a short snort of laughter. "I've actually met her in the last two weeks. I think you're confusing a political view with a personality. She's really very interesting. Considering her background, she's right, too."

"What's she look like in person?"

"Every bit as pretty in real life as she is on TV. But more importantly, she's smart. She's not just book smart from Princeton, but common sense smart, too. I'm not saying I agree with her, I'm just saying she knows what she wants and she understands the dynamics of getting it."

Chuck said, "I bet you didn't call on the secure phone just to chat with me about a freshman senator from Texas."

"As usual, you're right. I have a couple of single fingerprints. Probably from two different suspects that the local PD can't find in any database. One print is from a bullet casing, and one is from a thumb drive left at the scene of the shooting." She gave a slight smile as she heard Chuck laugh on the other end of the line.

"This is for a local crime?"

"A series of connected homicides."

"I'm sure they just ran the prints through IAFIS at the FBI. That's leaving out a whole lot of potential matches through job applications and the military."

"That's why I'm calling you. If I were able to get you a copy of these two prints, do you think you'd be able to check every possible database?"

"Of course I *could*. The more important question is if I *will*. Please tell me this has some link to an official investigation not conducted by some backwoods police department."

"It is part of something I'm working on officially. The problem is

I have not officially documented it, for legitimate reasons. Is that enough for you?"

"I was just asking."

"And for the record, Chuck, no one would call the El Paso Police Department 'backwoods.' I've been very impressed by how it handled the investigation of the murder of a witness under federal protection and the possible murder of an HSI agent."

"It could take a few days, but I'll pull out all the stops."

"Thanks, Chuck, you rock."

Tom Eriksen sat alone in the Border Security Task Force office while Lila was back in the secure telephone room. He had barely slept. Kat Gleason had made him promise that he wouldn't stay up and read the report from the thumb drive. She said he needed his rest and she wanted him to worry about it tomorrow. She emphasized the point by distracting him for more than an hour. Then, just before she left, she looked at him with those big blue eyes and extracted his solemn word that he would not touch the report until morning.

He would never break a promise, but it still hadn't kept him from tossing and turning all night.

Now he had the report on the information from the thumb drive in the neat NSA notebook opened on his desk. He had been poring over it for more than an hour. It was really nothing more than a giant spreadsheet but appeared to be the records of one entity—whether it was a person or business he couldn't be certain—and the money being spent was enormous. These were all expenditures, with no revenue coming in. At least none that was shown here. The key was trying to find out who controlled this main account.

There were hundreds of deposits into dozens of separate bank accounts, almost always in amounts less than $9,999. This was a figure that was often noted by Customs and narcotics agents because if a transaction under $10,000 didn't require the federal form known as a currency transaction report, or CTR. There might have been some reason to transferring the money electronically in this amount as well. Some of the accounts had as many as fifty separate deposits over the past year.

The second feature of the spreadsheet was that payments of all types, including ones as large as $65,000, were being made to businesses across the country, but especially in Southwest Texas.

It all came back to trying to determine the identity of the company paying out this money. Big money.

The individual accounts could be identified, but trying to find who sent the money would be tough. It could be filtered through a number of accounts.

The businesses were another story. Most of them looked legitimate and would have records. His concern was that if he went to one of the companies and started asking questions, he had no way to keep them from warning whoever paid them in the first place.

Then he saw a single payment of $13,350. There was nothing unusual about the entry in the spreadsheet except for the company that received the money. Lopez Building Supply. The last time Eriksen had dealt with Curtis Lopez, he was trying to save his landlord's son from a beating in front of the house. This was the opening he needed to unravel the mystery of the thumb drive.

THIRTY-EIGHT

Kat Gleason briefed her boss on the different intercepts she was working on. She had had to wait until Lila Tellis was finished in the secure telephone room. The NSA phone had an outstanding video feed, unlike the other secure phones. On the screen was her handsome supervisor, who had shown great confidence in her ability and let her work on a variety of things. He was in almost every respect the opposite of Tom Eriksen's supervisor at the FBI.

The tall former marine said, "Is the task force providing any good intel?"

"Not that much yet. But I've made some good inroads talking with the FBI and DEA representatives."

"Don't get too close to any of them. We operate on a different level. Plus if they knew the full extent of our communications abilities, they'd be hitting us up to tap every two-bit drug dealer in West Texas."

Kat kept a straight face, making a mental note to keep things cool with Tom around the office. She didn't want word getting back to headquarters.

On the video screen her supervisor said, "What's the status on your intercepts that show ongoing activity?"

"A fixed landline in Peru associated with the Shining Path has been talking to a cell phone in Colombia. We've got people working on the subscriber information. It looks like they may be trying to revitalize the cause and launch a new offensive. They've received new funding from narcotics profits and have noticed the cutback in

U.S. commitment to narcotics interdiction aimed at the poppy fields in Colombia. For a while the DEA hit the Colombians so hard it caused Afghanistan to be the key producer of opium without competition."

"It just goes to show you that the U.S. can't let up in any area without consequences. No one has given the DEA much thought since 9/11, but if they don't start hitting those poppy fields again, assholes like the Shining Path will use the profits to stir up all kinds of shit. Too bad the Colombian military didn't completely kick the shit out of them when they had the chance."

Kat said, "Should I put that in my report?" She was relieved to catch a hint of a smile from her supervisor. She went on to say, "I'm still monitoring the calls into Texas talking about killing a 'big mouth.'"

"Any ideas who they're talking about?"

"I haven't discussed it with anyone, but my guess is it would be an informer for law enforcement. The drug cartels have shown less reluctance to cross the border to deal with problems."

"Any corroboration?"

"None."

"Keep listening, and try to figure it out before we spread it around. Especially if any of the calls come into the U.S. We've gotta protect our turf."

Kat wasn't sure she agreed with the protecting-turf option most federal agencies exercised. But she respected her boss and knew that he'd been around a long time. She signed off the call and went back to her regular duties.

———

Tom Eriksen parked in the rear of Lopez Building Supply. There was a small walk-in office in the front of the sprawling complex with a warehouse and a huge loading-dock facility in the rear. He now understood how the three Lopez brothers had hidden the cost of the materials they had loaned to Marty. Eriksen had no idea the family-run operation was this large.

He sat in his car for a few minutes, watching the activity on the loading dock and hoping to notice one of the three brothers he'd talked to in front of his landlord's house. Finally he saw the stout Curtis yelling at someone on the loading dock.

Eriksen calmly slipped out of the Taurus, crossed the parking lot, and climbed the short flight of stairs onto the dock. He could tell by the way Curtis's eyes cut from the small Hispanic man he was yelling at in Spanish to Eriksen that the surly warehouse supervisor didn't recognize him immediately. Finally it sank in and Curtis said, "You come by here to pay up for your boy Marty?"

Eriksen shook his head and said, "Not today, but I promise it's coming. Even if I have to go to Marty's dad, you'll get the money."

Curtis had eased closer to him during their short exchange. Now he said, "Then I guess we've got nothing else to talk about today."

Eriksen didn't move. He had dressed casually in Dockers and a loose button-down shirt that covered his display badge and the gun on his right hip.

Curtis said, "Are you hard of hearing or just stupid? Because if you didn't come by to pay up the debt we should've collected a few weeks ago, then you need to understand you're about to get your ass thrown out of here. I'm better prepared this time, and I got enough boys on the dock to handle you."

Eriksen calmly scanned the dock and counted four men besides Curtis. It was probably enough, but he figured he could give them a pretty good run for their money. He slowly reached in his rear pocket, pulled out his ID, and let Curtis see the FBI logo.

"You're a cop?"

"Actually I'm with the FBI."

That changed Curtis's attitude. He looked around the dock and then focused back on Eriksen. "What are you doing here?"

"I need to have a look at your books again."

"Why?"

"It's part of an investigation. You guys aren't in any trouble, but I think you might be able to identify someone who bought some supplies."

"Why should I let you just walk in here and look at our books?"

"I'll give you a choice of reasons. The easy way is I could just kick you and your brothers' asses again. Or I could talk to your dad about the supplies you fronted Marty without telling anyone here. Either way it's gonna ruin your day."

Curtis put on his best fake smile and said, "Right this way."

———————

Hector showed his normal caution when he stepped into Pablo Piña's study. He'd avoided the most powerful man in the region for several days because he liked to focus on one issue at a time. His current employer would not appreciate the contact with the Dark Lord of the Desert, even though Hector realized Piña and Don Herrera had to be associates.

Hector didn't want to wait on his job from Herrera. He wouldn't have another window of opportunity to kill his target in the U.S. for a few more days, and he thought it was best to confront Piña about whatever the man wanted to talk about.

Hector appreciated Piña's security. He had the latest in scanners and technology to ensure no one could smuggle a weapon or listening device into the house. Hector had no doubt that he was on some sort of closed-circuit TV at that very moment. He still wasn't worried. If Piña had wanted him dead for some reason, he would've sent a dozen of his punks.

Piña followed the rules of etiquette scrupulously, offering Hector all sorts of refreshments, but the big man merely wanted to get down to business. Piña took the hint and said, "Without Manny, operations are suffering. I have no one with enough experience and intelligence to run things the way Manny did. I was hoping you might be interested in the job."

This truly was a surprise to Hector. He'd worked for different drug cartels over the years but had gravitated toward the enforcement side of the business after he found the management of people to be tedious. Too often they wanted to tell him personal problems and give him excuses that he cared nothing for. At least when he was offered money to kill someone, he either worked alone or with a few assistants. Just the thought of why he had switched to this profession made him miss his cousin. He had been crazy and unpredictable, but Hector could trust him. That was rare in this life.

Piña gave him time to think but finally grew impatient, saying, "You are respected and honorable. Those are two of the traits I look for above all else."

Hector listened to some more of the drivel that came out of Piña's mouth, then finally said, "I have a question."

Piña stepped out from behind his desk and gave him a big smile. "Of course, anything you want to ask."

"Why did you send Manny to kill Martinez in the U.S.?"

Piña went through the full explanation of how the doctor had allowed his son to die of a drug overdose. "Manny didn't necessarily agree with me, but he always carried out my orders."

"It was a personal matter that wasn't even a real debt of honor? My cousin died on that job."

Now Piña hardened his voice. "And you were all paid well for your efforts. Now I'm offering you a chance to make more than you ever dreamed of."

Hector wondered what such a job would be like. Living in a secure, nice hacienda. Not worrying about the ever-present slowdowns in his current profession. But on the flip side he'd have to deal with two-faced weasels like Pablo Piña. He was certain of his answer before he said it out loud.

———

It didn't take long for Eriksen to find the $13,350 payment on the Lopez Building Supply books.

Curtis had been very careful to shuttle him into a rear office and stand behind him the whole time he searched the giant spreadsheet that contained all of the company's expenditures and revenues. After Eriksen had scanned numbers for a minute or two, Curtis said, "So the FBI's working on a case that involves money transfers. Is it some kind of spy case?"

"No."

"A public corruption case?"

"No."

"Terrorists?"

Now Eriksen turned from the computer screen and looked up at Curtis. "Can you give me just a few minutes to focus on this?"

"Sorry."

Eriksen scanned column after column of numbers, looking for the magic figure, hoping he could trace it back.

Curtis said, "Is it some kind of serial killer case?"

Eriksen raised his voice. "Curtis, please—" but before he could finish his sentence his eye caught the figure 13,350. He froze and placed his finger on the screen, making sure he saw the right numbers. The date also matched the expenditure shown in the spreadsheet taken from the thumb drive. He let his finger drag to the left of the row of figures until he saw the customer's name. TARC, the Technology and Research Center. That was who controlled everything. And that's who Eriksen intended to focus on. Now he knew what he was up against.

THIRTY-NINE

Tom Eriksen and Lila Tellis sat in his government-issued Ford Taurus in the sprawling gas station directly across the entrance to TARC. He knew they wouldn't see anything of value to their criminal investigation, but he just wanted to get a feel for the place. It was the sort of thing he would've seen a cop do on an old TV show. But most of the cops on TV shows didn't have a woman who looked like Lila and had unbelievable connections sitting next to them.

So far they'd seen a dozen nondescript cars and two tractor-trailers pull into the fenced-in secure facility. TARC had bought cement and cinder blocks from Lopez Building Supply and had picked up the material in one of their own trucks. Curtis Lopez had no idea why they chose his company to deal with. He knew the name TARC but had nothing to do with the company.

Eriksen asked Lila, "Anything more on the source with the information about the assassination?"

"Nope."

"I'm getting an ulcer worrying about the senator."

"It'd be a shame if anything happened to her. Then you'd lose your big antiterror job."

"You really think that's all I care about?"

"I'm surprised you're looking to get out of El Paso. I thought we had a good partnership here."

"We do. That has nothing to do with any decisions I make. I joined the FBI to do something that made a real difference in the world. I can't think of anything more important than investigating terrorists."

Lila shook her head and said, "I was always taught to be careful what you wish for. There's always a catch."

Lila's cell phone rang, and she answered it with just her first name. After listening for a moment she said, "Thanks, Chuck." She turned to Eriksen and said, "I've got a name from the print on the thumb drive."

Eriksen looked over, shocked, and said, "The thumb drive from the market?"

She gave him a flat stare as if he were an idiot. "He couldn't go into much detail, because obviously my cell phone is not a secure line, but one of our specialists at Langley found an application for a computer engineer with the Department of Defense. They don't enter their prints into criminal databases."

"It makes sense we're looking for a guy related to computers. And having no criminal record explains why El Paso PD couldn't find anything. What's his name?"

"Eric Sidle."

Cash couldn't remember the last time he felt so relaxed. He just lay there, staring up at the ceiling and enjoying the sunshine washing in through the window. Carol's warm, naked body was snuggled up tight against his. It was soft and comforting and sapped him of any interest in starting his day.

When Cash had come over the night before, he'd expected more questions about her husband's death. Instead, Carol DiMetti greeted him with a warm embrace and a long, passionate kiss. He didn't want to stir up any trouble so he just went with it.

Now, in the quiet of midmorning, he felt like he had found what he was looking for. Maybe it was time to pull up stakes and get her away from the bad memories of El Paso. Carol stirred and rubbed her hand from the top of his chest all the way to his crotch. She propped herself up on one elbow and gave him a sweet smile. "It's been a long time since I felt that safe the whole night."

"You never have to worry about being safe while I'm around."

"You say that now when there's no danger, but what happens if TARC decides to treat me like they treated Vinnie?"

"That will never happen. Vinnie was trying to blackmail the company along with a guy named Eric Sidle. You were just his safety valve."

"You never completely asked me about what information Vinnie gave me in case he was killed."

"Because I never wanted to know the answer. And I still don't. I'm not the only one who does dirty work for TARC."

"But you would protect me from anyone else."

"I would. I probably should find you a gun to keep at the house, just in case."

"No need. I have a shotgun Vinnie gave me for the same reason."

"Do you know how to use it?"

Carol just smiled, then laid a long kiss on him. When she had finished, she said, "I need someone like you to take me away from here."

"Anytime you want."

"As soon as we get what's coming to us."

———————

Tom Eriksen sat at the table in the conference room of the Border Security Task Force with Lila Tellis sitting to his left and Kat Gleason sitting to his right. They'd been careful to keep the information they had on TARC between themselves because they still didn't know if there was a leak at the task force.

The two men Eriksen reported to sat next to each other. With Mike Zara in his dark gray suit and Andre's hulking form in a too-small Hawaiian shirt, they looked like opposite ends of the federal-supervisor spectrum. The one thing they had in common was that each had two phones on the table in front of him. A lot of federal agents carried a personal phone in addition to an issued phone, to keep their private calls private.

They were listening to a presentation by an assistant U.S. attorney about the subtleties of immigration law and how it would affect operations at the task force. The idea was for the task force to develop informants and sources of information, then pass on tips about large-scale smuggling operations to either HSI, DEA, or the Border Patrol. In theory it made sense, but in the real world, Eriksen died just a little bit every time he couldn't be in on a major arrest.

Andre, the task force supervisor, asked a few of the more pointed questions, making the young prosecutor fidget in place as he tried to come up with answers.

"Are you saying we can't make arrests, counselor?" Andre's deep voice added an ominous tone to whatever he said.

"Of course not. Any of you who are sworn law enforcement officers and have the authority to investigate crimes like this can make an arrest. All I'm saying is you have to document the sources of your information and be ready to use them at trial if needed."

From the other side of the room, Mike Zara who'd felt compelled to sit in on the meeting, said, "So you're saying the FBI doesn't have specific authority to investigate immigration."

The young attorney replied, "In this case it doesn't apply because everyone at the task force is officially cross-sworn and has jurisdiction over immigration if necessary."

Eriksen could see the answer frustrated Zara, who was still looking for ways to curb any chance of Eriksen's causing him more aggravation.

After the meeting broke up, but while everyone was still in the room, Eriksen's phone rang. He picked it up and said, "Tom Eriksen." He recognized the voice immediately.

"Tom, it's Ted Dempsey. I was wondering if you and a couple friends wanted to come by a little party we're throwing downtown at the Cattleman's Steakhouse. One of my producers just got a big job in New York, and we're going to take the crew out after the show."

Tom's eyes automatically cut to his supervisor and he hesitated.

Dempsey said, "Senator Ramos will be there. It wouldn't hurt to keep yourself in her line of sight while you're looking for a counter-terrorism job. Besides, it'll be fun. You can bring that lively DEA agent and anyone else you'd like."

Eriksen mumbled thanks and said he be there, then closed the phone. He looked up at Mike Zara and realized that even though he didn't like to lie, it could hurt to tell the truth in this situation. He went with his instincts. "Lila, Kat, and I are invited to a party thrown by Ted Dempsey tonight at the Cattleman's Steakhouse. It's a private event, and I won't be on TV. Senator Ramos is going to be there too." He looked from Mike Zara to Andre, basically the only two supervisors he'd ever dealt with in El Paso. "Do either of you have a problem with that?"

Andre shook his head immediately, but Eriksen could see Zara considering the implications of denying him permission to attend the party with a friendly senator.

Finally Zara mumbled, "Just don't show your face on TV."

———

Hector crossed the border through a pedestrian checkpoint where he knew the inspector. He didn't have to slip him any money—that was too dangerous—but he did make a monthly contribution to the inspector's family in Mexico City. That earned him the right to cross without scrutiny. He didn't take advantage of the situation. Hector never tried to smuggle drugs or weapons across the border when he came through. It was just a way to come across the border quickly, and he knew the inspector would make no record of the visit.

He glanced at Hector's passport and waved him on. No one at the Paso del Norte would ever suspect anything unethical had just occurred.

It was a cool day with a north wind bringing a little extra chill. Hector was dressed nicely with a blue blazer over his over starched white shirt and khaki Dockers. The outfit gave people the impression he was a casual professional with no need to impress. Hector didn't like the idea that he had to overcome the stereotype many *norteamericanos* held about Mexicans. If he dressed in jeans and a T-shirt, the Texans would often assume he was a manual laborer or ran a lawn care service.

Four blocks from the port of entry was a small shipping and mailbox store where he owned two boxes. The mailbox held mail that came for him or his associates, and the larger box was used to store weapons and other items he might need when he came across the border. Today they were two pistols and a container of black powder that had been in the mailbox for almost six months. He was originally going to use it in a false kilo of cocaine that was really going to be a bomb. Before he had to make the deadly package, the man he had been sent to kill was shot by a DEA agent during a minor drug transaction.

Hector made sure no one was paying attention to him in the corner of the store and reached past his favorite 9 mm Browning Hi-Power pistol to retrieve the .40 caliber Beretta. It was a very smooth gun that packed a punch. Years earlier he'd liked the Beretta 92F. But he had to adapt to the times, and the .40 caliber was slightly larger and fired a more powerful round. He tucked the gun into his belt under his jacket. He didn't bother with a second magazine. This was a simple approach to handling his assignment.

Based on the information he'd just been given, he could surprise his target in front of the fancy restaurant in downtown El Paso. He would be in place by eight o'clock and, if all went well, slip back across the border and be in bed by eleven.

FORTY

Tom Eriksen had never been inside a stretch limousine before. He liked the idea that Ted Dempsey had rented it for the night to make his producer, who was leaving for another job in New York, feel special. It said a lot about the TV news host. At the back of the limo, there was a long seat on the side as well as front and rear seats that all faced the middle, open area. A well-stocked bar had supplied everyone with a beer.

Eriksen also liked having Lila Tellis with him, but he was profoundly disappointed that Kat Gleason had gotten tied up at work and was meeting them at the restaurant later. The fact that he was disappointed and couldn't share the experience of the limo ride with Kat made him realize how strong his feelings for her were becoming.

Dempsey was studying something on his BlackBerry when he looked up, mashed the off button, and jammed the phone back in his pocket.

Dempsey said, "I swear I did just fine without this electronic tether for most of my life."

Eriksen and Lila had not really known a time as an adult without a cell phone. It was part of their nature to be in constant touch with other people.

Lila said, "There isn't a supervisor in the federal government without *two* cell phones. One for official work calls and one for personal use."

Eriksen let out a chuckle and said, "I did notice both Andre and

Mike Zara scoop up two phones each after the meeting this afternoon."

The senator said, "That's why I have an aide. He's the only one who calls me. Everyone else has to go through him. Even my husband."

Eriksen sank back into the comfortable seat and sipped on a Coors Light. He could get used to traveling like this.

———————

Hector had walked past the restaurant one time, then waited near the end of the street, out of sight. A little after eight o'clock he'd eased closer to the valet and nodded hello and greeted him in Spanish. The valet responded in Spanish and gave him a big smile. This was exactly what Hector wanted. He knew the valet was in the country illegally. After the job was complete this young man would not want to be a witness for the police. He'd probably flee the scene as fast as Hector.

Hector surveyed the area out of habit. No one in the office buildings this time of night, clear streets, perfect.

His pulse didn't even start to climb. This really had become just a job to him.

———————

Kat Gleason had raced around the empty office setting up equipment to monitor the lines she couldn't follow live. She had a backlog of calls to review and a stack of transcripts she had not yet read. But tonight she wanted to be with Tom Eriksen. It sounded like fun. She'd been looking forward to the party all day and realized it wasn't just because she was going to meet a celebrity like Ted Dempsey, but because she was going to spend time with Tom.

Even though she was always careful not to have any public displays of affection, and they were keeping their relationship quiet around the office, she loved spending time with him. As far as anyone in the office was concerned they were just friends. She didn't want any questions about her relationship and how she had used the resources of the NSA to come back and haunt her.

In the hallway Kat dodged Larry, the tech who'd had found the spreadsheet on the thumb drive. He gave her a smile and said, "You're here late tonight."

"I'm just heading out the door."

Larry looked at her awkwardly, then blurted, "Would you like to go out to dinner?"

She knew it was hard for him to ask, and she hated to shoot him down, but she gave him a smile and said, "I'm sorry, I have plans tonight already."

"Some other time?"

She hesitated, not wanting to lead him on but not tipping her hand about her relationship with Tom Eriksen. "How about lunch sometime?"

The young man nodded his head as he looked down at the ground.

It was about the only sight that could take the wind out of her sails. She was not in the mood she expected as she jumped into her Honda and headed off to see Tom.

———————

Cash had accomplished very little during the day except to avoid Ari. It was late now, and he had to talk to the little Israeli about their progress looking for Eric Sidle. He knew Ari had been at the corporate office all day and realized he was gaining the trust of their employers.

Now, as Ari approached him in the parking lot outside the little off-site office he said, "Any luck finding Eric?"

Cash just shook his head.

Ari said, "He's contacted Mr. Haben, because now Ari has been told to tie up all the loose ends and find a way to lure Eric in. They don't care if we do it quietly and cleanly or cause a big mess. He just wants Eric out of the picture, and then we can deal with anyone else."

"Just Eric? No one else?"

Ari gave him a chuckle and said, "Really? What do you think?"

Cash resisted the urge to pull his pistol and blow the short Israeli's brains all over the sidewalk.

———————

As the limo turned the corner, headed for the restaurant, Eriksen looked out the window and noticed a man who looked familiar. It wasn't so much his face as his demeanor. He was large and deliberate in his movement. It put him on edge. Once the limo had come to a complete stop in front of the restaurant's fancy facade, Eriksen stepped out of the car first, scanning the area, looking for the man. But he was nowhere in sight.

Eriksen followed the group inside, and settled in the back room at a long table.

Kat Gleason showed up about twenty minutes later, getting a quick introduction to everyone. She gave them a dazzling smile and said, "Sorry I'm late. I got stuck at the office."

Senator Ramos returned her smile, then pointed at Eriksen and Lila and said, "You should be like these two and take the office with you."

"What do you mean?"

"Look at them. They may be at a party, but they won't let the cop in them take a rest. They're so nervous about some vague threat against me I can't seem to lose them."

Kat found a seat next to Eriksen and said, "What threat?"

Eriksen explained what Lila's source had said.

"Why didn't you tell me?"

"We didn't say anything to anyone in the office. There was just so much going on, and we had been involved in one too many touchy situations." He hesitated, then decided if he couldn't trust Kat, he couldn't trust anyone. "We're also worried about a possible leak in the office."

"A leak. I couldn't imagine anyone in that office leaking information. Do you have any idea who it might be?"

Eriksen looked down and mumbled, "We think it might be Andre."

Kat seemed like she wanted to say something, but she just stared at him. It looked like she was caught in an ethical bind. He wondered if she had already said something to Andre about a case.

Eriksen decided to let it go. Kat would tell him if she thought it was important.

———————

Hector waited and calculated the odds. He knew he couldn't make his move in front of the restaurant when the young cop stepped out of the limo first. Hector had heard someone yell, "He's an FBI agent," when he tackled the man in front of Hector after the TV show. Regardless, it was a wrinkle Hector hadn't expected, and he needed some time to think. The pressure Don Herrera was putting on him was affecting his judgment. He wanted this over tonight. Now he walked as quickly as he could to the mailbox store to retrieve his black powder. He could find the other elements he needed at the Home Depot not far away. It would be crude, but he thought he could make a bomb powerful enough to ignite the limo's gas tank and handle two problems at once. He wasn't happy about the collateral damage, but he was starting to run out of time. Sooner or later his target would leave El Paso and he would have a much more difficult time accomplishing his assignment.

FORTY-ONE

Tom Eriksen had enjoyed the entire evening, even if it had stretched on a little too long. The food was phenomenal, and the presentation to the young producer was mostly funny, although it had way too many inside jokes.

As things started to wind down, the senator took a seat next to Eriksen and Kat Gleason, leaned in close, and said, "It's not my business, but I have to ask the question." Eriksen shrugged his shoulders and said, "Sure, go ahead."

"Are you two an item?"

Before Eriksen could answer, Kat volunteered, "No, we're just friends."

The senator gave him a smile and said, "So you won't have anything holding you here in El Paso. I think you'll get offered a position on a counterterror squad in D.C. I pulled a lot of strings to get you the job."

On one hand Eriksen was thrilled at the opportunity, but when he turned, he could see the surprise in Kat's face and wanted to explain. He knew she wanted to keep their relationship quiet around the office and figured that was why she had volunteered the "just friends," so quickly. The truth was, looking at her right now, he wasn't sure what he wanted to do.

Hector had taken advantage of the fact that the driver had left the limo behind the restaurant when he went inside to join the party. It had only taken a few minutes for Hector to duct-tape his makeshift bomb. He'd stuffed the black powder into a clear plastic container that had held some kind of fluorescent spray paint, then packed a number of small items including screws and roofing nails around the explosive. Then he closed the container and taped a road flare to it. He had it secured against the gas tank so that when the car moved it would ignite the flare, which would detonate the black powder, which, in theory, would detonate the gas tank.

It was difficult for Hector to move his bulk from the rear of the car, but he slid out, then retrieved his nice blazer from the trunk. The rear parking lot was dark, and he had no concerns about having been seen. He was going to watch the show from the alley not far away.

———

Kat Gleason had been shocked when Tom Eriksen told her about the threat to the senator. It coincided with her intercept about someone wanting to "deal with a big mouth." It was something she had to look into more closely. But all she could think about was her boss's admonition to keep quiet about the NSA's capabilities.

The news was so important, she was hardly processing what she had just heard about Eriksen moving back to Washington.

Eriksen seemed concerned that they had not been able to verify the threat and gain more resources to protect the senator. It was legitimate.

She could see Ted Dempsey paying the bill and knew the party was about to break up. She had to get Tom Eriksen away from the crowd so she could talk to him more about the threat and find a way to explain what she knew without violating her boss's order. It was the only thing that could have distracted her from asking more questions about the senator's comment about his counterterror job in D.C.

Everyone started to slip on jackets and collect purses. The whole group headed out the front door as Tom turned to her and said,

"Why don't you leave your car here and ride in the limo back to the set? I'll give you a ride back here in my car."

Kat just nodded her head, looking forward to a few quiet moments with him when she could explain what she knew about the threat.

———————

Eric huddled in his shitty hotel room and tried not to be terrified, but it wasn't working. He had made an overture to the corporation and told them that for two separate payments of a million bucks each, they could have back all information in his control. Sure, Mr. Haben seemed reasonable on the phone, but Eric knew he had guys like Joe Azeri, or Cash, working for him. He also knew there were people asking questions about him. Mainly street people and people connected to computers, but he wondered if it wasn't a way for the corporation to locate him.

He wanted to go by his sister's and have a home-cooked meal, but he didn't want her to get any more involved in this bullshit than she already was. If something happened to her, it would kill him.

Only one person knew he was at the hotel, and that was his buddy Kurt. Kurt had helped him out with a small loan and brought some food by one night. Other than that, Eric was a hermit and intended to stay that way until he could get out of town and head back to Chicago for good.

———————

Eriksen scanned the street as they stepped out of the restaurant. The image of the big man in the blue blazer hadn't left him. It was second nature. But at this time in the evening, in El Paso, Texas, on a weekday night, they all but rolled up the sidewalks. The driver whom Dempsey had invited to the party, slipped past the crowd and started toward the rear of the building where he had parked the limo. Dempsey grabbed him by the arm and said, "Hang on, Leo. It's a beautiful night, and my hotel is just a few blocks away." Dempsey looked to the rest of the crowd. "Would you guys do me the honor of walking with me to my hotel, where we'll have one last toast to America's hottest producer?"

Even though Eriksen wanted Kat to see the inside of the limo, no one could refuse such an eloquent and gracious offer. Everyone, even Senator Ramos, started walking toward the Marriott.

As she made her tenth call from her cell phone while walking with the group in downtown El Paso, Lila Tellis saw how her cover as a U.S. drug agent had real advantages. DEA agents were renowned for the cultivation of informants. It made sense because anyone working a narcotics case needed someone on the inside of a big organization. From early in the academy, the DEA preached the gospel of using informants to infiltrate drug gangs. They had the usual bureaucracy, but at least they realized an agent couldn't use a Boy Scout to crack a drug ring. Often the informants were either working off their own drug charges or they were former drug users looking for a way to earn some quick cash. Neither circumstance called for the highest quality of person. Lila had initially cultivated a number of thugs and smugglers in the El Paso area to solidify her cover with her coworkers, but her army of slimeballs willing to rat out friends had come up with good information over the last couple of years.

Now she was using her cadre of informants to reach out like fingers into the underground world of computer hackers. She knew that someone had to be talking to Eric Sidle, who might not even realize how badly people wanted to find him.

She had sent the word to so many informants that after a day of reaching out to the computer underground her phone had started to ring nonstop. She had met two of the computer people personally and had to all but spray them with a bottle of water to keep them away from her. Once they realized she was a real-life female and willing to interact with them, the computer guys became relentless stalkers.

She felt like she needed to make Eric pay for this inconvenience whenever she managed to find him.

It was funny how a guy like Tom Eriksen could inspire her to work so hard on a case not related to international terrorism and intelligence, which was her main assignment. She supposed that was what real leadership did. The guy was willing to work day and night and made others willing to do the same thing. She had grown to like the somewhat serious FBI agent and could see flashes of his real personality whenever he wasn't worried about someone else's safety. She really hoped he stayed in the Southwest. Lila would like to work with him for a good long time.

Hector watched in shock as his target turned with all the other people away from the parking lot and started walking down the main street. He couldn't believe his bad luck and what a wasted day this had been. Was he ever going to get a clean shot at the target?

Then he had another thought as he watched the lean, older limo driver walk by himself to the rear of the building. Hector realized immediately that wherever the group was walking, the driver was going to meet them in the limo. But as soon as the vehicle started to back out, it would start the chain reaction that would lead to a massive explosion. An explosion that would draw attention, tip off his target, and kill an innocent driver.

Hector hustled across the parking lot from the alley as the driver slipped into the limo and slammed the door.

He heard the engine start but was able to get the driver's attention before he moved the car. Hector always had the option of the pistol if he couldn't think of anything else to say that would stop the driver. The local cops would write it off as a robbery. He didn't want to resort to that, but he would if necessary. If for no other reason than to save the man's life. A bullet in the arm was better than instant incineration. Just scare him out of the limo and yank off the bomb after he flees.

As the limo's tinted window rolled down, Hector saw the dark features and black hair of the driver and called out to him in Spanish.

The driver held up his hand and said, *"No habla, amigo."*

"I'm sorry, I thought you were one of my people."

"No way, man. I'm Italian from Westchester County. Never learned a lick of Spanish. Whatchu need, my man?"

His friendly manner caught Hector by surprise, and he fumbled for words as he tried to think of an excuse to keep the car from moving. Then, in what he considered a flash of brilliance, Hector said, "I think my daughter's cat might have crawled under your limo. Hang on a minute while I look under. No?" He thought he'd gotten the comment out like a real American until he finished it with "No" as a question. He knew that was more a Latin habit.

Regardless, the driver nodded his consent, and Hector scrambled to the rear of the vehicle and was able to scoop off the bomb in a matter of seconds. He tucked it under his jacket, stood up, and called back to the driver, "Nope, it must've scampered past you. Thanks for letting me take a look."

The driver waved his acknowledgment as he backed the giant limo out of the spot.

FORTY-TWO

Tom Eriksen walked into the Border Security Task Force office and didn't even try to hide his smug satisfaction when he turned to Lila and said, "I've got a full background on Eric Sidle. I've got everything, including where he went to high school." He held up a copy of Eric's driver's license from Illinois. The photo was five years old.

Lila glanced at the photograph and said, "I've got one, too." She held up a small color photo that showed the computer engineer dressed in a suit like someone applying for a job.

"Where did you get that?"

Lila just gave him a grin. "You're so cute."

Eriksen had the impression she wanted to ruffle his hair as if he were a little kid. "At least now we can hit the streets and know who we're looking for."

Lila nodded slowly, then said, "Or we could go talk to the snitch that just called me and said he knew where Eric was staying."

Eriksen gave her a look and finally said, "Do you always have to upstage me?"

"C'mon, you're an FBI agent, it's expected."

Eriksen tried to stifle a laugh. He liked these interactions, and the feeling made him consider his options for the antiterror job the senator had hinted at. But he couldn't pass up a chance to fulfill a dream.

An hour later, Eriksen and Lila found themselves in a discount computer store in a suburb of El Paso known as Castner Heights. It was a nice, quiet residential neighborhood with a few upscale restaurants and businesses.

The informant, whose name was Kurt, knew one of Lila's contacts. She had sent out the message that they were looking for Eric Sidle. It was a common police practice, and in this case, the computer underground was so specific, it hadn't taken long to find the wayward computer engineer.

Eriksen noticed a tall, gangly young man standing in the rear of the store. He was wearing a black shirt that said something about hackers. "Looks like our man."

"Let's give it a second before we just walk up to him."

"This is a weird place to meet."

Lila said, "If we were working a narcotics case the meeting would be in a seedy bar late at night, but with computer geeks this is the kind of place we meet."

The young man spent a minute assessing the store, then walked directly up to them. "Are you Lila?"

She gave him a smile and said, "I am if you're Kurt."

They spent a minute getting to know each other, and Lila introduced Eriksen, emphasizing the fact that he was an FBI agent. Eriksen noticed Lila never mentioned to Kurt exactly what police agency she worked for.

Finally Kurt said, "And you won't tell Eric how you found him?"

"Nope."

"And you give me five hundred dollars cash."

Lila said, "That was the agreement."

"And you forget about my hacking into the UTEP computers?"

"The administrators will drop the charges, but you've got to knock that bullshit off. Getting the names of coeds out of the computer is just plain creepy."

"I was just using them for specific marketing. All I ever did was give their addresses to companies selling designer purses and perfume."

"As of today it's no longer part of your business plan."

"Got it." Kurt leaned in closer to the two federal agents, then scanned the store one more time before he said, "Eric is living in an old hotel on the west side of town. It's called the McLaughlin Towers.

Only four stories tall, but I guess back when it was built it was probably giant in comparison."

Now Eriksen asked, "Have you heard about anyone else looking for Eric?"

"Nope."

"And I don't have to tell you how important it is for you to keep this quiet."

"I completely understand."

Somehow Eriksen felt more comfortable dealing with narcotics dealers and killers. There was something about this guy he didn't trust.

———

Ari felt like a caged tiger as he fidgeted at the table in the Dunkin' Donuts. He hadn't been out to this area called Castner Heights before. There was no reason for him to venture out this way. Just a bunch of yuppies and comfortable houses. There was a time when he would have felt like spraying them with a burst from an Uzi. But now that he was getting used to the corporate environment, he realized these were potential customers. Not just for the shitty computers TARC made, but for the cocaine they smuggled in to bolster profits.

The only business close to the Dunkin' Donuts was a computer store across the parking lot, and it didn't surprise him when he saw the tall, goofy-looking guy strolling across the lot from there. An executive at TARC had connections with the local computer nerds and had found someone who might know Eric. Go figure, nerds all tended to stick together.

Ari was supposed to pass the information to Cash but instead thought he might take the opportunity to enhance his standing with the corporation. Not only would it help his chances for a permanent job, it would annoy Cash to no end. The guy thought he was the king shit, always telling Ari what to do. Not for much longer.

Not only did the guy walking toward the doughnut shop match the description, but he was wearing a black T-shirt that said HACKERS DO IT WITH COMPUTERS. It had to be him.

Ari gave him a quick wave as he stepped into the Dunkin' Do-nuts. The younger man hesitated, then slowly walked his way, eas-ing into the chair on the other side of the tiny table.

Ari didn't waste any time. "You got some information for me?"

"You got the cash?"

Ari plopped down a wad that contained fifty twenty-dollar bills.

The kid said, "Wow. Eric is at a hotel called the McLaughlin Towers."

Ari knew the place on the west side of the city. He didn't say anything; he just kept staring at the kid named Kurt.

Kurt said, "You won't tell Eric how you found him, will you?"

"For a thousand bucks I'll do whatever I want. And if you ask me another question, you'll be on the run, too." Ari kept his eyes on Kurt, then said, "Anyone else asking about him?"

Kurt hesitated. Finally he said, "No, not really."

Ari just nodded, stood up, and left the kid sitting alone at the table. It was part of his best badass move.

FORTY-THREE

Kat Gleason was working in her office at a frantic pace, rifling through stacks of transcripts and leaving messages for the translators to rush work on the phones she was listening to. When she had heard Tom Eriksen talk about the threat to Senator Ramos the night before, everything clicked into place. It was verification of the phone call she had heard earlier about dealing with a "big mouth." The intercept could be direct evidence of a plot against the senator.

Kat had a call in to her boss to explain things and knew she had to say something to Tom Eriksen. She just wanted to explain her position to her superiors in Washington first. They were fanatical about the secrecy of the work the NSA carried out. But this was exactly the sort of thing they were trying to stop.

She finally found the transcript for the number in northern Mexico she had been monitoring. A number from a prepaid, throwaway phone operating in the Chihuahua area had called the number yesterday afternoon. The report on the call said, "A male with no regional accent, speaking Spanish, told another male, with an accent consistent with northern Mexico, that 'the target is eating at the Cattleman's Steakhouse in El Paso. Probably after the end of the TV show around eight o'clock. This is one of your last chances.'"

Few calls were as obvious and specific as that. Kat felt ill thinking about it. The call occurred just after they'd discussed dinner in the conference room. There really was a leak in the task force. Tom was the only one she could talk to.

As soon as Eriksen stepped through the doors of the eighty-five-year-old hotel known as McLaughlin Towers, all he could think of was how accurate Kurt had been.

This place was a dump. The cheap linoleum was peeling up at the corners, and there were dark water stains on the ceiling. The hotel had a dank, musty smell, and he imagined a blob of mold growing at an exponential rate between the walls.

He glanced back down at the photo of Eric Sidle and read the description on the back. Six foot two, 180 pounds, smiling in his driver's license photo. Usually an indication that something was wrong with a person's cognitive ability.

Lila and Eriksen glanced over the empty check-in desk, then went to look for a manager. One older man, at the end of the corridor as they walked in, made them as cops and scooted out the ancient double doors as quickly as possible.

Eriksen was glad he was armed.

Ari didn't bother to call Cash for backup as he drove around in his Pontiac Firebird, looking for the hotel. He didn't need any help; it was just a computer engineer. He couldn't believe things had gotten this far out of hand. He agreed with the corporation's decision to kill Vinnie DiMetti. He had never met the man, but trying to blackmail the company like that wasn't a bright move. Ari would've taken care of the widow, Carol, as soon as he was done with Vinnie. But he wasn't in this position at the time.

The computer geek who started all of this, Eric Sidle, would've been the first on his list. But as he understood it, they needed to make sure he got back into the U.S. because the corporate officers needed to question him personally. They hadn't told Cash how important Eric was. He could've handled them both in the same night. Cash was an arrogant blowhard, but he seemed to make pretty good decisions.

This was going to be Ari's big score. He'd be the boss by the end of the day. He intended to go to this shitty old hotel, snatch Eric, and deliver him, alive, to Mr. Haben. That would give the corporate officer a chance to question him, and it would also prove how resourceful Ari was.

How hard could it be to grab one computer nerd? And he had his .380 with him in case there was a problem. A photograph of Eric with two in the head was his fallback position.

Now he just had to find the McLaughlin Towers.

———————

Eriksen and Lila turned the corner in the nasty hotel, still looking for the manager's office. Eriksen's phone rang in his pocket, and he dug with his left hand to find it. He saw that it was Kat Gleason calling from her cell phone. That was odd for this time of the day when she was in the office. He figured it might be something important.

Just as Eriksen was about to flip the phone open, the bell to the elevator chimed, and they both turned in time to see Eric Sidle step off into the corridor.

Eriksen faced him, not wanting to spook him into running. It was Lila who said, "Eric Sidle?"

The computer engineer looked directly at them, didn't say a word, then broke into an all-out sprint down the corridor until he banged out the rear doors.

Eriksen raced out after him. As soon as he and Lila had passed through the doors, they found themselves in the rear parking lot, which opened up into several others. They split apart, drawing their pistols, and moved quickly between the cars looking down the lanes trying to see the fleeing computer engineer.

Eriksen knew to control his breathing to keep up the chase as long as possible, but as he looked out over the expanse of the parking lots he realized it would be difficult to find someone who was trying so hard to evade them.

Then he had an idea.

FORTY-FOUR

Ari walked into the empty lobby of the old hotel. He could tell by the condition of the place that there wasn't a daily influx of guests and most of the residents lived here on a week-to-week basis, but he was still surprised no one was behind the front counter.

He leaned into the open space and shouted, "Hey, anyone around?"

After a full thirty seconds an elderly, heavyset woman shuffled in from the back and gave Ari a murderous glare. "There's been nothing but a ruckus this morning. If you want a room it's thirty dollars a night or a hundred and seventy-five a week."

"What room is Eric Sidle in?"

The old woman cackled and said, "You think I keep track of the names? This is a cash-and-carry business, my friend. If they pay the cash and carry their luggage, they can stay. And they don't have to worry about me talking to any half-pint strangers about them."

Ari let the "half-pint" jab slide, but he still felt his face flush at the insult. He reached into his pocket and pulled out a wad of money, then counted out three hundred dollars in twenties. He liked using twenties because the volume of bills was more impressive than just throwing down a few fifties.

The old woman stared at him for a moment, then said, "The tall young guy is in room 321. I haven't seen him this morning, but I heard someone hustling through the hallway a few minutes ago, and he's about the only one who lives here who could run that fast."

Ari didn't say a word; he just laid down another twenty.

The old lady didn't hesitate to turn, pull a key off the board, and slide it across the counter.

This was how things were supposed to work.

———————

Eriksen had slipped to the edge of the quiet parking lot silently. He had called Lila on her cell phone and told her to back off and let anyone who was watching see her leave. It was the oldest trick in the book, but it might just work. He crouched at the corner of the building, his Glock still in his hand, and waited. No one came or went from the hotel, and he knew that if Eric was hiding from them, every second would seem like an hour. Almost nobody had the patience to simply sit still. It wasn't like he was a marine sniper; he was a computer geek who was scared out of his wits.

Just when Eriksen was starting to think his idea had failed, he saw some movement near an old Ford Bronco. He heard a grunt, then saw Eric's face as he peeked over the top of the hood. It was actually a pretty good move. As soon as he had run out of the hotel's rear door he probably flopped to his belly and crawled under the high vehicle.

Too bad he didn't have the patience and conviction to believe in his ploy.

Eriksen used his natural ability to move quickly and quietly to slip up next to Eric. He didn't shout at him or yell "Police" or do anything else that would scare the computer engineer into fleeing. Instead, Eriksen had one handcuff on Eric's wrist before he realized anyone was nearby.

He said, "Don't try anything stupid, Eric. We just need to talk to you. I'm Tom with the FBI."

Eric, slightly taller than Eriksen, looked at him and said, "You're a cop?"

Eriksen nodded.

Eric said, "Thank God."

———————

Ari slid the key silently into Eric's hotel room door, drew his pistol from the small of his back, and then shoved the door open quickly. He stood in the doorway and scanned the room. Empty. A suitcase and a few shirts, but nothing of any value.

Ari shut the door behind him and stuck his head into the tiny, smelly bathroom to make sure there was really no one in the room. He glanced under the bed and was finally satisfied he was alone. He plopped onto the bed and considered his options, wishing he hadn't talked to the manager. There was no way she wouldn't warn Eric that someone had been looking for him. Killing her would also tip off Eric. He could wait right here, but he had a lot to do, and he wasn't sure that was the best use of his time.

As he sat on the bed, his eyes moved to the open suitcase on the floor and he noticed two framed photographs lying on top of neatly folded jeans. He sat up and slid off the bed to take a better look. He picked up the larger of the two photographs and immediately recognized Eric, several years younger, posing with a woman.

Then Ari recognized the woman. It was Carol DiMetti.

FORTY-FIVE

Eric Sidle fidgeted in an interview room at the Border Security Task Force office for almost an hour before he turned his attention to Tom Eriksen and said, "I guess maybe you guys really are cops."

Eriksen stared at him silently. Had that really been the reason the computer engineer had barely made a sound since they had grabbed him near the McLaughlin Towers? What the hell had scared him so badly? Now that he realized this was a legitimate law enforcement facility, Eric visibly relaxed.

Lila had stayed outside the room, watching the interview via closed-circuit TV. It wasn't like Eriksen had just sat there and stared at Eric for the past hour. He was a good interviewer who'd been through a dozen different interviewing and interrogation classes.

In a case like this, where they had no real clue what exactly was going on, they didn't have the leverage to scare someone. Right now the only facts Eriksen had to work with were that Eric's fingerprint was on a thumb drive at the scene of a homicide, the thumb drive contained financial accounts for TARC, and it appeared that some of the accounts were not legitimate. Not exactly a slam-dunk case. He didn't even know what the charge would be against Eric. No one thought the computer engineer had shot anyone. Based on how the guy acted now, he was more of a deer fleeing from a predator.

They had taken this interview slowly, not trying to provoke Eric into insisting he needed an attorney. Eriksen had let him stew by himself for fifteen minutes; then Lila brought him a sandwich and a

284 LOU DOBBS AND JAMES O. BORN

can of soda. Eventually Eriksen started asking a few simple questions, but Eric hadn't given any specific answers.

Now that he realized Eric had been afraid they *weren't* cops, Eriksen wished they'd taken him to a building that looked like a law enforcement agency. The Border Security Task Force was in a nondescript building that housed mostly administrative offices on the lower floors. He could see why someone would think it was a facade.

The other issue Lila and Eriksen faced was keeping the interview quiet. They were on the floor underneath their main office, and there was no reason for Andre to wander down this way. If he did, they could cover by saying Eric was just another informant.

Eriksen said, "Who else was looking for you? Did they ever pretend to be the police?"

"Dude, I deal in computers. This shit is all new to me. I just took on some contract work for TARC and things went bad very quickly."

"How'd they go bad, Eric?"

"I'm not even sure I want to talk about it." He looked away, obviously having enough confidence to think he could talk his way out of the office.

Eriksen was tired of the games and the violence and the assholes like this. He leaned in and said, "You don't have to talk about it with me. I'll take you down to the El Paso homicide bureau. They've got questions about the shootings in the market. At the very least you're going to be charged with accessory to assault on a police officer."

"What the hell are you talking about, man?" Now the fear was back in his eyes.

"You were present and dealing with someone who shot an El Paso police officer. We have physical evidence that you were there. No way around it, my friend, you're screwed."

"Hang on, hang on." The panic bled through his voice. "I might know something that could help you guys."

Eriksen decided to teach Eric a lesson. As he stood up and turned toward the door, he glanced up at the camera in the corner of the room and winked at Lila. Just as he placed his hand on the doorknob Eric started to cry.

He said, "Okay, I do know something that could help you guys. But you gotta keep me safe. Me and my sister."

———————

Hector's special phone rang in his villa outside of Ciudad Juárez just as he was about to take a siesta. Europeans and Americans scoffed at the traditional rest much of the Latin world observed around two o'clock in the afternoon. Hector found he could barely function without it. The countries that observed the siesta typically worked later in the evening. Hector found it a needed respite from the pressures of his chosen profession.

He had been called by Don Herrera and told his target would be at the Marriott in El Paso about six in the evening with only one assistant. Herrera told Hector to get it right and reminded him of all that awaited him if he completed the assignment.

Hector shook his head about the money spent just to keep someone from running off at the mouth. It was astounding. Assassins would always have work in a world like this.

It made Hector think about the FBI agent who interrupted his job the week before. It was odd that he was on the scene and able to act so quickly. Even if he did grab the wrong person. It had made Hector wonder if he somehow had a leak in his tight circle of confidants. He looked at everyone just a little bit differently and listened for any possible clue to tip him off. It was this sort of problem that had made him grow tired of being an assassin.

———————

Tom Eriksen looked at Eric. "Who's your sister?"

"My sister, Carol."

"Why is she in danger?"

"She has the contacts at TARC."

It was all becoming very confusing. This moron hadn't been clear on anything he'd said, and piecing it all together was giving Tom Eriksen a headache.

Eriksen said, "Is your sister's last name Sidle?"

"No, DiMetti."

Eriksen knew that name. It was the same as the dead coyote in Mexico. "Was her husband Vincent DiMetti?"

Eric nodded. "Yeah, Vinnie. The cops shot him last month. I was in the group trying to cross, and he was one of the scouts."

"Was Vincent—"

"Vinnie."

"Was Vinnie trying to blackmail TARC, too?"

"I wouldn't call it blackmail. It was a negotiation tool. He wanted a better job. I think he underestimated how annoyed the corporation could be with him."

"How'd you come by the information?"

"I took it off a computer at TARC."

"Did they know it?"

"Not until Vinnie told them about it and tried to use it to his advantage. My sister also has the information in case something happens to me."

"You take information off computers often?" Eriksen had a hundred questions he wanted to ask, but he now realized how big this case could be and wanted to start off right by getting a solid idea of what TARC was doing and what evidence the government would be able to use.

Eric thought about it for a minute, then said, "I took a bunch of information off of a drug lord's computer in Mexico, too. There really wasn't much to it except that it showed he did business with TARC. Turns out no one really cared about that information. The drug lord was too crazy to worry about something like that. He had a personal vendetta he was trying to settle."

"Which drug lord?"

"Pablo Piña."

Now it was all coming together in Eriksen's mind.

Eric said, "Two of the men at the market worked for Piña. He was pissed at my friend Luis Martinez, and I guess maybe me, too. But he was really after Dr. Martinez."

Just then Lila Tellis burst into the room. She apparently felt it was time to step in. She said, "This is interesting, but do you have anything that will help us with TARC?"

"I have a cell number that I called. It's for a big shot at TARC. I don't know his name, but he used to give me orders. I called him yesterday to make him an offer to sell him back the information."

Eriksen got the number from Eric and started planning their next move.

———————

Kat Gleason had pieced the transcript info together with things Tom Eriksen had said. She was pretty confident in her findings. Now she hustled through the Border Security Task Force offices, looking for the FBI agent. Her supervisor at Fort Meade hadn't called back yet, but she was afraid when she did speak to him he would tell her not to disclose what she'd learned. Turf wars and secrecy trumped virtually any other activity in the federal government.

She had a choice to make. Basically it came down to her loyalty to the NSA or her loyalty to Tom Eriksen. But really it was more than that. She had to do the right thing. Talking to Eriksen about the intercept might not be the smart move careerwise, but it was definitely the right move. She smiled as she realized it was exactly what Tom would do in the same situation.

She had scoured the third floor but found no sign of Tom. She didn't want to ask anyone where he might be or arouse suspicion about the contact between the two of them. His car was out back, and he wasn't answering his cell phone. That meant he had to be in the building.

FORTY-SIX

Tom Eriksen couldn't understand why Lila had interrupted his interview. She usually was very careful about letting other people do their jobs as best they could. It didn't seem like she had anything to add except that she didn't want Eric talking about Pablo Piña anymore.

As Eriksen was considering asking her to step outside the small interview room so he could discover the reason for the interruption, there was a deliberate knock on the door.

They exchanged glances, and Lila turned and opened the door.

Kat Gleason was there, anxiously fidgeting, and said, "I need to talk to you for a second."

Eriksen hid any irritation as he said, "Can it wait?" He wondered for a moment if this was a personal issue. Had he said or done something to upset Kat so much that she would interrupt an interview like this?

Kat shook her head no as she stepped into the room, virtually ignoring Lila and Eric, grasped Eriksen by the arm, and pulled him into the hallway.

Eriksen waited until Lila shut the interview room door again and said, "What's so important?"

Kat started slowly. "Anything I tell you in the next minute is unofficial, just between you and me, and you can never say officially that you heard this information. Understood?"

Something told Eriksen this was not personal as he nodded his head.

"I've been monitoring two phone lines in Mexico where someone's talking about killing 'a big mouth.' The calls are very specific, and I think it has to do with your concerns about Senator Ramos."

Eriksen absorbed the information as he stared at Kat's beautiful face. Then he said, "When did you know about this?"

"I've been following the intercept a couple of weeks, but I didn't make the connection until you said something at dinner last night. Tom, you have to understand the limitations I work under. I was specifically told not to let anyone at the task force know what our intercept capabilities were."

"This is the verification we need. We can get all kinds of security on the senator now, and she'll have to accept it."

Kat focused her beautiful blue eyes on him and said, "There's more."

Eriksen just stared at her, knowing a bomb was about to drop.

"I just went through the most recent intercepts on the phone line, and yesterday afternoon there was a very specific comment about the target being at the Cattleman's Steakhouse for dinner. The conversation was hours before we all went to the restaurant."

The news smacked Eriksen in the face like a cold hand. "Damn, Andre is the leak." Eriksen's head began to spin, but he realized he needed to take action. He stepped back into the room for a moment and snatched the sheet of paper with the phone numbers Eric had provided. He handed the sheet of paper to Kat and said, "Can you do anything with these phone numbers quickly?"

Kat nodded her head as she reached up and accepted the paper. She mumbled, "This is exactly what my supervisor said would happen, but I'll get you the information as soon as possible." She twisted her head in every direction quickly to make sure they were alone, then stood on her tiptoes and gave him a kiss. She whispered into his ear as she started to leave, "Please be careful."

As Hector ran the thousand little errands he needed to complete before crossing the border later in the evening, he recognized a black Chevy Tahoe rumble to a stop in front of a store where he was buying a leather notebook to help cover his pistol when he walked into the lobby of the Marriott in El Paso.

Pablo Piña stepped out of the rear door of the Tahoe and waved off the two bodyguards who wanted to follow him into the store.

Hector had been avoiding Piña until after he completed his assignment. He had no intention of taking the job with Piña's organization, but he didn't need the distraction before he completed his hit in El Paso.

Hector met him at the front door of the shop as a way to assess the two security men in case there was a problem.

Piña gave him a big smile and wrapped an arm around his shoulders, then walked him back into the store.

The shopkeeper saw who had come back inside with Hector and immediately scurried into the back room to give them privacy.

Piña said, "Few people ignore me, and when they do it's usually someone I'm trying to kill." Piña gave him a laugh, but Hector answered with a weak smile.

Hector said, "I'm sorry, Mr. Piña, but I have a job I've been trying to complete. It has taken all of my attention."

Piña shook his head and said, "You mean killing Senator Ramos?"

Hector thought it was an odd choice to pull out of the air. It took a moment for him to make the connections in his head. Then he stared at Piña and said, "Why did you think I had a contract for Senator Ramos?"

Then everything suddenly started to make sense to Hector.

Piña stared at him but didn't answer.

Hector slipped his hand behind his back and pulled his hidden knife, flicking it open as he pulled his hand from behind his back and placed the blade against Piña's windpipe. He pressed just hard enough to break the skin and let Piña feel a trickle of blood run down his neck.

Hector said, "You told someone in the U.S. about my assignment, didn't you? That's why the FBI man has been there every time I tried to complete the contract. He's following the senator for protection. I've seen him a number of times."

Piña was barely able to croak out, "What? Hector, this is madness."

"You're a snitch for the FBI."

"No, no, I swear I'm not a snitch for the FBI."

Hector read the man's face and listened to the tone of his voice. He had always been very good at picking out lies. "You know I don't make idle threats." He moved the knife a fraction of a centimeter, causing more blood to spill out onto the terrified man's throat.

Piña didn't say anything else, and Hector started to believe him. Then he thought of the key question.

"Then who did you tell in the United States that I had a contract on Senator Ramos? An FBI agent almost stumbled into me last week when I tried to complete the hit, and he was there again last night in front of a restaurant. He was there protecting Senator Ramos because you told someone I had a contract on her."

Piña, now shaking almost uncontrollably, said, "It was harmless, I swear. I have a contact at the CIA. I trade a few tips for information about what the DEA has on me. It's a very fair arrangement and necessary for business."

"Except I almost got killed. The FBI agent stopped me from getting at my target."

"I'm sorry, Hector. I'm truly sorry. I had no idea. And I meant no harm to you."

"No one ever does." Then Hector drew the knife across the drug lord's exposed throat. He heard the rush of wind as Piña tried to take a deep breath but found no way of getting it to his lungs. Blood poured down his expensive shirt as he tumbled into a display of purses and then twitched on the wooden floor of the shop for a few seconds.

Hector took a moment to calm down and drew his pistol from under her shirt. He couldn't leave the security men alive without worrying about retribution.

Now he really would move away with the proceeds from this assignment, but his honor had been satisfied. If he thought Ciudad Juárez was a violent place with Pablo Piña in charge, he could hardly imagine the carnage that would ensue when every thug in the city tried to fill the vacuum left by the Dark Lord of the Desert's death.

———

Kat Gleason was cautious when she approached Larry, one of the Three Wise Nerds in the NSA office, with the phone number Tom Eriksen had given her to find out about. Once again she didn't have a case number, and considering what was going on around the task force, she didn't want too many people to know what they were up to. She knew Larry had a little crush on her and hated to exploit it. But these could be desperate times.

She said, "Larry, do you think you could do me another favor?" She handed him the torn sheet of paper with the phone number. "We really are hoping to know what numbers were called from this phone, and what numbers made calls to it. We know it's a drop phone, so we probably won't get any subscriber information."

Larry took the sheet of paper but hesitated. Finally he said, "I guess I'll go through the same little dance we did before and ask if you have a case number or a reference number."

Kat gave him a smile as she shook her head.

Larry said, "Is this one good for lunch or just an occasional smile from you?"

Kat turned the smile into a glare. "No games, no dates, no bargains. We need this information and we need it fast. Can you help us or not?"

"Who is us?"

"Us, as in law enforcement."

"Not your FBI boyfriend?"

"He is a cop." She paused and then leveled another look at him. "Larry, I'm not kidding when I say this information could be vital. There's a lot going on you don't know about, and if you need me to explain it to you later, I'll be happy to. But right now I need you to shut the hell up, hide petty jealousy, and give me the information immediately. Do you understand?"

Larry nodded his head and scurried off with the paper in his hand. Kat tried to hide her smile.

FORTY-SEVEN

After they had made arrangements to hold Eric Sidle, Tom Eriksen and Lila Tellis jumped into his car and headed out to Canutillo, where Eric Sidle's sister owned a house. Eriksen was hoping Carol DiMetti could piece together some of the information. He also wanted to assess her credibility as a witness since they intended to put together a case against TARC immediately.

He appreciated how the whole task force seemed to be working together even if they weren't telling Andre what they were doing. Kat was getting the information on the telephones, Lila had made sure the IG at the Department of Justice knew exactly what was going on, and Eriksen was trying to contain his burning desire to clear this up as quickly as possible. This was exactly the sort of case that could make a difference in people's lives. This was what his father would encourage him to do.

Eriksen couldn't help but lean on the gas. He couldn't wait to hear if she knew anything about her husband's death. The whole thing had seemed unusual to him from the beginning. He was also desperate to know if she had any information on John Houghton's death.

Eriksen was looking forward to talking about Andre's role in all of this. Hopefully the IG would be able to turn the case over to the U.S. Attorney's Office. He was looking forward to explaining the whole case to Mike Zara, too. Eriksen was pretty sure his supervisor would find something in the complex investigation to complain about and somehow blame Eriksen for letting it get this far.

He pushed the Taurus through traffic and saw the exit on the highway. He didn't think it would take too much longer to find Carol DiMetti's house.

———————

Cash was finishing his sandwich on the couch, watching Carol straighten up around the house. It was the kind of domestic scene he dreamed about but had never experienced. As he reached for his bottle of water, the front door opened. Cash jumped but immediately decided it was probably Carol's elusive brother he had never met.

It took a moment for him to realize the stout figure in the door was Ari. Before Cash could say anything, the little Israeli said, "What the hell are you doing here? Did Mr. Haben call you about this?"

Just then Carol stepped back into the living room and froze.

Cash said, "Call me about what?" Now he noticed the small .380 pistol in Ari's hand. "Talk to me, Ari. What's going on?"

A smile spread across Ari's face. "You really don't know what's going on, do you?"

Cash didn't like where this conversation was going and was thinking how he could stall Ari until he could pull his own pistol from his waistband. But he knew from experience it was tough to beat someone who already had a pistol in his hand. Even if it was only slightly bigger than a peashooter.

Ari said, "You've been banging this broad?"

Cash looked over at Carol and saw she was too frightened to move.

Now Ari looked across the room at her. "Do you want to tell him or should Ari?"

Cash said, "Tell me what?"

"This whole blackmail idea came from her. Eric Sidle is her brother."

Cash felt a cold ball grow in his stomach that kept him from drawing his pistol.

Tom Eriksen tried not to push the government-issued Taurus too hard. Although he was excited about the information he'd learned from Eric Sidle and how things were falling into place, there was no reason to race to Carol DiMetti's house.

He muttered out loud, "What does it all mean?"

Lila Tellis, staring out the passenger window, said, "Probably means you didn't hit DiMetti that night on the border, which reaffirms my faith in FBI marksmanship."

"But TARC is such an ambitious target. It's gonna take a whole team to bring down that monster."

"What would you call the task force? You got Kat Gleason running information through NSA, me going through the Defense Department, and we've got half a dozen guys back at the office that would jump at the chance to work on this. We just have to make sure we can trust our leadership." After a moment she turned to look at Eriksen and said, "What do you care anyway? You'll be leaving the team to move on to your counterterror job in Washington."

Eriksen could sense the resentment in her voice. "I never said I was moving on."

"Whatever. I didn't see you tripping over yourself to tell the senator you weren't interested."

Eriksen just let the awkward silence hang in the car.

Lila finally said, "I think we need to scoop up as many witnesses as possible, because once this case gets rolling some are going to be hard to find and TARC will be able to get to the others. You got your work cut out for you."

Eriksen said, "What do you mean, *me*? I thought we were working as a team."

"You know how the U.S. attorney will view it. You're the one with the jurisdiction. You're an FBI agent. I'm technically not even supposed to be working inside U.S. borders, and even my cover as a DEA agent is limited to narcotics. You said you wanted to make a difference in people's lives. Now's your chance."

———————

Cash resisted every urge to turn and stare at Carol, who was standing in the doorway between the living room and the kitchen. Ari had made no move, but he wasn't shy about staring at the beautiful widow of his former partner, Vinnie.

Ari gave Cash one of his shit-eating grins and said again, "She really took you in completely."

Cash had to consider that comment as he slowly turned his head to Carol, looking for some denial. Any twitch or movement, even one of her adorable pouts, was all he needed to draw his pistol and put a few rounds in Ari before he knew what happened.

But Carol gave him nothing. She was scared, as anyone would be in this situation, but she was still thinking. He could see the wheels turning behind those beautiful dark eyes as she figured the odds.

He forced himself to finally say, "Is it true?"

Her hesitation said all that needed to be said. Then she shrugged her shoulders and said, "Come on, Joe. You know how the corporation is. It was our only chance to get what was coming to us. And it's not too late. You can come in on the deal with Eric and me."

Suddenly all the clues made sense to Cash. The men's clothes in the extra bedroom with the Northwestern logo, Carol being from the Chicago area, and the fact that Vinnie DiMetti wasn't smart enough to write a postcard told Cash it was all true and Carol had been the mastermind behind this whole mess. Now he had his hand resting comfortably on the grip of his Beretta 9 mm. He even thought about jerking it free and pointing it at Carol to show her how much she had hurt him. It would be a race between him and Ari to see who could pump more lead into that beautiful, curvy body.

Then Carol looked at him and said, "I didn't lie to you, Joe. I didn't want you mixed up in this. When I said you made me feel safe, I meant every word of it."

He studied her face. Every nuance of her expression held a clue. He wanted it to be true. More than anything he had ever wanted.

Cash took his time. Let Ari stand there and stew. He took one more look at Carol and decided she was telling the truth. He made a decision and went with it, pulling his gun from beneath his shirt and bringing it on target. As he looked over the front sight, the flash from Ari's .380 blinded him, and he felt a burning sensation in his neck where the round ripped through tendons and muscle.

He pulled the trigger three times but knew he was off balance from that first shot. He had a sense that the rounds went high and slammed into the upper wall and ceiling. Then he saw another flash. His ears were already closed from the first round fired inside the small living room. This time the round hit him lower in the throat, slicing through his windpipe and robbing him of any oxygen. It was like he had lost all his energy in a heartbeat.

Cash tried to keep the gun up, but his arm relaxed and the gun tumbled onto the thin throw rug, making a hollow thud. He flopped back on the couch and tried to cover the hole in his throat with the palm of his left hand.

Carol had scurried away from the doorway, and now Ari was marching toward the kitchen with his pistol held out in front of him.

Cash was aware of some conversation between them, shouted and screamed. He might've heard a strangled cry from Carol and felt regret that he couldn't protect her the way he'd thought he could.

Then Cash, who was so used to the name he'd almost forgotten his mom calling him Joey, closed his eyes and tried to think of all the decent things he had done in his life. He had no doubt he was going to have to explain a few things carefully. But he was hoping, on balance, God would understand.

FORTY-EIGHT

Sitting at her desk, Kat Gleason ran through all of the intercepts that had come over the line in the last two hours. Now that she knew what to look for, she didn't want to risk missing any more vital information.

Larry, the Wise Nerd, had come up with information on the phone number Tom Eriksen had given her. She was trying to keep it all straight in her mind when she came across the transcript time-stamped from earlier in the day. She read through it and realized it was the two people who had been talking about an assassination of "a big mouth."

The line that caught her attention was toward the end of the conversation where the man calling from a Chihuahua phone line identified the target specifically as "Dempsey"—and went on to say that he would be in the lobby of the Marriott about six o'clock this evening.

Kat considered the information and knew she had to act quickly. They had been wrong. Senator Ramos was not the target of assassination. Ted Dempsey was.

Just as she was searching for her cell phone, a secretary stuck her head in the door and said, "You have a call from Fort Meade on the secure line."

Kat didn't have time for this.

———————

Hector made it across the border easily. He suspected that by the time he returned, rumors about Pablo Piña's death would be running wild.

Hector had scooped up the bodies of Piña and the two security men, dumped them in the back of their own Tahoe, and left the SUV near the headquarters of a rival drug gang. If his reasoning was correct, the leader of the other drug gang would claim credit for Piña's death and reap the rewards of an undeserved reputation.

The only one that could connect him to the drug lord's death was the shop owner, and he could be trusted to keep his mouth shut. Hector wasn't about to start executing witnesses who had no involvement with any crime. It wasn't like he'd been given a contract for the shop owner.

Now, in El Paso, he had already retrieved his favorite pistol from the private postal center. He chose the Browning for this job. He didn't foresee other people around that he would have to shoot, and no one would be wearing body armor. It was tucked securely in his pants with a casual button-down shirt hanging over the butt of the pistol. He carried the leather notebook to hide the pistol when the time came. This was his last shot at the simple hit. There was no way he wanted to chase Dempsey all around the country while he did his show. There was going to be no fuss and no drama in the way he did it tonight. He intended to walk up to him in the lobby of the Marriott, draw his pistol, shoot the talk show host twice in the head, then dash back to Ciudad Juárez as quickly as possible.

Any plans after that were futile. For all he knew he might be in a private war with the survivors of Pablo Piña's organization.

Now he had to focus on his one assignment.

Tom Eriksen checked the street signs as he reached the outskirts of the suburb known as Canutillo. He didn't turn his head as he said, "How do you think we should handle this witness?"

Lila said, "I'll talk to her because she's female. But something tells me she's not just a witness. The way her brother referred to her makes her sound like she might be involved in this scam like he is."

"But she doesn't work for TARC."

"This isn't the Middle East. The enemy of my enemy is not necessarily my friend. You know how these shady witnesses can be. I think we need to come down hard on her first and show her who's the boss."

"I'll leave that up to you. But we should get our chance to talk to her in the next couple of minutes."

Lila started writing on a small notepad and said, "I'll have a few questions ready as soon as we see her."

———

Kat Gleason started talking the moment she lifted the receiver of the secure phone. She didn't want to give her supervisor a chance to cut off her explanation and make her shut down any information to Tom Eriksen at the FBI. She focused on not speaking too quickly, but she wanted to get her ideas across.

"I pieced together information from other parts of the task force to verify that there is, in fact, a plot to assassinate a U.S. citizen being discussed with someone who lives in Mexico. But now it looks like the target is Ted Dempsey, the talk show host, and I even have a time and place for it. I have to pass this information on immediately to the FBI."

Her supervisor said, "Wow, take a breath, Gleason."

Kat was quiet for a moment, but she was anxious to pass the information along to Tom Eriksen.

Her supervisor said, "So, essentially you're saying you're going to ignore my order and not keep our abilities quiet."

"I don't have any other ethical option since I learned about the time and place of the attempt. I'm paid to piece together all possible information. You have my official conclusion. There is no time to debate this. For safety reasons we have to pass on the information right now."

"And where is the FBI agent you want to pass information to?"

"Interviewing another witness. He and his partner are the ones that arranged protection for the senator, but not Ted Dempsey. We have to get moving on this right this second or it's gonna be a big mess."

Kat was a little surprised by the long silence. It didn't matter to her going forward. In about three seconds she was just going to hang up the secure phone and do what needed to be done. She had enough faith in Tom Eriksen and knew he would figure a way to stop the assassination.

Finally her supervisor broke the silence. "Very well. Call him. Write up a good report to explain your reasoning. Then—"

Kat didn't have time to listen to the rest of the bureaucratic bullshit. She slammed the secure phone back on its cradle and started frantically digging for her own cell phone.

———

Ari slipped through the kitchen, the pistol up in front of him. He wasn't scared or nervous. In fact, he had a grin plastered across his face. Cash had just gotten what he deserved, and Ari was looking forward to shutting up this DiMetti chick. She had caused way too many problems at the corporation. *His* corporation. He could call himself an executive at a computer company now. His mother finally had something to be proud about. Maybe he never finished college. Maybe he was never successful at anything except convincing the morons out here he was a hardened killer. But he was looking forward to a high-profile job with a decent salary so he could rub it in his mother's and sister's faces. They never believed in him. No woman had ever believed in him. And maybe that was why he was looking forward to planting a couple of rounds in Carol DiMetti's pretty face.

As far as his standing with the corporation went, bringing her in alive to confirm that Cash had been part of the conspiracy might not be a bad idea. They also might be able to use her as leverage to bring her nitwit brother back into the fold. Ari understood they needed computer geek types working at a company like TARC. He also understood that they should be the easiest to keep in line with a few extra bucks or a decent show of force. If they were all like the little dweeb that Ari had met at the Dunkin' Donuts who immediately gave up Eric's hiding place, he didn't think it would be too much trouble to conquer them all.

As soon as he was in the kitchen, Ari saw the closed door to the bedroom and silently shuffled across the kitchen's tile floor to try the door handle. Locked. Ari cleared his throat and tried to keep his voice even when he said, "Carol, I'm not going to hurt you. Come out and we'll clear this whole thing up." He thought he sounded very diplomatic.

Nothing but silence.

"It will help your brother, too." Ari figured that would sell her on the idea of surrendering and coming back to the corporate offices with him. In fact, Ari thought the whole family should be wiped out. He'd volunteer to track down her parents in Chicago if TARC would let him go.

He leaned in close to the door, hoping to hear something that might help. There was a familiar *clack* from behind the door, and it only took him a moment to realize someone had just racked a shotgun.

FORTY-NINE

Carol DiMetti was scared. She had backed into her bedroom and immediately scooped up the shotgun Vinnie had given her. How could her simple plan have gone so wrong? She just hoped her brother was safe.

She couldn't help but think back to the beginning when Vinnie didn't want any part of it. She pushed him when she found that her brother had information linking TARC with the drug dealer in Mexico. She just wanted money, or at least a chance for Vinnie to earn more money. Poor Vinnie wasn't smart enough to have ambition. She made him tell his boss he wanted a better job or he'd make public the information her brother had stolen on a thumb drive.

After Vinnie was shot, she thought Joe Azeri might be her ticket to a more comfortable life. Now he was dead in her front room. And she was facing this maniac in her own house.

She could hear him in the kitchen outside the closed door. The bedroom had two entrances, and through some odd design flaw from the 1960s someone had made a hallway into the rear of the kitchen. Her whole body shook as she held a Remington 870 pump shotgun that she knew was loaded with four rounds of buckshot. Vinnie had always said that 12-gauge buckshot was the only shot that could miss and still hit. He always laughed at his little joke, but Carol didn't really get it.

Carol knew she was going to have to shoot this moron and raised the butt of the shotgun to her shoulder, locking it in place, just like

Vinnie had showed her. Her whole body trembled. She picked a spot dead center of the door and slowly squeezed the trigger.

When the shotgun fired, the impact on her shoulder was tremendous, but the incredible explosion was worse. From practice, she knew to rack the shotgun's slide back and saw the empty casing pop into the air and onto the cheap carpet. She didn't hesitate to fire a second time, the gun blasting a second giant hole in the door. The whole experience felt like bombs going off.

Carol racked the shotgun again, but this time she took a second to peek through the two holes in her door. She saw the body of the man crumpled against the far wall. She leaned in and peered out the upper hole to see the pistol out of his hand and on the kitchen floor. His face had been nearly ripped off by the buckshot, and his exposed gums and teeth looked like bloody rags.

She didn't know how long she'd been staring through the hole when she heard a noise in the front room and what sounded like more than one person entering the house. She froze and finally heard someone say, "Police. Put down your weapon and come out the door with your hands where I can see them and you won't get hurt."

God, how she wished she believed them.

As Tom Eriksen stepped out of his government-issued Taurus, he noticed a Cadillac and a Chevy in the driveway in front of the small house in Canutillo occupied by Eric Sidle's sister, Carol DiMetti. Eriksen had been shot at enough in the past month that he had developed a good sense of tactics and attitude. He already had his hand near the grip of his Glock on his hip. His eyes scanned the entire neighborhood looking for any suspicious vehicles or people. It was late afternoon, and most of the driveways in this working-class neighborhood were empty.

His cell phone rang, and he glanced at the screen. When he saw it was Kat he realized it would have to be about the case. He flipped open the phone as Lila started moving toward the house slowly, just as cautious as Eriksen.

As soon as Eriksen answered the phone, Kat said, "I just got a new intercept on our line. The target of the assassination is not Senator Ramos, it's Ted Dempsey."

Eriksen took a second to process the information.

Kat didn't waste any time before she said, "Whoever is going to do it is going to try and catch Dempsey in the lobby of the Marriott at six this evening. Are you going to be able to stop it, or do I need to call the El Paso PD?"

A chill went down his neck. All he said was, "On my way." As he was about to call to Lila, Eriksen heard two heavy blasts. They were gunshots, either a rifle or shotgun. Immediately he drew his pistol and raced to the front door. Lila had already thrown herself against the front wall of the house and peeked in through the wide window.

Lila said, "Front room clear."

Eriksen was next to the front door, so he tried the handle. The door was unlocked, so he shoved it open and slipped into the house. He had his pistol up and scanned the room quickly.

There was a dead man with two bullet holes in his throat on the couch. Eriksen took a second to check for a pulse but found none. Out of habit he picked up a 9 mm off the ground and stuck it in the small of his back for safety. This man had not been killed by a shotgun, so that meant there was more than one person left in the house.

The confidence that came with experience made him move quickly and efficiently as he cleared each room methodically. He paused for a moment for Lila to come in and cover him as he headed toward the kitchen.

Before he was completely inside the cramped kitchen, Eriksen saw the buckshot pattern across a closed door and the wall. As he peered around the corner he could see a second body with multiple buckshot hits and blood pooling on the ground. The man's face had been partially ripped off, and his teeth were exposed where his lips should've been.

Even though he knew there was an imminent threat in front of him somewhere, all Tom Eriksen could think about was getting to Ted Dempsey.

———

Hector was early, so he walked around the entire building that housed the Marriott in downtown El Paso. The building also had some offices and stores around the front. It was like the hotel was an afterthought. There was nothing unusual about the late-autumn day. It was cool, but not unbearable, and there was hardly a hint of moisture in the air. He hated to admit it, but El Paso did feel cleaner and safer than his own home just across the border. He understood that Ciudad Juárez was a much bigger city, but still he wished they could clean it up so people didn't have to live the way they did now. He understood why everyone wanted to cross the border into the United States. If only they realized how most of the *norteamericanos* felt about them.

As he came around the corner toward the front of the hotel, he hesitated when he saw a marked El Paso Police Department cruiser on the street directly in front of the entrance. Although he realized it was likely just a coincidence, in his business anyone who counted on things being a coincidence ended up dead. If he had to, he could deal with one cop and Dempsey. But if he killed a police officer, he would get little sympathy from the police back in Mexico. Cops all tended to stick together no matter what country they were from, unless they had really lost touch with any aspect of what brought them into police work in the first place.

He watched a young patrolman, nearly as tall as Hector himself, unfold himself from the patrol car and walk into the hotel.

This could be a problem.

———

Eriksen waited until Lila was in a good tactical position behind the heavy butcher's-block island in the center of the kitchen. He called out in a loud voice, "Police. Put down your weapon and come out the door with your hands where I can see them and you won't get hurt."

There was a long pause as he held his position, staring down the barrel of his Glock .40 caliber. Anyone who came to the door with gun in hand would be dead in a matter of seconds.

Finally, a female voice from the bedroom answered him. "How do I know you're the police?"

The question took him by surprise for a moment, and then he realized the position the woman was in. He called out, "I'm Tom Eriksen with the FBI. Your brother is safe at our office. He told us where you live."

"That still doesn't prove you're a cop. You could be lying."

"Then pick up the phone and dial 911. Call the cops. We'll be happy to wait for them to show up. In fact, I'm telling you right now I need you to call 911."

He heard movement in the bedroom and realized that was exactly what she was doing. She still wasn't convinced to come to the door. Finally he heard the lock click, and the door opened a crack. She popped her hands out and said, "I just called 911, but I believe you. I'm coming out."

He stole a glance at Lila to make sure she was still in a safe and tactical position. "Step past the body and towards me." He watched as she shuffled out of the room.

It was clear she was terrified, and she was surprised when Lila popped up from behind the kitchen island and wrapped the woman's arms behind her back, handcuffing her and pushing her to the carpeted floor of the living room in a matter of seconds. It was a standard move for safety until they verified what was going on.

Now Eriksen could move forward and clear the rest of the house.

Hector risked walking by the front of the hotel and peeking into the lobby. The last thing he wanted was a witness who could identify a big Mexican guy casing the place just before a nationally known talk show host was shot in the lobby. But it was a chance he would have to take. He had to know exactly where the cop was and if he could wait for the patrolman to leave before he took action.

There was no sign of Dempsey, and the cop was near the front door, leaning casually on a counter and flirting with a very pretty concierge. Hector shook his head. How many great endeavors were derailed by romance?

The cop paid no attention to anything but the blond concierge. The lobby looked empty behind him, which made Hector think he could wait, unless the cop's pickup line didn't work and he overstayed his welcome. The other thing in Hector's favor was that Dempsey could linger in the lobby.

Hector found himself standing and staring through the front door. Not a professional tactic. As he was about to move on he noticed the elevator at the far end of the lobby open and Dempsey step out.

The cop wasn't moving.

Hector couldn't let another opportunity pass him by. He turned and pushed through the heavy, ornate front door.

Eriksen had to leave Lila at the house in Canutillo with Carol DiMetti and two dead men. Someone was going to have to explain to the local cops what the hell had happened. Lila was on her cell phone trying to reach an El Paso cop she trusted.

Eriksen punched the gas of his Taurus, feeling alone since he couldn't tell any supervisors what was going on without the risk of his being grounded or the information being leaked. He was truly on his own.

He blew through a red light and took a corner a little too fast, feeling the car fishtail to his right. If ever he had a reason to speed as an FBI agent, this was it. He couldn't believe he was caught up in this kind of case and was getting information from agencies like the NSA.

He had tried to call Dempsey several times and left a message telling him to wait for him no matter what. That might have been a little cryptic, but he didn't know how you tell a guy he'd get killed if he left his hotel room.

The downtown district of El Paso seemed way off in the distance as he thanked God for the light traffic and punched the gas again. He hoped he wasn't too late.

Ted Dempsey liked El Paso. The network sometimes put too much emphasis on doing remote broadcasts from big cities. They felt it would broaden their demographics and attract more new viewers. But El Paso was the kind of town that was just small enough that he could connect with people and get a good feeling for what concerned them. That was one of the reasons he had started on his crusade against the outsourcing of jobs a decade ago. Then he realized the dangers of illegal immigration and addressed both issues on the show, educating first himself, then his audience, and then Washington, if indeed those in either house of Congress or the White House would ever willingly look beyond the Potomac for understanding or answers. He was sincere about both issues, but they also resonated with the public. He became more popular with the people whose interests he truly represented in his broadcasts and commentary, and he rankled more than a few corporate leaders who didn't share his enthusiasm for straight talk about the shortcomings of some business practices and public policies that had to be changed if the middle class were to survive.

Another reason he liked coming to El Paso was his new friend, Tom Eriksen, the principled young FBI agent. It was young people like Eriksen and his partner, Lila Tellis, that gave Dempsey hope for the future of the country. If young people like that were still seeking careers in public service, then America could still overcome a lot of challenges and prevail.

As he stepped off the Marriott's elevator into the cavernous lobby, Dempsey realized he'd missed two calls that had gone right to voicemail. As he looked down at the screen of his BlackBerry, his assistant said, "Need me to call someone for you?"

Dempsey shook his head. "No, thanks. It's my FBI friend. I'll call him on the way to the airport." He turned to say his good-byes to the desk clerks, who had been very helpful to him. One in particular, a tall young man originally from Mexico, had shown great interest in Dempsey's schedule and tried to help any way he could.

He noticed a lanky uniformed cop flirting with the knockout at the concierge desk. The young blonde worked a shift in the late afternoon, and he could see why a patrolman would want to take a break to chat with her for a few minutes.

Dempsey looked down at the time on his BlackBerry. He was early for a change and told his assistant, "Let's get a coffee before we head out." He was looking forward to a smooth, easy flight back to New York.

FIFTY

Hector decided he had to act, cop or no cop. He'd already lost sight of Dempsey and the young man who had trailed him. That was probably the assistant the desk clerk who called in the tip had overheard. Hector wondered how much money Ramón Herrara had spread around the city to have eyes and ears everywhere. It was a valuable resource but also dangerous to have others know parts of your plans.

Once in the lobby, Hector stopped in front of a TV playing ESPN. It was a story on the San Antonio Spurs. Hector had a difficult time understanding basketball. It had no relation to any of the games he had played growing up in Mexico.

The cop didn't move or acknowledge his presence as Hector scanned the entire lobby, noting the location of possible witnesses before seeing Dempsey and his assistant at the Starbucks counter in the corner.

Now he considered a true tactical problem. Was it better to shoot the cop, who had a pistol handy, and risk scaring his target, or was it better to shoot the target, then have to confront an armed cop?

Hector pondered the question for a few minutes while he stood in the lobby and hoped the cop would just leave.

———————

Now Eriksen could see the Marriott just a few blocks away. But he knew there were a number of turns, and traffic had picked up considerably once he was in the downtown area. He pulled an extra magazine of .40 caliber bullets from the glove compartment and slipped it into the pocket of his jeans. He pulled the tail of the shirt away from the handle of his Glock on his right hip. He wasn't trying to hide who he was this time.

He was leaning over the dash and looking out the top of his windshield when a Lay's Potato Chips step van pulled through the intersection. By the time he looked up, the tall van blocked the light, and Eriksen had no idea if he was running a red light or not.

He slammed on the brakes and felt the Taurus drift sideways as it slammed into the van and came to an abrupt, violent stop. It wasn't much of a collision, but the car was wedged under the van, and the heavyset driver of the truck hopped onto the asphalt, already screaming obscenities.

Eriksen didn't have time for this sort of foolishness.

———————

The waiting was killing Hector as he slipped his hand under his shirt and pulled out his well-balanced Browning 9 mm, sliding it into the leather notebook he had bought in Ciudad Juárez. The notebook was now a keepsake, which would remind him of the time and place he slit Pablo Piña's throat. It also hid the gun from the view of anyone walking past and provided quick access. Then Dempsey was paying at the counter, getting ready to leave. Hector intended to wait until he was right next to the cop and shoot them both at the same time. He didn't like the plan, but that was his only option.

In the distance, he could see Dempsey say good-bye to the young woman at the Starbucks counter and slowly turn to make his way through the empty café and into the main part of the lobby.

Then Hector saw something that, to him, constituted a miracle. The young concierge handed the police officer a business card with her number scrawled on the back. At the same time, over his radio there was a report of a car accident apparently close by.

The handsome young police officer gave the concierge a parting smile, then jogged out of the hotel lobby to show how urgent his radio call had been and leave her with an idea of just how important his job was.

As soon as the cop banged through the doors, Hector looked up to see Dempsey talking with his assistant at the far end of the lobby.

Finally everything was lining up for Hector.

———————

Tom Eriksen abandoned his car, flashing his badge briefly and telling the furious van driver to save his complaints for the cops. He turned and sprinted toward the Marriott a few blocks away. As in most cities not on the East Coast, the sidewalks were nearly empty, and he only had to dodge the occasional pedestrian. He got a few strange looks for running so hard in street clothes.

It felt like the farther he ran, the farther away the hotel got. It was similar to running toward a mountain. But finally he was on the same street as the Marriott. An El Paso police cruiser pulled away from the curb just as Eriksen arrived. He tried to get the patrolman's attention, but the car turned the corner headed toward where Eriksen had left his own government vehicle.

Eriksen approached the door to the hotel ready for action. Now that he was used to gunfire he didn't hesitate. Experience really was everything. Now, as his father would say, it was time to answer the bell. This was the sort of thing he had dreamed about since he was a little kid.

———————

Hector was patient after the cop rushed out of the hotel. He allowed Dempsey to complete his slow stroll down the middle of the lobby, stopping to chat with anyone who wanted to say hello. Hector figured if he took the shot when Dempsey and his assistant were closer, almost in the small area where the TV played, he could shoot, turn, and walk out the door. He'd be on his way without any eyewitnesses. It made his month of trying to complete this assignment seem worthwhile. He'd learned a lot each time he had tried to catch Dempsey in his crosshairs. To be able to complete this assignment when the police were at least partially aware of it was a testament to his ability and made him swell with pride.

He knew that when he was older, relaxing on one of the western beaches of Mexico, he wouldn't be able to resist bragging about how he had gone up against the famed American FBI and still completed his assignment. He never liked to say he *killed* people. He preferred to think of them as business transactions. Aside from the first few times he pulled the trigger, he really felt no rush of adrenaline or excitement. There was no actual enjoyment in it, other than the satisfaction he got from a job well done. And the money.

Hector pretended to be watching the TV, still not understanding the first thing about American basketball, then glanced into the lobby and noted that Dempsey and his assistant were now walking at a steady pace and on a direct route. Dempsey was sipping his coffee and chatting leisurely with his assistant. Hector knew it was time. He still had the pistol in the notebook. He opened it as if reading a page. The gun was visible to him but still obscured to anyone else by the notebook cover.

A few more steps and he would fire.

———

As soon as Eriksen dashed through the front door of the Marriott he recognized the big man between him and Dempsey. This time he didn't have to search his memory. It was the guy from the Cattleman's Steakhouse. Kat's information on the conversation that mentioned the restaurant told him why the man was here. He could articulate it later when he was questioned about pulling his service pistol.

Eriksen ducked toward a pillar in front of the door as he drew his Glock and started to bring it on target, shouting, "FBI, don't move." He had a good position and the advantage of surprise, and he was pissed. He was pissed about what he'd gone through the last month. He was pissed that he couldn't talk with his partner John Houghton, and he was pissed that guys like this thought they were above the law.

All that ran through his head instantly as he developed a good sight picture of the assassin. Eriksen was shocked by how quickly the man dropped a notebook, raised his right hand, and fired two relatively well aimed shots into the concrete-and-marble pillar. It hardly affected Eriksen's concentration. He was now a veteran of gunfights. He let out a breath and realized a stunned Ted Dempsey and a young man were directly behind the big assassin. Eriksen had to make these rounds go exactly where he intended them to or he would hit Dempsey.

He focused on the front sight of his barrel and fired. Once, twice, three times.

The big man froze where he was. Then the pistol slipped out of his hand. It felt like time had frozen, and the giant lobby seemed silent after the sound of gunfire. The assassin turned his head slightly as two separate splotches of blood blossomed just like an opening flower on his shirt. His whole body seemed to twist as he tumbled to the ground, bouncing off the chair and falling into the wide flat-screen TV.

Someone in the background screamed, and Eriksen snapped out of his tunnel vision. He scanned the lobby quickly to make sure no one else was working with the assassin. Once he was satisfied, he stepped from behind the pillar and quickly retrieved the Browning from the floor next to the dead assassin.

His heart was already resuming a steady pace. He took a deep breath to clear his head.

He'd done it. He had prevented an assassination. His father would be proud. And maybe some of his dead ancestors as well.

––––––

It was dawn by the time Eriksen made his way to the Border Security Task Force office. He had stopped answering his cell phone and knew that a number of the bosses would be at the office waiting for him to be debriefed.

He and Lila were completely exhausted. Pulling an all-nighter was a little different now than it had been in college. The scene at

Carol DiMetti's house was complicated, and the El Paso homicide unit came out to assist the local cops. They wanted to get finger-prints from both the dead men and see if they could link them to the recent rash of murders in the city. Clearing an open homicide was like heroin to the average homicide detective. The more cases they cleared, the more they wanted to clear. They had already con-nected one of the dead guys at the house to the shootings at the market and the Martinez apartment and, by extension, to the mur-der of John Houghton. That meant with some effort everything could be tied together and maybe Eriksen would get the answers he'd been looking for.

Eriksen had been cleared by the El Paso police to leave the scene at the Marriott. Dempsey turned out to be a good eyewitness and explained in great detail and with a little flair what he had seen. Eriksen knew it would be a nonstop parade through different news outlets for the popular talk show host today. How often did someone in the media get to witness something like this?

During the police debriefings, Dempsey found time to comfort the tired Eriksen, telling him, "Don't worry about me. Someone try-ing to shoot me means I'm doing my job and ruffling feathers."

Now, at the task force office, all Eriksen could think about was nailing Andre for his role in the conspiracy. Eriksen owed it to John Houghton. Andre had pretended to be his friend just like he had pretended to be a good supervisor. He wondered how long the big man had been putting on an act. Certainly he hadn't started out his career providing information to smugglers and other criminals. Eriksen wondered what turned a guy like Andre from the path of protecting and serving to the path of corruption. It was a sad situa-tion, and the fact that Andre was able to act like a decent guy didn't help things at all.

Eriksen waited outside the conference room, taking in a glare from Mike Zara as he filed in behind the pudgy Department of Jus-tice inspector general.

Lila leaned in and whispered, "I invited the IG. I thought we might need him at some point."

Eriksen nodded. "Good call."

"How're you holding up?"

It was a question Eriksen couldn't answer with confidence. "I'm tired, but we need to handle this as quickly as possible."

Lila turned and headed into the conference room.

Between his exhaustion and the prospect of what he was about to face, Eriksen felt a little dejected. Then he looked up and saw Kat Gleason waving him to the end of the hallway. Just the thought of some interaction with the beautiful NSA analyst lifted his spirits.

FIFTY-ONE

Waiting in a hallway in the Border Security Task Force office, Kat Gleason was in a tricky position. She absolutely had to get Tom Eriksen's attention before he stepped into the conference room, but she was hesitant to let any of the bosses see her talking to the embattled FBI agent. He had been in a shooting just a few hours ago and still had work to do. As he walked toward her, a weak smile forming on his face, she ducked into the smaller secondary conference room, and he followed.

The first thing she did was hug him hard, trying to feel every part of his upper body and his beating heart. She gave him a kiss on the lips and leaned her head against his muscular chest. "My God, this is scary. Are you all right? This isn't anything like the movies. Sometimes I forget that. You could've been killed."

"That was one of a number of outcomes I tried not to think about."

Kat couldn't help herself as she squeezed him again. Then she said, "I have some information you need before you walk into the conference room."

"I'm all ears."

"Basically, a number from a prepaid drop phone purchased here in El Paso has called the same number I heard talking about the hit on Dempsey. I compared the calls to our intercepts. The phone in Mexico was called right after the meeting here at the task force where you said you were going to see Dempsey at the Cattleman's Steakhouse."

Eriksen looked at her and said, "Damn, that proves it was Andre."

Her engineer mind couldn't argue with that logic.

He said, "We still need something more before we can make our move. And we've gotta do it fast. If he threw the phone away there would be nothing to connect him to it. That's our only link."

Kat's specialty was electronic surveillance, not building cases that would be acceptable to a jury. She considered the problem in her analytical mind.

Eriksen looked at her and said, "He doesn't suspect anything now. He'll have the phone with him in the meeting. Can you call in exactly fifteen minutes? I'd like to hear what he has to say first."

"Are you sure?"

Eriksen nodded and said, "We can't let him get away with this. The Department of Justice inspector general is in there. He'll have enough clout to hold him if I can articulate our suspicions. But I need to hear his phone ring in exactly fifteen minutes to know I have enough to act on."

"Be careful." She was just now beginning to realize the dangers of actual law enforcement. Anything could happen. Tom had already had someone shoot at him tonight, and he had seen three dead bodies. One of them he had had to shoot himself.

Eriksen said, "I'll have Lila for backup. She'll watch out for me."

Kat couldn't resist one more kiss after she whispered in his ear, "You've got to let Lila in on our plan. Tell her to be careful, too."

As soon as Eriksen left her to go into the main conference room, Kat rushed to her desk and started counting the minutes.

The meeting started the way Eriksen had expected it would, with lots of introductions and false statements of support for Eriksen's actions at the Marriott hotel. Everyone wanted to support a hero unless something turned up to make his actions seem less heroic. No matter how many managers or attorneys said they were glad he was all right and safe, Eriksen wondered how many were like Mike

Zara, secretly hoping he would fail. That made the group sitting around the massive conference table that much scarier. Eriksen had faced enemy gunfire this evening, but somehow that seemed trivial compared to what he was about to pull off.

This was no game, and there were far too many variables. He had relied on his training and experience to guide him in his confrontation with the armed killer. The federal government was good about training its law enforcement people on tactics and marksmanship. But the lesson Eriksen had learned over the past month was that experience carried the day in a time of crisis. Now he really did feel like a hardened veteran. John Houghton had stayed so cool under fire because he had *learned* to stay cool under fire. Now Eriksen had to learn to be patient and let things develop.

He couldn't help glancing up at the clock on the wall. A little less than two minutes had gone by. In thirteen minutes he expected to hear Andre's phone ring, and then he'd have to talk fast to keep the big DHS supervisor from saying it was all bullshit and walking out of the room to destroy any possible evidence linking him to the mayhem that had occurred in and around El Paso in the last month.

No one in law enforcement shut off their phones during a meeting. They needed to be available for emergencies. The whole profession accepted the practice, so Andre would be vulnerable when the call came to him.

The assistant U.S. attorney, who was dressed very casually and had obviously been called out from home, had a concerned look on her face. Her intense eyes conveyed apprehension—logical enough since she thought she was dealing with a rogue FBI agent who held the keys to a blockbuster case. Eriksen had already mentioned TARC and Eric's statement in case something happened to him and he couldn't pursue the matter, either because he was in custody or the conspiracy was bigger than he realized and he was dead. Eriksen didn't like to consider either idea.

The lawyer looked directly at Eriksen, cleared her throat, and said, "Agent Eriksen, the U.S. Attorney's Office is not looking into the shooting. That's the El Paso Police Department's jurisdiction and has to do with FBI policy, but you've raised some questions about TARC, and we need to have a unified statement when we face the press." She looked around to make sure the rest of the group agreed with her premise. Only Mike Zara looked appalled at the idea that they were skipping over the part where Eriksen shot someone in a hotel lobby.

The assistant U.S. attorney continued as if she were presenting a witness in front of the jury. "How did you learn about the assassination attempt?"

That question caught Eriksen by surprise. He hesitated, not knowing how much he could divulge and not wanting to put Lila in an awkward position. He spit out a few unintelligible syllables before Lila spoke up.

Lila said, "The information came from one of my snitches in Mexico. It started out vague, but we were able to narrow it down as the days passed."

The lawyer turned to Lila. "Do you consider this a reliable informant?"

Eriksen's eyes flicked up at the clock. Eleven minutes until Kat called the phone. Lila didn't hesitate at the attorney's question. "The informant had been reliable in the past, but he was murdered yesterday in Juárez."

From the end of the table Mike Zara mumbled, "How convenient."

Eriksen watched Andre for any reaction. The big man was calm and taking notes.

The assistant U.S. attorney turned her attention back to Tom Eriksen. "And the witness against TARC, he's credible?"

"Very."

There was still no reaction from Andre.

Eriksen threw in, "And the witness is related to others involved in the case. I also have a number of bank records to back up some of the assertions."

322 LOU DOBBS AND JAMES O. BORN

Now Mike Zara cut into the conversation. "And who have you been updating on this information? Did Andre know about the alleged assassination attempt?"

The assistant U.S. attorney looked at Zara and said, "Seriously? *Alleged* assassination attempt? There was a man waiting in the lobby of the Marriott with a pistol. If it weren't for Agent Eriksen, we'd have a dead nationally known talk show host and everyone would be looking at El Paso as an extension of Juárez. I think we're past the alleged stage in the assassination."

Zara's face flushed red as he said, "Did anyone else know about the investigation?"

Eriksen realized that Andre was deferring to him to answer. Maybe he suspected something. It was Lila who said, "There were security issues with the informant—now that he's been killed, I'd call them legitimate security issues—that required us to maintain the strictest possible confidentiality. We did alert the Texas Department of Public Safety when we thought the target of the assassination could be Senator Ramos. In addition, we maintained relatively close surveillance of both the senator and Dempsey during the investigation."

Eriksen suppressed a smile at how well played and well worded Lila's comments were. He glanced up at the clock. Eight minutes left. Now he started wondering about the tactical questions related to his impromptu and imaginative ploy. Would he have to draw his gun? Right now he was carrying a backup Glock model 27. His duty pistol had been taken into evidence, which was policy of any police shooting. How would the other people at the table react? God, how he hoped it wouldn't come to gunplay. If it did, he could count on Lila, and probably the IG would help cautiously. Mike Zara would freak out.

Seven minutes. Eriksen felt his stomach tighten as he considered everything that could happen.

The assistant U.S. attorney snapped her fingers to get his attention. He had apparently spaced out more than he realized. She said, "Are you all right, Agent Eriksen?"

He nodded his head. "Yes, ma'am. Just a little tired."

"I can imagine. We should be able to wrap this up quickly. In fact, if you're that tired we could do it another time."

Eriksen realized he needed to make this last at least another seven minutes. "No, I'm fine. I'd rather get some of this out on the table now while it's fresh in my mind."

The attorney said, "What else have you discovered that links TARC and these different incidents together?"

Eriksen had been ready for this question. He'd even practiced the answer. As he spoke, he turned to the whole group, but it was really more a ploy to be able to look at Andre and see his reaction. "The thumbprint of the man killed with a shotgun at the house in Canutillo matches the print on a casing found at the market shooting and a casing found in the Martinez apartment." He waited until everyone absorbed that information, then added the bombshell. "That same print was found in the apartment of HSI agent John Houghton, and the El Paso homicide unit has reclassified his death as a homicide."

Now Andre looked up, but he appeared to be personally interested rather than concerned. Mike Zara had his usual sour expression, apparently upset that Eriksen had uncovered anything at all related to another federal agent's death.

Eriksen continued, "We still haven't identified the suspect, but that connects a lot of activity that's occurred the past five weeks. The other man at the house has been identified as Joe Azeri, also known as Cash. He was a small-time hood from New Jersey, and we are working on his links to TARC. El Paso homicide told us that it appears the man shot by Carol DiMetti with a shotgun murdered Azeri with two shots from a .380 into his throat."

Five minutes left.

The attorney said, "Who told you to investigate TARC?"

"Part of my job description."

Mike Zara said, "I never told him to go on any fishing expedition. If this case is as big as he says, it should be on an FBI squad supervised by an FBI supervisor."

Everyone in the conference room turned toward Andre, the supervisor on the task force.

Eriksen hoped Andre's cell phone didn't ring right now, because he was interested in what the big man had to say.

Andre considered Zara's comment, wrote another note on his pad, then said, "This kind of investigation falls under the broad purview of the task force, so as far as I'm concerned, Tom and Lila are covered."

Now Zara leaned forward in his seat and said in his usual loud voice, "But did you tell him to investigate?"

Andre remained placid. "I don't have to. They're professional law enforcement officers. If they can't do something like this, what good are they? My job is to help them, not to hinder them." He glared at Zara. "That's a lesson you might wanna learn."

Eriksen thought it was a nice speech. Too bad Andre was full of shit. It was almost time for Kat's call. Eriksen let his hand drift down to the pistol in a holster on his hip.

He would be ready for any surprises.

FIFTY-TWO

By Tom Eriksen's calculations it was now a minute past when Kat was going to call. In his mind, Eriksen had imagined Andre's phone ringing, the DHS supervisor reaching for the phone, then Eriksen and Lila taking action. It was a good plan. But Eriksen was beginning to learn that good plans rarely worked out as planned.

Now there was an awkward silence, and people around the table looked at Eriksen as if they expected him to say something. He shot a glance to Lila, who was also looking up at the clock on the wall. He had no way of checking with Kat. Once Andre left the room, if he had any concerns about being suspected, he could just chuck the phone.

Then Eriksen heard a low ringing sound. It sounded like an old-time telephone, but it was clearly electronic. This was it. He looked at Lila, who also acknowledged the ring.

Eriksen turned to his right and looked at Andre, who matched his gaze but didn't move. The phone rang again. It took a moment for Eriksen to realize the ringing phone was to his left. He spun in his chair. Mike Zara reached into his jacket pocket. Then the ringing stopped. Zara looked around the table and mumbled, "Sorry."

Eriksen caught Lila's eyes.

The leak wasn't Andre. It was Mike Zara. That made Eriksen pause, confused and stunned.

The assistant U.S. attorney cleared her throat and said, "Go on, Agent Eriksen. I'm sure there's a lot more we need to hear."

Eriksen hesitated as he tried to process the information he had just learned. Lila stood from the table, excused herself, and rushed out of the room. He knew she was going to confirm the phone call with Kat.

Eriksen had to stall. He started slowly, "Well, we . . ." All he could think about was John Houghton and duty. He had a duty to his friend, and to his friend's widow and children, just like he had a duty as a law enforcement officer. He also was human, and anger started to build in him as he looked to his left at Mike Zara. The FBI supervisor still held that smug expression.

Lila stepped back into the conference room, looked at Eriksen, and said, "She got what she needed."

Eriksen said, "I'm afraid we have a leak in the office. That's one of the reasons we didn't tell anyone exactly what we were doing."

It was show time.

FIFTY-THREE

It was the portly Department of Justice inspector general who looked at Eriksen with a very calm expression and said, "How about giving us some details on this serious allegation?"

Tom Eriksen was careful to keep his eyes directly on Mike Zara. He noticed that Lila stepped around the room to a spot where she was behind the FBI supervisor. There was a clear sense in the room that Mike Zara was the focus of their attention.

Eriksen looked at his supervisor and said, "Do you mind pulling the phone out of your coat pocket?"

Zara didn't change his expression and slowly folded his arms across his chest. "Yes, I do mind. I mind very much being part of a frivolous investigation. I mind wasting my time in a meeting like this. And I really mind having someone like you level any sort of accusation against me." He unfolded his arms and placed his hands on the arms of the chair and slowly started to stand.

In a firm, loud voice Eriksen barked, "Sit down. Do it now. Keep your hands on the table where we can all see them." It was a subtle variation of a normal police command. But instead of telling Zara to put his hands where *he* could see them, Eriksen made everyone in the room feel like part of it by saying, "Keep your hands on the table where we can *all* see them." The ploy worked. Andre was definitely leaning forward, ready for action, as was the IG. Now Eriksen had to make his case clearly and concisely.

Eriksen said, "We've seen a consistent leak of information using a number of different investigative resources available to us. Two minutes ago an NSA analyst called one of the phones that had been used to pass on information. I believe it was the phone in Mike Zara's coat pocket that just rang. All I want to do is look at the phone and see if it's the switchboard number from the office. If it's not, then I will have nothing to hold Mike on." He noticed out of the corner of his eye Lila slide toward the IG and whisper into his ear.

Andre weighed in with his deep, commanding voice. "Come on, Mike. It's no big deal. Show us the phone, then you can skate right out of here. You can go join the other FBI supervisors in your secret nap room or whatever you guys do to fill the day."

Zara said, "You're crazy if you think I'm gonna do anything like that. The whole idea is beneath contempt and doesn't deserve my attention."

Andre reached into his own coat pocket and pulled out two cell phones. "I'll do it." He held up a BlackBerry and said, "This is my Department of Homeland Security phone." He carefully set down the BlackBerry, then picked up a smaller Android phone. "This is my personal phone. You guys can look through either one and see how many times I called my wife and my kids. As long as it doesn't leave this room, you can even see where I called my girlfriend. I have nothing to hide. At least from you."

The IG said, "I only have one phone, but you can certainly look through it." He pulled out an iPhone and set it on the long table.

Eriksen dug his phone out of his front pocket and set it on the table, followed by Lila doing exactly the same thing. Finally, the assistant U.S. attorney, who had been watching all of this unfold in silence, pulled her phone from her purse, then dug deeper and pulled out a second phone. She said, "One's the Department of Justice phone, and one is my private phone. And I don't care if you see that I called my husband on it several times. I have to confess I even texted him once during this meeting. I had to make sure my kids got off to bed on time."

Now they all stared at Mike Zara, using the power of peer pressure.

His eyes darted around the room, and a bead of sweat formed on his forehead. Finally, after a long pause, Zara said, "I'm not showing any of you anything. This is an outrage." Somehow he still managed to keep his usual arrogance in his voice and make his argument sound righteous.

Eriksen made his decision and knew he had to get the phone before Zara left the room. He said, "In that case, I'm placing you under arrest. Per policy, incident to that arrest, I'm going to search you and take your firearm and anything else you have concealed in your pockets into evidence." He worded the statement carefully because it was rare you had an assistant U.S. attorney as a witness. When this came to court in a year or more, Eriksen didn't want there to be any mistake about how he obtained evidence. Once he had the phone in his possession, he could always get a search warrant to look at the numbers, but the key was to grab the phone now.

Zara gave no hint that he was going to comply.

From across the table the IG stood up and said, "You heard him, Zara. You're under arrest."

Zara stiffened in his seat, then slowly dug in his pocket and pulled out his cell phone. Lila stepped toward him from behind him and jerked his pistol out of a molded plastic holster. Once he had emptied his pockets, Zara slumped back into the chair, looking like he had been through a battle.

Eriksen wasn't proud that he had been hoping he'd have a reason to punch the smug son of a bitch. Anytime a law enforcement officer was found to be involved in criminal activity it was a sad day for the entire profession. Corrupt police practices got so much airplay when they occurred, but no one stopped to consider how rare it was in the big picture. No news director ever played a news story about how virtually every other cop in the country was honest and ethical. Even Ted Dempsey would have to mention this incident.

The inspector general looked across at Zara and said, "Do we have permission to look at your phone? If it's not the right number, I'm sure the assistant U.S. attorney over here will authorize your immediate release, and you will receive an apology from my office for your temporary detention."

Zara knew he was done. He nodded slowly, then slid the phone across the table to Andre, who caught it with one hand.

Andre examined the Boost prepaid phone. Then he opened the flip phone and spent a moment searching the call-log numbers. After a couple of seconds he looked up at Eriksen and solemnly nodded his head.

Zara let out a breath and dropped his head to the table.

Eriksen pulled a card from his wallet, looked down at his broken supervisor, and said, "You have the right to remain silent."

FIFTY-FOUR

Ramón Herrera tried to relax as he read an electronic version of the *El Paso Times* on his iPad. He shook his head as he read the story again, taking a bite out of an English muffin and poached egg the chef had left on the table next to him on his ornate balcony.

The FBI had arrested that idiot Rich Haben, and based on the exorbitant bond and the fact that he was still in jail, Herrera thought he probably had not cooperated. Yet. He could deal with the American businessman in a few days. Killing a prisoner in a U.S. jail could be a challenge, but he'd done it before.

His normal contact inside the FBI was offline. No calls were going through to him and no news coming out.

He knew that his assassin, Hector, was dead. The paper described him as an "unidentified gunman" who was shot by an FBI agent in the lobby of the downtown Marriott hotel. His contact at the Marriott had confirmed it was Hector. Worse, Ted Dempsey was empowered by the arrest of Haben. The talk show host was infuriating.

On the bright side, someone had dealt with Pablo Piña in Juárez. He'd find a better man to replace the thug. Pablo was also his biggest tie to TARC. Herrera had tossed the phone he'd used to contact Haben and Hector, and he was secluded as well as secure in his mountain retreat. The Mexican Army couldn't root him out of here. But it wouldn't come to that.

Herrera looked up as his assistant came out onto the balcony. The attractive young man was holding one of the hacienda's portable phones and said, "You have a call, sir."

"Who is it?"

The young man looked nervous when he said, "It's the president of Mexico."

———————

More than a week after the awkward arrest of Mike Zara at the Border Security Task Force office, Tom Eriksen found himself once again at the Cattleman's Steakhouse, this time having dinner with Ted Dempsey and Senator Elizabeth Ramos. The three of them sat comfortably around a table in the corner of the popular restaurant as he filled them in on the details of the case. There were still some things he couldn't talk about until they became public record, but both of his dinner companions were smart enough to fill in the blanks.

Eriksen said, "I know you saw on the news that my former supervisor at the FBI had been arrested. He really didn't say much once he had an attorney. But we had just enough to make an arrest over at TARC. We went right to the top and grabbed a guy named Rich Haben."

Dempsey cut in and said, "That jerk. You should hear some of the things he said to me. Is he the one who paid for the hit?"

"He's associated with the person who made the call, but we still don't know who that is. Haben is too terrified to say anything yet."

Dempsey seemed to process the information.

"You definitely got his attention, and, according to the border talk, TARC was the centerpiece of a criminal empire. It looks like Haben was behind a lot of things. He directly supervised the two men involved in the different shootings around town who were found dead at Carol DiMetti's house. But even he has a boss."

"You guys working on him?"

"Trying to, but they want to prosecute Mike Zara, too. That's always one of the FBI's priorities. They can't ever risk having even a hint of corruption. That's why the employment process takes so long."

The senator said, "How was a criminal able to get to a supervisor like that?"

"No one knows yet. It could've been money or something else. The FBI is looking hard into it."

The senator said, "Do you have any ideas how we might combat that in the future? Is it a pay issue?"

"No, ma'am, I think it's just one guy who fell through the cracks. I've never had any reason to doubt the integrity of another FBI agent. In fact, it was my own institutional bias that kept me from ever even considering Zara as the possible leak. I just assumed it was the task force supervisor from HSI, Andre." He let out a short laugh and said, "I had to explain the whole thing to him and apologize at the same time."

Dempsey was smiling when he said, "How'd he take it?"

"He thinks I'm just a typical dick FBI agent now, but he appreciates that I solved the case that involved the murder of our mutual friend, John Houghton."

Dempsey said, "What about the two witnesses? The brother and sister."

"Carol and Eric are now under the protection of the U.S. Marshals in Witness Security. This may turn out to be one of the biggest cases ever worked in the Southwest, and when you look at the number of people who died, the Marshals want to make sure nothing happens to their star witnesses."

Dempsey nodded and said, "You've done a remarkable job. I'm glad everything worked out, and I'm proud we're friends."

Eriksen was touched by the sincerity of Dempsey's words.

The senator said, "I've heard all I need to. That antiterror job in Washington is all yours."

Eriksen wanted to jump out of the seat and kiss her, he was so excited. It was the culmination of his dreams and exactly what he wanted to be doing with his career. It also put him much closer to his family, whom he'd missed more the longer he was away.

He was able to remain composed and said, "Thank you very much, Senator."

She gave him a politician's smile and said, "My only caveat would be that you keep me in the loop on all of your big investigations."

"Excuse me?"

"I think being a U.S. senator makes me trustworthy enough to confide in."

"Yes, ma'am, I'm sure it does. But we have rules and policy that dictate who I report to. And reporting to a senator is way above my pay grade."

Now the senator became a little cooler and said, "I *make* the pay grades."

"I understand. But I still couldn't ethically accept a job like this if the condition went counter to my training and oath of office."

Now the senator let out a manufactured laugh, patted him playfully on the arm, and said, "Luckily you'll be in Washington, D.C., where none of that will matter to anyone."

"It will matter to me."

"Are you saying you no longer want the job?"

It was tough. He was embarrassed that he had to hesitate before he answered. But finally, reluctantly, he said, "I appreciate the offer, but I'm afraid I'm saying exactly that."

———

The next afternoon, Kat Gleason met him in front of his apartment. She greeted him with a warm hug and a kiss on the lips, something she was careful to avoid doing around any of their coworkers.

Eriksen said, "What was that for?"

"I'm just glad you're not under any dark cloud and that you made it through the case without being killed."

"I have to say I'm glad about all of that, too."

"I'm also glad you're not moving back to the East Coast." She gave him another kiss.

He tried to act casual when he said, "I'm not sure I was ever considering it too strongly."

They both had to laugh at that.

Just as Kat and Eriksen were about to get into his personal car, Marty, the oldest son from the family in the front house, raced down the driveway toward them. Immediately Eriksen recognized the hefty forms of Curtis Lopez and his two brothers behind Marty.

Marty panted, "Please, Tom, can you help me?"

All three of the Lopez brothers skidded to a stop when they saw Tom Eriksen. Curtis Lopez held up his hands and said, "We don't want no trouble. But you said this jerk-off would pay us, and we still don't got no money."

Eriksen gave Marty a hard look.

The young man said, "I've tried everything. I offered to put a free pool in at their house. They're just being unreasonable."

Eriksen said, "Pay them. You promised me you would, and I promised them you would come through."

Curtis looked surprised by the show of support. Marty said, "I don't have that kind of money."

Eriksen said, "I bet you have fifteen grand in equity in that new Camaro of yours. There's your money right there."

Marty said, "I'm not gonna sell my new car. I love it."

Eriksen smiled and said, "Way to stick to your guns, Marty. Good luck with these three. My girlfriend and I are going out to dinner." Before he slammed the door of his car he heard Marty meeting his obligations.

Eriksen was glad he'd decided to stay in El Paso.